WHERE DREAMS GO

RAIN TRUEAX

Where Dreams Go
by

Rain Trueax

There is a pleasure in the pathless woods.
There is a rapture on the lonely shore,
There is society where none intrudes.
By the deep sea, and music in its roar:
I love not Man the less, but Nature more."
Byron

Book 2
Oregon Historicals

Where Dreams Go

is an original work of Rain Trueax.

ISBN: 978-0-9898075-9-3
Paperback

Prepared and presented by:

Seven Oaks
Monmouth, Or.

Sign up for new release notifications at http://raintrueax.blogspot.com

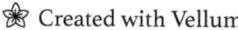 Created with Vellum

CHAPTER 1

Early Summer 1855, Oregon Territory

Martha Stevens stood on her porch, leaning against a hand-hewn, cedar post, as she gazed at a view, which never ceased pleasuring. Their—no she had to stop thinking their-- *her* log and frame cabin stood on a knoll. Behind it was a dark and thick fir and cedar forest. To the east, snow-capped Mount Hood loomed over the heavily forested Cascade Mountains. Nice views but not what had led her to want the porch. That was for the view toward the south east where the land sloped to rolling oak and grass covered valleys and far below, the Clackamas River.

When she and Amos had chosen this piece of land, they thought they would grow old here. Instead, she had found herself a widow, but a widow unwilling to give up on the dream that had meant so much to her husband. She could do this. She would do it. The roof of the nearest cabin, the Lance home, was barely visible from one corner of the porch. To the southwest, a scant two miles away, her daughter and son-in-law, Amy and Matt, were available if she had problems. Close enough but not too close.

Martha pushed back a wisp of long hair, tucking it into the loose bun at the back of her neck. She didn't have to look in a mirror to know there were silver strands hidden in the black. She was forty years old-- not old exactly but certainly not young. Today, she felt old.

She glanced toward the small log barn, feeling a twinge of pain as she realized, although Amos had been dead well over a year, she still half expected him to step away from the door, to come striding toward her with his long-legged gait. But Amos would never come that way again-- only in her memories. Memories she both cherished and shrank from remembering. The worst was of that sunny afternoon, summer nearly at an end.

For the first time in over twenty years, she and Amos had been alone as their youngest daughter had left for Portland to prepare for boarding with friends and attending school. She and Amos had laughed over the strangeness of a home with no laughing children, of the freedom to make love at odd hours of the day, at the new beginning.

After a light lunch, he'd lingered over a second cup of coffee, unusual for a man who normally could barely wait to get out the door and back to his work. Could he have sensed there would be no tomorrow for him, for them? She didn't think he had a premonition, even as she'd combed the words they had last said for any such hint.

"Matt and I'll be falling those trees we talked about," he said as he finally rose, bending to lightly kiss her cheek.

She frowned, not liking the idea, never liking it when they felled the gigantic cedar and fir trees, but Amos and Matt knew what they were doing. She had no reason to object. It was the kind of thing men did.

He walked out the door, waving good-bye with a jaunty grin.

No, as many times as she'd gone back over it, there'd been no clue that within an hour their lives would be irrevocably changed, his ended, hers hewn in two. She wished she could stop remembering those moments. She couldn't keep the memories from returning.

She had been pouring molten wax into candle molds when she heard the groan at the door. She turned, shocked to see Matt stumble into the room, nearly falling, his left arm hanging loosely at his side, blood on his forehead.

"Good Lord, what happened to you?"

"It's not me. It's Amos... Tree split... Go to him."

She didn't know how she made it out the door, down the steps. Never remembered running across the meadow or her first sight of Amos. He had lain half under wood and branches, the tree above him broken off at an odd angle.

"Amos," she screamed. "Oh my god, no."

His eyes were open, glazed with pain and the knowledge of life force fleeing. "I love you," he managed. "It's been good with us... Don't mourn me long... Not good woman... alone out here. Write..."

Before she had been able to respond, could say such a thing was unthinkable, she felt his spirit go. The man, with whom she'd slept, loved, borne children, for whom she'd traveled across the whole of a country, was only a lifeless body.

Over a year had passed since that horrible day and the days following when they buried Amos in Oregon City's Mountain View Cemetery. She could have had him buried on their land, except, what if the land didn't stay hers. No, best was a town nearby. She had left many graves when she traveled west. It wasn't where Amos was anyway.

Miss him didn't describe all she still felt. He was the one who knew her totally and loved her anyway. She had shared her dreams and nightmares with him. He had encouraged her in whims like the long front porch.

The loss had cut her in two, but slowly she learned to smile at a wonderful sunset, laugh at the antics of the crows, and watch the swooping formations of the swallows, nesting near the barn. It wasn't the same. It would never again be the same, but she had found, if not happiness, at least contentment.

Walking to the barn, she began singing an old hymn. She hardly realized she'd been altering the words until halfway through, when she realized she had been singing a teasing parody Amos had taught her. His words turned the saintly old hymn into a rousing, bawdy ballad. Of course, he'd never sung it around their three daughters, but he'd taught her the alternate version; then shown her what the words meant. For a moment she felt the old sadness sweep over her. She stopped and mentally shook herself. That wasn't what he would want. She had to let herself remember those good times but not dwell on them.

By the time she gathered the eggs, she was loudly singing a rousing marching song, and the hens were looking at her uneasily.

"It's all right, I'm not crazy, and you're safe. At least for today," she said, laughing at their cocked heads. They had stopped their cackling and were studying her, trying to decide whether to run or hold their ground.

"Of course," she warned, "if I feel like chicken pot pie, tomorrow might be a different story."

The hens scattered until she poured a large can of cracked corn into their feeder. Immediately they converged in a melee on the golden nuggets. Her old rooster stood back to allow the hens to feed, while keeping a watchful eye canted toward the young rooster who was trying to sneak in among the hens. When the young rooster realized he was being watched, he scurried to the back of the pen and waited respectfully for his turn. The expression on his blank face was as close to wistful as it ever got on a chicken.

Walking back to the cabin, eggs in the basket, Martha, still in a reminiscent mood, thought how it had been living alone. She, who had gone straight from her parents' home to that of her husband, had expected to be frightened. Oregon was still mostly unsettled territory. The forests were deep and dark. Strangers sometimes wandered through.

"You really should move to town," her neighbor had warned, shaking her head and folding her arms over her chest. "It's not safe or seemly. We would buy your land, you know. My brother..."

Martha had stopped her. "Eunice, Amy and Matt are nearby. I am staying." Her smile was the one that Amos always said meant the subject was closed. Perhaps because she had a shotgun and rifle by the door, and a revolver in the chest beside her bed, or because so few people stopped by, she had not lost a night's sleep because of fear. There had been lonely times, times when she'd paced the floor, but even those times had lessened. She was too busy to whine or feel sorry for herself.

She had been fortunate Amos had left her financially well off. She could afford to pay for her needs. In the Willamette Valley, with so many families arriving, there was no shortage of those short of funds and needing work. Sometimes, bartering got her what she wanted as effectively as money. A finely stitched dress for the wife or daughter could lead to the husband or eldest son plowing and planting her garden space or building a stretch of fence. A few men had hoped to barter for something more personal; but no naive girl, Martha had soon set them straight.

Helping with allaying loneliness, St. Louis, their wagon master on the trip west, had settled less than a mile from her cabin with his own home to the north. He came to check on her nearly every day. His gentle wit and comforting concern had eased her through the most difficult of times.

It wasn't a perfect existence. Perhaps the time would come when she would be forced to give it up. For now, she had no thought of leaving. Amos had built this home for her. She had proved it up after his death, and now held title to it. Here she would stay as long as possible.

After she had put the eggs in the kitchen cabinet, she went back out to her garden. In Missouri, she'd had a large garden of flowers and herbs. She and her daughters had enjoyed reading the Bible and Shakespearean plays and sonnets, then searching for plants or seeds to add the appropriate flowers or herbs. When she had known they would go to Oregon, she had collected as many of the seeds, bulbs and cuttings as she could. Most had taken hold and thrived in the moist Northwestern climate.

Crawling down the row, pulling grasses and chickweed from among the daisies, Martha felt pleasure in the work. No matter how low she'd felt, her garden always eased the pain. Unfortunately, both garden spaces had to deal with the depredations of deer, birds, rabbits, raccoons, and even an occasional herd of elk; but between her homemade deterrents and the proliferation of plants, there'd been enough to keep all satisfied.

Behind the string beans, squash and cucumbers grew her medicinal herbs--borage, chamomile, golden seal, garlic, yarrow and others whose names she'd forgotten but not their uses. In an herbal circle, she'd planted hyssop, parsley, fennel, rosemary and lemon balm. Surrounding them were daisies, anemone, columbine, irises, pansies, lilies, primroses, and violets. On each of her infrequent trips into Oregon City, Martha kept her eyes open for the herbs she still needed, as familiar plants were making their way to Oregon.

Healers some called the women of her family. Most likely others had called them witches. Her great-grandmother, grandmother, and then mother had walked with her in the woods, teaching her to recognize the plants and how to use them. When she had first arrived in the Willamette Valley, she and St. Louis, who knew the Indian herbal remedies, had walked the hills, looking for recognizable plants, roots and barks. Gathering, drying and labeling them, Martha planted some in her garden and stored others against future need.

In the south west corner by the porch, protected from the harshest of the winds and winter freezes grew her Rose of Sharon. It was a descendent of her grandmother's large bush, and she'd carried the cutting with her from Missouri, hoping that it would survive, unsure if she'd end up with only a dead stalk. The first year she had mulched it heavily through the winter unsure if it would see spring. It hadn't looked like much. By the second year, it had established its roots and was now rewarding her with healthy new growth and the first waxy buds.

The sun shone warmly on Martha's face. There would have been a time when she'd have worn a bonnet to protect her face from what now seemed to be a life giving force, but here, living alone, she'd learned to take her pleasures as they came. Sometimes the simple ones, like sunshine, were the best.

By afternoon, the sunshine was gone. Clouds built up against the mountains; and as the wind whipped up, a thunderstorm seemed likely. Martha looked out the window toward the barn, wondering if she should get the sheep under cover. On a knoll, lightning could present a danger. Before she could make up her mind, she saw a horse and rider coming steadily up the hill from the southwest. Although she'd yet to have a problem with strangers, she checked the load in the shotgun before she stepped out onto her porch.

The rider came straight for her cabin, as though it was his destination. His hat brim was pulled low, shielding most of his face. He was a tall man, not one she recognized as local. She edged back a little and brought the shotgun out, resting it loosely in her arms.

The stranger reined his dark brown horse up in front of her

porch and leaned his elbows on the pommel of his saddle. "That for me?" he asked, gesturing toward the weapon. White teeth flashed in a handsome, heavily tanned face, a week's growth of black beard on a strong jaw. When he pushed the hat back on his head, she saw the intense dark blue eyes.

"Adam!" she cried, leaning the shotgun back against the wall. He slid from the horse in time to catch her flying embrace.

"I guess it wasn't." He grinned, lifting her from her feet and swinging her around before he set her back on the ground.

"It's good to see you. So good. It's been a long time."

"A few years."

"We weren't sure how to reach you. Did you get our letters?" He tied his horse to the porch railing and looked at her, his eyes alight with his smile. She couldn't seem to stop her questions. "Did you stop at Amy and Matt's?" she asked.

"I got there about noon. Nothing would do, but they had to feed me, wouldn't let go until I'd heard all their news."

"Then you haven't seen St. Louis yet." He shook his head. She smiled more broadly. "He'll be so excited."

Adam laughed at that. "In all the years I've known that man, I haven't seen him excited at anything. I doubt this is going to be the first."

"He talks about you a lot. About how you were the best scout he ever had."

"That wasn't what he said at the time."

"Well, you know his ways."

He grinned. "That I do."

She stepped back then to look up at him. "You look good, although thin, tired."

"A motherly thing to say," he said with a short laugh.

"Well, I was almost your mother-- at least in-law."

"Amy had something to say about that," he reminded, his eyes glinting with humor.

8

"Is that why you stayed away these years?" she asked, looking into those eyes, trying to decide if she saw pain there.

"No." He grinned as he rubbed his bristly jaw. "She was right about that-- for both of us."

"It didn't hurt to see her with Matt?"

"Indirect as always, aren't you, lady?" He laughed. "No, and it didn't hurt to see that she is, as they say, large with child."

"I'm glad. I imagine they told you that Belle's in San Francisco, visiting with a classmate's family, but Loraine will be home in a couple of weeks for a visit."

"They said she was helping the Collins manage their dry goods store in Portland. The three of them seem an unlikely combination."

Martha smiled and ushered him into the cabin. "Come in. It's getting cold outside."

Once inside, she stepped back to look at him. His size and energy seemed to fill the cabin. The features were as she'd remembered-- a Greek Apollo could have been no more darkly handsome. There was a bit more hardness to his mouth, sadness in his eyes, but otherwise, he was the Adam she remembered.

"It's worked well for Loraine with the Collins," she said. "Jacob has not been well. He's aged so much in this last year, and Agatha-- Well, Agatha is still Agatha, but Loraine manages them both. Since their children live so far away, she's like a daughter to them, and she seems to have a knack for business."

"Good for them all then." He gazed around the living room, the glance taking in the Spartan furnishings. Martha wondered what he thought of her rustic home. She wouldn't ask.

"I think there's still coffee from this morning." She walked to the cook stove. "Would you like a cup?"

"I've been up since before dawn. Coffee sounds good. By this time of the day it ought to be almost as strong as Clem's."

"It would be hard to top his." Martha laughed, remembering how strong the wizened old hired man's coffee had been.

They sat at the table as he sipped the coffee. He grimaced. "Might be as strong as Clem's."

"We wrote you several times," she said, her elbows on the table, chin resting on her hands.

"I got one of them. That letter chased me around until it caught me at Fort Jones. I was sorry to hear about Amos. Real sorry."

"We felt you'd want to know."

"He was a good man. I always liked him."

"He liked you too. We'd have both been happy if Amy had chosen you, but then Amy and Matt are so in love, and he's a good man too. He's good to me."

"Sounds like Matt."

She glanced out the window at the darkening sky. "You got here just in time. It looks like it's going to storm."

"I saw the thunderclouds building up."

"You will stay for supper, of course. It won't take me long to go outside and put the animals in the barn."

"I'll take care of your stock when I put Joe under cover."

"I can help." She reached for her shawl.

He stopped her, his large hand taking the shawl from her fingers. "No," he said with a crooked grin. "I'll take care of the stock."

"But that's silly," she protested. "It'll be faster if we do it together."

"Humor me, lady," he said laconically, taking her shawl from her shoulders and throwing it back over its hook.

She smiled, shaking her head. It had been awhile since she'd had a man boss her around. She'd almost forgotten what it was like. "All right, this time," she agreed, giving in with relative grace. "I'll have supper ready when you come back."

He grinned at that and headed out the door.

CHAPTER 2

Outside, the rain was a gentle drizzle. Adam looked up at the black clouds overhead and hurried to unfasten Joe's reins from the porch rail. "Come on, fellow," he said as he walked him to the barn. "We better get you under cover. It's going to blow hard here in a few minutes."

He led his gelding to a stall and went out into the fenced corral to drive Martha's cows and mare back through the gate to the lean-to. By then, the rain was driving down hard, soaking everything with its force, and the animals were eager to get under shelter.

In the barn, Adam took off Joe's saddle, throwing it and the saddle bags over a gate and rubbing him down, all the time, talking reassuringly. "This is better fare than you're used to, eh boy." He patted the horse's neck. Joe whickered, nuzzling him before he looked over the rail toward the mare. "I think you're going to like it here," Adam said with amusement. In the loft, he found loose hay and pitched down enough for all the animals.

Only then did he hear a baaa from outside the barn. Looking out the backdoor, he gave a snort of disgust. What the hell was Martha doing with sheep? Five of them huddled plaintively against the far side of a fenced enclosure. The wind and rain were driving against the side of the barn with a force that told him this was no casual storm. Overhead, lightning flashed across the sky, followed almost immediately by a loud clap of thunder.

He doubted spending a night out in the storm would hurt the woollies, but he'd promised to take care of all her stock. If he didn't, she'd be out doing it herself. He pulled his brim down low to keep the hat from being blown off and went into the driving rain.

The five sheep were either unbelievably stubborn or stupid. Of course, they didn't know him, but that didn't excuse their bolting first one way, then another. As he chased after them, he was grateful none of the soldiers at the fort or Martha could see him. There were some things better done in privacy and chasing sheep definitely qualified as one.

"Dumb as sheep," he grumbled, as he finally latched the gate behind them, securing them safely in a corner of the barn. "I should've left you out there. She'd of been better off if you did get hit with lightning or a tree fell on you."

The sky was nearly black by the time he finished, and he was cold and soaked to the skin. The lightning came down with multiple prongs and thunder crashed again as he ran back across the yard toward the promising light of the cabin.

Opening the door, the warmth hit him with an almost physical blow. Candles were lit on the mantle, and the fireplace had a blazing fire. He slammed the door against the rising wind and stood, reluctant to go further with his buckskins dripping water on the wood floor.

Martha took one look at him before disappearing into what he guessed was the bedroom. She came back with a patchwork quilt, which she put on a chair by the fire. "You have to get out of those wet clothes. I probably should have kept some of Amos' things, but this will have to do while yours dry."

"I'm fine. I'll be dry in no time."

"You're already shaking. Adam, don't be so silly. You're like one of the family. I'll step into the bedroom while you change, but you better have taken off those wet clothes before I get back, or you'll be catching lung fever." Her voice was level and casual as though she had often suggested to men who came in her home that they should strip buck naked and wrap themselves in a quilt.

He watched her walk back into the bedroom, heard the door close firmly. He was soaked and chilled. She was right. It made sense to strip. He would after all have the quilt, but he felt uneasy about it.

Even with warm fingers and when the leathers weren't wet, peeling himself out of his fitted buckskins took some work. Now it seemed almost impossible. He pulled the shirt off over his head, fighting it every inch before he threw it onto the ground behind him. His boots were soaked and seemed glued to his feet. When he finally got them off, he discovered even his socks were soaked. Hands still shaking, the tight fitting breeches were even more difficult, and it seemed to take forever before he'd managed to peel them down his hips and throw them onto the sopping pile at his feet.

Looking around, he saw the quilt where she'd placed it on a nearby rocker. He was reaching for it, when the bedroom door opened, and she came through.

"I have some--" Martha stopped in mid-sentence, her mouth hanging open as she looked at him—all of him.

He dropped the quilt from his still badly shaking hands as he let out a mild oath.

"Oh my!" She quickly whirled to face the wall. "I'm so sorry. I thought I'd waited long enough."

He grabbed again for the quilt. "It's nothing," he said, then stopped abruptly he realized what he'd said.

Martha gave a self-conscious laugh. Cheeks still flushed, she turned to face him. "No, it's not. I mean, it's not nothing. It's —Oh my".

She straightened her shoulders. He could see her make an effort to normalize her voice. He felt like a fool. He'd humiliated them both. He wished for words to make it better but how do you normalize being seen naked by a woman who you should have regarded as a mother... except...

She shook her head. "I'm so sorry."

He walked over to the fire. "My fault."

"No fault in it. I..." She stopped again before taking a deep breath. "I heated up stew, if that's all right."

"Sounds fine. Better than fine."

She hurried over to the cook stove and began ladling stew into bowls. He wished he could read her mind, but then maybe it was better he couldn't. She must be regretting asking him to stay for supper. He wanted words to make it better for her but some things you couldn't go past. He should never have come, but how could he have stayed away when he knew.

When they sat at the table, she bowed her head and said a simple blessing over the food. Looking up, she smiled. "What are you thinking?" she asked.

"How do you know it's anything?" He managed a smile.

"You had a look on your face. I can't decide what it was."

"Difficult to explain." He hesitated a moment, but she waited. "It just seemed good to be in a room like this, sitting at a table, hearing you say grace. It reminded me of all the times I've missed."

"By your own choice-- which you can change at any time."

"Maybe. Anyway, it's just good to be here."

"Tell me what you've been doing with yourself."

He took a bite of the stew to avoid having to answer. When the quilt slid off his shoulder, he reached to pull it back up. "It's good stew," he said hoping she'd forget her question.

"I'm glad you like it. I do add some spices that not everyone likes. I didn't expect company."

"It suits me."

14

"I'll have you know that I not only cooked it. I shot, cut up and dried the deer meat."

"Seriously?" He knew his voice had to reflect his surprise.

"I've learned to do a lot of things I never thought I could." He could hear the pride in her voice. "I didn't like shooting such a beautiful animal, but I can't expect others to look out for me all the time."

"I'm sure Matt would."

"He would, but he's got a homestead to run, a family of his own to look after. I either have to be able to do things for myself or can't expect to stay out here." She sipped her coffee and watched as he helped himself to another bowl of the stew.

"I can imagine that this last year had to be hard on you." *Dumb thing to say, fool.* He was struggling for words he didn't have.

"It was." She put her plate by the tin sink and refilled his coffee cup, before she picked up his wet buckskins.

"I can take care of that," he said, then watched her ignore him and move closer to the fire.

"You could, but this is the kind of thing a woman likes doing."

Trying to keep his mind on his food, he found it constantly drifting along with his gaze to her slender back as she dried his leather shirt and pants with a flour sack towel, then put them over a chair, safely back from the fire where they wouldn't dry too quickly. She opened a tin of oil and kneeling again, picked up his boots, using her fine-boned hands as competently as any man, she rubbed the oil into the leather.

She was as beautiful as he'd remembered-- her skin a creamy gold, cheekbones high, eyebrows finely arched, dark eyes slightly slanted, and bodily curves womanly and gentle. When he saw her push back a lock of black hair with her wrist, he caught himself fantasizing about that long hair loose, flowing down her back, lying spread out across a pillow. He wondered what her breasts would look like if the fabric straining against them was stripped away. He swallowed hard as he realized where his thoughts were taking him. Castigating himself, he turned back to finish the stew. *You've been too long in the wilderness. You're not fit to be around a lady.*

When he finished eating, he stood, grasped the quilt securely, and walked to where she was now sitting on a little stool in front of the fireplace, a piece of embroidery on her lap. She looked up with a smile as he sat in the large rocker. "So," she said, "tell me what you've been doing."

"Not that much to tell," he said, liking the smooth way her fingers worked the needle and thread in and out of the design.

"I don't believe that for a moment, but I knew being a man, you'd not want to talk about it until you'd eaten and had your coffee."

"Think you know quite a bit about men, do you?" he teased, then wished he hadn't. The last thing he wanted to do was remind her of Amos.

She smiled at him, her eyes clear and showing no sign of sorrow. "Being married to one man for twenty-two years teaches a woman a bit."

"I shouldn't have--"

"Brought up Amos?" she finished for him. "It's all right. I think about him. He is still a part of me, a part I don't want to lose. The sadness has lessened, and I tend now to think more about the good times."

He sat back, rocking a little, staring into the fire. "It's something to have," he said finally. He had no memories like those. The women in his life had been only fleeting events, thoughts for the moment. A long time ago, he'd realized that was even true of what he'd thought had been his love for Amy. He'd wanted a wife. She had fit his image of what one should be, then had come Matt's challenge to his competitive nature, and that had been all there was to it.

Martha was looking at him again, her large eyes somber. "Can't you talk about what you've been doing after you left us?"

He smiled faintly. Fortunately, she was not a mind reader. "I could, but it's not a pleasant bedtime story."

She frowned. "And are you only supposed to share the pleasant side of your life with women?"

"I might I have thought that."

"Then perhaps, Mr. Stone, you're the one who doesn't know so much about women." She smiled.

"Most probably true. I haven't spent much time around ladies."

"Then we'll start your lesson now. I, as an example of one woman, like to hear what a man's been doing, to hear about his work, and don't care if it's pretty or not."

"You sure?"

"Has it been so terrible?" she asked, frowning and laying aside her needlework.

He swallowed, staring into the fire. "You know I was tracking and scouting for the federals in the Siskiyous."

"St. Louis learned that much when he tried to find where to write you."

He shook his head. He didn't like thinking about what he had been doing, all he'd seen. Still, when he met her level gaze, he knew she wasn't a woman to put off.

"If there's a good side, I've yet to see it." How does one tell a gentle woman about senseless death and destruction, about hatred so strong that it leads to the slaughter of children, about the stench of death permeating the air around you, until there is no clean place left? Some of the Indian tribes had rituals for dealing with death. He wished he remembered what they were.

"Where is this Fort Jones where our letter finally reached you?"

"In Northern California, near Shasta, but the Indian trouble's been mainly north of there."

"A lot of fighting?"

Too much. "It's not so much the actual times in battle, such battles as there've been. At least then you don't have time to think."

"Your voice sounds so bleak. Is there no hope for it?"

"The white man won't leave that area. It will take eliminating every Indian there, I think, to have peace. There've been-- maybe a hundred whites killed in that area last year and who knows how many Indians. No one big attack, no big fancy war with glory for warriors or soldiers, just a dirty little murder here and there, then retribution."

"We don't get a newspaper out here except when someone goes to town and then we trade it around with news that's probably old. What we have heard about the situation has seemed so mixed up with sensationalism there's no way to decide what's true."

"It's probably better you don't hear. When people read about an Indian attack, they automatically group all Indians into the same bunch. Some idiot would be shooting peaceful Molallas up here to punish the Takelma, Shastas and Modocs down there."

"That's unfortunately probably true."

"The last treaty in the Rogue country might have held, except for an unprovoked attack on a party of Indians. There's so much hate." Enough to make a man physically sick. He swallowed hard, not wanting to think about the carnage, the burnt cabins, the Indians left hanging from trees. Too many innocents on both sides. Whatever he'd thought he knew about life, in the Siskiyous he'd learned he'd had no clue. He tried to think what he could tell her without giving her nightmares like his own.

"It's been a kind of hell the last few years. A lot of miners and settlers think the only good Indian is a dead one. Any excuse to kill is enough. So an Indian robs a miner of his gold dust or a couple of them attack a cabin. The vigilantes grab somebody, anybody whose skin isn't the color of theirs, and shoot or hang them. The tribes retaliate. Nobody on either side cares who was guilty."

"And you've been with the military through all this?"

"Most of the time, one patrol or another." He took a deep breath, strangely finding it did comfort him to talk to her about it. There was something good about having someone care, someone listen.

"From what I can tell, there isn't enough good land to satisfy both the Indians and the settlers, which leads to broken promises, attacks." He smiled humorlessly. "So far as I've been able to tell, there are no heroes, no villains. Just victims."

She sat silently, her knees drawn up beside her, her eyes not leaving his face as he talked, as he told her briefly about some of the battles, of an officer he'd served with and liked and who'd been killed at his side.

"Is that why you left?" she asked.

"No. Although I admit, it makes a man think, being that close to death. No, the truth is less dramatic. I was sick of the politics, our inability to do anything concrete about the problem. Then I got the letter and read what had happened to Amos. I was on a monthly contract. When I finished what I'd promised, I left."

"Matt said he wrote you two months after it happened."

"I saw the date. I haven't stayed any place long enough for it to catch up to me. Mail is pretty undependable in my world—or what was my world."

"You are a rolling stone," she said with a small smile. "Would you like some fresh coffee now?"

"Sounds good."

Outside he could hear the wind assaulting the cabin, rain coming down in torrents, and thunder occasionally crashing farther in the distance. He sat back in the rocker, soaking in the heat of the fire as he looked around the room. The stone fireplace had a long mantle made from what looked like a thick, sanded and polished slab of oak Besides candles in pewter holders,

Martha had a cut glass vase filled with wildflowers. Hanging on the wall was what Adam assumed to be her needlework-- colorful, fanciful flowers, worked around the words of a poem. Smiling, he stood to read it, half expecting a Bible verse. It wasn't.

To see a World in a Grain of Sand
And a Heaven in a Wild Flower,
Hold Infinity in the palm of your hand
And Eternity in an hour.

"Hmmm," he said, as she returned, handing him a cup of coffee, "kind of a deep thinking for a piece of fancywork."

"And what should be on a piece of stitchery?"

"Roses are red. Jesus loves you and violets too," he suggested teasingly.

Her laugh was low and sweet. "Well, in this case, I happen to love that verse. It expresses so much in so few words."

"Who wrote it?" He leaned against the mantle, his gaze steadily on her.

"William Blake."

"Do you read a lot of poetry?"

"I read almost anything that I can get my hands on. We had to leave most of our books in Missouri, but I'm accumulating a few." She pointed to a small shelf with what appeared to be a dozen books on it. "They've started a lending library in Oregon City. It's not big or anything, but it has liberal borrowing policies. I can take a book when I go into town and send it back with whoever is heading into town next." She took a sip of coffee.

"I've never understood poetry."

"Some are difficult to understand, but I think the one by Blake is self-explanatory."

He raised his eyebrows and grinned with mock disbelief.

"It's about seeing the perfection in the small things, the small moments and realizing that sometimes an hour is all we will have." She smiled. "Or am I making too much out of it?"

"No, that makes sense."

"Often men don't think so much of poetry and think it's for women. But a poem, like a painting, expresses so many ideas with so few strokes."

"We should all do so well," he agreed with a wry grin. Somehow when it mattered, he never seemed to find the words. He had justified his lack by deciding it was the fate of all men. But then along would come one of those fancy poets, managing to put deep and profound thoughts on paper. Of course, he didn't know how they managed in talking to the actual women in their lives.

She sat back on her stool, beginning again to work the needle in and out of her stitchery. "You said something about politics adding to the Indian problem."

He leaned his arm against the mantle, staring into the flames. "There are different factions arguing over what to do. You have the volunteers made up of locals, the miners, the farmers, and the military. Every time there's an incident, they're at each other's throats faster than they are at solving the problem.

"If a white man is murdered, the first thought is it must be an Indian did it, no looking for evidence—kill the first Indians they see. If white men kill an Indian, no one pays attention. Vigilantes believe if they wipe out a whole village, women and children, you'll teach the rest a lesson. No clue as to what that lesson might be when it's a baby slaughtered," he said bitterly.

"You can break it down again. Those who want war, and those who are pacifists. Neither have much respect for the Indian people as having a culture or right to the land on which they have lived for generations." He shrugged and smiled self-deprecatingly. "I swore I'd leave it behind, forget about it when I came up here, but it keeps coming back to haunt me." He wondered if he'd ever be free of the memories coming back at the worst times or the nightmares.

"Then you haven't made up your mind what you want now?"

He moved from the fireplace to sit in the rocker. "It's not what I want. It's what I can have." He forced a smile he didn't feel.

"Do you intend to go back?"

He shook his head. "No. I'd only go back if I thought I could make a difference. Right now, I don't see that any man can. That region is on a collision course with disaster."

"Is there no glimmer of hope in it?" Her eyes were dark with sympathy.

"Maybe one. There is a new Indian agent, Joel Palmer. He seems like a good man and is trying to find a peaceful resolution —as peaceful as seems possible anyway. To be honest, right now I just want to forget about the whole mess."

"I guess I'm not helping that."

"You've helped more than you know. It's good to sit here, talking, having somebody listen and care. Your cabin is a home. It's been a long time since I've been in any home let alone felt such a sense of peace." He stretched out his legs, his gaze holding hers until he turned back to watch the flames flickering. Outside he saw a flash of lightning and heard the resounding answer of the thunder. Rain pelted against the window, driven by the wind.

"You will stay here tonight, of course."

He laughed at the firmness in her voice. "It hardly seems proper, Mrs. Stevens."

She smiled at him. "Proper doesn't seem all that important when it comes to getting soaked in that rainstorm, hit by lightning, or a tree that is blown over by the wind. Besides, no one except possibly St. Louis will even know."

"I don't want to hurt your reputation with your neighbors."

She snorted. "I don't worry much about what people think. Those, who are always judging someone else's behavior, aren't ones I want for friends anyway. There's a loft where Belle slept before she left for school. The bed will be short for you, but you can angle across it."

"All right... How is St. Louis?"

"He's well and been a godsend to me-- helping when he can, finding men who are willing to work for me. I don't know how I would have managed without him."

For the first time, Adam wondered if there was more between St. Louis and Martha than just friendship. "Lot of work here for a woman alone," he said, trying to read her expression and failing.

"I manage." Rising gracefully, she handed Adam a candle and holder. "It's past my bedtime, but you stay up as long as you want. You can use this when you go up. The bed's ready."

Adam stood up, wrapping the quilt more securely around his body. "Anything you want done before I turn in?"

"No," she smiled. "Just-- I'm glad you came."

"I am too."

As Adam lay in bed that night, he heard the heavy sound of the summer rains and thought of Martha lying in her own bed. The thought and the accompanying images kept him awake until nearly dawn.

CHAPTER 3

Before first light, when Martha walked out of her bedroom, Adam had already been up, had a fire lit, and she smelled coffee. As she walked into the kitchen, he was full dressed again in his buckskins and leaning one hip against a counter, long legs crossed in front of him. "Good morning." He poured her a cup.

"This is very nice." She took a sip. "And you make good coffee." She reached into the pantry for the bowl of eggs. "I haven't had anyone here for breakfast in a long time."

"And I haven't had breakfast with anyone like this ever."

"I can't believe that."

"Sure you can." His tone changed as he added softly, "I've had more lonely mornings than you'll ever know."

"Do you hear from your family?" she asked, uncomfortably aware she needed to change the subject—except what would be safe? Why did it feel so awkward with him now? She knew the answer to that. She had seen him naked; and ever since, she had been unable to forget the sight of his muscular frame lit by the fire's glow as he had reached for the quilt. *Dear Lord.* She tried to think of something else, set a bowl on the counter, and began breaking eggs into it.

"I wrote my mother once, left an address, but living like I have, on the move, I don't know if they tried to write or have just given me up as a bad job."

"You haven't been back to Ohio at all?"

"A long time ago. I've had no reason to go since."

"You must want to see your mother, your sisters."

He shook his head. "I guess that sounds pretty cold."

"A little. Even though we're not together all the time anymore, I would hate not ever seeing my girls."

"Not all families are the same."

"So tell me about yours."

He grinned. "I am not going to let this turn into an examination of me, my motives, or lack thereof. Did you notice the sun was shining?"

She wrinkled her nose at him. "Yes, I did, but don't you think you've heard the last of this."

He rubbed his bristly jaw and ignored the threat. "I lost my razor. Maybe my Bowie knife would do." He chuckled.

Martha looked at him for a moment, before reaching into the back of the dish cupboard. She handed him a razor, strope and shaving mug. "I couldn't bring myself to give these away. Amos' mirror is on the back step."

He looked at her thoughtfully. "You don't mind."

"They should be used."

She poured hot water into a basin, adding enough cold from the pump to make it bearable and handed it to him. She told herself she wouldn't watch as he went out back, drew off his shirt and began working up the lather to spread over his jaw and cheeks. As he continued talking to her, it was hard to concentrate on what he was saying and ended up being impossible not to see the sinewy muscles of his arms as they flexed. She'd ever seen such a chiseled chest. Whatever else Adam Stone may have been doing, it had been hard work.

Swallowing hard, she poured the eggs into the fry pan, stirred vigorously and concentrated on them. Beating egg yolks didn't have the interest that a muscular male torso did, but they were a hundred times safer to watch.

About the time the eggs were cooked, she breathed a sigh of relief as he slid his buckskin shirt back on, finally covering all that bronzed skin. She thought then about what she had seen the night before and to distract herself began scooping eggs onto plates, only aware after she stopped that she'd put all the eggs on one plate.

Oh Lord, she sighed redistributing the eggs. It had been way too long since a man had been in her home. It irked her that she was reacting like a silly school girl, not the responsible middle-aged widow that she was.

Adam sat at the table, complimented her lavishly on the scrambled eggs and took an extra biscuit with his second cup of coffee. He sat back then and smiled, teeth flashing white. "I haven't eaten better in months."

"From what I've been told about army food, I'm not sure that was much of a compliment." She had forgotten how handsome he was or had age and experience hardened his face into one of sculptural beauty in the most masculine sense?

Adam laughed, opened his mouth to say more, when they heard a loud halloo from outside.

By the time Adam got to the door, St. Louis had already gotten off his horse and was halfway across the porch.

"You son-of-a-gun. Matt told me ya was here," the older man bellowed. Although St. Louis stood almost a head shorter than Adam, he grabbed him in a nearly painful bear hug, almost lifting him from the ground with his strength and exuberance. "Why didn't ya tell us ya was comin'?"

"Because, you old coot, I didn't know myself when I'd be able to go until I was on my way," Adam said, answering again all the questions he'd already answered for Amy, Matt, then Martha. When he'd finished, St. Louis was sitting at the table, shaking his gray head and drinking coffee. "Gonna stay a spell this time?" he asked.

"I am thinking that way," Adam said, glancing over at Martha, who was putting fresh candles in their holders.

"It's good to see you, boy. Plumb good. Can't believe it's took ya all this time to get back to us."

"It's as hard to get away from the U.S. government as it was from you," Adam retorted.

"Do tell! Shore ya wanted to get away?" St. Louis asked astutely.

"I had had enough."

"Trouble with you is ya need excitement all the time. Can't stand still. It's what brought ya to leave home at not even fifteen, then sent ya across the prairies all them times. Won't never let ya sit still."

"Things change." Adam sipped his coffee, his gaze following Martha as she moved around the room.

"How old are ya, boy?" St. Louis asked, his steady gaze drawing Adam's back to him.

"Almost thirty."

"Time ya found yoreself a wife. Ain't that right, Martha?"

"Marriage was good for me," she said, agreeing with a smile.

"This here boy needs to go out and find a little gal. Settle down someplace."

"If marriage is so great, how come I don't see you with a wife?" Adam retorted.

"Uh, I been married."

"And not too old to do it again."

"Nah, I'm an old man now. Too old to go puttin' up with all that havin' a wife'd ask of me."

Adam snorted incredulously. "You're not that old."

"Wal, I'm too old for startin' over, but ya never got started at all. Time ya did."

"Maybe," Adam said, with a small smile.

"No maybes about it."

"What? You're looking at me like you're expecting me to start going on the hunt today."

St. Louis grinned. "Wouldn't be none too soon. Look how Matt's gettin' ahead of ya. He's havin' himself a son one of these days."

"You that sure it's going to be a son?" Adam leaned back in his chair, stretching out his legs.

"Shore, and what else! I got to teach that lad all I know about the woods and about livin'."

Adam laughed. "You could teach a girl just the same."

"Wal, it's gonna to be a boy child."

"I am not so sure about that," said Martha, coming to sit with them. "Our family's been pretty strong on girls."

"Wal, then ya had enough of 'em."

"Matt said he didn't care what it was. All he wants is for the baby to be healthy and for it to be over," Adam said. "I think he's ready to have a breakdown just thinking about Amy having any kind of baby."

"And ya think that's funny, him worryin' like that?" St. Louis asked, taking a swig of coffee.

"Knowing Matt. No. He always could imagine anything wrong that could go wrong especially when it came to her."

"Childbirth's a mystery to a man. Scares him aplenty just thinkin' about it."

"Well they lost one baby before it got developed enough," Martha said. "He'd naturally worry it'll happen again."

"I am sorry to hear that." Adam crossed his legs at the ankle. "Life is a risk."

"Matt has nothing to worry now. It was early before, when things go wrong; but she's been fine this time as I've told him more than once." She didn't mention Matt's injury and Amos's death might have been a factor because she wasn't sure they were. Birthing was a risk whether a woman was healthy or not, and she worried some herself whether Amy would be fine this time.

St. Louis chuckled. "Wouldn't dare with ya lookin' out for her."

"Absolutely right," Martha retorted making her voice sound confident.

St. Louis turned back to Adam. "Been up to Portland yet?"

Adam shook his head. "I've been there but not recently, Why?"

"To see Miss Loraine, o' course."

"Well, the answer to that is no, I haven't and don't intend to. I don't like cities." Adam rose, walking to the doorway and looking out at the river far below.

"Portland ain't all that much of one yet."

"Too much for me."

"She likely to be wantin' to see ya," St. Louis said, refilling his coffee cup and following him to the porch.

"They said she'd be visiting down here. I'll see her soon enough." Adam leaned one shoulder against the sturdy beam.

"She's a good woman." St. Louis lowered himself to the porch step.

Adam shook his head. "You old matchmaker," he hissed. "Forget whatever crazy idea is whirling around in that grizzled head of yours."

"Yore problem is ya are afraid of settlin' down."

"And your problem is you got Matt settled and won't be satisfied until you've done the same with me."

"Maybe so. Maybe no."

"I'll do my own courting, if and when I decide that's what I want. If I'd felt that way about Loraine, I wouldn't have gone south when I did."

Martha followed the two out onto the porch. "You two quit bickering. Look down at the silver ribbon of that river. Isn't it the prettiest thing you ever saw?" She perched on the railing, swinging a leg. "I never get tired of looking at it."

"Ever been to where it comes out of the mountains?" asked Adam smiling, despite his determination to hide his thoughts, at the picture she made with the sunlight glinting off her hair which had been loosely tied back with a ribbon, the ebony mass falling nearly to her waist. Adam knew he was staring, his thoughts such that he had to turn away before he revealed himself to her or St. Louis.

"I suppose you have," she said a question in her statement.

"Some time back. It's a paradise. Tallest, biggest trees you ever saw, big ferns that look almost tropical with the size of their fronds, wildflowers of every kind, little streams coming in from all sides, the mountains seem to cut right down to the river."

"Sounds wonderful," she said wistfully.

"High up, there's hot springs, coming straight out of the ground."

"Like we saw along the Oregon Trail?"

"Some, but better. These are little springs at the edge of the river. It's easy to take rocks, dam up a little piece and make yourself a hot bath to whatever temperature you want."

She made a little purr of pleasure, the kind he imagined she might when a man touched her just right.

"You soak in it up to your neck. There's nothing much closer to heaven than that. Lie there, watch an eagle soar by, look at the fluffy clouds as they sail past."

"I would love to see that someday," she said with a sigh of relinquishment, "but I don't suppose I ever will."

"It's only two days ride."

"Might as well be a week."

He worked to keep his voice neutral. "I'll take you. I'd like having an excuse to go back up."

"You might be able to, but I couldn't. I can't leave the place that long."

St. Louis had been watching Adam, a small smile on his face, which Adam didn't bother trying to decipher. St. Louis grinned more broadly. "Shore ya could, Martha. I'll look after yore place here. What's to stop ya?"

"Well," she stuttered, "it wouldn't look right for one."

"Why not?" Adam asked. "You said, I'm like your son." His knew his voice took on a sly slant but couldn't sound innocent to save himself. "Who could find fault with that?"

"But--"

"Looky here, Martha," St. Louis said, a gleam of humor in his dark blue eyes, "Nobody'd even know. Who's goin' to see ya headin' up in the mountains like that?"

"The Lances for one. You know what a gossip Eunice is."

"They won't know where you're goin'."

"Besides," Adam reminded her, "didn't you say you didn't care what people thought?"

"I don't know, but it just wouldn't-- I've never done anything like that."

Adam laughed. "All the more reason to do it now. It's beautiful, Martha. There are also a couple of good sized swimming holes, heated a little by the hot springs."

"I admit it's tempting, but--"

"No buts," Adam ordered firmly, "I need something like this. I wouldn't go if I had to go by myself. Come on. Let me show you your river."

She looked from his eager face, almost boyish even with the square jaw and hard lines these last years had added to his face. She knew she was wavering, tempted almost beyond saying no. Then she remembered. "There's Amy's baby. I can't be gone when it's due."

"When's it due?" asked Adam.

"In seven weeks, maybe less."

"Then, we should go right away. You'd be back way ahead of time. It'll take us two days travel to get up there. Two back. If we spent two or three days, fishing, swimming, enjoying the springs, there'd be no problem."

"I don't know," she said, wanting to say yes, but still unsure of the propriety of the expedition.

St. Louis smiled, looking from one face to the other. "I'll tell ya what I told Matt, a couple of years ago. If ya get a chance for somethin' good, reach out and grab it. Ya just never know when it might come along again or if it will. This here trip sounds like that to me. Ya might never get another chance to go up. I hear it's plumb pretty."

"You could come with us," Martha said as she considered something she truly would like to do except it felt irresponsible and was there another concern, one she should be taking more seriously as to why it wasn't a good idea?

St. Louis grinned, eyes twinkling. "Somebody's got to take care of these places. I figure it'd better be me since Matt's as near to crackin' as a man can get."

Martha looked at him, then back to Adam, suddenly making up her mind. She did need something like it, something she'd never done, never dreamed she would do. "If you would keep an eye on Amy-- you know so much about medicine, I'd feel better. The baby hasn't dropped; so I am sure she's not going to deliver in the next few days."

St. Louis grinned broadly. "I'd do that anyways. Go and don't worry about a thing."

"You'll explain everything to Amy and Matt?" she asked, still anxious.

He chuckled. "I'll do 'er."

"What would we have to take with us?" asked Martha, looking down toward the tempting river, then to the dark mountains in the distance, the mountains she had so often admired and never thought to see close up.

"I've got a tent in my gear. You can use that. I'll sleep out in the open," Adam said, listing off what they would need.

"What if it storms again?" she asked skeptically, as a sudden and unwanted picture of Adam, standing magnificently naked, flashed with disturbing effect into her mind.

Adam grinned easily. "I've slept out on lots of bivouacs. It's nothing new to me. I'll find a tree to get under if nothing else, or I can wrap up in a tarp."

"Well then." She rose and nodded. "I suppose I should get together the food." She walked back into the cabin.

When she was gone, St. Louis grinned broadly at Adam, who was leaned back against one of the porch posts. Adam's own smile disappeared at St. Louis' steady look. He frowned. "What?" he asked knowing the answer.

"Nothin'."

"What do you mean nothing? That look says something. What?"

St. Louis laughed, looked down at the river, and began to hum.

"You old coot," Adam said, shaking his head, "you're hopeless."

"Yep," he said, still laughing.

Martha stuck her head back out the door. "You will have dinner and stay the night, won't you, St. Louis?"

"Wouldn't miss it," he said, still chuckling at Adam's scowl. "What are ya fixin'?"

"Well, I thought maybe chicken. There's a young rooster I've been saving for a special occasion, and Adam's homecoming definitely qualifies."

St. Louis laughed again as he headed for the chicken coop. "It does at that. Yes sir, it does at that."

CHAPTER 4

With the sun barely lighting the east, Adam saddled and began packing their horses. He had been a little surprised she wasn't using a sidesaddle, but it made sense given the rough country. She came out of the house wearing a plaid wool jacket and handed him the last sack of foodstuffs. Not looking up until he had tied everything down, Adam turned to ask if she had everything and stopped his mouth gaping open. "Whaaa?" He closed, then reopened his eyes.

"Don't tease me," she protested, pulling the coat more tightly around her slender form.

"No. It's just."

"Haven't you ever seen a woman in pants?" she asked, her cheeks flushed.

"Of course, at least-- yeah, I think I have." Nobody though had had a figure like hers. The pants fit loosely but only tended to emphasize Martha's slender legs and softly curved hips.

"I-- when Amos died, there were so many things I had to do, and a skirt got in the way. I bought a pair of boy's pants, and it simplified everything, but if you think I shouldn't wear them."

"No," he said grinning broadly now that he was over the surprise. "It makes sense. Easier riding, and you won't get caught up on the blackberry vines."

"It seemed like a reasoned thing," she repeated, looking uneasily away. "Nobody usually sees them, and I figured we wouldn't be around anybody on this trip either."

"You don't have to explain it to me. I approve-- completely."

She glanced back at him as though trying to read his expression, then gave it up and looked toward the door where St. Louis now stood, a broad smile on his bearded face.

"Have a good time, you two," he said, meeting Adam's hard gaze with a twinkle in his own. "And don't ya worry about nothin' here."

"It might seem we're going out of our way," Adam told her as they rode south, "but the route straight up the Clackamas is blocked by steep cliffs, making it difficult at best to get horses through. By cutting south to the Molalla River, following it until we hit an Indian trail that cuts across the mountain, we'll drop almost straight into the valley of the Upper Clackamas."

"Indian trail? Do they still use it?"

"Do I hear a little worry in your voice?" he asked with a laugh.

"Well, if it's their trail, maybe they won't like others using it."

"I don't think they'll mind. There aren't a lot of them left around this area, but those here are not looking for trouble."

"I haven't had any trouble with them, no stealing or troubling the stock when they have come past. If they've come to the door, I've offered food, and they've seemed satisfied with that."

"That was a good thing to do. It's a sign of friendship, something they will offer also."

Adam and Martha rode most of the morning. He stopped once, to give her a chance to stretch her legs. "I'm not tired," she said gamely.

"I know, but you don't often ride all day, do you?"

"No."

"Well, then you'll be some sore tomorrow anyway. We'll make it a little easier by giving your muscles a break now and then."

As they climbed higher in the mountains, the country grew more heavily timbered. First they followed above the river he said was the Molalla, then angled almost due east.

"How did you come to find this way?" she asked when he again insisted she stop and exercise her legs.

"I was with a band, the Molallas. We went hunting up here. It's a place they regularly used in the summer and fall."

"Did they speak English?"

He shook his head. "Not much, but some Chinook which is the usual trade dialect. I had worked with a tracker once who was a breed. He taught me enough to get by. Sign language also is pretty common."

"You know that too?"

He grinned. "Tracking, trying to bring people together in a peaceable manner, it pays to be able to communicate anyway you can. Sign language isn't that difficult. A lot of it's commonsense, making gestures that tell what you're trying to communicate. For instance, fingers walking is walking."

With the sun beginning to set, he looked for a sheltered spot and found it, a small stream below the camp. "Looks good to me. How about you?" he asked, although he'd already decided it would be their campsite.

"I'd be in love with anyplace that got me off my horse." She dismounted stiffly, finding every muscle sore.

"Walk it off," he said, pulling their packs from the horses. "I'll take care of the animals. We can fix supper later."

By the time they sat down to a meal of beans and cold biscuits, she was feeling more like herself. "I suppose," she said, as she settled herself gingerly on the ground, "that at my age I shouldn't even be doing this."

He chuckled. "Ah, I see. So old. About to be a grandma." She had discarded the coat but wore a bulky shirt tucked into the belted pants. Looking at him, she was surprised to see an admiring gleam in his eyes.

"I will be in a few weeks."

"You'll make a beautiful grandmother."

She smiled, feeling a little nervous at the compliment. She set herself to devouring her food, amazed at how ravenous she was.

After he'd eaten, he cut fir boughs, placed them on the ground, then set up the small tent on top of them. "Not a feather tick, but it'll soften the ground some."

"Thank you." She bent to pick up her blankets.

"My pleasure."

She looked up and again caught that glitter in those blue eyes. What was there about the husky tone of his voice that caused shivers to run down her spine? His gaze, intent on her, demanded she meet it.

"Aren't you using any for your own bed?" she asked.

"I'm used to sleeping on the ground." She knew he watched until she pulled the flap of the tent closed.

Lying back in her blankets, she tried to assess the strange sort of vibrations she had felt at being close to him. Ridiculous. She was being a foolish old woman. He had been a friend of her son-in-law, a suitor to her daughter. Whatever she was feeling, it had to be because she hadn't been around such a good looking man in a long time—make that ever. On the wagon train, he'd been just another young fellow. Out here, the dynamics between them had changed.

Then she thought about what he had looked like naked that first night. She scrunched her eyes closed, angry at herself. Whatever this was, she would get control over it.

~

When Adam saw that the trail ahead crossed an old rock slide, he stopped their horses, studying it to determine its safety. It looked stable. Although there were rocks on it, the trail was clear enough for passage. He didn't like it. "We'll have to take it easy here. Let the horses pick their way," he warned. He led the way, listening for any sign that the slide was moving as he rode. Soon they were across and back in the forest.

Late morning found them higher in the mountains and crossing the divide that separated the two river basins. "Pretty, isn't it?" he commented, pointing to the north. Looming seemingly almost above them was Mount Hood. Even in late summer, its slopes were covered with white, although patches of rock were visible.

"It's as though we're under its wing," she said staring at it.

"Almost. The Clackamas drains off the slopes of Hood. The Indians have a legend about the mountain."

She smiled. "And you know it, of course."

"So happens I do."

"I guessed you would."

"Woulda made me look bad to bring it up if I hadn't wouldn't it?"

Her laughter joined his. "So?"

"Saghalie, the chief of the gods, had two sons, Wyeast and Klickitat. These two sons visited the Columbia River and saw it was beautiful. A good place to make their homes, but like a lot of gods and humans, they decided it should be divided up, but couldn't figure out a fair way. That led to a fight.

"Saghalie, disgusted with their squabbling, put a stop to it. He said, 'You two idiots can't work this out; so I will.' He shot an arrow far to the west and another to the east, then said, 'Each of you go in a different direction, find your arrow, and settle where it is.'

"Wyeast went west where he found his arrow in the Willamette Valley and was the forefather of the Multnomah tribe. Klickitat went east and found his arrow in Yakima country and became the father of the Klickitats. Since these sons still couldn't agree and bickered over everything, Saghalie, who wanted a little peace, raised up the Cascade Mountains between them; and so they could still visit each other, he put an arched stone bridge across the Columbia."

"Having had children, I can understand that solution," she quipped.

"Do you want to hear the rest of this or not?"

"Ooops, sorry."

"It's all right. The story gets complicated here, so you need to pay attention. We have the entry of the woman. In this case in the form of a witch, Loowit. She was old and ugly but had a good heart. She was the one who created fire and gave it to the People. Saghalie wanted to reward that generous deed and gave her one wish, which could be for anything. What do you suppose she wished for?"

"Hmmmm, power, riches, beauty, or how about love?"

"Too many answers. She wanted only one thing. To be turned into a beautiful, young maiden."

"Figures," she said, shaking her head. "That way she can have it all."

He laughed. "You're getting ahead of the story. The chiefs from all over the region fell in love with her, including--"

"Uh oh, Wyeast and Klickitat. I can see where this is going."

"You pick this stuff up fast. Well, Loowit loved them both. Being a typical woman, she couldn't make up her mind, which she wanted. So, both the chiefs and their tribes began making war on each other."

"Only a woman could cause such grief," she said, shaking her head and pretending sorrow. "Every tradition seems to find a way to blame us for all the world's problems--Eve, Pandora, Helen, and now Loowit."

He chuckled. "Let me see. Where was I? You do play with my mind, Mrs. Stevens. All right, it's coming back to me. Saghalie was so mad at the renewed fighting that he shattered that stone bridge across the Columbia. The huge stones fell into the river forming rapids. He put Loowit, Wyeast and Klickitat to death; but because they'd been beautiful and majestic, he decided to turn them into mountains. Loowit became Mount St. Helens, Wyeast Mt. Hood, and Klickitat Mt. Adams."

"It was a good story, but a bit sad. Separated forever, huh?" She glanced across at him as he leaned forward on the pommel of his saddle.

"True. Well, for what it's worth, there actually had been a stone bridge across the Columbia. The first explorers, trappers saw it before it collapsed You can still see the huge chunks of rock under the water."

"Thank you for telling me the story. Although, I will probably never be able to look at those mountains again without thinking of Loowit. I'm not at all sure I like women always being portrayed as the cause of all man's trouble."

"Uh huh. Beautiful women. It is an undeniable fact of life that beautiful women are."

"What about handsome men? Might they not also cause such grief?"

"Between two women?"

She nodded.

"Women are too sensible to let that happen." He grinned.

By evening, they began descending into the Clackamas River drainage. The trees were gigantic, making it difficult to see into the distance. Martha was glad Adam knew where they were going, because it was all too easy to see how they could become lost in this country.

"The Indians come up here in the fall for huckleberries," he told her as they eased their horses down a particularly steep grade.

"I'll bet they're the only ones." She looked at the ground, searching in vain for a sign of a trail ahead. "Are you sure we're still on the trail?"

"Oh ye of little faith. Not many white men up here, so not the heavy traffic, but don't worry, white man'll get here, build a big, rutted, muddy road, throw out garbage, then you'll have no trouble telling where you are. Of course, it also will never be the same."

"Divine progress, I guess," Martha said, "but it does seem a shame to spoil this beauty by cutting down the trees."

"I've never seen any place in the Bible where it said cut down the trees as a way of fulfilling some kind of divine mandate."

"Well, people do say it was when God gave man dominion over the earth."

Adam's smile was sardonic. "I've heard that used. Except dominion means care, not slaughter, not abuse, not misuse. If there is a god, which I personally doubt, He made this world beautiful. It's humans who mess it up. I don't think He'd much appreciate people destroying what He made perfect."

"You don't have to convince me," she said with a sigh. "I don't like the cutting down of trees even when sometimes it's needful." She saw him cast her a curious look, but she didn't feel like spoiling the moment by explaining herself and so concentrated on watching the narrow way down and hoping her mare wouldn't stumble.

When they finally came out onto what seemed a level grade, she saw the river almost directly in front of them. Although not so large as she was used to seeing, she knew before Adam told her that it had to be the Clackamas.

A few hours later, Adam reined in his horse, smiling as he pointed. Martha saw steam rising off the river. "One of the hot springs," he said. "We'll make camp above it."

Together they put up the tent, built a fire, then cooked a simple meal. "We'll have fish tomorrow night," he promised as he took the last sip of his coffee.

She smiled. "Pretty confident about it, aren't you? I mean, the fish are still in the river."

"A man's got to believe in himself if he expects to catch *anything*." He grinned at her, inhaling deeply of the fresh mountain air. "When I come up here, I never want to go back."

"It is peaceful. It would be an easy place to forget there is a world--elsewhere."

"About all that lives up here year round are the eagle, deer, cougar, elk, wolves, and bear."

"It would be wonderful for humans--until the first snow fell," she said.

"This country doesn't get as much snow as you might think. Of course, more than the valley below, which some winters doesn't get any, but not so much as say Ohio."

One by one, the stars appeared as the sky darkened to ebony black. Martha pulled her coat around her shoulders, glad for the extra warmth. Even with the campfire in front of her the night had grown crisp. Adam leaned against a rock, one knee bent, a vision of raw masculinity and power.

"Tomorrow, I'll build you a bathtub."

"I haven't been able to submerge in a big tub since Missouri. We left a lot of luxuries behind when we came west."

"You didn't want to leave Missouri?"

"I'm not complaining."

"Amy said you never wanted to come."

"Not to begin."

"But you went where your husband dictated?"

She laughed. "Amos wasn't the type to dictate. It was more that I saw how important it was to him to come out here. I didn't want to be the one standing in the way of his dream."

"How about your own?"

"I'd already had that. Women aren't so hard to understand, Adam. Most of us want simple things--a man, children, a home. I had all that. When he convinced me going to Oregon was important to him, that he'd had enough of keeping the store that his parents had built. It had been their dream. I didn't want to deny him his."

"And is he now dead because he had a dream and got it?"

"Possibly, or possibly it was simply the time God called him home. It might as easily have happened in Missouri. But at least this way, he'd lived his dream first."

"He was a lucky man then, to have that," Adam said reflectively, staring into the flames of the campfire.

"Do you have a dream?" She cocked her head a little as she studied him, the lean planes of his face, the black hair curling down over his forehead, the bristle darkening his solid jaw.

"Once I thought so." He stopped for a moment, seeming to think. "I wanted to see this country. I've done that-- most of it anyway. The last few years I've been caught up in other men's dreams or maybe nightmares."

"How did you come to do that?"

He shrugged. "I saw the need and thought I could help."

"It wasn't your dream?"

He shrugged. "Maybe I'd been leading other people to their dreams too long to know my own."

She looked up at what appeared to be thousands of stars flickering overhead. "A place like this could help a person figure things out."

When she looked back at him, he was smiling, the firelight reflected in his eyes. "I thought it might, which is why I wanted to come here again." His smile disappeared. She wished she could see into his thoughts, but maybe it was best she could not.

"I think I should go to bed now," she said, uncomfortable with the long silence.

He rose in one graceful motion and pulled her to her feet, quickly dropping her hands. "See you in the morning."

CHAPTER 5

I n the morning, Adam, garbed in a cotton shirt and pants, instead of the usual buckskin, proved as good as his word. After breakfast, he pulled off his boots, threw off his shirt and rolled up the pants to wade out into the shallow part of the river. Piling the rocks, he built a basin, allowing a stream of river water to mingle with the piping hot spring coming up through the ground.

Legs spread wide apart, hands folded over his chest, he surveyed his work proudly. "If it's too hot, make this opening bigger."

She dabbled her fingers in the water. "It feels perfect." Half of the pool was overhung by large cedar and fir trees; the other half looked straight up into a brilliant blue sky.

Adam grabbed his gun belt from his pack. "I'll leave this with you. I don't expect you to have any problems, but if you do, make a big bang, and I'll come running."

She grinned, conjuring up a picture of herself cowering behind a pile of clothing and shooting off the gun, while being menaced by a bear.

"I'll be around the bend of the river, catching us dinner,"

Adam said dressing and pulling on boots before he deftly assembled the pieces of a bamboo fishing pole. Martha smiled as she saw his mind was already gone from her. He waved and headed down river.

When he'd gone, Martha picked up around the camp before she took her towel and headed for the pool. Unbuttoning her shirt, she hurried as cool morning air hit bare flesh. Quickly boots, socks, pants, and undergarments joined the pile of clothing on a large rock.

Naked, she knew she'd never felt so free in her whole life. Slowly, she lowered herself into the hot water, sinking until only her head was sticking out. In moments all the soreness from the long ride had been magically whisked away.

She looked down at her body, shimmering under the water. Her breasts were firm and round. Even with three babies, they didn't sag, possibly because they weren't particularly large. Her waist was almost as slim as when she'd married Amos. Her hips were definitely fuller, but for the most, her figure hadn't changed much from seventeen.

Martha sat up abruptly, angry at herself for fretting over her figure at her age. She couldn't deny the surge of restlessness, the quickening in her body when she thought about the reason. It was because of him. It was ridiculous, but there it was.

It'd been so long since she'd thought about a man as a man. Her marriage had been long and happy; but because it'd been comfortable, many things had been taken for granted. The early passion had morphed into a comfortable awareness of each other, a shared intimacy that was in many ways stronger than those early, more volatile feelings. Then when Amos had died, she had wanted all feelings to die. She had believed they had.

She tried to think how this could've happened. It all seemed to go back to seeing Adam naked. The feelings at that memory were raw, sexual, alive, and they arose in the most unexpected times with no way to prepare for their effects. A part of her had awoken. Now, whenever she heard his step or his deep voice or saw his tall, rangy body, her stomach tightened, her heart quickened.

Of course, the situation was impossible, but she had to admit the foolish thoughts, at least to herself. Adam could be her son; except, of course, he couldn't. But ten years stood between them-- ten years going the wrong direction.

Coming up here had been a mistake. She should have thought before she went off with him for a week in the wilderness. Or was that why she'd gone? That was a disconcerting thought. Had she gone because she'd known exactly how she was feeling and wanted more time with him, time alone when no one could see, no one could know? She began breathing more quickly.

She rose out of the water and reached for her towel. As she dressed, she repeated it over and over—ridiculous, impossible, silly. There were so many reasons, not the least of which was that Adam himself could never be thinking any of these foolish thoughts. She had to get control of herself, remember she was a middle-aged woman. These kinds of feelings were in her past.

By the time Martha saw Adam striding back up the bank of the river, she was sitting on the bank above the river and had herself well in hand. She would allow no traitorous thoughts or feelings to ruin the friendship they had.

Proudly, Adam held out a string of freshly cleaned trout for her to admire. "I'll cook tonight," he said with a grin.

"That sounds wonderful." Impersonal, that was the key.

"I think I'll use the pool, if you don't mind." He smiled.

"Oh!" She scrambled to her feet, her skin feeling flushed. "I'll-- I'll take your fish up."

He handed them to her and began to unbutton his shirt. She gaped at him. Surely he wouldn't undress right in front of her. She slammed her mouth shut and turned stiffly. It took all her

47

willpower to walk, not run up the slope. The last thing she needed was another glimpse of that oh, so tempting muscular body. She gripped the string of fish tighter than was necessary as she successfully fought the urge to turn around for one quick look.

Adam had packed the trout into clay, and then set them into the coals at the edge of the fire. The two of them sat back watching the flames. "I loved the hot spring. Just like you said I would," she said with a sigh, remembering the weightless feeling floating in the sulfuric smelling water.

"I thought you'd like it."

"I just thank God for it and that we could use it," she said.

"You think some god went out of His way to make something like that just for us?" Adam asked with a chuckle.

She had just said it without thinking. Her own beliefs were a bit unorthodox. She was in no mood to be so serious and decided instead to tease him back. "Of course and knew we'd be here today. He provided this whole place just for our enjoyment."

"Kind of like a banquet or party setting?"

"Of course."

"Maybe he set those fish onto my hook too," he teased.

She raised her eyebrows. "Some consider God a fisher of men."

Adam straightened, waiting a moment before he answered. "I might as well say it right now. I don't think there is no god, not after all I've seen. If there is a god, just saying *if*, I don't think he, she or it cares what we do, not on a personal level anyway."

"I remember you saying that on the wagon train when we were heading out here." She watched as he shifted position to feed the flames.

"Matt and St. Louis, they were always talking about how they saw it, always trying to talk me into seeing things their way, but..."

"It didn't change how you felt," she finished for him.

"No. I've seen too many things--awful things--to believe there is a god involved with daily living. If there was, and it was a good god, he or she'd change things, not sit up on some cloud looking down and not caring. The way some think, he'd instead be taking joy in suffering like with Job."

"So if not a god, what do you believe in Adam?"

"Myself. You. What I can touch, see, and hear. I believe in that river over there. That above us right now there are thousands of stars. I believe in life and death, in pain and happiness, in hate, and love."

"You're poetic."

"No, but I see that there is reality and then there's hope. God comes under the category of hope-- and that only if you don't think you'd be one heading for hellfire and damnation at the last judgment."

"You know the words. You must have gone to church at one time?"

"Religiously, until I was old enough to escape."

"Escape?"

"A little melodramatic," he said, smiling, "but basically covers it."

"What were you escaping from?"

"My mother was in the church every time the door opened. She used scripture on us like a battering ram. Remember the verse where it says spare the rod and spoil the child. She really believed in that one." If his laugh was supposed to be humorous, it failed; instead reflecting a lingering anger.

"That's not a good way to learn about God."

"Tell me about it," he quipped, laughing again. Reaching down, he took a fork and gently thrust it into one of the fish, breaking apart a section. "It's ready."

"And smells delicious."

"Trout is one of the few perfect foods." He broke off the clay shells and put the fish onto one of the tin plates.

"I can't agree with that," she argued. "It has too many bones."

"That's what makes it so special." He broke off a piece and held it in front of her mouth.

"How can that make it special?" she asked as she opened her mouth and let him feed her.

"Because," he said with a smile, "it's like a rose. Rose has thorns. Right?"

"Yes," she said, watching as he picked up another chunk of trout.

"Why has it got the thorns?"

"Because that's the way it's made," she retorted. "And it's made that way for a reason. The thorns protect the flower, not so easy for rodents to crawl up and eat the blossoms."

He grinned. "Doesn't stop the deer."

"Well, true."

"The thorns on a rose make you appreciate its beauty more. A little pain in the plucking and then you can enjoy the blossom."

"What's that got to do with trout?" she asked, eating the bite of trout he again fed her and deciding he would never eat if she didn't feed him too. She reached down for a piece, struck by the simple sensuality of having him take the food from her fingers with his teeth. She was playing with fire but wasn't ready to deny herself the simple pleasure. She felt alive, like a woman for the first time since Amos had died-- maybe even from before that.

"Trout's like that. The bones make you appreciate the taste. You have to work a little, but it's worth it for that delicate, delicious taste." He smiled and added, "Most worthwhile things are that way."

She couldn't decipher the smile on his face, then decided she didn't want to try. She reached for another bite of the fish and ate it herself. Something was changing between them. She wasn't comfortable with that change, yet wasn't willing to stop what was happening.

~

When Matt saw St. Louis ride into the clearing, he strode out of the cabin, watching the older man dismount.

"How ya doin'?" St. Louis asked.

"All right," Matt said, as St. Louis patted him on the shoulder.

"And the missus?"

Matt felt himself tense. "She says she's fine, but..."

St. Louis laughed. "Matt, I never knowed a braver man than you, but when it comes to that little gal, you're a positive coward."

"It's easier when it's me. When it's her, like you said, I go nuts."

Amy followed him onto the porch, her belly preceding her by some distance. "Want some coffee?" she asked, unconsciously rubbing her back.

"Ya got some?" St. Louis responded with a broad grin.

"Would I ask if I didn't?" Her smile was quick and teasing.

The three of them sat at a table in the small cabin, almost a replica of the one Martha lived in on the hill.

"How's Mama," Amy asked, sipping on a glass of water.

"Just fine when last I seen her," St. Louis said, eating a freshly baked cookie.

"Did you see Adam?" Matt asked.

"Yup," St. Louis said, beginning to chuckle.

"What's funny about seeing him?" questioned Matt. "I was glad he finally got back here. I didn't know if we'd ever see him again. He say anything about how long he'll be stayin'?"

St. Louis laughed again. "Could be awhile."

"What does that mean?" asked Amy, uncomfortably shifting in her chair.

"Nothin' much."

"I don't think so," Amy probed, looking at his eyes. "What is so funny here? Is it something we ought to know about?"

51

"When ya do, I got a feelin' ya will," he said, refusing to say more.

When Amy excused herself to lie down for a nap, Matt pushed St. Louis out the door and demanded, "All right, what is goin' on?"

St. Louis smiled. "What do ya mean?"

"I mean, there's somethin' you ain't tellin'. You might put Amy off with that sly grin of yours, but I want to know what's up," Matt drawled.

"There's things that a man can tell another man. And there's things a man can't," St. Louis said, again with that smug smile that said definitely something was up. "This one ain't mine to tell."

"You are lookin' like the fox that just swallowed the hen whole. I don't get it."

"Nope, but I'm thinkin' ya will."

"All right. We'll play twenty questions. Is this somethin' to do with Adam?" Matt questioned, rocking back on his heels, thumbs in the pockets of his jeans.

"Yup."

"Is he goin' to settle around here?"

"Possible," St. Louis said, looking off toward the mountains.

"All right, old man, I've had enough. What are you tryin' to tell me without tellin' me?"

"No big thing." He grinned again. "Oh by the way, I forgot to tell Amy, but maybe ya can do it for me. Her ma's gone up to the mountain."

"The mountain?" Matt repeated. He tried to think how that fit into the conversation. What was Martha doing going up the mountain. What mountain?

"Yup. I'm stayin' up at her place, lookin' after the stock and all. She went up the river for a campin' trip."

"A campin' trip? Now? Now with Amy due? What's goin' on?"

"Amy ain't due for over six weeks. She'll be back in plenty of time, but she asked me to look in on here anyways just to be safe."

Matt put his head back, studying St. Louis. "Martha went up the river?" He paused before he realized there was only one answer. "Adam took her?"

"Ya find that so hard to believe?" He chuckled again and Matt felt like strangling him as he tried to think through what was going on—what had been said and not said. "You tell Amy."

"Hold it just a minute." Matt frowned, staring at the wooden porch post, as he tried to take in what St. Louis was really saying. When he looked up, he knew he had paled. "Adam and..."

"Now ya ain't even hearin' yoreself." St. Louis raised his eyebrows with mock concern, patting his shoulder understandingly. "This business of havin' a baby is sure hard on a man's brain."

"Maybe so," Matt said succinctly, staring into the distance and then back at St. Louis, "but if you are sayin' what I think you are saying, I don't want to be the one tellin' Amy!"

~

The next morning the sun already high in the sky, Adam washed up the tin dishes. "Today, I'll take you swimming. You do swim, doin't you?"

She nodded. "But how can we swim? You mean going in clothes and all?"

He grinned. "We'll figure out something. Come on."

"I'm not sure I want to," she equivocated, uncomfortable with the banter that seemed to arise so easily between them now. Their relationship had changed from what it had been. Now what was it?

"Sure you do. It's a special place, almost magical. Prettiest spot on the river. You can't turn that down."

"Would we ride there?" she asked, gesturing toward where the tethered horses were grazing on the tall, mountain grass.

"Nope. It's an easy walk."

"Everything seems easy to you," she grumbled, but followed when he started up the river. As they walked, she kept an eye on the large rocks underfoot to avoid a twisted ankle.

"Now it's your turn to tell me something," he said.

"All right." She followed as he edged around a large boulder.

"Have you ever thought of going back to Missouri now that Amos isn't here?"

She shook her head. "My children are here. Well, not Belle so much but the other two. Besides, I like it here. It's a beautiful country, as Amos thought it would be."

"Are you lonely? Living alone?"

"Not really. I do have Matt and Amy close by, St Louis. The Lances live not far away."

"It's not the same as having someone living with you."

"No, it's not. All right. I suppose there are times that, truth be told, I am lonely, but it's not a bad kind. With a homestead, there's always something to do. I think though that was a strange question coming from you."

"Why do you say that, Martha?"

She stopped, then continued walking. It was the first time she'd heard him use her name since he'd been back. It sounded, intimate somehow, then she realized how silly she was being, making something out of simply hearing her name from his lips.

"You're alone. More than I," she said to get her thinking back on more comfortable ground. "You don't have family. You move around too much even to make friends. You don't have a home."

"In the past I never wanted one," he said, tossing a rock at the water.

"Why not?"

"It wouldn't seem like there was much point unless there was a woman there."

"And there's never been a woman that you wanted to be there?" she questioned, and then quickly regretted it, remembering too late that he had. He'd wanted Amy, but she'd chosen Matt.

He looked at her thoughtfully for a moment. "There was a woman, but she had a husband."

"Not Amy?"

"No."

"Maybe there'll come another one-- someday."

He grinned, his gaze intently on her. "Could be."

"Marriage is a good thing, Adam," she said, walking on.

"For some people," he agreed.

"When it's good, it is very, very good."

"And when it's bad?" He laughed.

"All right. It's very, very bad."

"You know more about the good than bad though, don't you?" He asked the question, not really wanting or needing to hear the answer, which he already knew. He'd seen it when on the wagon train west he'd watched Martha and Amos together. They had been two halves of a whole.

"Yes. I loved Amos. He treated me like an equal. We had something rare together. He was always there for me. It's a good feeling; one you should experience. You really should do as St. Louis suggested and find a woman of your own."

"Could be. Someday. Do you still miss him?"

"Of course, but not like I did in the beginning. It's hard, knowing I don't have anyone that close to share with, to argue with." She didn't add make love with, but it was also on her list.

"Are you happy now?" he questioned, as he helped her over a large fallen tree.

"As much as possible, I think. You just accept what has to be. Sometimes I've thought I'll have to move into a town eventually, that I can't keep living alone; but for now, it works."

"There aren't a lot of women that could live alone."

"Women are more resilient than you think. Only our own expectations stop us."

"Sounds like you're one of those women who believe women ought to run things and even vote just because they can wear pants."

"I don't think women want to run everything, but voting is a sensible thing."

He laughed. "Women voting? You seriously think women want to vote? Let alone should?"

Her breath came out in an irritated hiss. "What makes you think women shouldn't vote?"

"Well, they would be bored learning about the men running for office for one thing. What woman cares about politics?"

"Men running for office? Why shouldn't women run for offices too!"

"You are joking." The surprise in his voice further irked her.

"You are insufferable. Typical of a certain type of stubborn, narrow-minded male!"

"You're proving my point. Women can't keep cool like men. That's part of their problem."

When he reached up to help her across another rock, she glanced down, deciding that the water was deep enough. Yanking hard on his wrist, she caught him off guard. When he stumbled, she gave a solid push and laughed as she heard the loud splash followed his curse as he hit the water.

Sitting down on the rock, she watched for him to surface, spouting water and another oath. "What was that for?" he asked, shaking his head and sending water in all directions.

"Just-- you said, women couldn't keep cool enough. I thought I'd just make sure that you at least stay cool."

"You're a cruel woman, Mrs. Stevens," he grunted as he climbed out of the water, shaking like a bear.

"It wasn't me that said, men shouldn't vote, that they couldn't handle the complexities of it."

He laughed, complaining, "I was teasing."

"Maybe I was teasing too."

"Maybe?" He grinned. "Martha, come here," he commanded, standing at the edge of the river, water running in rivulets down his neck and disappearing under his dripping shirt, his hands on his hips, legs spread wide. He looked ruggedly handsome and the thought of doing just as he asked and then some was nearly unbearably tempting.

She backed away. "I don't think so," she retorted, moving a little farther up the bank. In a flash, he was after her, and they both ran through the woods. He probably would have caught her except his wet boots slipped on the fir needles, and he went head over heels.

She stopped, watching as he raised himself up on his elbows. "Are you all right?" she asked from a safe distance.

"Definitely not."

"Did you hurt yourself?"

"Yes."

"What did you hurt?" she asked, edging a little closer to assess his condition.

"My pride," he said laughing. "And if you want the vote, I'm all for it."

CHAPTER 6

The swimming hole was bordered by huge boulders. The water, an intense blue-green, formed a deep pool with tall fir and cedar trees overhanging it.

"It is gorgeous," she said as she stood looking down, "but I still don't see how we're both going to swim in it."

"First of all," he said with a wry grin, "I'm already wet. So I don't have a problem except maybe drying my boots."

"You brought that on yourself."

"Might be, but I sure didn't expect it."

"If you'd have expected it," she pointed out with a pert smile, "it wouldn't have worked."

"This is true. Anyway back to swimming. If you take off your boots and pants, you could swim with that big shirt. It'd cover you plenty good enough; and I promise not to watch-- too closely." He grinned.

"I don't know."

"You said you can swim."

"Well, of course, that is, I swim a little. There haven't been a lot of chances to work on it, but when the girls were small, we found a place to make sure they learned. Actually Matt taught Amy."

"Who taught you?" he asked, not really wanting to hear that it was Amos but tempted to ask the question anyway.

"My father."

"Ah, I don't think I've heard you talk about him. What kind of man was your father?"

"Big, rather like you except he farmed."

"And that was his dream?" he asked, helping her down a little slope to the pool.

She deliberated for a moment. "He loved books. Perhaps his dream was wanting me to go back East to school. I'm not sure he ever quite forgave Amos for marrying me. He didn't approve of him to begin."

Adam smiled at that. "The saintly Amos?" he questioned, his voice taking on a tinge of sarcasm, "why would anyone not approve of a man like that for his daughter?"

She looked down at Adam speculatively. "That's an odd thing to say."

"Was it?" he questioned, not meeting her gaze. He put out his hand to help her again as they climbed around a huge boulder.

"You know it was."

"Wasn't Amos the perfect man?" he asked his voice cool as he looked out toward the river.

"No, of course not. He had his flaws like every human being who lives."

"You believe that?" He turned to face her, his gaze searching her face.

"I was married to the man for twenty-two years. Of course, I believe that. He was just a man, a good man, but just a man."

"Sometimes when people die they become canonized. No living person can live up to them, or what they've been."

She smiled at him, trying to understand what was beneath

the words. "I suppose that's possible. It is easier to think about the good things than the bad, but I do remember both."

"Tell me more about your father," he asked as they stood at the edge of the river.

She knelt to dabble her fingers in the water. "It's cold," she assessed. "Well, he and my mother were happy as well as I know it anyway. He was a good father. I didn't have any brothers or sisters, and I suppose it could be fairly said that he invested too much of his hopes in me, but he was supportive eventually even in my marriage. He adored his granddaughters."

"That's important in a parent-- being supportive," he mused, beginning to unbutton his soaked shirt.

"What-- what are you doing?" she asked, as she watched him peel it off, throwing it the ground, revealing once again his sculpted chest and sinewy arms.

"I thought," he said, sitting down and pulling off wet boots, "that I was going swimming. What do you think I'm doing?" He threw her a frown. "This would have been easier if they weren't soaked."

"Well, I uhh... can't you swim in your clothes?" she asked, nervously looking away from the sight that gave her eyes too much sinful pleasure to feast upon. And if she looked at him, she would be feasting upon it.

"I suppose I could, but why should I?" he asked, grinning as he seemed to recognize her discomfort and found it humorous.

"Just it would look more proper."

He shook his head ruefully. "Lady, nobody is going to see us up here, and it's going to feel more proper this way." He spread his shirt over a rock to dry. He unfastened his belt and put it on a rock. Giving a little run, he dove cleanly into the water, swimming below the surface before he came up half way out into the pool.

Swallowing, she began to pull off her own boots, trying to decide if she could really swim in her pants. They didn't fit her like a second-skin as Adam's did. Loose, heavy fabric would hamper her movement in the water, and she was not the world's best swimmer. On the other hand swimming without them would reveal so much leg.

But not if I go in fast, she thought, ending the debate and beginning to unbuckle her belt. Nervously, she looked out to see where he was. He had made it to the other side and seemed to be standing on some sort of rock shelf.

"Come on in," he yelled. "The water's great."

"I am," she muttered, pulling her shirt from the pants and deciding it would come mid-way down her thighs. *If I'm just fast enough,* she thought again, walking down to the edge of the river before she began pushing down her pants.

In moments, she had done a quick step, thrown the pants back on the shore and was in the water up to her hips and watching the shirt float up in a disconcerting way, but the water did feel good against her bare legs, giving her a sense of freedom she hadn't known in a long time. At least he's clear across the pool, she thought comfortingly, but when she looked back, he was gone, the surface of the water, showing only a ripple where he'd entered it. *The man's like a fish.* She frowned as she pushed her shirt down, holding it to her legs.

Just as she'd feared, he soon erupted, almost beside her. "I'll swim across with you," he said grinning broadly. "Just in case you've forgotten how."

"I haven't forgotten how," she hissed, watching the water run in rivulets down his chest, glistening like diamonds on his skin.

She knew if she wasn't careful how she pushed ahead in the water, he'd be seeing white pantaloons, instead of the shirt. She kicked out. "Why don't you go first," she suggested.

He grinned, obviously aware of her maneuvering. "Ladies before gentlemen," he insisted, his eyes glittering from more than the water on his lashes.

"Really. I'd feel ever so much safer," she protested.

He smiled, shaking more water from his hair, but kicked off

into the deep water, floating on his back like an otter as he looked back at her.

Her own stroke was not as smooth and clean as his, but it competently brought her from one side of the pool to the other. He swam along, floating and watching her all the time with that little gleam in his eyes.

"Did uh anyone ever warn you about the river monsters we have up here?" he asked, grinning as he helped her from the water onto the rock ledge.

She realized if she stood up, her thighs would be exposed to his gaze, and she had little hope that he would be enough of a gentleman to look away. "No." She settled the problem of modesty by tucking her knees up inside her shirt. He stood above her, wet pants riding low as they clung enticingly to muscular thighs and slim hips, making it impossible not be aware of his masculinity, all too aware.

"The sea monster, well actually, he comes from under the water. Kind of grabs beautiful women by the ankles and drags them under to a cave, where he lives and they can breathe air because, of course, he doesn't want to hurt them."

"Of course not. So what does he do then? Or dare I ask?"

He frowned, stared pensively back at the water, then down at her. "Well, I'm not sure I can finish the story, now that I think about it, because it would doubtless offend your ladylike sensibilities."

"Oh my. Is it possibly one of those fates worse than death that is so prevalent in some literature?" she asked, amused in spite of knowing it wasn't wise.

He looked at her carefully as though trying to assess her ability to handle this information. "Yes, I'm afraid it is," he admitted in a somber tone.

She laughed. "Is this another Indian legend?"

He sat down a little below her on the rock shelf, his shoulder almost, but not quite, touching her. "Nope. I made this one up all by myself."

"Very inventive," she said, complimenting him on his illusion. "Is there a moral to this legend?"

"Of course, there's always a moral to legends," he explained as though speaking to a child who knew nothing. "The moral to this one is beautiful women should always have men around who can protect them from the river monster."

"I see. Any particular type of man or will anyone who comes along do?"

"He must be very particular."

Curly hair fell in glistening ringlets on his forehead, making her wish she could reach out and touch the hair, stroking it back into place. Uncomfortable with her thoughts, she tried to lessen the inner tension she was feeling. "So if I need such a man, for protection, of course-- what should I look for?"

"Tall would be good," he said, leaning a little toward her, his blue eyes intense, demanding.

"I can see where that might be useful-- for protection that is," she agreed.

"He should swim well." She knew his eyes were telling her more than his lips, but she ordered herself to ignore those messages. *Do not be a fool.*

"Is that it? Doesn't he need any sort of magic or a sword or something to help him overpower this river monster?"

"Magic would be good. There's a kind of magic that people make together. Maybe that kind. Very powerful stuff."

She looked at the surface of the river, and knew with certainty that if she stayed on this ledge, he would lean over further until she would be in his arms. *I can't let that happen,* she argued with the part of herself that wanted to be reckless, that wanted to feel his lips against hers, wanted to be held by a man, loved by a man.

Laughing, she jumped up and dove cleanly into the water. When she surfaced, she said, "I think maybe a woman should just be a very good swimmer herself. That might be better than depending on a man. They can often be quite unreliable."

She watched with trepidation as he dove into the water. *Swim for the opposite bank. Swim as fast as you can as if your life depended on it,* she told herself. At all cost, she didn't want him to catch her in the middle of the pool where she would be vulnerable, more vulnerable than possibly he had any idea.

Pulling her strokes more cleanly, she began kicking hard, knowing she could never outdistance him, but that she had to try.

Soon, he cleared the water right in front of her. "Sure you don't need a rescuer?" he questioned, blowing out water like a spouting whale.

"Positive," she gasped, still swimming hard. She watched with ill ease when she saw him jackknife in the water and disappear beneath its surface again.

Oh no, She was not the least surprised when she felt a firm grip on her ankle, a grip that was pulling her down, down to where she knew he would be waiting. She kicked out, trying to break the grip, all the time knowing her strength was no match for his. He gave a yank, and she held her breath. She was going under.

Looking into the clear water, she saw him, saw his long arms, reaching out for her. For a moment, she let him think he had won, that she would yield to what he clearly wanted and then at the last moment, she kicked out again, not really landing a blow through the water but startling him enough that he let go of her ankle.

Surfacing, she headed for shore, watching nervously for where he would emerge from the water. When he didn't, she became concerned, perhaps she'd kicked him harder than she had realized. Ducking her head back under the water, she half turned, looking to see where his body might lie when he again had her, his arms around her.

When they broke the surface, she gasped, "That was unfair trickery."

"River monsters are never fair," he said, letting her go and swimming easily alongside her. "Didn't I tell you that part of the legend?"

"No, I think you left it out."

"Funny, because it's the best part. River monsters are tricky, and they *always* get what they want."

Her feet touched bottom, and she began wading up to where her clothing lay. "Always?" she questioned as she began pulling pants on over her wet legs and shirt.

He grinned. "Well, almost always, and they prefer not to remember the few defeats they suffer."

When dinner was over, they sat comfortably at the campfire, enjoying the quiet of the forest and the bedtime sounds of the birds in the trees above them.

"Adam?" she asked after a moment.

"Uh oh," he said, shaking his head, "this's got all the earmarks of a typical *woman's* question."

"What is a woman's question?" she asked with a smile.

"You know--probe into a man's gut and try to figure out what makes him tick."

"And you knew it was going to be one by the tone of my voice?"

"Of course."

"Well, if mine was," she said with a grin, "than yours was a typical male response. Divert attention from anything you don't want to discuss. Even before you know whether you want to or not."

He smiled. "Fair enough. All right, go for it. What is it you want to know?" He leaned back against a log, one knee bent; his cool blue eyes intent on her but giving away nothing of his thinking.

"I'm curious about your family. Whenever you talk about them, there's something that makes me think something is wrong there. Won't you tell me more about your people."

"There are better things to talk about."

"Not really. Do you have brothers or sisters?"

He nodded. "You know this is going to get boring. There's no big story here. Nothing much to say about my family."

"But--"

"There goes that but again," he interrupted, shaking his head. "*Women* are always doing that."

"Maybe it's because *men* are always putting women off," she suggested with a toss of her head.

Ignoring her question and frown, he said, "Do you ever wear your hair down?"

Her frown deepened. "What does that have to do with anything."

"Nothing much. Do you?"

"Not often."

"I'll bet it's real pretty when it's hanging loose down your back." Those cool blue eyes seemed to be seeing right into her very soul.

"It gets tangled. And it is more proper for a woman my age to wear it up."

"You worry too much about what's proper," he suggested with a small grin.

"It's..." She stopped, aware she'd been about to say the proper thing to do. She glanced up at him and saw he was silently laughing at her. "I never knew you were a tease," she said, shaking her head ruefully.

"There's a lot you don't know about me," he said. The expression in his eyes changed to one she recognized but hadn't seen for a long time in the eyes of a man.

"I suppose that's true." She licked her lips nervously; all too aware they were very alone up in these mountains only the towering trees witnesses to whatever might happen. She felt no fear of him but rather of herself. He was so handsome, so ruggedly masculine; and she could only think how good it would be to touch the black curly hair, stroke her fingertips along the edge of his strong jaw, watch his blue eyes darken with passion. She turned away to avoid giving away any of her thoughts.

"There's a lot I don't know about you." His voice was deep, intimate.

She looked back and then couldn't turn her gaze away. "There's nothing all that interesting." She stopped unable to finish, unable even to remember what she'd wanted to say. She swallowed, knowing she had to break the mood, the mesmerizing force of his blue eyes. "I think I'll go for a walk along the river."

She stood, watching with a little flutter in her stomach as he rose in one fluid movement. "Sounds good to me too."

As they walked, picking their way along the rocks, she tried to put the conversation back on a more comfortable footing. "Loraine will be coming to visit soon so as to be here when Amy's baby is born." At all cost, she had to remind him of her children, of her age.

"That so?" he said, tossing a small stone into the river.

"Yes, she's anxious to see everybody. I got a letter just a week ago." She was rambling but couldn't stop herself. It seemed as though only a flow of words would protect her from whatever was happening between them.

She felt his hand on her arm as he reached out and stopped her. Looking down, he smiled faintly. She realized he knew what she'd been trying to do, and for some inane reason, it seemed to amuse him. The pressure of his warm hand on her arm was faint; yet she could feel it all the way through to her bones.

"You feel it too," he said.

"No, I-- That is, this is silly."

She pulled her arm away.

"Not silly," he said, not attempting to touch her again. "I'm a grown man, and you're a grown woman. We're old enough to know what we want."

"But--"

"There you go again," he complained, "always with those buts."

Flustered, she broke away and walked down to the river. The water, hurrying downstream as though knowing where it was heading, then deflected back upstream by rocks, before attempting again to find another path, seemed as misdirected as her thoughts. It was definitely as mindless. Bad enough had been the way her own mind tripped her up, seemed to be betraying her with its thoughts, its temptations, but to think he might have been carried away on the same pipe dreams made the whole situation filled with unacceptable possibilities.

She knew without looking that he had followed her, knew he was standing only inches behind her, not touching and yet touching her in a hundred impossible ways.

"I knew it was different as soon as I got to your cabin," he said softly, his voice a husky temptation. "When you ran into my arms, it wasn't like before."

"Of course, it was. This all seems so silly, Adam," she repeated finally not willing to look at him. "I should have never come up here with you."

"Yes, you should have." His hands were on her arms as he pulled her back against him. "You know it was right to come with me. You know it, and I know it."

She should move away; but oh Lord, it felt so good to feel his hard length, to rest for just a moment against his strength. "We're both just lonely," she whispered, trying to find an argument that would war against the feelings rushing through her body at his touch. It was all physical. It was too long without a man. It was impossible.

"It's not that, and you know that too." His breath now was against her ear as he bent, his words a soft litany.

If she didn't break away immediately, she never would; and with a strength she hadn't known she possessed, she jerked from him, turning to face him, to keep everything that he was suggesting at a distance, a safe distance. "This is ridiculous, Adam. I'm way too old for you. You were in love with my daughter for heaven's sake."

"I wasn't ever in love with Amy," he said flatly. "I played with the idea for awhile; felt I should have a wife."

"You wanted to court her," she argued, her breath coming shakily.

He grinned. "I got into a little competition there with Matt. I never have liked losing."

She grasped at another straw. "We haven't known each other long enough."

"We've known each other a long time. It's just what we're feeling now that's new." He stopped then, studying the river before he went on, "But for me the feeling isn't new. Do you understand it's why I stayed away so long? I knew how I felt, what I wanted on the wagon train, before we got to Oregon. You were married, happily married."

"I can't believe this."

"Believe it or not, I don't care, but I know what I feel. I can see in your eyes now that while it's new to you, you are starting to feel it too."

"No!" She put her hands over her ears. "This is not true. I am about to be a grandmother. You are still a young man."

"Martha, you are not an old woman. You had your children young. You're not all that much older than me."

"I am. And it's not just our ages. There's the way Loraine feels about you."

"She should've gotten over that a long time ago. There was never anything between us. I knew it and never let it happen."

She shook her head. "That isn't the way Loraine sees it. She still talks about you. She'd never forgive me-- if." She couldn't go on, couldn't admit what she was thinking.

"You can come up with all the excuses you want," he said, seeming to tower over her, "but none of it matters. It's what we feel that matters, and you know that."

"I'm not going to let you talk like this, Adam."

"You're still in love with Amos?"

"Of course, I still love him."

"I didn't ask that. You are still in love with him?"

She wasn't sure, but she did know this was impossible between them.

"You can stop me saying the words, but you can't stop what I feel, and Martha, I think you are ready to live again, to feel again."

She turned, hurrying back up the river bank. He was wrong. She could stop the feelings; stop it all. She had to.

CHAPTER 7

With morning, heading the horses back the route they had taken, Adam and Martha fell into an uneasy silence. He was in no mood to make idle chitchat and kept Joe in the lead, his eyes carefully watching the trail, not allowing himself to look back at her. Repeatedly he castigated himself for coming on so forcefully, for trying to convince her of everything in only a few moments.

Idiot, he thought. *You couldn't give things a chance, could you? Not you, smart guy. You have to shout out everything you're thinking! Ruin any chance you might've had.* He had no idea what he could do to mend matters, and so he decided to leave it alone, maybe try to talk to her again in a week or two. More likely, he thought glumly, it'd take a year or two.

When they came to the narrow slot in the mountain, he glanced uneasily at the clouds overhead. They had to make camp soon, but if it was going to storm, he wanted to get across the rock slide first. He looked back at her, trying not to see the soft curve of her breast under the flannel shirt or the way those damned pants hugged her slim hips. "You think you can ride another hour?" he asked.

She nodded. "It does look like it's going to storm."

He nodded. "Better if we get across the high ground before it does."

She followed as he reined his horse to the right, edging them up into the hills.

When they reached the slide, he studied it tensely, trying to decide if there'd been more rock fall since they'd come across two days earlier. From all he could remember, there was no good way around this point. If it was a big storm coming, the situation wouldn't get better.

"Look at the loose rock," he said, pointing out the bad spots. "When we go across, take it easy on your horse. In fact..." He dismounted. "You ride Joe across."

"But why?"

"I trust him more than your mare."

"But..."

"Quit butting me, Martha," he snapped, reaching up and lifting her from her mare. "Trust me."

She shook her head angrily. "I don't have much choice."

"You're right about that." He helped her up into Joe's saddle. "Let Joe pick the footing."

"Aren't you going to lead?"

He shook his head, not wanting to explain that the first animal across would be safest. If more rock was going to be dislodged by their passage, he didn't want her behind him.

Mounted on Martha's mare, he was glad he'd made the change, as the horse seemed determined to trip her way across the rock. They were two-thirds of the way across when he saw the mountain start to move above him.

"Ride," he yelled at Martha, slapping Joe on the rump. There was no point in taking their time now. The faster they got across the better. Joe moved with all the agility for which Adam had purchased him, carrying her onto solid ground.

When the ground slid out from under his own horse, Adam jumped, trying to free the horse and himself to make it to the safety. Hitting hard, he felt something give painfully in his left shoulder as he began sliding with the rock, tumbling down the hill. Somewhere in the distance, he heard Martha scream, but he could do nothing except reach out, trying to grab onto something solid, something that would stop his downward momentum. Rock, moving faster than he was, bounced off him painfully; until one struck him in the head. A savage jolt of pain was the last he knew.

When Martha saw the slide start and realized Adam wasn't going to make it clear, she screamed, the sound swallowed by the angry roar of the landslide. Reining Joe in, she turned in the saddle only to watch helplessly as Adam went off the mare. Horse, man and rock were one in a tumble down the slope.

She jumped from Joe's back, scrambling down the side of the hill, unsure of what she thought she could do but knowing she had to get to him. *I will not lose this one too,* was her only thought. By the time, she was halfway down the hill, rock and man had stopped, and the roaring sound had changed to a deadly silence. There was no sign of her horse, but Adam lay twenty feet or more out onto the slide, lodged against a large boulder, half draped around it, blood flowing from a cut on his forehead.

"Dear God," she cried as she stumbled across the rock, heedless that more rock might come down. "Adam, Adam are you all right? Oh please, be all right."

She watched as his eyes blinked open, unfocused and glazed with pain. "Whoa," he grunted.

"You're bleeding." She struggled to keep her voice level, not to give into the panic she felt. "What can I do?"

"You asking me? You're the healing woman." She saw him force a smile.

She reached out, touching his face. "Where does it hurt?"

"Besides everywhere, you mean." He stopped, as she saw him try to assess his condition. "I think I dislocated my shoulder," he grunted, grimacing as he tried to shift his position without the use of his left arm.

"You've got to get off this rock fall before it moves again."

"Moves?" He stopped and appeared to realize if he was still on the rock fall, she had to be too. "Martha--" he began before she cut him off.

"Don't you dare say it. I am not leaving you here."

"Damn it, get--"

She put her fingers across his mouth. "Can you stand up?"

"You're a stubborn woman, Martha Stevens."

Ignoring that, she got her arms around him, trying to help him sit.

"Lord," he swore softly again. "I'm dizzy."

"Maybe I should bandage your head before you try to move."

"When we get to solid ground," he muttered.

"You're bleeding."

"If we stay here, it's apt to get worse," he said, attempting another smile. "Give me your arm." He managed to lever himself to where he could stand.

She put her arm under him, lifting with more strength that she'd known she possessed. Swaying and unsteady, he stood, but she was unsure for how long. Slowly, they made their way across the treacherous face of the slide, both aware that any wrong step could send them to the bottom of the canyon. She became aware of the sound of a fast moving stream below them. If they rolled into that, they'd most likely die.

When she finally felt solid ground under her feet, she knew Adam was barely aware of his surroundings. She lowered him to the ground as the first drop of rain hit her face. She groaned with frustration. She had to get him into a shelter, bandage his wound. She ran his hands over his limbs for broken bones. The dislocated shoulder and head wound appeared to be the main injuries if there wasn't anything internal. She had to pray there wasn't as then she could do nothing for him.

She ran back up the slope to where Joe patiently waited. Searching through Adam's saddle bags, she found a scarf that looked clean. Grabbing a canteen, she scrambled back to Adam. She looked toward the rock slide, wondering for the first time what had happened to her mare. Half their supplies were on her. Joe had carried Adam's gun, clothing, the tent, a single bedroll, cookware, but only part of their food. With the weather turning cold and wet, what had started out as a simple outing in the mountains was taking on a new cast as she assessed what supplies they had.

She would need Joe's help. By the time she got Joe to him, Adam was unconscious again. A steady drizzle was falling. She secured the horse loosely to a nearby tree, then bent to Adam. She needed to stop the bleeding. Stitches would be hard to do, and she hoped she could close the wound with out them as she placed a scarf over the slash, tying it tightly around his head. More of concern was that his clothing was soaked. Shelter was essential.

Groaning, his eyes opened. She lifted his head and held the canteen to his lips.

"You've got to get on your horse," she said, easing him back down. "It's too steep down here to set up the tent and we're going to need shelter."

"All right," he mumbled, seemingly barely aware of what she was saying.

Between their efforts, he crawled to Joe. At that point, her imagination deserted her. He was such a tall horse and Adam such a big man. She had no idea how she was going to get him up into the saddle, and Adam didn't look like he would be much help.

"Stirrup," he muttered.

"What do you mean?"

75

"Tie my right wrist to the stirrup. Ties in my saddlebags. Let Joe do the work."

"Drag you? He could hurt you."

He opened his eyes, trying to smile at her. "Well, I don't think I can drag myself into that saddle just yet. Joe's a good horse, no stumble foot. He'll be careful."

"But."

He closed his eyes and gritted his teeth. "Can you trust me just once," he muttered sounding angry.

"All right, all right," she snapped.

"I know I made you mad. I... am just too mad at myself right now to have the patience you deserve."

"Mad at yourself?"

"For putting you in this position."

"Not even you can control a rock slide." She stood, found the rawhide straps, and made a loop around his wrist tying the other end to the stirrup. "I only hope you're right about your horse," she grumbled, thinking his body was going to be awfully close to Joe's hooves.

"Just lead him up slow and easy and make sure *you* don't step on me."

She laughed as she knew he had intended.

With each step of the horse, Martha was sure Adam would be kicked in the head, but somehow, they made it. At the top, she unfastened his wrist. She wanted to wrap her arms around him and sob, but this was no time to collapse. Things had to be done.

Adam grunted and rolled onto his side, clearly intending to stand.

"No way, mister!" she snapped, pushing him flat again. "I can handle this. Lay there and be quiet."

"Damn, if I just wasn't so dizzy," he grunted, putting his good hand to his head.

Somehow, she erected the tent and carried in the single bedroll. For a moment, she wondered how they would sleep, but she knew there was no choice. He would need her body heat. For this night, they would sleep wrapped together.

When she had half dragged, half helped him into the tent, they were both soaked to the skin. She had to get him out of his wet clothing but was reluctant to hurt him, as she was sure pulling off his shirt over his head would do.

"Martha," he said, shaking violently, "bring in my saddlebag. It's got my gun in it, and something for you to change into. You're shaking nearly as bad as me."

"I know. I know." She ducked back out of the tent, unsaddled and tethered the loyal Joe under the shelter of a tree, with even some grass, then brought back the saddlebag. In the tent, the rain was beating a pattern on the canvas. She reached over to check Adam's bandage.

"Get out of those wet clothes," he ordered. She was only mildly surprised that his tone was arrogantly forceful despite his pain. "Put on my extra shirt."

Kneeling at the foot of the tent, even in the dim light, she knew he would see her, but she also knew this was no time to be missish. She was a grown, mature woman. She could do this and whatever else was needed.

By the time she had removed all her clothing, she was grateful for the shirt, not only for modesty but because of the cold. Still shaking a little but immediately warmer, she faced the next major obstacle. "We've got to get you out of--"

"I know." He shifted his weight, then grimaced and laid flat. "I can't."

"It's going to hurt." She crawled up to kneel at his head. "We should cut it off."

"I'm not going to have this shirt cut to ribbons," he grunted, his blue eyes showing outrage at the very suggestion of damaging his precious buckskin shirt.

"I could open up the seams and sew them back together later."

He swallowed, obviously torn between saving his shirt and facing the agony that moving his left arm was going to cost.

"You think you could do it without cutting the leather?" He sighed giving in to the inevitable.

She drew the large bowie knife from its sheath on his belt and began delicately attacking the threads before she decided delicate was not going to do it. Careful not to cut him, strand by strand, she sawed the seams apart, and finally was able to lift the shirt from his shaking body.

If she was to have any hope of warming him and stopping the shaking, his boots and pants had to come off too. The socks and boots presented little difficulty, but when it came to unbuckling his belt and sliding down the buckskin pants, she was beginning to shake more strongly and not just from the cold.

You're a married woman, or were. You know what a man's built like, she told herself sternly as she began edging the buckskins down his hips. *Don't be a ninny about this. He'll die from shock or pneumonia if he doesn't get warmed.* Perhaps she could have convinced herself to stay impersonal, if she hadn't looked up and seen his cool blue eyes watching her, the expression in them unreadable.

"Remember," he murmured with an attempt at a smile, "it's nothing."

She laughed, tears coming again to her eyes at his attempt to lighten the moment. "That isn't the way I remember it," she said with a tightening in her stomach.

"Ah--" He grimaced as she eased the pants off. "I wondered if you did remember."

"I wish I didn't." She looked as impersonally as she could over his naked body, assuring herself that other than many red marks, which would soon be bruises, he didn't look badly hurt—other than his shoulder and head. Quickly she pulled the bedroll blankets over him. They alone would never warm him. If he had asked for more, suggested in any way what she had to do, she couldn't have. She slid under the blanket. He shuddered, as she wrapped her arms and legs around his icy cold body. She set to rubbing her hands over his arms and then chest, applying the friction and human warmth that alone might save him from the shock his system had endured.

As her warmth went into his body, as she felt herself becoming more and more aware of the feel of him, the hard strength that lay within those muscles, the vulnerability of his body's reaction to her touch, she knew she couldn't deny what she felt, couldn't pretend the man beneath her fingers was only a friend of her daughter's.

"Lord, Martha," he sighed as his good arm went around her. "You know what you do to me?"

"You are warming up?" she asked teasingly, bending down to work on his feet.

"You could say that, lady. Ahh." She felt the warmth come back into his body and knew hers was becoming overheated.

Lying back, she put her arms loosely around him. He had to be in considerable pain; but with the darkness and heavy rain outside their tent, she would be unable to ease that before morning. She felt his hand tentatively reaching out for her, pulling her fully against his hard length. They were safe, had come through danger and found safety and warmth in each other's arms and she felt the rightness of being with him.

"You know now that I love you," he whispered against her hair.

She nodded. It didn't seem possible, but she had known and maybe from the moment he had stepped down from his horse at her cabin. She might've even seen it when they were on the trip west, except then she'd have never let herself look. She wondered now if Amos had known.

Against all sense, knowing a match between them was impossible, still a magnetism drew her toward him. It was not all on his end. It wasn't just because she was lonely. She felt an energy in him that called out to her. He was too young. She was too old, but against all that, she did know. She kissed his temple. She could only give him one thing—the truth. "I love you too."

He exhaled as though he'd been holding his breath. "Marry me, lady."

"We can't talk about this now."

"You just said you love me. We're not children. Marriage is the next step."

"Maybe sometimes it is, but." She stopped and kissed his shoulder. "Sometimes it can't be."

"I want you."

"I know." She raised herself on one elbow and looked down at his face, the blue-black shadow of a beard covering his jaw. She lightly touched her lips to his-- just tasting what a kiss would be like with him.

His fingers tangled in the heavy mass of her hair, pulling out the pins, letting the wet weight fall down over them both. His lips reached out for hers, hard and searching, demanding the response, that she was all too eager to give him.

He stopped, his eyes searching hers. She looked up at him puzzled, then remembered his injuries. She should never have kissed him as she had.

He smiled. "It's not that. I want you. I want you like nothing I've ever wanted in my life, and it'd take more than a dislocated shoulder to stop me. Except, if you can't promise to marry me, you'd hate me and blame yourself if I took what I know you'd give in this moment, when we've just cheated death."

He was thinking more clearly than she. She swallowed. A part of her wanted to say she could marry him, wanted to deny all the things that stood in their way, but she couldn't. She was not a free woman to take whatever she wanted and let the devil count the cost. She had children, responsibilities. She couldn't just think of her own desires.

He pulled her down beside him, nestling her against his side. "Sleep. We'll work this out tomorrow."

Unbelievably, cradled against him, she did just that.

When she saw the light of morning, she realized first that she was warm, and then that she was cuddled against a naked male as though they'd slept together for years instead of only this once. His eyes were open, filled with pain, but somehow he managed to find a smile and she knew it was for her.

"What are we going to do?" she whispered.

"Long term or short term?"

"Let's go for short term first."

"Then, I think," he said with a groan, "You're going to have to put my shoulder back into its socket."

"I can't do that."

He smiled faintly, his finger reaching out to push aside a long strand of hair. "Yes, you can. I've had this happen before. It's not much fun, but you can do it."

"It will hurt you terribly."

"I know, but it's going to hurt worse if we don't get it back. If it healed this way, I'd never move it again normally. You can do it, Martha."

She sat up and looked out at the sunshine. "All right," she said, then crawled out of the tent, aware, wearing just his shirt, she was presenting him with a vision of a lot more of her body than she would have chosen, but then she'd seen all of his.

She took their wet clothing and spread them over a bush in the sunshine, hoping they would dry quickly. Looking down the slope, she tried again to see if her horse was visible, but all she saw was rock and the river at the bottom. Possibly her mare had been killed and swept away with the current.

Adam, wrapped in a quilt, had maneuvered himself into the sunshine by the time she'd turned around. "How do you feel?" she asked.

"When we get this shoulder popped back in, not bad," he assessed. "I'm sore just about everywhere, but the dizziness is less."

"How do I do it?" she asked, looking at his muscular shoulder and the malformation. This would not be easy.

"Get a grip on my wrist. Hold it straight out, then give a solid yank."

"But that's going to--"

"Yes, it is. Like hell, but then it's going to start feeling better."

Although Martha had done a lot of nursing, assisted in many births, she didn't ever remember feeling the inner sickness that came knowing she was going to be hurting him, but he was right, she had to do it.

She grabbed onto his wrist, pulling it out as he instructed, trying to ignore his harsh intake of breath. "Now pull hard," he said through gritted teeth.

When she did it, despite his determination to be stoic, a groan slipped past his lips. He closed his eyes, gritting his teeth, but never lost consciousness. She knelt beside him and stroked his forehead. "How is it?" she asked when he opened his eyes.

He smiled at her. "You look like a little girl in my shirt."

"I do, huh?" She felt tears in her eyes but didn't brush them away. Maybe he wouldn't notice.

He tried flexing his arm, moved it in a circle. "You got it," he said, sitting up, the quilt falling to his waist.

"Shouldn't I bind your arm to your chest?" she questioned, frowning a little at the way he flinched when he moved.

"Not yet. Where is your horse?"

"I don't know. Maybe she was killed in the slide, swept off by the river, but I saw no sign of her afterward."

"We have to get out of here." He stopped as she began gathering her hair back into its bun. "No," he growled, taking the pins from her fingers. "Leave it down."

"It gets in the way," she argued, the cloud of black hair around her face proving her words.

"Just for now then. The teaspoon of honey to make me forget the hurt." He grinned. Lord, his smile was at once so masculine and boyish. How would she ever resist the forbidden fruit he represented?

She shook her head but said, "All right, but just for now."

His bigger smile made the inconvenience of the mass of hair almost worth her while. "We need to get our gear together," he said after a moment. She realized he was readying himself to stand.

"You don't intend to ride?" she asked with disbelief.

"I sure don't intend to walk," he quipped, gathering the blanket more securely around his body and rising unsteadily to his feet. "Joe can carry both of us if we take it slow, and I don't intend to take it fast."

"I think we should stay here a day. You need to rest. You might have a concussion from the blow to your head, and you definitely lost blood."

"It looks to me like we'll get another thunderstorm this afternoon. Maybe we won't be able to make it back before it rains, but the sooner we get started the better. Half of our supplies were on your horse. We can't stay up here."

"We could wait a day," she insisted, stubbornly.

His smile was crooked. "I don't think so."

"Why?"

"Because another night in that tent with you, and we won't be waiting for a preacher."

"Adam," she retorted, "I told you."

"I know what you told me. Do you hear what I'm telling you?"

"Yes." She looked down.

"Well then?"

"Well then, I still think we have to wait a few hours."

"Why?" he asked with that stubborn mulish expression she'd seen so often in men.

"Were you planning on riding out of here like you are?" she asked, smiling as his sheepish expression told her that he had just remembered what he wasn't wearing. "If we wait for a little, and you rest. Our clothes will be almost dry. See the steam rising off them in the sunshine."

"You win this one." He smiled and lay back down. She realized how hard it was for him to admit weakness. "It's my fault you are in this mess," he said with another grimace.

"Things happen. It wasn't anybody's fault. You need to rest. Let me help you back into the tent." She knelt beside him more at ease now with him seeing so much of her bare legs. She wondered if he'd touch her, instead he sighed and then nodded.

Inside the tent, she adjusted the blankets around him. "Martha," he said, his eyes closed.

"Yes."

"Did you really say you loved me?"

"Yes."

"Did you mean it?"

"Yes."

"But you won't marry me?" He opened his eyes.

"I can't."

"That doesn't make sense."

She sighed, bent over him and lightly kissed his lips, but ducked back before he could react. "It wouldn't work," she said, sitting back with her legs tucked under her.

"Why not?"

"There are too many differences-- important differences."

"What's more important than love?"

"Age, religion, lifestyle. You name it, and we don't agree on it, and then there are my children."

He smiled, his eyes glittering a little with what she suspected was the beginning of a fever. "It would make for an interesting marriage," he said.

"Or an interesting divorce, or *murder*," she countered.

"You violent, lady?" he asked, his voice drifting off as his eyes nearly closed.

"Maybe I could be," she whispered, stroking the black curly hair away from the heat of his forehead.

"I think," he said, rousing himself and smiling at her again, "I knew that."

CHAPTER 8

With the sun high in the sky, Martha was able to dress in her own clothing. She concentrated on gathering whatever dry wood she could find because it was obvious Adam was running a fever. They would not be going anywhere with the afternoon.

When he said they had to leave, she only smiled, before pushing gently on his chest to show him his own weakness. "Hell, Martha," he groaned, "what have I gotten you into?"

"Cursing won't do any good," she said primly, putting the canteen to his lips. "Save your energy to fight this fever."

"I can draw you a map. You take Joe and..."

She laughed, putting her fingers across his lips. "You are joking?"

He frowned at her. "It's the logical thing."

"In the first place, I am terrible with maps. In the second, I might not find you again, in the third, other people's logic has never appealed to me, and fourth, I won't leave you alone up here. Suppose another monster came long-- the rockslide monster?"

"But..."

Smiling, she reached down, lightly kissing his dry, hot lips, before nipping lightly. "Don't you have a thing about the word *but*? Seems to me you said it shouldn't be used. So, save your breath because I will not leave you up here alone."

"Geesus," he groaned. He tried to sit up but sank back almost immediately. "Dizzy," he groaned in an angry voice. "You're right. I couldn't stay on a horse... even if I could get up there." He sucked in another angry breath.

"Give it time," she said, tucking the covers back around him. Outside, she built a fire in the lee of the wind, watching a little uneasily as the thunderclouds built up again. She kept thinking it would rain. She worried if it did that Adam would get wet even in the tent. Fortunately, the rain did not come to them. She could see it falling across the canyon, but their side stayed dry.

Cautiously making her way down to the river, she filled a small pan with water, brought it back and put it on the edge of the fire. With Adam's knife, she stripped off a patch of outer bark from a willow and scraped the inner bark into a tin cup. When it was ready, she poured boiling water over the bark, allowing it to steep into a strong brew. She allowed it to cool some before she carried it to where he was sleeping restlessly.

"Adam," she said, touching his bare shoulder. "Can you drink this?"

He blinked, trying to focus and then smiling when he saw the cup in her hand. "What," he asked with a grimace, "is that?"

"Horrible tasting but good for you," she promised.

"I don't remember anything horrible tasting ever being good for me," he argued as she lifted his head and put the cup to his lips.

"This is. It fights fevers."

"In that case." Reluctantly, he allowed her to help him drink him the bitter brew.

When she let him back down, she felt again of his forehead, worried that his temperature was rising dangerously high. She came back with a damp cloth and began lightly sponging his arms and chest, hoping she could bring the fever down a little.

"Uhmm," he sighed, "that feels good-- so good."

"I'm glad," she whispered, enjoying being able to touch his body, having such a good excuse to do it.

As night settled in around them, she gave him more of the bark tea and offered him food, which he refused. Trying to set a good example for him, she forced herself to eat one of the biscuits, before she slid back under the blankets, putting her arms around him. There was so little she could do, so much chance that he would get pneumonia if it rained again. Tears rolled down her cheeks onto his chest.

Restlessly, he stirred, his arm going instinctively around her. "Don't cry," he whispered.

"Why not?" she asked, her hand resting on his hard chest.

"Don't like it."

"Oh," she retorted in the darkness, "and that's a good reason for not doing something. Just because you don't like it?"

"Uh huh."

"You know what I think?" she whispered, wondering how aware he really was.

"I have never known what you think," he said. His lips brushed against her hair, his kiss light. "I want to though."

"I think you are a very superior male."

"Can't argue with that," he agreed with a smile in his voice.

"No, I mean, you think you are a very superior male."

"That too."

Martha fell asleep in his arms, waking in the morning only when she heard a loud, "Halloo the camp."

She looked at Adam who was reaching for his gun.

Both of them got to the flap of the tent at almost the same time, Adam barely clinging to the blanket.

Looking out, they saw the face of St. Louis as he leaned over the pommel of his saddle and looked down at them. "How ya doin'?" he asked with a broad grin as he saw their dishevelment and the gun in Adam's hand.

"What are you doing here?" snapped Adam.

"Bein' a rescue party, I thought," the older man quipped with a chuckle. "The mare come home last night, looked a little banged up. I figured somethin' went wrong... Course if I was wrong." He stopped, chuckling again as Adam ducked back in the tent, cursing as he hurt his shoulder while wrapping the blanket around himself more securely.

Embarrassed, Martha crawled out of the tent. "You were right, St. Louis. We got caught in a rock slide. That's when Adam was hurt. We weren't sure what became of Mabel."

"She's fine." St. Louis dismounted and came over to the tent, now seeing the bandage on Adam's head and the stiff way he held his shoulder when he re-emerged. "Ya all right, boy?" he asked.

"Yes," he growled, grimacing as St. Louis probed his shoulder, rotating it as he assessed for himself the seriousness of his injuries.

"He's had a fever," Martha said, watching uneasily as St. Louis manipulated the arm, causing Adam to flinch away from the pain.

"It's all right," Adam growled. "I've dislocated it before. It pops out too easy."

"How about yore head? That pop out now and again too?" St. Louis asked with another grin.

"It was fine until you started yelling."

"Got a headache, have ya?"

"It's getting worse by the minute," Adam muttered.

"You got food for breakfast, Martha?" St. Louis asked, turning back to his horse.

"We have two biscuits left."

"I brought some, figurin' ya might be hungry by now. We'll

get a fire goin' and in no time at all I'll whip the two of ya up a breakfast ya'll never forget." He looked over at Adam's clothing, still hanging on the bush and said wryly, "Maybe, ya want to give those to the boy." He smiled to himself as he turned back to the business of rekindling the fire and fixing food for them.

Adam struggled into his pants and, with only a few groans of pain, put on the shirt that Martha had worn so attractively, a shirt that still carried her scent. "How'd you find us?" he asked, as he walked barefoot to where they both sat by the fire.

"I figured the way ya'd go up here. There was no followin' your trail. Not after that last thunderstorm. I don't think even you coulda found a trace of it."

"Probably not." Adam lowered himself cautiously to the ground.

"Got caught in a slide huh?" St. Louis repeated. "Lucky ya weren't both killed."

"It was close," Adam acknowledged, "closer than I'd like to think."

"All's well that ends well," St. Louis said with another grin. "I got some hot water here, and we'll soak off that bandage, take a look at yore head."

"That's not necessary," Adam grumbled, although they both ignored him as St. Louis handed Martha a cloth and the pan of warm water. Gently, she soaked around the edges of the wound, until the scarf could be pulled away without starting it bleeding again.

St. Louis pushed Adam's head back, as he carefully studied the raw edges. "Don't think it's goin' to need stitches, but ya might get a scar out of it."

Adam shrugged. "Think it'll spoil my luck with the ladies?" he asked St. Louis with a wry grin, not looking at Martha.

"Wal, for an ugly cuss like ya, probably won't make no difference atall. What do you think, Miss Martha?"

Martha smiled, pretending to consider the question seriously. "Some women like scars," she responded judiciously.

"How about you?" Adam asked, his blue eyes now on her. "You like scars?"

"I can take them or leave them," she quipped, "but I'd prefer--personally--that you not acquire any more."

He laughed. "I aim to please," he quipped. "I'm not over fond of getting them myself."

"Did you see Amy and Matt?" Martha asked, sipping a cup of St. Louis' hot coffee.

"I did. She's fine. I don't know if Matt's gonna make it though."

"He's got it bad," Adam agreed as he took a plate fried salt pork and a slab of fried bread from St. Louis.

"Worse case I ever seen," St. Louis agreed. "Poor man even went through mornin' sickness."

Martha laughed. "Worse than Amy's," she agreed accepting her own plate.

"He won't be good for nothin' 'til that baby's born safely."

"Ya still look a mite peaked," St. Louis observed as he watched Adam eat. "Ya got a fever?"

"He had one yesterday and last night," Martha said. I think it's down now though."

"Think ya can ride out of here?"

Adam looked up and smiled. "Do you have a better idea?"

St. Louis chuckled.

"Did you tell Amy where I was?" Martha asked, her voice reflecting her concern.

"In a general sort of way. I told Matt."

"He was going to tell her though?" Martha asked.

St. Louis considered that a moment. "Maybe. Maybe not. He didn't look to be overeager to be telling her."

"I can imagine," Martha said, looking at the ground.

"What's this all about?" Adam growled. "There's nothing wrong with what you did or have done or are doing."

"Of course, but--"

"Martha," he interrupted, "you are a grown woman. You have a right to a life of your own."

"It's a normal thing for a mother to be concerned about what her children think."

"To a point. You're carrying it too far."

"Easy for you to say," she snapped.

St. Louis smiled as he watched the two bicker. After a moment, he said, "How was it up the Clackamas River?"

"Beautiful," Martha muttered, staring at the ground again.

Adam shook his head angrily, rising too abruptly and staggering before he steadied himself. "You got the horses ready to go?" he growled, glaring at Martha though his question was clearly directed at St. Louis.

"After we eat," St. Louis said placidly. "And I'm not gonna choke down my food neither; so settle down and relax. Nothing's gonna nowhere all that fast."

Martha watched, as Adam began pulling out the tent stakes, wishing she could explain how she felt to him. He had no children, couldn't possibly understand how she felt about her worry that she would let her daughters down in some way, not be the person they expected her to be.

She hadn't totally made up her mind about what she would do anyway. She felt half irked that he wanted to force her into a quick yes or no. She needed time to think about what had happened, about the new emotions raging through her heart and body. A few days ago, she had still been thinking of her loss of Amos. This was too sudden for a sensible decision. Adam though didn't want to give her the time she needed. He wouldn't even understand the need for it. All he would understand was that she seemed to be backing away, that she wasn't willing openly to declare her feelings.

She looked toward St. Louis, who had been such strength after Amos died, and wondered how much of this he understood.

He smiled. "I'll get the horses saddled. Ya go talk to the boy," he said as he went off to saddle Joe.

Martha moved cautiously toward Adam, unsure of what she wanted to say, or if there was anything she could say. "You could try and understand," she said, not impressed with the only thing with which she'd been able to come up.

"Are you trying to understand?" he asked, winding up a length of rope.

"Is it so unreasonable to ask for some time to think about all this, about what you've said?"

"What is there to think about? We love each other. Are you going to deny that now?"

"No."

"But you don't want to tell your children. You don't even want to tell St. Louis. Are you ashamed of loving me?"

She turned away, aware that he had come too close to the truth of it.

"And what is it about me that you're ashamed of? I don't have a lot of money, haven't got a job. Is that it?"

"It isn't you," she retorted, irked at him for implying she'd be looking at his material worth as a consideration. "It's me. Don't you understand? It's us together. I just don't know... I never dreamed."

"Well, I have, lady," he retorted, his eyes narrowed. "I've dreamed of it too many times, laid awake nights thinking about it and knowing it was never going to happen. I wasn't glad when I got the letter about Amos. I felt bad because I knew him, and he was a good man. But it wasn't my fault he died. It isn't my fault that I'm alive, but there it is."

"I never implied that it was."

"Martha," he said, stopping to take her arms in his hands, to force her to look up at him. "I want you. I want you for my wife. It's that simple."

"That is not simple. If you were older, you'd understand that."

"How much older you think I'd have to be, Martha?"

"I'm sorry. I wasn't meaning years but experience. You haven't been married, don't understand what that is like. There is more to marriage than feelings. There are the little things like conversation at night, like going to church together, like having the family over for Thanksgiving dinner."

"And those things are more important than love?"

"Not more important, but maybe just as important."

"I've lived too long, without any of those things, for me to agree with you. I know what matters, and it's what we feel for each other. To hell with the rest of it!"

"Easy for you to say. You have nothing to lose," she snapped.

He shook his head with a bitter smile. "That's funnier than you know, lady. Maybe it's you who doesn't know so much about love as you think." He turned his back on her, beginning to roll up the blankets and then tent.

"Adam--" She started and then stopped, as she realized she had nothing more she could say. He didn't understand. It was evident she wouldn't be able to help him see what this all meant to her.

St. Louis came from the trees, leading Joe. "You about ready?" he asked, looking from one to the other. His expression, half hidden by his beard, gave Martha no clue as to how much he understood.

"This is your favorite pinto, isn't it?" she asked St. Louis, trying to inject some normality into the situation, as she mounted.

"I seen yore horse got cut up some and went back to my cabin afore I started out. This here's Lady. I been talkin' about breedin' her. She's a beautiful handlin' little animal. Meek as can be, but she can go the distance."

"Sound like good traits," Adam said sarcastically, "in a horse or anything." He mounted Joe and looked back at them with a hard smile.

Not that she was a violent woman, but Martha wished she

was close enough to slap him. Fortunately, she was too far away to do that or to yield to her second impulse, which was to grab his ears and drag his head down to where she could kiss his lips and anything else she could reach until his anger was gone and its fire redirected.

St. Louis glanced at Adam. "Ya think ya can hang on 'til we get home?"

Adam snorted and kicked Joe lightly in the side to lead off, leaving Martha and St. Louis to follow in his wake or fall behind.

"He's a stubborn one," St. Louis said, letting his horse fall in beside Martha's, "but he'll see things clearer when his head and shoulder stop hurtin'."

She sighed, feeling close to tears. "Seems like there's no way for this to get clear."

"Things have a way of straightening' themselves out with time," he said, his tone sympathetic enough to nearly have her bawling.

"Some things can't be worked out, not ever."

St. Louis smiled and nodded. "True. Amazin' though how few of them there are."

"You make it all seem so simple."

"Pare it down to the bone, and it is."

"How can a person know what matters? There are so many things to consider."

He grinned at her, his eyes on the tall man, riding so stiffly before them. "Follow your heart, Martha, and you'll see it's not all that hard to see what matters."

She glanced at him, realizing she didn't need to tell him anything. "My heart takes me a lot of directions. Thank you though. You're a good friend," she said with a teary smile.

"Bein' a friend to you, that's right easy, Martha." He grinned. "Now that stubborn cuss ridin' ahead of us, him, it's a little mite harder, but I'll do 'er."

95

"Do you think this ride will hurt him?" she asked, noticing that Adam's shoulders weren't quite as stiff as they had been.

St. Louis chuckled, "If I know him, and I think I do, there's nothin' gonna pull him out of that saddle right now. We'll keep an eye on him, if he starts a waverin' we'll get to him before he falls off and hurts himself worse."

But he didn't waver and with late afternoon, they rode into Martha's yard. As she dismounted, Adam sat in his saddle and said, "I'm not goin' to be stayin'. That is, I figured it'd be better if I stayed with St. Louis." He looked over to St. Louis to see his nod of approval.

Martha had not expected to have to say good bye so soon and not this way. "You could both stay here," she said. "Just for tonight."

"No," he said firmly, his jaw set with determination. "It wouldn't be *proper*. And you know how important that is to you."

She again felt that urge to slap his face as St. Louis gave him some quick instructions to his cabin. "I'll just stay and help Miss Martha get herself settled in. You get there, take the second bedroom."

"All right," Adam said, his eyes on Martha. "Good bye," he said, then wheeled Joe and rode out of her yard.

Martha dismounted and handed the reins to the mare to St. Louis. "You go with him. He does need you even if he doesn't know it."

"I'll just--"

"No, if he falls out of the saddle, I'd like to know you'll be there to catch him. I'll be fine. You know I will."

He looked at her for a moment, and then smiling at what he saw in her face, he nodded. "I'll be back tomorrow to check on yore mare." With that, he rode off, catching up with Adam.

CHAPTER 9

Martha sighed as she finished putting away her gear. All she wanted was a bath and all she could think about was the hot springs and having Adam with her to enjoy them. As she heated water for her tin tub, she thought about how he had torn her tidy little life into shreds. He came along, demanding she instantly rearrange her entire existence for his convenience. What if she did it? What if she yielded and estranged her children all for him? How long would he be with her? He was an adventurer, a rolling stone. He'd be gone, leaving her to pick up the pieces. She would not be the first woman to whom that had happened.

She filled the hip bath and put it in front of her fireplace, stripping out of her bedraggled clothing and sinking into the water, savoring the warmth, the cleansing power of the water and soap.

"The whole thing's ridiculous." She worked the soap into a lather. "I was right in what I told him. He can't come here like this and tell me. Oh God," she whispered, "just what was he telling me? That he's loved me for a long time, since the wagon train. Could it be true? Wouldn't I have noticed?"

She knew she wouldn't have seen it. Married to Amos, she'd never have let herself look toward another man. She had seen Adam only as a suitor to her daughter and then as a friend of Matt and St. Louis. She wouldn't have considered him in any other way-- even if she had seen it in his eyes.

Toweling off, she only hoped she'd be able to sleep, as despite all she'd been through it seemed her mind was spinning with possibilities and impossibilities. Slipping into her bed, she lay for a long time staring at the ceiling beams.

With first light, she got up and stared into her wardrobe trying to decide what to wear. Since she'd come to Oregon, she'd had time to sew, sometimes too much time. Dresses for herself and maternity clothing for Amy had been an activity that kept her fingers busy and her mind occupied during the wet Oregon winter. Thanks to that, she had many options from which to choose. Thoughtfully, she picked a lavender print. Fitted in bodice and waist, a simple embroidered white collar and cuffs for adornment, the dress was simple but pretty. Maybe a little dressy for wearing to gather eggs, but this morning she needed the comfort of something feminine and attractive.

Dressed, her hair neatly coiled back on top her head, she wandered out into the main room. She didn't let her eyes look toward the loft or allow her mind to remember how completely a man had seemed to fill this cabin, his deep voice making the house seem like a home again. To be honest, at least with herself, she knew it wasn't just a man. It was that man.

"Don't be ridiculous," she ordered as she fixed a simple break-fast then worked on straightening the cabin, dusting the floors and furniture. She refused to think of the things Adam had said to her, the questions he had raised. In a few days, it would be easier-- she hoped against hope.

A light tap at her front door caught her completely off guard. She'd heard no one ride up or perhaps she had been so lost in her reverie that she wouldn't have heard if it had been a whole army. When she opened the door, Eunice Lance was standing there, a smile on her round face and a basket in her arms.

"How are you, Martha?" Eunice asked.

"I am well," she said, ushering her into the part of the cabin that functioned as a parlor. "What brings you here, Eunice?"

"Well, actually a couple of things. For one, I have something for you in this basket." Eunice giggled, reminding Martha of one of the woman's more annoying habits. Laughter with Eunice seemed to have no bearing on humor. Eunice pulled back the cover on a basket to reveal a sleeping, black kitten.

Martha looked at it, then back to Eunice. "Yes?" she asked, unsure of what Eunice had in mind.

"Living alone like you are, When Angel had her last litter I just knew I had to save one for you."

"Uh... a kitten. Well, I'm not sure I have time for a pet, Eunice."

"Cats don't take much time," she said giggling and plopping the kitten down into Martha's arms. "You'll just love her. We named her Heaven."

"Heaven?" Martha repeated. How on earth could she get Eunice to take her back with her?

"Naturally you can call her whatever you want. She's the prettiest of the litter and Heaven just seemed a good name for such a sweet little mite."

The kitten began to squirm in Martha's arms. "I don't think she likes me," Martha said, trying to think of a polite way to refuse the gift.

"Of course, she does." The nervous giggle again. "Kittens just like to run around, that's all. She'll be a mouser for you." Eunice plopped herself down in the large rocker, looking up at woman and kitten with a contented smile. "Just get a box with some dirt, and she will be no trouble at all."

Martha set the black ball of fur on the ground. "Well, maybe." Realistically, she'd never be able to get her neighbor to take her back. Perhaps having something willing to go after mice would be a good idea. She sighed with defeat. "Can I get you a cup of tea?"

"I'd love that, dearie," Eunice said, smoothing out her skirt and watching as Martha moved to the stove and began making the tea. "So, what have you been up to lately?" Eunice asked with a sly smile.

"Why?" Martha asked, smiling back, uncertain of how much Eunice observed of what went on up the hill from her cabin.

"Oh, just we saw a stranger come riding up your way. He was on a big brown horse. Went on past our place, but Horace said he thought he ended up here."

"Adam Stone," Martha said, determined to keep her voice casual as she brought back a small tray with the teapot and two cups. She poured Eunice a cup. "Adam is a friend of the family. He was the scout for our wagon train."

"You don't say? He certainly seemed to be a big fellow, dressed like a mountain man." She giggled. "I don't think I've seen him around."

"When we got to Oregon, he went on south. He's not a man to settle down." Martha sipped her tea wondering if she had said the last for Eunice or to remind herself.

"Roams around, doing nothing much then?" Eunice asked, cocking her head.

"Adam does what he's always done. He's most recently been a tracker and scout with the Federals."

"Oh my, an Indian fighter?" she asked, her eyes growing large with undisguised interest.

"I don't think Adam would appreciate being called that. He has a great deal of respect for the Indians."

"But if he's with the soldiers."

Martha smiled faintly. "He is trying to do what he can to bring peace."

Eunice looked down at her tea and then back to Martha. "How well do you know him?"

"Hard to answer that, Eunice," Martha said, thinking with amusement *I've slept with him naked in my arms.* She smiled as she imagined the expression she'd see on Eunice's face should she say that aloud. "I'm not sure many could say they know Adam Stone well."

"He seemed to be a very attractive man. Handsome actually," Eunice probed.

"You got quite the look at him for his just riding past." Martha smiled.

"Well, strangers don't come through all that often. Uh, where did you say he was staying?"

"I don't believe I said, but he's at St. Louis' for now. Or was when I last heard. He could be gone for all I know."

"I was just thinking."

I'll bet you were, Martha thought with a widening smile. "If you are thinking of a match for Fanny," she said, mincing no words, "I'm not sure Adam will be settling down anytime soon."

Eunice giggled nervously. "Well, it isn't easy for our girl to meet eligible men."

"We are a long ways out," Martha agreed, smiling and thinking it would probably help Fanny's meeting of young men more though if she didn't take after her mother in her love of rich food. Both women weighed at least fifty pounds more than seemed healthy.

"It might be nice just to have a little social gathering for Mr. Stone, help him meet people and maybe encourage him to settle around here," Eunice suggested.

"Might be." Martha's smile broadened as she imagined just how thrilled Adam would be at such a prospect.

"Speaking of daughters, how is yours doing? She must be more than ready for that baby to be born."

"Another five weeks or so. You know how it is with a first baby," Martha said, finishing her tea.

"And then you'll be a grandmother," Eunice said. "Must make

a woman purely proud to be a grandmother. Of course, it also means we're getting along in years-- when that happens." She twittered.

"A new chapter," Martha agreed. "And yes, I am looking forward to the baby."

"Are you going to deliver it?"

"So long as everything seems to be progressing normally, we saw no reason for her to try to get into Oregon City. Amy did visit Dr. Bloomington there though, and he felt she would have no problems. If there is, Matt will ride into town and doubtless bring the doctor out one way or another." This time Martha was the one to laugh.

"Exactly how long did you say Mr. Stone would be staying?" Eunice asked, returning to the real topic of her interest.

Martha smiled again, shaking her head a little as she looked over and saw the kitten using her sharp little claws to attempt climbing a table leg. "I don't think I've heard it mentioned. Did I tell you that Loraine is going to be home for a visit next week?"

"Oh."

Martha knew that after Eunice digested all the information, she would doubtless come up with a plan to get her daughter to meet Adam as soon as possible. She couldn't imagine Fanny presenting any serious competition to Loraine, and then she stopped smiling as she realized with her changed feelings for Adam this whole situation held no humor.

After Eunice had walked out the door, Martha looked down at the small kitten, trying to decide how she'd been left with an added responsibility and wondering what she could do with her. "You are a pretty, little thing," she murmured, scooping the ball of fluff up in her arms.

An instant purr was her reward as she smoothed the long dark fur. "Maybe this relationship between you and me will be all right after all," Martha said as she carried the kitten over to sit in the big rocking chair. She settled Heaven on her lap. "After all, shouldn't all grandmothers have cats? And you'll be a good excuse for talking to myself. You will make an excellent conversational partner. You'll listen to anything I want to tell you and you can't repeat a thing." She smiled down at the little black mite.

～

Adam sat glumly on St. Louis' porch, staring out across the valley, his thoughts not printable.

"Ya thinkin' of headin' out?" St. Louis asked as he came to sit beside him.

"What makes you say that? You want me to go?"

St. Louis smiled. "It ain't that. You're welcome to stay as long as ya want. In the last week, you chopped up more firewood for me than was good for you. I got nigh unto two winter's supply now."

"I needed the exercise."

"It hurtin' ya?"

Adam rotated his shoulder. "Not to speak of."

"You want to talk about it?"

"It's fine."

"Didn't mean yore arm. I meant what was driving ya to split all that wood with a banged up shoulder."

"There's nothing to talk about," Adam said, getting up and pacing restlessly the length of the porch.

"You never been a liar, Adam. Leastwise not a good one."

"Look, I--" Adam stopped as he saw a rider heading toward them. "You expecting company?" he asked St. Louis as he watched the figure grow larger.

"Nope, but I never expect company. It just finds me."

As the rider grew closer, Adam smiled, humorlessly. "I think this is *my* company."

When the man dismounted, he reached out to shake Adam's hand. "Man, I was hoping you would still be here."

"As you can see, I am. St. Louis, do you remember John Pollard?"

St. Louis put out his hand in greeting. "Did we meet ya in Portland afore we headed here and Adam went off to the south?"

"You remember correctly," John Pollard said with a broad smile. He was a man of medium height, his hair, prematurely receding from a high brow. A sandy mustache, matched what little hair was left. Although it was obvious by his bearing that he was military, he wore civilian clothing.

"So, what brings you here?" Adam asked, leaning back against a post, one knee bent as he studied him.

"Got any water?" Pollard asked St. Louis, ignoring for the moment Adam's brusque question.

"Shore thing. Got coffee too if ya want a cup?"

"Sounds marvelous."

When St. Louis went into the house, Pollard turned back to Adam. "You're right, of course. I am here for a reason."

"The Captain send you?" Adam asked, his eyes narrowed.

"In a manner of speaking."

"I told you both I was through."

"I remember."

"It's only been three weeks since I left. You military men are like vultures. Circle a dying animal hoping it'll be a carcass soon."

Pollard smiled. "Unpleasant analogy to say the least. Could we not come up with something more agreeable?" He considered a moment as he sat on the porch step. "Perhaps eagles, yes, I like that much more." Adam snorted but smiled reluctantly.

St. Louis came out balancing three mugs of coffee, handing one to Pollard and the second to Adam. He plopped himself into the chair beside the door.

John Pollard took a drink of the coffee and grimaced. "What the blazes is that?"

"You don't like it strong?" Adam asked with a crooked grin.

"I thought I did." More cautiously, Pollard took another sip.

"Well, let's have it," Adam said.

"There has been trouble."

"There is always trouble."

"This is a little more serious."

Adam cut him off. "Everything is serious. Unless something catastrophic changes it, that mess in the Rogue Valley is going to go on for years and there's not going to be a month of that time that something *serious* isn't going to happen. I don't need to hear more."

"You can't just quit," Pollard retorted.

"I fulfilled my contract."

"We need you."

"There are others who can do the job as well as me. I'm tired of seeing Indians hung on a tree and babies butchered in their beds. I'm sick of the stench of death, John."

"It's not going to get better if men like you turn away from it."

"The deceit and lies are so deep that there's no way to stop what's happening. No man can. I've had a bellyful."

Pollard sighed with resignation. "I told him you'd say that."

"Then why'd you come?" Adam asked.

"Maybe I needed a vacation." Pollard smiled and leaned back against a post.

Adam laughed. "You do need a vacation. Well, I was thinking about going into Oregon City, and getting stinking drunk, more drunk than I've been in ten years. Want to come?"

Pollard pretended to consider, rubbing his jaw thoughtfully. "I've nearly forgotten what the morning after is like. Maybe I just might consider it--except for getting back on my horse with a hangover. How far is this town?"

"We just follow this river down, and we'll both find out," Adam said. "Want to come along St. Louis? but if you do, no damn lectures."

St. Louis chuckled and gave a loud sigh. "Wal, I got other things I could be doin' but can't let the two of you go by yoreselves. I'll just have to ride along and make sure you stay out of trouble."

"That would spoil the point of it," Adam retorted. "No mother hens allowed."

"How 'bout I just go along to pick up the pieces and drag 'em back?"

"I heard another version of this, but mine is that there are three times in a man's life he's entitled to get drunk," Pollard said with a laugh. "When he has a son, when he doesn't, and when he just feels like a son of a bitch."

"Well, then we better saddle up," Adam said with a grin, pushing off from the wall. "At least two of those fit this occasion." He looked back at St. Louis. "There are establishments to get a whiskey in Oregon City aren't there?"

"Last time I was there looked to be," St. Louis said. "Never been in one though to be sure."

"Don't you drink?" Pollard asked.

"Not much anymore. I ain't young enough to take the aftereffect," St. Louis said with a grin.

"Don't you ever think about getting out, John?" Adam asked as the three of them rode their horses west. Because of the men's distraction, the horses picked their own gait and compromised between Pollard's tired gelding and Adam's eager Joe from a fast walk to a gentle trot.

"In my family the men are military through and through, but yeah, there are times when the rides are long and the nights cold, that I think that, but then I wonder what I'd do if I did."

"Find a wife, settle down someplace, build a home for yourself," Adam said, staring blindly into the distance and thinking of his own dreams—dreams that seemed more unlikely of becoming reality than ever.

"I've thought of it, of course, but I've never met the woman that would make it into more than an idle thought, sprung up like a small plant that is planted in the wrong spot only to wither and die."

"You need to get out of that mess down there, and you know it. Do it before it's too late," Adam said. "Get that family you used to talk about."

"Can't believe this," St. Louis snorted, "Adam Stone tryin' to talk another man into settlin' down."

Adam raised his eyebrows but ignored the dig as he turned his attention back to the rutted road in front of him. "I never said I didn't want that. I've just never been able to get it."

"Maybe ya just ain't stayed still long enough. Patience, boy. Patience, that's the ticket."

"I think some men aren't cut out for families," Pollard said. "Once upon a time I thought otherwise, but now I can't see myself with wife and child. Hell, even the military bores me after awhile. I get somewhere and want to move on."

"You should move on from this one, John."

"I have a job to do."

"It will kill you if you stay with it."

"So will old age." He grinned. "If I live long enough."

"You won't if you go back."

"I realize you weren't happy with what we were doing down there, but it had to be done."

"It's not going to be done. Not in a way you or I will want to see."

"Perhaps not but orders are orders. Because of your arguments, I came close to ordering you put in irons."

"Orders are orders. I've had a bellyful of hearing that. It's what I have against the military," Adam growled. "No sense. Just do what somebody, who isn't even there, knows nothing about it, has ordered. Don't consider right or wrong. Just do it."

"Our superiors are trained to know what's best," Pollard tossed back.

"Hate to interrupt yore argument, but which one of you is gonna to tell me what the heck happened?" said St. Louis.

After a moment, Pollard answered. "I suppose the last campaign explains it as well as any."

"How can you choose one example from so many," Adam asked as sarcastically as he could.

Pollard ignored him. "We were chasing a band of Takelma led by none other than the man we call Chief Sam, an important leader. We must have chased them up one side and down the other of the Rogue Valley. They ran into a bunch of volunteers before we caught up with them. There was a battle--if you could call it that. Several volunteers were killed which escalated the local rage."

"If we'd just been able to cut across country. We knew where they were going," Adam said. He didn't like thinking about any of this. Talking about it was worse.

"We had to follow the trail, be sure we had the right men," Pollard argued. "Anyway, we continued to follow them. It was. Well, there's no easy way to say this. One of the cabins we came across had had children." He didn't finish.

"Life was lost because we had to follow orders."

"There was something more at stake here than saving a few lives."

"Not in my mind, there wasn't," Adam snapped. "The so called bigger picture is lost when you see a little girl, maybe six or seven butchered."

"Some things are meant to be," St. Louis said. "I lost my own family, only family I had and nobody can explain why. Ain't no sense nor reason to it, but it's the way life is."

"Not the way *this* had to be," Adam said coldly.

"Adam had asked to take a few men with him and cut the band off," Pollard explained. "If he had done so, I admit that he maybe, might could have saved the settlers, the children, but he might not have gotten there in time anyway." He turned in his saddle to face Adam. "You could also have gotten killed. There were quite a few men with Chief Sam."

Adam's breath came out with an angry hiss. "At least we would have had a chance, maybe the innocents would have had a chance." He shifted his shoulders, trying to ease the discomfort in his left shoulder.

Pollard sighed. "Maybe."

"Been pretty ugly for any caring folk then," St. Louis said, shaking his head. "Seems like that's been the story of the American Indian and our people all the way along, wherever they are."

"You said it well," Pollard agreed wryly. "It doesn't get better. We didn't give up even though we lost the trail. Then we came across another trail, coming from the west and another confrontation. There were more innocents lost; this time Indians. We pieced together what happened. Some of the miners, mad over what they'd been seeing, they came across a peaceful band of Shastas, who looked to have been hunting, not looking for trouble. There was a fight. Some would call it that but the Shastas were lightly armed. The ones who weren't shot were hung."

"Left hanging from the trees," Adam added. "One was a seven year old boy." He took a deep breath, not wanting to remember any of this, let alone talk about it.

"We stopped and buried what we could and then we went on," Pollard said, clearing his throat noisily. "When we finally caught up with Chief Sam's bunch, there was another fight. But we got him, except when for reasons beyond my comprehension, we were told to let him go. So all of it was for nothing. I have no blame toward Adam for his bitterness. Just..."

"Orders were orders," Adam growled.

"That is how it is. We often don't know the full reason behind them."

Adam cut him off. "First of all there likely isn't a reason. If there was, I wouldn't want to know it. I don't want anything more to do with any of it. If saving lives isn't what it's about. If ending the fighting fairly isn't what we were there for, what the hell were we doing?"

CHAPTER 10

They fell into a moody silence as they crossed a creek at its ford and then rode past more small farms. The road widened as they dropped down into the community surrounding Oregon City. The town lay on the banks of the Willamette River. Tall, steep cliffs rose immediately behind the main business district, providing an impressive backdrop to saloons, hotels and general stores.

"Nice little town," Pollard said as they rode down what obviously was its main street, "bigger than I expected."

"Town's even got steamships visiting it," St. Louis said proudly. "It was the capitol of the Territory, 'til Salem stole it. Some say it might yet be when Oregon becomes a state."

"You think it will become a state?" Pollard asked.

"The folks mostly shore want it. It'll happen. Progress, that's what they call it."

Looking past the signs for one that appeared to offer what he wanted, Adam turned in his saddle to look at St. Louis. "You want to come in with us, maybe order a milk, or should we meet up with you later?"

St. Louis grinned. "I got a few errands I should run, a friend, who hasn't been well to check up on. I'll be back in an hour or so."

Adam and John tied the reins of their horses to the hitching rail. Adam grinned. "I haven't had a cold beer in... I don't remember the last time."

"What makes you think you're going to get it here?" asked John. "The place looks pretty primitive."

"Portland's got a brewery. I don't ask it to be fancy, just has to have ice," Adam said with a grin as they stepped through the door.

Inside, they leaned on the bar, sipping what proved to be lukewarm beer. "Sorry," the bartender had said, "but this time of the year, we can't always get ice. Nobody been up to Mt. Hood in too long. Lots of whiskey though iffn' you want it."

"No thanks," Adam said, shaking his head.

"You liking it here?" Pollard asked, watching as Adam ordered another beer.

"As saloons go, it's all right."

Pollard laughed. "Wasn't what I meant, and you know it. I remember what you told me."

"I never should've told you anything," Adam said trying to put an end to the conversation.

"Maybe not, but you did. On a lonely night when we were both feeling under the weather, you talked about a woman that you loved but couldn't have. When you left so abruptly, and I remembered the letter that had been waiting for you. I made some assumptions."

"Dangerous thing to do."

"Possibly but was I wrong?"

Adam shook his head, taking a deep breath. "Leave it be, John."

"Trouble with you, Adam, is that you keep everything bottled up inside. Let it out, talk about it. It helps."

Adam laughed cynically. "Isn't that the pot calling the kettle black? I don't remember you ever even sharing any of your personal life. Hell, I don't even know where you come from."

"St. Louis."

"You serious?" Adam asked, drinking his beer in a few long swallows and ordering a third.

"You can't keep drinking like that," Pollard said, shaking his head. "You'll be sick."

"Don't mother me."

"I am not trying to do that, believe me. I just want to be a friend. We are friends, aren't we?"

"We are, one of my best friends, but I'm planning to get drunk. I want to wipe some images from my head. It's not easy to do. I have nightmares about the ugliness at night, think about all the mistakes I've made during the day. The only thing that takes it away is when I'm so tired I don't dream. "

"Well, alcohol isn't going to help."

Adam shook his head mournfully. "I can't believe this. I leave St. Louis behind so I won't have to hear a lecture; and what happens-- I get it from you! Life is very unfair."

"It's just I care."

"Definitely the story of my life." Adam laughed without humor. "People care. Not enough, of course, but they care."

"If you came up here for a woman, was it because she sent for you? Did you see her?" Pollard asked, ordering another beer for himself. Adam gave him a look but said nothing. "If it was the woman. What happened?"

Sighing, Adam looked away from the bar, toward the window and the gray, overcast sky revealed above the falls and river. "You know, something, John," he said as he finished the third beer, ignoring the question, "I've seen too many people die these last two years. Way too many. I've seen too many children have their lives ended for something they didn't understand or have anything to do with. Straight out murders by soldiers, on both sides of a war, who don't know why they're doing it either.

Those babies, Indian or white, they didn't get a chance at life and why?"

"I can't argue with that."

A large man, standing not far from them slammed his shot glass down on the bar. "You two Injun lovers?"

"What would make you ask that?" Pollard asked putting his hands up in an attempt at peacemaking.

Adam straightened and looked across to meet the man's eyes. An unusual experience for him. "And if we were?" he asked, his words beginning to come with a little difficulty.

"I figured as much. I hate Injun lovers. Fools like you two'd give the whole valley away to the Injuns."

Adam smiled. "Give it away? Why, *friend*, it was already theirs."

"I knew you was an Injun lover," the man said, turning slowly and fully facing Adam as he carefully placed his glass on the counter.

"Gentlemen," the barkeep said, his voice raised, "if there's going to be a disagreement, I suggest you take it outside."

"No disagreement," Adam said, still smiling, "this man is just ignorant, another ignorant farmer. Can't blame a man for ignorance."

"What'd you call me?" the man snarled, beginning to move toward Adam.

"Nothing," Pollard said, trying to pull Adam back, "he didn't say anything. Come on Adam."

Adam shook his head. "I said you were an ignorant farmer. You don't know what you're talking about when you start talking about the Indians. All you types are the same-- stupid!"

"I don't know nothin' huh? I know they're thievin'. I know they're dirty, and they all oughta be hung."

Adam nodded softly, sighing as he looked back at John for a brief moment. "You heard him," he said. "This is something he brought on himself."

"I am so scared," the big man said with a sneer. "Brought it on myself." He guffawed. "That's a good one."

"Nobody's breaking up my bar. Outside," the barkeep said, a shotgun pointed first at Adam and then at the big man.

"Sure," Adam said, beginning to walk toward the door, when the big man jumped him from behind, rabbit punching his neck.

Half stunned, he twisted around to meet the challenge. "Won't be no trouble, George," the big man said. "This here won't take no time atall." Before the man could throw another punch, Adam had lashed out with his right fist, landing a solid blow to the big man's chin, followed rapidly by second to his stomach.

For a moment he thought the man would fold, but he only smiled and unleashed a left hook that caught Adam on the jaw and hurled him against the wall.

Smiling now, savagely aware that a fight was going to be better for blowing the cobwebs from his brain than alcohol, Adam moved forward, his own fists landing as the two of them exchanged blows, each absorbing and dealing out jolts that would have leveled smaller men.

"You still think all Indians are dirty savages?" Adam asked, wheezing for breath as the man stumbled backward, nearly landing on his back before he saved himself, lunged forward, and grabbed Adam in a violent bear hug.

"Amen," he growled, as he began squeezing, stopped only when Adam kneed him viciously in the groin. When he was released, he pounded the big man in the stomach and followed that with a strong connection to his jaw.

Staggered back by a flurry of jolts to his own midriff, Adam stopped protecting himself long enough to lash out with a right upper cut that finally sent the big man to the floor.

The blast of a shotgun, stopped them both. "Enough," the barkeep yelled. Even through the haze of battle fervor, they stopped. Adam was on his knees, weaving a little and the man was lying on the floor, his fist raised up for one more blow as they both froze.

"I told you both no fighting in here!" the saloon keeper repeated to make sure they'd both heard him. "If either of you take one more punch, I'm going to blast you with this bird shot, and that means you too, Crane. You'll be pickin' it out of your butt for a month of Sundays."

Adam began to laugh as he staggered to his feet, reaching down to give the big farmer a hand up. By now, his opponent was smiling too, as he watched Adam rub his hand over his jaw, tentatively trying to decide if those hard fists had loosened any teeth.

"Who are you?" the big man asked as they both returned to the bar, their drinks still setting undamaged on the bar.

"Adam Stone. This is John Pollard."

"I'm Tom Crane. What makes you think you know so much about Injuns?"

Adam took a sip of his beer, finding it had lost its appeal. John responded for him with a touch of grandiosity. "He's an Indian fighter. That's who he is. Who are you?"

Crane grinned and reaching into his pocket pulled out a shiny, silver badge. "I'm sheriff. That's who I am."

Adam did a double take. "You are joking."

"Nope, I'm off duty. Never wear it when I'm off duty, but--"

"But," the bartender said, wiping down the bar, "you don't mind breaking up my place once a week."

"I always pay for damages," Crane said with a sheepish grin.

"Do you always fight over Indians?" asked Adam, moving to evaluate his shoulder. No damage from what he could decide.

"No need to. Always something though. See with my job, I got a lot of pressure. Leaves me feeling like I'm going to blow up, but every once in awhile there's just nothing like a good fight to let off the steam. Man likes to test hisself."

"Hmmm," Adam said, catching a glimpse of his damaged face in the bar mirror. "You two in town long?" Crane asked.

"No," said Pollard quickly. "We're practically gone."

"Hey," Crane said with a grin, "don't worry about it. That was the best fight I've had in six months. The next round's on me."

Adam almost said no but decided he didn't feel like another fight.

"You really an Indian fighter?" Crane asked as the three of them moved to a table.

Adam grimaced with disgust. "No," he growled, glaring at Pollard.

Pollard grinned. "He's tracker and scout for the army down in the Rogue River valley."

"Was," Adam reminded him.

"Down on the Rogue, huh? That's rough country. I been there. Was trying my hand at gold mining. I done a little bit of everything."

"You been sheriff long?" Pollard asked.

"A year. I don't know if I want to stay with it. Seems like no matter what I do, I make somebody mad at me. Too tough, not tough enough. Not enough money to make the dang thing worthwhile while other folks are getting rich with gold."

St. Louis came through the door, looked a moment and saw them. "What ya been up to?" he asked Adam, staring straight at what was promising to become a black eye.

"Just meeting the sheriff here. Tom Crane, St. Louis Jones."

"St. Louis huh? What's your real name?"

"It's been my name for enough years, I don't 'member the other."

Adam sipped at his beer. "I can't believe it. I've known you for what, seven years at least, and I've never heard your real name either. What is it?"

St. Louis grunted, "Might as well tell ya because ya ain't goin' to let go of it 'til I do." He hesitated before he said it quietly. "Elijah."

"Elijah? Like in the prophet," Adam said, beginning to chuckle.

"Wal, I can see I made yore day. Looks like I ain't the only one. What'd ya do to yore face?" Before Adam answered, St. Louis got a better look at Tom Crane's face. "Holy Moses, ya both been in a fight. Where's the other guys?"

Adam smiled sheepishly. "We're it."

"Ya are it? The two of you been fightin' each other? "

"That's about the size of it," Crane said, through stiff lips.

St. Louis chuckled, shaking his head. "Who won?"

"The bartender," Adam grunted. He was beginning to feel the effect of the beer and didn't want to move too quickly for fear he'd end up on his face. It'd been quite a while since he'd had anything alcoholic, and he realized this had all been on an empty stomach. Pollard was right, if he wasn't careful, he was going to be sick, very sick.

"Is there a hotel here?" Pollard asked, looking toward Adam with what now appeared to be concern.

"Sure, right down the street," Crane answered. "Nice, clean place, cheap too."

Pollard looked at St. Louis. "I don't think he's going to be up to riding home today."

St. Louis grinned, nodding his head in agreement.

Adam laughed. "I cannot believe this. Now I got two of you doing it. You ought to at least take turns."

St. Louis chuckled. "Wal, then me first. Let's get us a room."

Adam shook his head. "You two do what you want, but I'm riding back to the cabin."

"If ya do, ya are goin' to end up flat on yore back," St. Louis told him.

Adam grinned. "If I fall off my horse, you can bury me on the spot."

"Is that a promise?"

"It sure is. I haven't fallen off a horse since I was four years old."

"How about up the Clackamas?" St. Louis asked with a grin.

"Not even then. I jumped when the mare stumbled—to avoid having her roll on me. Bad landing, but it wasn't a fall."

"When was this?" asked Pollard with interest.

"Never mind," Adam growled, standing and putting out his hand toward Tom Crane. "I'm glad to have met you. Ever get out our way, stop by." He stopped then and realized what he'd said. "That is for as long as I'm there."

"You heading out?" Crane asked.

Adam shrugged. "Not sure. Might go to Alaska though."

Crane's eyes lit up. "I been thinking about that myself. I heard there's gold up there just lying on the ground."

Adam chuckled as Crane rose, his body looking even more bull-like now that Adam understood the muscle behind the bulk. "Good meeting you. Maybe we can do this again sometime."

Adam grinned. "Not 'til I forget about how much this hurts afterward."

"Ya go doin' that many times, and ya won't have the same face," St. Louis said as they rode past the houses on the outskirts of town.

"Did you see your friend?" Adam asked to avoid hearing more about his foolishness.

"For a few minutes is all. He's not feelin' good."

"Do I know him?"

"John McLoughlin. Do ya?"

"Heard of him but never met him. What's wrong with him?"

"Heart sick, I'd say. After all he done to help folks, the government here got it put into the 1850 Homestead Act a clause that took his homestead land. Dang them. John's getting up there, but I think this was a stake through his heart. A lot of folks come out here and got to Fort Vancouver, and even though he wasn't wanting Oregon to be a Territory, wanted it to be its own country, he helped them. Gave out of his own pocket."

"Hudson's Bay, right?" Pollard asked.

"Yep. Then he served as mayor here, that was about the time we got here. Then he gets a kick in the butt by them as want power more than doin' what's right."

"He own the big house on the hill?"

"He's still fightin' for what's his but for now, it's about all he's got. I swear sometimes I hate government." He ended with a growl before he looked over at Adam. "Ya look pale. You sure you shouldn't stay in town?"

"By tomorrow I might be too stiff to sit a horse," Adam admitted with a short laugh.

St. Louis smiled. "Ya go into town to get drunk, get in a fight, now nothin' for it, but ya got to ride home. What's got into ya, boy?"

"It's a woman," Pollard confided.

"Don't say," St. Louis said with interest.

"Exactly."

"John, shut up," Adam growled.

Pollard laughed. "But, of course, my friend."

"Some friend," Adam groaned, giving Joe a little kick nudging him into a gallop. "See you two at the cabin," he yelled over his shoulder as he gave Joe his head.

As Adam felt the power of his horse under his thighs, he felt the first stirrings of freedom and release in years. He'd forgotten what it felt like to have the wind with him, to be sailing through time. Life was suddenly sweet. Maybe there'd be a tomorrow after all.

Bending low over Joe's neck, he urged the horse on. Joe was as caught up in the joy of movement, the rapid pace they were cutting across the land, as Adam. There was no need to urge him to greater efforts. They hit the creek crossing and didn't even slow, sending water high in the air.

As though the fight and now this wild ride had burned the alcohol, the death, anger, and frustration from his system, Adam could think clearly for the first time in months. Finally, he slowed his horse. Stopping to look at the country through which he'd been riding, he absently stroked Joe's neck as he looked into the distance. Far below he could see the silver ribbon of the river; above loomed the mass of the mountain.

This last week, he'd decided he should leave, head north, but something had stopped him and now he knew what. He'd come here for her; then had acted like the child she thought he was. Rushing her and then not giving her time to think about something that had to be all new to her. He had wanted her for too long. He was too close.

She had said she wouldn't marry him, but she had also said she loved him. He wouldn't give this dream up without a fight. If he lost, it wouldn't be because he'd run with his tail between his legs. For once in his life, he was in reach of what he'd thought would never be his. Only a fool would run off before he knew for sure there was no hope.

CHAPTER 11

A dam debated how to proceed for three days, driving St. Louis and John Pollard crazy with his pacing and need to keep active. He debated different ways to talk to Martha, all the time hoping she would come to him, but she didn't. Then one day, Matt rode into the yard.

Slamming his ax into the stump, Adam, sweat dripping from his brow, rolling down his bare chest to his belly, threw on his shirt, and strode to where Matt was dismounting.

"Howdy," Matt said as they shook hands.

"Everything all right?" Adam asked because the bleak expression on Matt's face made him suddenly afraid that something had happened to Amy.

"Yeah. Maybe. I don't know. The baby's dropped," he said.

"That's good, isn't it?" Adam asked. His own knowledge of birthing was limited to animals.

"Amy's ma says it is, but it means it won't be long."

"So? It had to happen within nine months. Didn't you expect this when you decided you wanted a child?"

"I never decided that," Matt said with a sigh. "Just it's what happened."

"I have heard that," Adam said suppressing a smile. Obviously Matt was in misery and laughing at him would be unkind.

"Where's St. Louis?" Matt asked, looking around as though he suddenly became aware of his surroundings.

"He and Pollard are out trying to find a calf that didn't show up with his mama. You want to talk about what's wrong?"

The two men sat on the front step, Matt staring off into space for what seemed a long time. He buried his head in his hands before he said, "This is hell! Pure hell! If I'd known what was coming, I'd never have touched her."

"You're talking about the baby?"

Matt nodded.

"It's the kind of thing most women do just fine, Matt. They're built for it. You got to get hold of yourself for Amy's sake."

"I know. That's what Martha tells me too." He stopped and seemed to consider before he said, "My ma died when I was born."

"In childbirth?" Adam asked, suddenly understanding more of Matt's fears.

"No, but for years that's what everybody said. She died a few months after, but I can't get it out of my head all the years that I figured birthin' was a death sentence."

"I've never seen a baby born, not human that is," Adam admitted, "but with the animals, generally it's not that difficult."

"I just look at Amy, and then I look at me and I wonder how she can carry a child of mine. She's so big right now, hard for her to get around. How can all that get out without tearin' her apart?" Matt ran his hand over his eyes, seeming to be wiping away a picture of something that he couldn't bear to see.

Adam tried to think of words that would soothe, but he didn't know enough to reassure Matt. "You know most of that size, it's water."

Matt took a deep breath and then said, "I didn't come to moan about it. I come because Amy's ma, she's havin' a supper for folks. Kind of a celebration. Loraine's home."

Trying to keep his voice steady took more effort than Adam expected. "Martha ask you to invite me?"

"She come down to check on Amy, and she sent me over. She's visitin' with her while I'm gone, otherwise I wouldn't leave." Again his voice reflected his edginess.

Adam put his hand on Matt's shoulder. "Matt, you have to calm down. Amy's a strong woman. Isn't that right?"

Matt nodded.

"Has Amy seen a doctor?"

"Yeah."

"Well, what did he think?"

"That'd she'd have it with no problem but what does he know?"

"He knows because he births a lot of babies and Martha thinks it'll be all right with her, doesn't she?"

"Uh huh."

"Then you got to pull yourself together. Martha had three babies with no problems, didn't she?" Again the sad nod. "And what about Martha's mother, she ever have any problems with her babies?"

"Not that I heard."

"Then it's like livestock, Matt. You pick a good breed, and look to see what kind of stock it comes from. You've done that with Amy. She's a strong woman, out of strong women. Quit fretting this. I got a good feeling. Soon, you're going to have a son or daughter. Whichever it is, it's going to be healthy, and Amy's going to make a beautiful mother."

"I reckon you are right."

"I know I am," Adam said, putting every bit of force into his voice that he could manage. After a moment, he couldn't resist asking, "How's Martha?"

"Fine," Matt drawled, not appearing to be thinking about his answer. "She's happy Loraine's home for a visit, but Agatha Collins came with her, and I think she's drivin' Martha a little crazy. That old woman hasn't changed a bit."

"How long's Loraine staying?" Adam asked, not really caring, but wanting to hear more about Martha without having to ask specifically.

"Probably 'til after the baby's born. I'm not sure. She hasn't said much, just got in two days ago."

It was obvious to Adam that he wasn't going to hear anything more unless he directly asked. Matt was so preoccupied with becoming a father that his brain had gone into hibernation.

St. Louis and John Pollard rode into the yard. After everyone was introduced, and Matt had told them about the invitation, St. Louis said, "Looks like a mountain lion got my calf."

"Not good. You had any other losses like that one?" Adam asked.

"Not that I knew of anyway, but once one starts takin' stock, it won't likely stop."

Adam stood up. "Show me where the carcass is. Maybe I can find the track."

"I was hopin' you'd say that," St. Louis said. "I don't hold out much hope though. Them critters is smarter than us, I swear."

"Maybe so," Adam nodded with a little smile, "but we do have guns. It evens it up some."

"What about Martha's celebration supper for Loraine being home?" Matt repeated the invitation.

"It shouldn't get in the way. What time was she planning?" Adam asked, trying to keep his voice level, aware that St. Louis at least was listening intently to every word whenever it concerned Martha.

"Come at noon tomorrow."

"See. No problem," Adam said with a faint smile. He gestured toward John. "But the two of you go on ahead if I don't make it back in time."

"What do ya mean the two of us?" asked St. Louis bristling. "I figure to go with you in yore trackin'."

Pollard added, "Me too."

"Well, you aren't, neither of you. We might as well announce our presence if we all go tromping out in the woods. If I have any chance of killing that cat, it'll be by myself and on foot."

"It don't make sense to me," argued St. Louis.

Adam laughed. "I'm the tracker, and I'm the one that's going to see what I can do. If I lose it, or can't get it before it's time to leave, I'll come back down and go with you. Otherwise, I'll meet you there."

"Without your horse?" questioned St. Louis with disbelief.

Adam grinned. "How far away is the carcass?"

"Maybe half a mile."

"I am not taking Joe up there to be cougar bait. I'll come back for him. You and I can ride up to the site of the kill, but you bring him back with you."

"Who's this Martha and Loraine," Pollard asked, "and are you sure I'll be welcome to dinner there?"

"All are welcome, most especially Adam's friend," Matt responded, explaining the identities of the women.

Adam walked into the cabin and began gathering his gear. Reaching into his saddle bags, he brought out his holstered Walker Colt and belted it to his hips. He was pulling off his boots as St. Louis overshadowed him. "You sure ya want to do this? I don't much like the idee of you goin' by yoreself."

Adam laughed. "I'll be careful, Ma."

"Wal, I know that. It's just--"

Shaking his head, Adam put on moccasins. "I'm tired of hunting men, St. Louis, real tired. Going after a big cat is just what I need."

"If ya don't make it back in time for dinner, Martha's goin' to have my hide," St. Louis grunted as he watched Adam rise to his feet.

"I'll be back. If I lose the track, I'll quit. If I don't, I'll have it by then. I expect it to be bedded down somewhere near the kill, and tonight I'll be there too. Most likely, if it has a full belly now, it'll be back tomorrow at light."

∾

Martha hovered over the table, rearranging a bouquet of flowers for the second or third time and knowing she was being foolish in her nervousness. She glanced over at Agatha who was rocking back and forth, staring into the dark fireplace. "Are you all right?" she asked, walking over to the old woman.

"Fine. Just fine. Still bone weary is all. That is a long trip for an old lady. Longer than I'd figured."

"You didn't have to come," Loraine interjected, coming in from the bedroom.

"I didn't think it'd be right, young woman traveling all alone," she grumbled.

"I'd have been fine."

"Well, it's too late now," Agatha snapped.

"What time are they coming?" Loraine asked, smoothing her skirt and looking up at her mother, who had just pulled two pieces of sword fern from the vase.

"I don't know. I said to come at noon, but I don't know."

"How does Adam look?" questioned Loraine, fussing with her brown hair in front of the small hall mirror by the front door. Her lovely face was oval shaped, her hair curly, a reddish brown with bronze highlights, pulled into a bun.

"He looks fine," Martha said.

"He's been healthy?"

"Well, I didn't ask for a full report, but as best I could tell, he was tired, but-- yes, I think he's been healthy." She didn't mention the accident on the mountain because if she did, she'd have to answer many questions with which she wasn't prepared to deal. There would be no way to explain it without admitting she'd been alone with him, and what would Loraine think of that—let alone Agatha?

Besides, he should be fine by now. Probably he'd been laid up in bed for a week or so, possibly still be taking it easy, but should be showing no effects from it anymore.

"Who all did you invite?" asked Agatha from the rocker.

"The neighbors, the Lances--Eunice, Horace and their daughter Fanny. Fanny is a bit younger than Amy. Of course, Amy and Matt, St. Louis and I believe Matt said that they had a guest, a John Pollard, or Bollard. Something like that."

"Someone's coming," Loraine said with excitement, tucking in a few stray hairs before she went out on the porch.

Martha sighed, shaking her head. It was to be expected Loraine would be excited at the prospect of seeing Adam. Would she be disappointed if Adam wasn't equally enthusiastic about seeing her? He'd said he didn't care for Loraine that way, or might that have changed over these last days? Had the anger he'd felt at her refusal to consider marrying him given him a changed attitude about other things.

"It's just Amy and Matt," Loraine said as she ushered them into the house, hugging her sister as best she could around her burgeoning belly and then her brother-in-law.

"Just Amy and Matt?" Amy retorted with a grin. "What a greeting, Raine." She laughed at Loraine's attempt at a contrite expression as the sisters hugged again.

Moving over to the table, Amy said to her mother, "The flowers are very pretty."

Martha smiled. "Seeds came from Missouri." She pulled up one of the daisies to adjust the arrangement for what seemed the hundredth time that morning.

Heaven woke and came out from behind the stove, stretching and looking sleepily up at all the people who were gathering in her home. She yawned broadly showing off tiny sharp teeth.

"Who's this?" asked Amy, reaching down and picking up the kitten.

"Heaven. Eunice decided I needed a pet. Either that or she had one kitten she couldn't get rid of any other way. Whatever the case, here she came, and it looks like here she'll stay."

"I can't believe you have a cat," Amy said, stroking the smooth fur and listening to the loud purr. "I didn't think you liked cats."

"I didn't either," Martha admitted, "but I guess I do this one."

"You don't need to defend it to me. I think it's a great idea."

"How are you feeling?" Martha asked, as Amy put down the kitten and absently rubbed her back.

"Like this baby can't come any too soon. I'm not sure Matt's ready though."

"He does look a little peaked," Martha said with a smile. "Maybe I ought to mix up some tonic for him."

"The man is going to have a breakdown if he doesn't relax-- either that or drive me to one."

"He's not handling this well." Martha began stirring a large pot of beans on the stove.

"Just all those old fears. Then when I miscarried our first one, well, it's made him feel doomed, I think." She laughed. "It helped some after he talked to Adam yesterday. I guess he needed masculine support. Not that St. Louis hasn't been great, but Adam's always been a good friend." She grinned. "Well, almost always."

"He talked to Adam?" Loraine asked.

"He went over there to invite them. How'd you think he did that without talking to Adam?" Amy smiled; her eyes twinkling with amusement.

"Well, uh how is he?"

"He's fine, or at least he was yesterday."

"When will they be here?" Loraine asked nervously.

"I think St. Louis and Mr. Pollard just rode up."

Martha stopped stirring the pot and turned to look at her daughter. "Adam might not come?"

"It seems St. Louis lost a calf to a cougar. Adam was going to track it, and he might not be back by the time they'd be leaving."

Martha felt the blood rush out of her head. "Track it at night, by himself?"

Amy shook her head at the vagaries of men. "That's what they said. It didn't make sense to me either, but there was something about one man having a better chance than several, and it not being that dangerous, and I don't know."

Matt, who had gone outside, came back in with St. Louis and John Pollard. As soon as Matt had finished introducing Pollard to them all, Martha could not resist asking, "Adam didn't come?"

"He'll be here," St. Louis said with a frown. "He said he'd get the cat or give up in time to make supper."

The Lances came through the door and introductions had to be repeated. Fanny, pretty but easily as heavy as her mother, looked around the room shyly. Eunice surveyed them all. "Wasn't someone else going to be here?" she asked. When the explanations had been given, she turned her interest and questions to John Pollard.

As she returned to her stove, Martha tried to hide her worry. His shoulder could be reinjured. It hadn't been that long since the dislocation. He shouldn't have been allowed to go from a sick bed to hunting a cougar.

"Were you out of your mind, letting him go off by himself?" she hissed at St. Louis when he made the mistake of coming back to talk to her.

"I'd like to of seen anybody stop him," St. Louis said defensively, keeping his own voice low. "He was set on doin' it his way."

"It's foolishness. Just plain foolishness," she muttered. She stopped, concerned that she might be overheard and her words misconstrued or worse correctly read.

"Maybe so," St. Louis responded, putting his arm around her shoulder, "but he knows his business, and I don't think even *you* could've stopped him."

She stared into his eyes, realizing that no matter what she said or didn't say, he knew the truth of her feelings for Adam. He knew and didn't seem to condemn her. She shrugged her shoulders. "I suppose you are right, but..."

"He'll be all right," the older man said, his voice for her alone, "in every way."

Martha went onto the porch for seemingly the fifth time, trying to not to appear as though she was looking for him and all the time anxiously scanning the horizon. She was convinced something had happened, and it took her a moment when she first saw man and horse coming across the field, racing the wind, before her brain could accept who it was. She stopped, momentarily stunned by the impact just seeing him had on her. Loraine, quickly at her side, said, "It's him! It's really him."

"Yes," Martha said her eyes unable to release him as he pulled up the big horse by her front porch as he had done only three weeks earlier. He'd turned her life upside down since that time, gone off and left her, and now was back and dismounting, his eyes on her.

He looked hard and lean, the bristle on his jaw only accentuating his raw masculinity as it had before. And more importantly, as she scanned his long length, he was unhurt, seemingly undamaged in any way as he moved like a big cat himself toward where they waited.

Martha stood, unable to move as she watched Loraine run down the steps and throw herself into his arms. *Was it only a few weeks ago that I did the same?* she mused, amazed again at how her life and thinking had been turned around in that short span of time.

Adam kissed Loraine lightly on the top of the head. He looked up at Martha, his gaze held hers in that unsettling way of his "Am I late for supper?" he asked, his voice dark, intimate and somehow erotic despite the simplicity of his words. Or was it that anything he said would cause her stomach to flutter and her heart to skip beats.

"We waited." She swallowed, knowing that if anyone had been watching her, they would have seen, known everything that she didn't want known. Don't look at him, she sternly ordered, put this all from you. Don't think. Don't. As she turned to go back into the cabin, she saw that St. Louis was standing in the doorway, his gaze missing nothing.

"You all right?" he asked, allowing her to pass.

"Of course," she said briskly as she hurried into the room. "I'll have the food on the table in a minute."

Behind her, she heard St. Louis asking, "Did ya get it?" And Adam's answering deep laugh as he told them about the long night he had spent and the final success of his hunt.

Amy and Martha put the food on the long table Amos had made for their cabin. Although ample in length, they could not all sit at it.

"You overdid yourself," Eunice said, complimenting her on the lavish spread.

Martha wished she could take some pride in what she saw displayed on the table. Fried chicken; scalloped potatoes; a corn soufflé that even she had doubted would turn out, but had; tomatoes from her garden; pickles that she had put up the year before; and the first of her green beans. Over on the counter were the dried apple pies for dessert.

All of it should have made her feel good, having her family with her should have made her feel good, but somehow all she could think about was one man and the young women who should be his interest.

She asked St. Louis to say the blessing; then some settled at the table, others on the porch or by the fireplace. Eunice and Agatha seemed to have found something in common. Half of the men, Matt, St. Louis and Horace were on the porch, talking about their homesteading problems as they ate, while John Pollard stuck nobly to Adam's side as Fanny and Loraine vied for his attention at the table.

Martha swallowed, aware Amy was watching her, curiosity in her large eyes. "Are you all right, Mama?" she asked.

"Of course, why would you ask?"

"You seem pale."

"Could be the heat-- of the stove," she suggested, aware that Adam's gaze had settled on her again. He sat back, apparently having eaten all he intended.

"Is it true you are a scout for the military?" Fanny asked.

"It was," he said, not taking his eyes from Martha.

"I can't believe it's been almost four years since I saw you last," Loraine said, "but you don't seem to have changed much."

"I don't change," Adam said, smiling faintly, "about things that are important."

Nervously, Martha moved back to the stove and picked up the fresh coffee pot. She carried it out onto the front porch to the men. St. Louis looked up. "Let me take that. You just rest a mite. I'll pour everybody their coffee."

She nodded gratefully, aware that to go back into that cabin was to face those eyes and to watch Loraine and Fanny vying for who could fawn over Adam the most.

She walked a little ways from the cabin, trying to settle herself enough to face what she must, to deal with her unrealistic heart, which kept betraying her at every opportunity. Why did he have to look so handsome? Damn that rugged bristly jaw. He ought to look unkempt like any other man would, not so masculine! So--

At that moment her heart seemed to stop as she realized that he was walking behind her, his height towering over her.

"How have you been?" he asked his voice low, husky, intimate.

"Well, I... How is your shoulder?" She would keep everything casual. It was the only way this was going to be bearable.

She glanced up into his face and saw by the twitch of muscle in his jaw that he was tenser than he had sounded. He glanced down at her and then off toward the mountain. "That's a pretty dress. I like how the blue makes your skin look like porcelain." *Damn! No way could she handle this. Not possible.* "I would've shaved," he apologized, rubbing the bristles on his jaw but still not turning to look back at her, "but then I'd have been late, later, that is."

"That's fine."

She gave herself permission to just for a moment look fully on him, take in the way the hair curled around his collar, the strong brows, drawn into a frown, those intense eyes, which seemed determined to see into her heart. Loraine's voice interrupted the moment. "There you two are. What are you doing down here?"

Adam glanced up at Loraine and then finally at Martha. "I was telling your mother about the big cat."

"How exciting. Suppose you tell us all?" Loraine asked, hooking her arm into his and steering him away and back toward the cabin.

Adam looked back at her for one long moment. She felt his words as though he was saying them, but she knew he wasn't. One sign from her and he'd tell them all what she meant to him. All she had to do was give it, but she could not. She cast her gaze to the ground. She couldn't face the demand nor see the disappointment she imagined would be on his face. She was not the right woman for him. She knew it. She just had to convince herself.

The rest of the afternoon seemed to stretch on forever as

Loraine and Fanny demanded Adam's full attention, something he seemed charmingly ready to give them. Martha kept herself busy washing dishes, visiting with Eunice and Agatha, consciously making herself part of the older generation, and trying not to let herself think.

She heard the voice behind her, not turning around as St. Louis asked, "You need some help?"

She cut the pie into wedges. "You can give these out," she said instead of what she was thinking, "and see if anyone wants coffee with it."

"I reckon I can handle that," he said, his eyes on her. She knew he recognized her subterfuge. Because he was her friend, he said nothing.

Amy went around with the big pot of coffee until Matt took it from her. "Sit," he ordered, his gray eyes narrowed.

Adam laughed at him as he accepted a refill of his cup. "Ya think it's funny," Matt said, looking from Fanny to Loraine and back to Adam's laughing face. "Just you wait. One of these days. It'll get you too. I can see it comin'."

Adam sat back, stretching out his long legs. "You can huh," he said as he glanced up at Martha.

"Surely you are not opposed to marriage, Adam," Fanny said, settling her plump body as close as possible.

"No ma'am, but I haven't met the lady who'll have me."

"Or is it," inserted Loraine, "the lady you'll have?"

"Whatever the case," Adam said, "I guess it's the same in the end. But for now I have the freedom to roam, do what I want when I want. Maybe it's not such a bad trade off to be alone."

Eunice looked at him smiling, "Marriage is a wonderful institution, Mr. Stone."

"I've heard that, Mrs. Lance." He smiled then, his eyes twinkling. "With the right woman, a lady like you for instance, I'm sure it would be paradise."

Eunice grinned broadly. "There are many eligible young ladies around. Surely one caught your eye."

"Actually," Adam said, glancing again at Martha, frustration in his eyes, "often the women I've wanted, don't want me."

Loraine stared at him with interest. "Women? You met someone in Southern Oregon."

"Did I say that?"

"Well, lord love a mystery," said Eunice." Are you going to tell us anything about this mysterious lady of yours?"

Martha came up behind her; interrupting before anything more could be said. "More pie or coffee?"

"No," said Fanny, "although that pie was just delicious. May I have the recipe? I always collect good ones for when I have my own home."

"Of course," Martha said, heading outside to ask the men if they wanted more to eat or drink and avoid thinking of Adam's provocative comments.

CHAPTER 12

Adam felt an anger surge inside him at Martha's stubborn refusal to admit what he knew she felt, what was so right. He rose abruptly and walked onto the back porch, feeling like leaving and never coming back. He inhaled deeply, trying to steady himself; then realized he'd been followed outside and was only partly relieved to see it was John.

"Is this the smoking room?" Pollard asked with a grin.

"I didn't know you smoked."

. "Don't," Pollard said.

Adam rotated his shoulders, trying to take the kinks from them. The long sleepless night was beginning to catch up with him, and he felt as though a lead weight was attached to his body.

"So that's the lady," John said with a smile.

"What lady?"

"Don't play dumb with me. I saw the dusky beauty, how you looked at her and by the way, she at you. She'd be enough to tempt any man."

Adam started to say something, to deny it, but it would be pointless, besides there was something good about having someone who understood. "For all the good it's doing me."

"She's aware of you every moment."

"She's hiding it well."

"Only for someone not looking. If I were you and I realize advice is easy to give and hard to follow, but I think I'd hang in there. Her situation is complex to say the least. Be patient. Give her time to work it through."

"It's not easy."

"What good things are?"

"Ah the cavalry philosopher."

Pollard grinned. "You are an impatient man, Adam Stone. You don't like to wait for anything. You reach out with both fists to take what you want, fight for it, but this is something you can't fight that way. Women like her, you can't grab them with your fists, and that's got you frustrated, doesn't it?"

"Some," Adam admitted, chagrined that his old friend had read him so easily.

St. Louis wandered outside to join them, a cup of coffee in his hand.

"I'm beat and heading for your cabin," Adam told him.

"Want me to say yore good-bye to the gals... and Miss Martha?" St. Louis asked, emptying his cup.

"I'll do it. He didn't want to go back into that cabin, but common courtesy said that he could not just leave; moreover, he didn't want Martha thinking that a retreat meant the end of the battle. "Don't the two of you feel like you have to leave now, but for me it's been a long day."

St. Louis looked at him with understanding. "I see that."

"I imagine you do." Adam straightened, girding up his nerve to re-enter that cabin. Right now, shooting another mountain lion would be easier.

When he walked back inside, he was relieved to see that only Martha stood at the counter, a dish pan in front of her, her hands deep in the suds. He swallowed hard, as he walked up behind her, stopping with only inches separating them. "Are you leaving?" she asked, not turning.

"Yes."

"I realize you must be tired."

"Yes." He considered not saying more—for all of a moment. "Tired and frustrated."

She turned around, almost in his arms, but he kept his arms at his side, not drawing her against him as he wanted.

"With me?"

A lock of her hair had fallen from the bun and he pushed it back behind her ear. He let his hand drop before it did something that would make her mad.

"I am sorry, Adam."

"You know what you're doing to me?"

"I'm doing what I believe is best for both of us."

"I used to dream of having you in my arms, of holding you as we both slept. It was only a dream then. Now it's been real, and it's worse than a nightmare to think about it."

"I said I'm sorry." She glanced past him toward the open door and the front porch. "Someone could come in."

"And why would we care?"

"You might not, but I would. I have responsibilities, family."

His laugh was angry. "Do you love me?" he asked after a moment. "Did you really say it that night? I've wondered that a hundred times since then."

"I said it," she whispered, tears beginning to come to her eyes.

He was tempted almost beyond resisting, to reach out and brush the teardrop from her cheek.

"It's just so impossible. Can't you see that? Didn't today show you that?"

"Is that why you set all this up? To show me?"

"Not at all. That is, I don't know. It just seemed like the right thing to do."

"And you always do the right thing, don't you?" he asked, his voice husky, deep. He leaned toward her, his breath almost brushing her forehead.

She would have turned away, but he reached out, grasping her arms, holding her so that she had to face him. "I try," she said finally.

Before he could react to that, she broke away from him and hurried through the door to the porch where everyone else was sitting, enjoying the early evening air. He heard her asking if anyone needed anything as he slipped out the back door.

Manners or no, he'd had all he could take for this one evening. All he wanted to do now as to get out of there, to get where he could think. Only on Joe, only with the air flying past his face, did he think that would be possible. He tightened Joe's saddle girth.

Pollard came up behind him. "I think I'll leave now too."

Adam gave him a hard smile and said, "I don't think you'll be able to keep up," as he stepped into the saddle.

Pollard grinned. "Maybe not, but I'll give it the old military try."

"The two of ya left some disappointed young ladies behind," St. Louis said when he got back to the cabin. "Tough job, me trying to make it up to 'em"

Adam was sitting slouched by the fireplace, half leaning against a large pillow, staring morosely into the flames. Pollard sat on a narrow chair, cantilevering it backward and rocking. "I doubt they missed me," he said when Adam said nothing.

"You feelin' left out, Pollard?" St. Louis chuckled.

"Didn't Mrs. Stevens tell them I'd said I was leaving?" Adam didn't look at St. Louis, not wanting him to see into his eyes, to read between the lines to the source of the tension. He needed more time to school his features and put pretense back into place. He ought to be able to do it. He'd had more than enough practice.

"Must've slipped her mind," St. Louis said.

"A lot seems to be doing that lately," Adam muttered.

"What'd ya say?" St. Louis asked as he sat down with them.

"Nothing. Absolutely nothing."

"Not goin' into town for another drunk are ya?" asked St. Louis with a little grin.

"Didn't help much last time." Adam yawned, not anxious to go to bed-- afraid he wouldn't sleep. If he didn't sleep, he'd think. If he slept, he'd dream and that was often worse.

"I got a little medicinal whiskey here. Purely, o' course for health, but if ya boys want I'd pour ya each a shot."

Pollard grinned widely. "Well, I'd appreciate it, even if my morose friend here doesn't. Even the Bible suggests a little now and then for the stomach if I recall." He chuckled.

St. Louis grinned as he poured a small amount of the amber liquor into two glasses. He handed one to Adam. "If it'll make ya feel better, made her miserable too."

"What are you talking about?"

"Don't play no games with me, Adam. I seen it right from the start; and although Pollard over here might be one of them by the book military types, he's a bright boy and he's seeing what's goin' on too." Pollard gave an offended and dramatic grunt of protest. St. Louis grinned. "Now you might fool folks too wrapped up in baby makin' to see anything else, or them what's wantin' to catch themselves a man, but ya ain't foolin me."

Ignoring his probing, Adam took a sip of the hard liquor, grimacing as he swallowed it. "You are right about this being medicinal," he said as he half choked. "How long's this been evaporating on your shelf?"

St. Louis smiled. "Brought it with me from Missouri. Can't recall when I bought it, but it's been awhile, that's for sure."

Pollard coughed but grinned widely. "Well, I for one, appreciate it. It is, if not smooth, definitely effective. My stomach has not felt so *warmed* in months."

Laughing, St. Louis lit a fire in his cook stove and poured water into the coffee pot before measuring out the proper amount of coffee. "Now a cup of hot coffee, that's what does it for me. Nothin' like it on God's green earth. Got the smell, the taste and gives ya a jolt of pick-me-up."

Adam shrugged. He remembered all the late night cups of coffee he, Matt and St. Louis had shared. All the times he'd sat at the Stevens fire talking to Amos and Martha. It had been a good right up until he'd realized why he liked the Stevens fire so much, until he had come to realize what had been drawing him to their hearth again and again. At that point, he had stopped going.

"How ya feelin' tonight?" St. Louis asked.

"Fine." He shrugged, wincing as he irritated his left shoulder with the movement. "I'm stiff as a board though." He realized if he got St. Louis involved in diagnosing his old injury, he'd likely forget everything else. The problem with Martha was a thing he didn't want to discuss with the older man. It would not help.

"That shoulder ya dislocated, hurting?"

"Some."

St. Louis stood up and bent over him, reaching down, manipulating the shoulder a little. "Hurt?"

"Yes." Adam twisted away from painfully probing fingers. *Okay, so that hadn't been such a good idea.*

"Likely irritated it, sleepin' out last night."

"Probably."

"By the way, how big was the cat?"

"You can see for yourself," Adam said, sipping from his glass. "The pelt's in your barn."

St. Louis grinned. "In the barn?"

"You heard me. You aren't getting deaf in your old age are you?"

"Ya skinned it?"

"That's the usual way you get a pelt," Adam quipped sarcastically.

"What for?"

"Maybe I wanted a rug."

"Ya salted it down and nailed it to the wall yet?"

"I figured I could do that in the morning."

"I'll do it for ya. An old trapper like me's got a way with furs."

"I don't doubt that," Adam said, smiling faintly. "All right, go to it. I've never been overly fond of the smell of a raw hide anyway."

"Any special purpose in mind for it?"

Adam refused to offer him the truth that he'd seen it as a lady's muff, trim for a coat, or maybe even a rug in front of a hearth, and so he said nothing.

Pollard rose and yawned. "I hate to have to say it, but I have to leave tomorrow."

"You never said anything about that before."

"I suppose I was thinking if I didn't mention it, it wouldn't happen. I don't want to go back but duty calls."

"Quit the military, John," Adam said. "Quit while you can."

"I've thought about it especially after seeing this country, meeting your people. I've still got a year and a half left on my enlistment though... So, I have to go back for now."

Adam shook his head and threw another chunk of wood onto the fire, staring broodingly into the flames. "I see your future in this fire, John. Don't go back. Leave it for someone else."

"Desert?" Pollard laughed.

"De-enlist," Adam said with an answering chuckle. "I don't know. Just don't go back. It's going to explode down there, and when it's done it'll be ashes. Get out while you can."

"I know this won't make sense to you," Pollard said, "but I see it as my duty."

"I understand duty; but to have an oath of allegiance worth anything, it has to be to a higher good."

"I never knew you were a spiritual man," Pollard said.

"I'm not the way you mean it, but I just see there's a way to live, to be, and what's happening there is ugly and no part of good. It's no place for you."

Pollard sighed deeply. "Whether you were right or wrong, I'd still go back. I don't know any other way. You are a law unto yourself, Adam, but I follow the laws of others. It's the difference between us. One of the things I've actually admired in you-- why I suppose I sought you out as a friend. A friend is the one who fills out those places in a man where he knows he'll never be able to."

"You are setting yourself up to be a martyr. You go back, and you'll die there."

"If I do, it'll be for what I believe in, my code, and my death will mean something."

Adam snorted. "Bullshit. There will be many deaths down there. None of them will mean anything."

"This is where we must agree to disagree," Pollard said with a faint smile.

"What do you think, St. Louis?" Adam asked.

"Ya really want to know?"

"Would I have asked if I hadn't?"

"Men do sometimes. Wal, I'll tell ya." He poured his coffee. "There's a path for each man. The man who finds the one he's supposed to be on is a lucky man. I'd say ya could both be right and be doin' different things. It's the way life is."

"Each man's truth is different?" Pollard asked.

St. Louis nodded. "Some of that, but there's *truth* and there's truth. Some of it is forever and would be true for all of us. Others is part of what we come here to find and do, and we each have a different chunk of it."

Adam poured himself another shot of St. Louis' whiskey. "The philosopher wagon master. Well, in my opinion, men say things like that when they don't want to face their truth."

"Could be," St. Louis agreed. "I can't argue with you. Truth is what men fight and die over."

Pollard rose and stretched. "I keep it simple. I follow orders. Do what I have to do. It's easier than trying to sort it out for myself."

"You'll be the one paying for your choices," Adam said.

"If I wasn't doing this, I'd be keeping a hardware store somewhere, and I don't see how that'd have more value than what I'm doing down on the Rogue. I am trying to make a difference there-- hoping to make my life count for something."

Adam shook his head. "Six feet under, it won't count for anything."

"Maybe. Maybe not," Pollard said. "Someday maybe we'll both know."

"I doubt it," Adam said, feeling a surge of frustration. "I'd rather not be around to pick up the pieces after this one."

"Someone has to."

"Maybe so, but it doesn't have to be me or you." He looked at St. Louis. "I think I'll be leaving in a day or so."

"You not staying 'til the baby's born?"

"Damn." Adam grimaced. He felt trapped and didn't like it. Being around Martha this way was proving to be even harder than it had been before. Someday there'd be a man for her, one she deemed proper. She was too beautiful to stay widowed. It was not going to be him. It was obvious she'd never see him as a fit mate.

Maybe she was right, and he wasn't fit for her. He would not stay around while she was with another man, not going to endure that again. No way! Alaska, that was the place to be-- adventure, gold. No woman to haunt his dreams. No woman to remind him of what other men had, but he never would. He didn't care about gold. He just cared about escape.

He looked up to see St. Louis staring intently at him and knew without words being spoken that the old man had read all the thoughts that had passed through his mind.

"Don't go now," the older man said. "You want to talk about

this or ya don't, fine with me. I know though, like an ache in my bones that this ain't the time for ya to leave. If nothing else, Matt needs you."

Adam sighed. "I'll stay until their baby is born."

"Good."

"Maybe I could ride over, and do some work over there," Adam muttered as he stared back into the fire.

St. Louis chuckled. "Good idea. They could use three year's supply of firewood just like I got now."

Martha lay beside Loraine on the bed in the loft, having turned over her bedroom to Agatha. She found sleep almost impossible. When she wasn't busy, her imagination was filled with the images and scents of Adam. She kept picturing him sprawled across this very bed. The image in her mind was naked, muscular, male and tempting her with dreams that she knew were wrong but couldn't escape.

You've been too long without a man, she told herself as she stared fixedly at the beam in the roof over her head and instead saw him rising from the river, water running in rivulets down his body. She imagined herself doing what she'd wanted that day, walking toward him, instead of running away, catching those rivulets with her tongue.

"Mama," Loraine whispered, "are you awake?"

She didn't want to answer her. This was her daughter and she couldn't deny her. "Yes."

She heard Loraine swallow. "I don't understand Adam. I don't know what's going on with him. He treated me like a stranger. Like he knew me no better than Fanny."

Martha didn't want to talk about this. Not any of it. How could she when she was swollen with desire for the same man?

"It hurt. I didn't think it would after all this time, but it still hurt."

"Are you in love with him?"

146

There was a silence. Martha thought perhaps Loraine had fallen asleep. "I don't know," her daughter's voice came from the darkness, deeper, throaty. "I never knew before, and it isn't any easier now."

"What do you mean?"

"Well, sometimes, I think yes. Once, when we were coming west still, I thought maybe he might be starting to care for me, but he never said anything, never even kissed me. I think I was reading into it something that wasn't there."

Martha hurt for her oldest daughter, who was still her baby.

"When he stopped coming to our wagon, stopped visiting us at all. I thought. Well, I didn't know what to think, but it had to be because of Amy and Matt getting married."

"A logical assumption for you to make," Martha said.

"When we got here, and the Collins offered me the chance to live in Portland, I thought I'd meet someone, find a man who loved me back. It's been good there. I like running a business, far more than I expected, but there's been no man. Then, when you said Adam was here, I admit, I hoped-- again. I feel like a fool now because I know if he felt anything, he would have been different today. I'm not a fool about men. At least, I hope not."

"I'm sorry, Loraine. It's hard when the man you want doesn't want you back."

She gave a sad little laugh. "He treats me like a kid sister, which is the way he's always treated me. That isn't the way he'd treat me though if he loved me, is it?"

Martha gritted her teeth against the tears. "No, probably not." She felt helpless to help either her daughter or Adam. Both were hurting. Except, so was she. She was hurting in a way she had hoped never to hurt again. When Amos had died, she thought she had died too, the part that could love. Then it erupted to life in the most shocking way. She hadn't wanted those feelings to come to life. They had the potential to hurt too much.

She felt disloyal to Loraine and even to Amos though she

knew that was foolish. To have those feelings for another man seemed wrong. When she'd married Amos, she never expected to love another man, never to want another man's hands on her body, or to want to stroke his. Now she could only lie in the darkness and fight against remembering how Adam's hard muscles had felt beneath her fingertips, lie there knowing she wanted to touch him again. She tasted the desire as it flooded through her.

"What should I do, Mama?" Loraine asked.

"About what?"

"About Adam? Do you think there's a chance for me with him? How did you read him today? Am I wrong in thinking he doesn't care for me?"

Tears flowed down Martha's cheeks as she fought to keep Loraine from knowing she was crying.

"Mama, are you awake?"

"Yes, I'm just thinking." There were no right answers. No matter what she said it would be unfair to someone. Was there a chance for Loraine with him if she convinced him he could not have her? She knew that was not so. If it had been, he'd have moved that direction years ago when she was married. She wondered what she could say to Loraine that would help if... Then she realized with a shock what she'd been about to think. If. What could she possibly be thinking? There was no if for Adam with her.

"Loraine, I think you have to follow your own heart on this. I can't advise you, not in this. The way of a man or a woman's heart is something each person can only know for themselves."

"It's just all so hard."

"I know, sweetheart," Martha reached over and put her arm around her daughter, drawing her into her arms. "I know it's hard, but I can't answer for you. I don't know." She felt Loraine's tears through her flannel nightgown, then felt her own start to flow again.

CHAPTER 13

Days, then two weeks, passed with no change in anything, and Martha began to think Adam must not care about any of them. If he was still around, he was avoiding her and Loraine.

They were all sitting at the kitchen table, Agatha, lamenting her stiff bones, Loraine moping, when Matt burst through the door. "Land sakes, boy," snapped Agatha, "you near scared me to death."

"It's come early," Matt said, panting. "Amy's in labor. Is it too early?"

She shook her head. "An exact time is just guess work, Matt. It has been long enough. Please saddle my horse." She rushed to the bedroom. "I'll be right with you." She changed quickly into her pants. When she came out, belting them securely at her waist she heard Agatha give a yelp. "Martha Stevens! You're not going anywhere looking like that."

Martha smiled as she picked up the pack of medicinals she had gathered for this day. "Can and have, Agatha. It is very practical. I think someday women will wear them everywhere."

Agatha gaped at her.

Loraine smiled. "They are actually quite becoming, Mama. It's the sensible thing for a woman to do."

"Well, I never. What's this world coming to?" Agatha shook her grizzled head. "Mark my words. Women take to wearing pants, and the whole shebang is gonna be over. Woman can't be showing her legs thataway."

"Do you need me, Mama?"

"Not now. If you like, you can come later. I'll know better." She crossed the threshold at a near run, racing out the door and quickly mounting the horse that Matt had brought to her porch.

"How long has she been in labor?" she asked as she kicked the horse into a gallop.

"Two hours," he said, his face so pale that she wondered if he was going to faint. "She wouldn't let me come earlier. Said she wasn't sure, plenty of time, she said."

She cast what she hoped was a reassuring smile. "Amy will be fine."

"That's what she said." His face full of woe. "I wanted to come for you earlier, but she made me wait," he repeated.

"I'm sure she was right. The first one usually takes a long time, you know." The trees raced by as they galloped down the road. "Did her water break?"

"Yes."

"Well, try not to worry, Matt, babies are born easily in our family. I've told you that before."

"But I'm so big. She's so little."

Martha, having heard this all before and having answered it again and again as delicately as she could, managed a smile despite her own worry. There would be no reassuring him until his baby was in its mother's arms. Although Matt wasn't comfortable discussing any sort of intimate issues with her, she decided a little frankness, coupled with some distraction, was worth a try. "It is not the outside that matters in a woman and much as you might lust after Amy's slim hips, in this case, it's the distance between the pelvic bones. Our Amy is nicely sized in that area; so quit worrying!"

"But--"

"Matt," she interrupted repeating what she had told him so many times before she added, "Quit torturing yourself. Have some faith."

At their cabin, she reined in the mare and looked at Matt, knowing that for the moment, the further he was away from the cabin, the better for Amy, besides she needed St. Louis. "I want you to ride for St. Louis," she told him as she dismounted and began untying her medical supply bag.

"I can't leave again, not now."

"You have to because I may need him. He knows Indian things about births that I might not."

"I thought you said it was all going to be fine."

She gave a frustrated laugh. "It is, but I've talked to him about this, and he's said he wants to come when it's time. Now, you ride and get him for Amy."

"Shouldn't I go in first?" he asked, his normally strong voice broke on the words.

"No, go now." *Before you pass out on me.* She gave the rump of his horse a swat. "The sooner you go, the sooner you'll be back," she reminded him as he yielded to her pressure and took off at a fast gallop toward St. Louis' cabin.

Martha walked into the darkened cabin and headed for the bedroom. Lying in the middle of the bed, her black hair plastered to her head, Amy lay, looking almost relaxed for the moment. "Where's Matt?" she asked as Martha bent to kiss her forehead.

"You two," Martha teased. "You worry about each other like nobody I ever knew. I sent him to get St. Louis."

"Do you expect trouble?" Amy asked anxiety in her eyes now that the moment of birth had arrived.

"Not at all, but I know Matt's going to need someone to hold him up, and St. Louis will do that. Now quit worrying about him. How many minutes between contractions?"

"A while. Maybe eight, I think."

"Good. Sounds right on schedule then." She felt lightly of Amy's abdomen. The baby's head was still in place. "Real good. You know what I told you before, the contractions will come closer together, more intense."

"Yes."

"Are you resting between them, letting them do the work when they come, breathing deep, letting those muscles do what they were made to do?"

Amy nodded. "I'm trying. It's not easy."

"Nothing good ever is. All right, I'll go real quick into your kitchen and get some hot water started."

"It's already going." Amy said, managing a smile.

Martha smiled. "Then I'll make you some of that herbal tea I told you about. You have been drinking the tea I already gave you?"

"Yes, yes. I know what's good for me." Amy gave a little giggle.

"Good. I'll be right back with this tea."

In the kitchen, Martha emptied a small packet of blue cohosh root into the pot and poured nearly boiling water over it. She was only grateful she had brought a goodly supply of it with her because she had not seen the tall plant in any of the woods since she'd gotten to Oregon, and she'd looked everywhere. Probably there was something, which would do the same thing, but she didn't know the local herbs well enough yet to be sure of what was safe. Into another cup, she sprinkled little pieces of the inner bark from the wild black cherry and poured hot water over it too. Outside, Martha heard horses riding up and knew Matt was back with St. Louis. She only wished she had something she could give him but was grateful that at least St. Louis would be here now to help.

She carried the teas into Amy, encouraging her to drink some of each, but in particular the black cherry. "It tastes bad," Amy complained, sipping it while making a protesting face.

"And what have I always told you?" Martha asked with a smile.

"What is good for us isn't always what tastes good," Amy repeated with an answering smile. "I suppose I'll say the same things to this wee one."

"I suppose you will." Martha heard footsteps behind her and knew Matt had entered the room. "You hold her hand for a minute," she said as she looked up into terrified gray eyes. "Which is to reassure you that she's all right. Give her more of the tea on the left when she can take it."

She walked out of the room and nearly into the arms of Adam who was standing at the door. Startled, she almost threw her arms around him before she heard St. Louis' voice. "How's she doin'?"

"She's fine," she said, looking straight up into Adam's strong face. "I didn't know you were still here."

He smiled, his gaze soft. "Didn't you?"

She felt her eyes filling with tears. "Well, maybe." Then she remembered Loraine's tears and moved away. She wrapped her arms around herself and looked at St. Louis. "It's going to be awhile."

"I don't know how much help I'll be," Adam said, leaning back against the wall and watching, increasing her nervousness. To still her restlessness, Martha paced across the floor. A little distance might help to quiet the tumult that she felt whenever he came into a room, when she saw him, when—

She glanced over at St. Louis and saw he was smiling at her, his eyes twinkling. She looked quickly away. Darn. St. Louis was altogether too good at reading faces and seeing behind the words.

She swallowed, determined to put some normalcy into her voice. "You're here to help Matt," she managed, glancing back at

Adam and attempting a small smile that seemed polite and impersonal enough.

"Hey, that's the toughest job," Adam complained, his crooked grin making her want to put her arms around him before she reminded herself that he was to hold Matt up, not her.

The morning wore on and Amy's pains grew closer and closer, their strength increasing. Martha gave her a piece of a limb to bite down on. "Do what makes you feel best. If you want to yell, yell."

"Matt would die."

"Faint maybe. Not die," Martha teased.

Amy gritted her teeth. "It has to be getting close--" She broke off as another pain grew in intensity. She bit down hard on the wood, squeezing Martha's hand painfully enough most likely to leave bruises.

"Now remember what I told you," Martha said when the pain had eased. "When the pains change, when you begin to feel like pushing, push." Martha smoothed back Amy's hair, wondering how Matt was holding up. She had told Adam to stay near him to catch him if he fainted. The last thing they needed was for him to sustain a head injury from cracking his head against the floor or a table.

"Mama, it's! Yes, I feel the pushing... Ahhh." Amy's body grew rigid with the contraction and then she let go, panting.

"Now, baby," Martha said, "when it comes, bear down, hold onto me and bear down."

"Lord, this hurts!"

"I know. I know, but this very afternoon, you'll put your child to your breast and never remember anything about the pain for the joy you'll feel."

"Ahhh... I don't know... I--" She gasped.

Martha put some of the tea to her lips. "Drink this... Come on, baby..."

As another pain shot through Amy, she gave out a cry, which brought Matt and Adam to the door.

"She's dying, isn't she?" Matt cried.

Martha gave him a worried glance. His face was tinged with green. "It's going well. She's doing fine. It's almost time."

"But she's..." Tears ran down Matt's cheeks.

Martha felt pity for him, but her concern had to be for Amy. "She is birthing a baby, Matt. Your wife is a strong woman. She is doing fine. Now, did you fix the licorice tea, like I asked?" Boiled in water, it would encourage the afterbirth to come quickly and completely.

"I... I don't know." Matt's voice was little more than a cracked whisper.

"Go find out. We will need it soon."

He started to object, then stopped as Amy cried out again. Matt swayed against the door as Adam quickly put his arm under him for support.

"Right now, Matt. I need it. Your child is going to be here any moment."

As Matt swayed against him, Martha realized Adam also looked pale. Perhaps he wouldn't be able to hold Matt up. "Where's St. Louis?" she asked, glancing beyond them into the living room.

"Why?" Matt asked, straightening himself."

"Because, we'll soon need that tea and neither of you seem able to make it."

"I'll do it," Adam said, dragging Matt with him.

She turned back to Amy. "That's good. That's very good, baby," she murmured, putting her hands over Amy to send her energy. "It's coming now. I can, yes I see the head. Push down, baby! Push down for me."

"I can't. It's tearing me apart." She screamed.

"No, no it isn't. You're doing wonderfully. A few more screams and pushes and the wee one will join us."

She knew the men were at the edge of the door, but she had no more energy to give them. "Here your child comes." And it was true, the head emerged, deep red, the rest quickly followed. Martha gave a little laugh. "Well," she said, "I guess you fooled St. Louis."

"I... I did?" Amy gasped.

"You have a daughter." The baby's mouth opened with a sputter and then a ringing, almost angry cry, assuring the world she had been born and was alive but not pleased with the situation in which she found herself. Martha laughed in relief as she put her up on Amy's tummy.

Amy swallowed, reached down and touched the tiny face. "She's-- She's all right?"

"Perfect." Martha washed her own hands in the basin of water, and then without looking behind her, asked, "Where's that tea." She knew even as she felt it being put in her hand who had given it to her but she didn't turn. She put the cup to Amy's lips.

"Where's Matt?" Amy asked, frowning and looking past her mother.

"He's uh resting," Adam said. Martha glanced back and saw that Matt had slumped down against the door frame, St. Louis kneeling at his side.

Martha wiped Amy's forehead with a damp cloth.

"He should be here to see her. Look how beautiful she is, Mama, and her hair, it's blond."

"I don't know how you can be sure of that," Martha said as she turned to cleaning up the baby, her grandchild. "I don't think I've ever heard what you're going to call her." She wrapped the still complaining baby in a clean blanket and handed her back to Amy.

"Laura. It was to be Laura if it was a girl for Matt's mother, and Amos if it was a boy."

"That's fine," Martha said with a smile. "They'd have both been happy about that." She felt a pang of pain that seemed to go through her, as she knew how much Amos had wanted to see this first grandchild. She sucked in a breath forcing her thoughts from what wasn't meant to be. Maybe he saw from heaven.

"But where's Matt?"

A groan from the floor alerted Amy as Adam went back to help Matt to his feet. "Wha...?" he asked.

Martha grinned at his pallor, his dazed gray eyes. "You have a daughter, Mr. Kane. What do you think about that?"

He looked at her, then at Amy, holding the baby who was now making little mewling sounds as Amy put her to her breast. The afterbirth followed swiftly and Martha tied off the cord and cut it.

Stumbling Matt came to the bed and fell on his knees. "Thank the Lord. It's over," he cried as he held his wife and daughter in his trembling embrace.

"I'll make some breakfast," Martha said, stepping away from the bed, "and give you three some time to get acquainted."

Moving out of the room, she was not prepared for the clasp into which she was enfolded. The hard pressure of firm lips, which asked nothing and demanded everything. For a fraction of a heartbeat she thought of pulling back and then she was lost to her own reaction, her arms coming up seemingly of their own volition to draw him against her, as though she could somehow make him a part of her.

His lips were passionately claiming what was his by right. It didn't matter then that St. Louis was in the room, that she shouldn't be doing this, as her fingers dug into his back, her body arched into his. She heard him moan, as she thrust her hips against his. Their kiss was at once a celebration of life, the giving and the receiving of it, and an acknowledgment that no matter what words she said, her feelings were real and at least for this moment--undeniable.

"Oh Lord," he moaned into her ear.

"Yes," she whispered.

"Lady, I love you," he murmured in return.

Tears were running down her cheeks as she looked up into his eyes, knowing the truth of his words and feeling again the hopelessness in them. She stepped from his arms, wiping her eyes and trying to steady herself. She hardened herself even as she saw the plea in his eyes, knew that once again she was rejecting him, but she had no choice. It had to be this way.

Adam met her gaze, his own stormy--reflecting the passions he'd just shown and the awareness of what her pushing him away meant. "So be it," he said.

She glanced away, saw St. Louis stood by the stove, looking down at the teapot.

"Matt's a lucky man," Adam said, walking out the door. Martha's gaze followed him out, tears again threatening to erupt.

"Wal, dang it gal, go after him. You ain't a complete ninny are ya?"

"I can't." She wrapped her arms around herself as though to hold herself together, protect herself from the feelings that still surged within, that urged her to run after him.

St. Louis snorted. "If you're half the woman, I know you to be, ya can't not."

"Amy needs me," she snapped.

"Right now that girl only needs her husband and baby and you know it, but there is a man what needs ya. You know I'm right. Get out that door. I'll fix Amy and Matt some food in a bit when maybe they're wanting something more than just to hold each other. You go talk to Adam. You two got things need saying."

She looked at St. Louis for a moment, seeing the knowledge and wisdom in his eyes. It was not possible. She could not go after Adam. Just couldn't. Then she smiled, wiped her eyes, and headed for the door.

CHAPTER 14

The sunlight outside the cabin was monetarily blinding to Martha's eyes, then she saw Adam walking down the slope behind the cabin toward the little stream that Amy and Matt had named Hope. She called his name but whether he didn't hear or chose not to, he kept walking, forcing her to run to catch up. When she was only a few steps from him, he turned.

"Something wrong?" he asked

"Nothing. Or maybe everything."

"Amy?"

She shook her head. "She's fine. She doesn't need me. Where were you going?"

"I just need to clear my head."

"St. Louis said you needed me."

He stared at her a moment. "And you want to help someone in need?"

This wasn't going the way she had expected. "You're twisting my words."

"I'm trying to find out what they are. You say a lot of words, Martha. What do any of them mean? It seems to me you make a habit out of taking care of wounded things. If I'm wounded, will you care for me?"

"It's not like that."

"Isn't it? Isn't it that you put everyone ahead of your own needs? Does Loraine need you now, Martha? Is that what you're using as an excuse to run from your own feelings?

"I'm not the one who stalked off."

His eyes were glacial with anger and something that went deeper. "No, you're not. You just made sure I'd walk off."

"Oh blame me," she snapped. "I just... I'm trying to do what's right."

"Are you? Or are you scared of being hurt. Maybe the truth is that you don't trust me. Or is the real truth that you don't trust yourself, and you're reaching for any excuse you can find to protect you from being hurt?"

She glared at him wishing to say something cutting, something that would wipe that angry smile off his lips but knowing deep within her heart that all he'd said was true.

"If I was, it'd be logical," she said finally.

He gave a snort. "Logical, huh? When are you going to quit being logical?" He turned from her to walk away.

She ran after him, grabbed his arm and swung him around half out of his own surprise and half out of the force of her emotions. She grabbed hold of his neck, pulling his head down and before she let herself think, she reached up and pressed her lips against his, feeling his astonishment, and then his reaction as he bent and scooped her into his arms. His kiss was passionate, demanding, his lips first hard and angry, then softening and hot, heady with the heat of his body. His tongue went into her mouth, surprising her at first as Amos had never kissed her that way. She felt the erotic power, of that kiss, move all the way through her body.

He lowered himself to the ground and settled her onto his lap. Kissing her, he slanted his mouth across hers, teasing her lips apart with his tongue. This time, eagerly she darted within, meeting his thrusts with her own. His hands were on her breasts, teasing the nipples through the cotton layers, making them hard and wanting more, as she knew he was by how his erection was pushing against her.

"You are going to kill me," he said when the kiss ended.

"I know. I know," she whispered. She moved away, heard his protest, but she was going nowhere. She knelt before him and leaned forward. Resting her palms on his broad shoulders, she kissed first his brow and then his nose, working all around his face until she hovered above his mouth, sensually promising with her breath and denying with her lips.

"What are you trying to do?" he muttered, "destroy me completely?"

"I will," she agreed, her lips coming down to deliver the promise of sweetness. He pulled her back onto his lap. "I want to destroy you," she whispered as she kissed his ear, her fingers teasing along the rugged jaw to nestle at the back of his head. "Just as you're destroying me."

"How have I done that?" He cradled her in his arms.

"By coming into my life. Upsetting everything. Making me think of things I'd forgotten existed. Making me want what I shouldn't." She pulled back a little to study his face. "Why did you do that?" she asked, grabbing him by both ears and kissing him again.

"Because I couldn't stay away. Do you have any idea how many times I've been camping in the mountains and thinking stupidly that if I died the next day it'd have been without ever doing this?" He parted her lips, his tongue invading her mouth, as he seemed to enter into her very being. Meeting him with a quickness that felt as though she'd always done this, always known how to please him, what he liked, she allowed her own tongue to dance against his, teasing and promising.

"I wish," she sighed, then, "if only..." She yielded to a greater temptation and reached out to slowly, sensually unbutton his shirt, kissing where the hard chest was revealed to the touch of her lips. Taunting his nipples with her lips and then her tongue.

She heard his moan of pleasure, and it made her want more. He bent to kiss the hollow between her neck and shoulder. Slowly, his gaze on her eyes, he began unbuttoning her shirt, pushing it from her shoulders, then the straps of the thin chemise. "So beautiful," he said when he finally had her breasts free to his touch, his gaze.

"I can't get enough of you. Of having you touch me, of touching you." Her fingers on his neck stroked down his back.

"You have to marry me," he murmured.

She felt as though someone had thrown cold water on her. She pulled back. "I can't promise that."

"You can."

She stood, pulling her clothing back together, brushing off her pants. She pressed her lips together and walked up the hill a ways to the stream to stare at the moving water, listen to the riffles. "You don't know what you're asking," she said as she felt him come to stand just behind her.

He didn't touch her physically, but his presence seemed to envelope her. She felt a shiver as she realized it would be that way with him if she let him into her life. There would be no subtle, halfway measures. He'd swallow her in his world, with his energy. She'd have to make adjustments, learn to have a man to think about, to cater to. Then there would be when he would go off, when she was alone and more alone than she was now. There was when she finally lost him, whether to a cold death in some lonely canyon far from her or to a younger woman. She couldn't go through any of that.

"What is the real problem?" he asked.

She shook her head. "Just this is so fast. I can't deal with it. Amy, her baby. You asking me to marry you again."

"What do you want from me then?"

She tried to think of an answer. "I don't know. Yes, I do. This time, right now. Could you give me just this afternoon?"

He waited a moment to answer. Long enough that she wasn't sure he would. "No promises?"

"None. Just a few hours of there not being anyone else, no other time, no other people. A few hours when we are mates in the truest sense, but then we both go back to what was before it."

"You're asking a lot," he said sternly. "I want more than an afternoon, Martha."

"I know you do, but there are so many things to consider. My daughter is in love with you."

"I am not in love with her."

"I know."

"So like your little poem-- eternity in an hour?"

He had remembered that. "This moment is really all anyone has anyway, isn't it?"

When he didn't answer, she turned to look at him to see his expression. It was thoughtful, a bit bemused.

"Well?" she asked.

"I'm thinking."

She laughed. "It takes that long to figure something out like an afternoon, but you could ask me to marry you and expect an answer right away."

"I at least had had longer to think about that one." His smile was crooked.

"You are wasting our precious time."

"There could be a lifetime and one afternoon would just be the start."

"It would still be all you'd have right now, right this moment," she corrected.

He chuckled. "I won't promise you not to ask for more, won't promise to stop asking you to marry me."

He was a persistent man. "But not today. Not right here and now."

163

His smile was sweet, almost boyish. "So you want just this afternoon."

"It is yours too."

He sucked in a breath and she wondered if he'd ever give her an answer before he finally cleared his throat. "All right, lady, if this is it, this is all there is ever going to be, just these few hours, I'll take them." He pulled her into his embrace, then said, "Walk with me a ways, Grandma."

Arms entwined, they began to walk up the little stream. After a little way, the fir trees enclosed them on all sides, blocking out the sunlight and the rest of the world. She felt relaxed, at ease, totally feeling the moment but aware in the back of her mind that she was considering the possibility of more.

"Tell me what you've been doing," she said to distract herself from her erotic thoughts.

"So we came up here to talk?" he asked. Arm around her, he pulled her against him. She felt his long length all the way through her body as he bent and kissed her.

She laughed. "For awhile perhaps."

"So what have I been doing? Well I chopped a lot of firewood."

"What about your dislocated shoulder? I can't believe St. Louis let you do that. How is it now by the way?"

"It's fine, little mama. You're as bad as St. Louis." He laughed, but she wasn't sure he found it humorous. "It hurt my shoulder some to begin, but other parts of me hurt worse."

She ignored that. "What else did you do?"

"Went into Oregon City intending to get drunk as a skunk and got in a fistfight."

She stopped walking and put her hands on her hips giving him one of her looks of outrage.

"You are so beautiful when you are mad," he said with the smile that seemed to move her whole body. "When you look like that it's all I can do to not strip off your pants, shirt and anything else you shouldn't be wearing."

"Wait! I am trying to understand. You got drunk and got in a fight?"

"Met the sheriff of Oregon City too."

"You got thrown in jail because of a fistfight and being drunk?"

"You are fun to tease, but no, wrong again. Had the fistfight with him."

"I am confused. So then he arrested you?"

"We had another drink together. I liked him."

"I will never understand you, that's clear," she said with a wry twist to her lips. Obviously knowing one man really well did not prepare a woman for a different man.

"Then I got the cougar and came to your little shebang, which was by the way more torture than spending a night in a tree waiting for a cougar."

"Food that bad?" she teased

"It's what I wanted to be eating and couldn't," he said with a sensual smile that turned her heart upside down. "I was in the same room with you, could smell your scent—herbs, flour and you under it all." He bent to put his nose against where her neck and shoulder met, kissing her, then unbuttoning and pushing her shirt apart. "I could feel the heat of your skin even across the room."

She sighed, bending her head to one side to give him further access as he slipped her shirt from her shoulders this time, leaving her breasts barely covered with the chemise.

"I wanted you so bad," he said. "You will never know how much."

"I won't?" she asked with a little purr as his lips and tongue worked over her bare skin, to the fullness of her breasts where they swelled above the chemise.

"For years, I knew I'd never have you; then got so close to you again, only to lose. Damn, Martha, you'd drive a man crazy." He slipped the chemise straps down her shoulders.

She was so aroused she'd lost touch with all else they were talking about as she felt his hands on her skin. She wanted him now. She didn't need time to be prepared for him, but he was determined obviously to take his time, to torture her by these slow sensual touches.

"I stayed away, but the feelings didn't leave. You haunted me by every mountain stream, every night was filled with your big eyes."

He smiled then and pulled her down to the ground. They sat along the stream, the bubbling sound was soothing but nothing could distract her from how he was now sucking on her nipples through the thin chemise. She knew her hands were shaking but she unbuttoned his shirt until his chest was bare and she could push against him, rubbing her breasts against his.

"I wanted you too, you know?" she said sighing as she felt her chemise being pushed down, her breasts bared to his touch, his kisses.

"You did?" His voice was husky.

"From that first night, when I walked out of my bedroom and saw you naked. My pulses jumped, and my body began to demand something I knew was ridiculous." She had heard of love at first sight but never dreamed it might be real until that moment. Or was that just lust at first sight?

"Ridiculous huh?" He began unbuttoning her pants, then pushing them down, her boots were taken along with them and in moments, she was lying nude in his arms, feeling the grass under her back, his hands as they stroked her body, his eyes as he looked at her with so much intensity, that her body throbbed with need for him.

"Adam," she begged.

"What? What do you want, lady? What can I do for you?"

"You know what I want. I want you."

He was touching her now in her intimate places, suckling her breasts. He bent and kissed her again and she pulled at his clothing, unbuttoning his pants, sliding them from his buttocks. Soon they were both naked, their limbs entwined, their hands learning each other's secret places. She was so on fire for him, needed him so badly that she spread her legs, pulling him closer, stroking his shaft, and then guiding him to her.

Adam entered into her as though it had always been this way-- that they had made love a hundred times and yet each time was as if the first. She picked up on his rhythm, moving with him, touching, sucking and playing with his body as he did hers. As she began to feel her climax building, she saw the same happening to him as they exploded at nearly the same time.

Afterward they lay entwined, their breath slowly evening out. Adam played with her hair, taking out the clip, spreading it over the grass. "I love you," he whispered against her temple.

"And I love you." Having this day had seemed such a good idea. Let them both have something to remember, to take with them, but she didn't know how she could let go of what she had found with him. She had to. Somehow she had to. This wasn't meant to be.

"I'd walk through fire for you, lady," he whispered as though reading her mind, "but I don't know if I can do this, have this, and then what? What am I going to be left with?"

"Memories."

"Memories? What the hell good are they in exchange for what you and I could have?" His deep voice darkened with frustration.

She didn't want this ruined. "Memories don't hurt anyone else," she said defensively.

"Are you sure that it's others you are worried about?" He separated himself from her and began pulling on his pants.

"What we have couldn't last, Adam," she said dressing slowly, her fingers shaking as she tried to do buttons.

"Is that what you believe? That your feelings are so shallow, so insignificant that they'd fade away at the first sign of trouble? Or is that you think that's what mine are?

She sighed, looking away. "Do you have to ruin what we just had?"

"What is ruining it is not having more," he said. "It's being afraid to claim this for more than one afternoon. You know that too. Yes, I guess that I am different than you. I'd rather reach out for what I want, wrench it from the ground if I have to, face whatever risks were needed to get it. I'd rather do that, than just give up, just lie down and die."

"We're different—too different," she admitted, "and that's part of the problem."

"It isn't all of it though," he argued, his blue eyes glittering with anger. "Most of it is other people, isn't it? You're still too afraid of being seen as anything but proper."

"It's not just that."

"Yes," he interrupted, "it is exactly what it is. You're choosing what you're afraid they will think, over even trying, over even taking a chance with me."

"You're not being fair."

"You said you love me. How fair are you being to me or to you?
"

"It would hurt Loraine," she said through gritted teeth.

"Loraine has made a dream out of me. Just like I'd done with you. The difference is there is no chance for her and me. No matter what happens between us, I'm not going to be with Loraine. Do you understand that?"

"Yes, of course," she said.

"Then what are you gaining by being afraid to tell Loraine the truth?"

"She would never forgive me."

"For what? Is she so shallow, so much a little girl that she couldn't see all she had with me was a fantasy?"

"It's a lot easier for you. What do you have at risk here? You didn't have Loraine's tears falling on your shoulder. You don't have to face the possibility that your own children might come to hate you."

"What do I have at risk?" he asked with a bitter smile. "When I ride out of here, I ride alone. I don't have anyone and most likely never will. I'll spend a thousand more nights alone, and all because you don't have the courage to admit you are a human being, a flesh and blood woman."

They glared at each other for a long moment before they realized that St. Louis was yelling their names.

Adam, his eyes still on her, yelled back. "Up here."

"Loraine and Agatha are riding in to see the baby. I figured you oughta know."

Adam quickly pulled on his shirt, tucking it in. "We'll be right back. Just taking a little walk to clear our heads." He looked back at Martha, the muscle in his jaw throbbed with tension. "And I guess we did that, didn't we?"

She looked down, unable to look at him or she knew she'd be crying, as she nodded.

CHAPTER 15

Adam sat at St. Louis' table, watching him polish off a breakfast of pancakes, salt pork and coffee. He looked down at his own plate, nudging the food with his fork, wishing he had an appetite. It seemed that in the week since he'd seen Martha, nothing had tasted good.

"Ya ain't eatin' much, boy," St. Louis noted.

"Not particularly hungry."

"You're losin' weight." He stopped and took a swig of coffee before he added, "Get outta here. Go on over and talk to her."

"Talking does no good."

"Not when you're here, and she's there."

"She's where she wants to be."

"You two are powerful stubborn people."

"One of us is." Adam agreed. He got up from the table and walked to the door, staring out at the woods surrounding the cabin. A dewy mistiness hung around the trees. Late summer, warm, humid, air that told although the day would be hot, somewhere in the not so distant future lay autumn.

He sensed that going to Martha would only make things worse. He knew now he could have her body, but he wanted more than that. He wanted her to be the other half of his soul. She was the woman who could do that, not only warm his bed but his heart. It was painful to realize all she was willing to offer him was sliding in the back door of her life, hiding and lying about what they had, eventually profaning it.

She would never publicly acknowledge him as her lover, as the man whose name she would take. She had done that for Amos but not for him. Whatever her reasons were, his age, worry that he wouldn't be stable, what her children might think, her own lack of love, still in love with Amos, whatever it was, to be near her would lead to pain and frustration.

"It's about time for me to take off," Adam said, turning to look back at St. Louis.

"Where for?"

"Don't know. Don't much care. Maybe I will head to Alaska. It's one place I haven't been."

"Runnin' ain't gonna do you no good. Long as you know she's livin' in this world, walkin' on God's green earth, you're gonna be thinkin' about her, and maybe even if she wasn't, it'd be that way."

"I hope you're wrong."

"But I'm not. I've loved a woman that way once, and I know what I'm talkin' about. You've loved her a long time, ain't ya?" St. Louis walked to the stove and refilled his and Adam's coffee cups. He walked to the door and handed Adam's his, then went out onto the porch to sit on the homemade bench.

Adam walked past him and sat on the step, took a sip before he answered. "A long time."

"Knew it."

Adam smiled. "I doubt if you know for how long."

"I saw it on the trip out here. When ya pulled away from everybody, I thought like everybody else it was on account of Amy, then I caught that look in yore eyes one time when ya were lookin' at Martha. I told myself I was a crazy old man, but I saw it

again and knew. It's why I didn't try to argue you into stayin'
here then."

"It was hopeless, and it's still hopeless."

"It *was* hopeless," St. Louis said, raising his eyebrows, "but it
ain't now."

"That's not how she sees it."

"Maybe. Maybe not. I seen her look at you the same way now,
that same longing is in her that's in you, boy. She's a strong
woman, but a lots been dumped on her. She was widowed when
she never figured it'd happen. Made a life for herself out here
where it takes a man usually, raised the youngun she still had to
get off into the world, then lived alone when she needed to. You
come back here, and you throw the whole shebang into turmoil.
Tell her things she never expected to hear. She's had a lot to chew
on. Give her some time to work it through her cud."

Adam smiled despite himself. "John said somewhat the same
before he left."

"He was right."

"Maybe. He's been a good friend. One night on bivouac I
talked too much and so he knew about a woman, recognized it
had to be Martha when he saw her."

"Man needs a friend."

"John has been all of that—like a brother more than a friend."

"Just give her some time, Adam."

"She's made up her mind. She thinks it'd cost her her daughters. You know she won't give them up for me."

"Sure, she's afraid, not thinking straight. She raised those girls
up better'n that. It might be they'd have a little upset over it. It'll
be new to them, somethin' they never figgered. It's something to
figure out your parents are human too, but they'll get over the
knowledge, and they'll get a life lesson in the bargain."

"I think it's more than them. She doesn't trust me. Maybe
doesn't really love me. Maybe she still loves Amos, and she'll
never really be able to love any other man."

"You are drivin' yourself crazy."

"You think?" Adam retorted with a self-aware smile.

"If you love her, like you say, give the woman time. Don't go rushing off."

"When I see her, it's like taking a knife and ripping it right up through my gut."

"Wal, that there's a solid point, Adam."

"It is?" Adam looked up at him, suspicious at the tone in the older man's voice.

"Shore is. No woman's worth being gutted for. Course, she's not happy neither. Over there yesterday, I seen dark circles under those pretty big eyes of hers. I ain't seen her so sad since Amos died; but that ain't no problem of yours."

"I didn't want to hurt her. I offered her everything I had, and it wasn't enough.

"Everything but patience."

Adam felt angry as he saw how the older man had twisted this around to force him to see it from Martha's view. The trouble was whenever he started to think about her, about how this might be affecting her, all he could see was how she had looked when he was making love to her. He shook his head, trying to dispel the image.

St. Louis hitched up his pants as he rose from the bench. "Wal, I'd like to sit here and jaw with you, but I got work on that lean-to. I told you I was figurin' on addin' that onto my barn, didn't I?"

Adam smiled. "And you need my help?"

"Could use some of that grit of yours," St. Louis agreed, grinning as he reached up to pat Adam's muscular shoulder.

"If we don't talk about my personal life, not Martha, not anything but just work."

St. Louis rolled his eyes to the sky. "Now is that appreciation? I ask ya?" He shook his head as he picked up his hammer and tools.

"I appreciate you," Adam said, rising in one lithe motion, "just I appreciate you more when you're not telling me what to do."

"You sayin' I'm nosing in where I'm not wanted?" St. Louis asked with a chuckle as they headed for the barns.

"You've been known to."

"Just tryin' to be a friend." He pointed to a pile of peeled logs, mostly six inches across or less. "How about putting some of that muscle of yours to work into draggin' them logs over here."

"A better idea is putting Joe to work," Adam suggested with a grin as he rigged up a harness to let his gelding help. "I know," he said to the horse, patting his nose, "it's degrading to a horse of your abilities, but we all got to do what we got to do."

"What'd ya say?" St. Louis asked, taking his head out of a barrel of nails.

"Just explaining to my horse why he's being turned into a work animal."

"Ya goin' to get him to dig the holes to sink them into too?" St. Louis asked with a grin.

"I would if I thought I could," Adam said, tossing his shirt over the fence rail, "but I expect this is one for me.

An hour later, Adam had dug four holes to St. Louis' satisfaction, and they'd sunk the first of the poles into them and were nailing cross pieces into place. "What's this lean-to for anyway?" Adam asked, sweat rolling down his back.

"Sheep. I figure to get me a couple ewes and a ram," St. Louis said then chuckled at Adam's groan of disgust.

"Sheep!" Adam repeated. "Lord, how a man gets taken down by life. I who have led wagon trains across the prairies, scouted for cavalries-- building a lean-to for sheep!" He looked over at Joe, who was munching contentedly on some grass beyond the barn. "How the mighty have fallen, boy."

As they were cleaning up after lunch, the lean-to walls in

place, Adam looked down the hill and saw a rider approaching. He squinted, trying to recognize the big form on the horse.

As the man came nearer, Adam grinned. "Tom Crane."

"Wonder what the sheriff wants with us?" muttered St. Louis, stashing the tools into their box and wiping his hands with a rag.

"You got a past that makes you dislike sheriffs?" asked Adam as he cast St. Louis a sideways glance.

"Nope. Just never found one yet that brung me good news."

Crane dismounted-- his bulk as impressive as Adam had remembered. With the pleasantries out of the way, the sheriff took off his hat, wiping his brow. Adam noted the badge. So this was no social call. "Here to arrest somebody?" Adam asked with a grin.

Crane laughed. "Maybe. Got something' in your past that's worrying' you?"

"Not me," Adam said, gesturing toward at St. Louis, "but he might."

St. Louis headed for the cabin. "I'll put on some coffee. Ya stayin' for supper?"

"That depends," Crane said.

"On what?"

"On your friend here." He smiled at Adam. "I need help."

In the cabin, St. Louis quickly stoked up the fire and started the coffee. "I'm relieved you're still here," Crane said.

"Is that good for me or bad?"

"There's been a robbery in town."

"Oregon City?" asked St. Louis in amazement, as the three men sat at the table.

Adam leaned back in his chair, teetering it on two legs, studying the big man. He'd come to recognize a man's nervousness, his uneasiness, even when it was hidden, and with Crane it wasn't hidden very well.

"While I was out of town checking on some gold claims I'd heard about up the Santiam, three strangers rode in, robbed the

Oregon City Bank just before it closed, killed the teller, and took off before anybody realized what happened. I got back by nightfall, but they'd had too much head start, and I'm no tracker."

St. Louis shook his head, "Robbin' banks. What'll they think of next? Lord, what's this world comin' to?"

"It happened yesterday?" questioned Adam.

"It took me awhile to find anybody who knew who St. Louis was, and then where he lived, and I kept thinking about you talking about Alaska—figurin' comin' out here might do me no good. Riding off every which way wouldn't neither though."

"You're hoping I can track them."

"It's the only chance we got of getting back the money. My deputy's got a bum leg, but he said he'd hobble around and talk to the men in town while I get you. I figure we can get two or three to go with us, and when we catch up with them, I wouldn't expect you to take part in the arrests."

Adam smiled. "If I say yes, it'll only be if there's a realistic chance of tracking them. Which way they'd go when they left town?"

"First south for sure. The men who rode after them thought maybe up toward the hills. That's where they lost them."

"No point in wasting time." Adam stood up, walked over to pick up his saddlebags, and pulled out a holstered gun and belt, checking its load before strapping it to his hips.

"I'll deputize you if you really mean to go with me all the way."

"Guess you better do that." He looked up when Crane didn't say anything.

The big man looked worried. "Uh, do you have any sort of criminal record?"

"Only when I murdered my wife, but, of course, there was no evidence," Adam said with a chuckle, "and so, they had to let me off."

"Murdered your--"

"Don't listen to him," St. Louis interrupted, coming to watch

Adam stuff an extra shirt into his bag. "He ain't never had a wife. Not that he ain't been tryin'."

"Oh, I get it. A joke." Crane chuckled weakly. "Tell you what, I'll swear you in now, and it'll save us some time later."

"What about supper?" St. Louis asked, rising from the table.

"Too much time has already gone on the tracks. They'll be mixed up with everybody else who traveled that road. No time to waste," Adam said as he grabbed six of St. Louis' biscuits and stuffed them into the other side of his saddlebag.

Crane looked longingly toward the pot of stew on the back of the stove. "You sure about that?" he asked but gave up with a shrug when Adam stopped and looked at him coolly. "You want me or no?"

"Maybe I oughta go too," St. Louis interrupted.

"You're getting too old to be running around like that," Adam said, "besides who's going to look after things here?" He carried his bag outside and went to saddle Joe.

"Ya think this is gonna be dangerous?" St. Louis asked Crane.

"Since they already killed a man, I'm not expecting it to be easy."

"You be careful, ya hear," St. Louis ordered as Adam returned, mounted on Joe.

Adam adjusted the brim of his hat leaning forward on the pommel. "You keep an eye on things here. If those three double back, I want you at Martha's. Warn Matt. I'll be back." With that, he nudged Joe in the side and rode off at a gallop, Crane at his heels.

Loraine and Martha crawled along the row of string beans, picking and talking. Mostly it was Loraine doing the talking, she chattered about the things she'd done in Portland.

"It sounds like life in a city is making you happy?" Martha said as she dumped an apron load of beans into the basket.

"Mostly." Loraine nodded. "There's always something to do at the store, and then I have friends with more parties than back in Pine Bluff. I like the stores. Someone asked me to be in a play. I didn't do it but might."

Martha smiled faintly. "Have you met anyone-- special that is?"

"Well, there is a man, who seems interested in me, but it's not someone I could be serious about. I feel so silly saying that. I guess I should just take someone. Every woman's supposed to get married."

"Don't do that, honey. The wrong marriage can be a terrible burden."

"I had thought that too but seeing Matt and Amy makes me want what they have, but just marrying anyone wouldn't do that anyway would it?"

"Could your confused feelings for Adam have been the problem with this other fellow?"

Loraine laughed. "I don't think so. I'd honestly almost forgotten Adam until I heard he was back. Although Adam does tend to make everyone else look tame and boring by comparison, doesn't he?"

Martha picked up the beans they'd gathered and carried them into the cabin.

"Nice mess of beans, you two got there," Agatha commented as she ran her bony fingers through them; then settled at the table to do the snapping.

"Company, Mama," Loraine said coming quickly through the door.

Martha's heart skipped into her throat as it had done so many times when she'd thought it might be Adam riding up. It settled back down when she saw Eunice come through the door, followed immediately by Fanny.

"We brought you some of our preserves," Eunice said with a pleasant smile handing Martha a small jar of rich red fruit jam.

"It looks delicious. Thank you," Martha said.

"It is one of our favorites. My great-grandmother first made it in Virginia, and the recipe just kept being passed down, one generation after another."

Fanny looked around the room. "Uhh has Mr. Stone been by?"

Loraine smiled. "No."

Her face fell. "He hasn't left the area has he?"

"We have no way of knowing what Adam is up to, do we Mama?" Loraine said as Martha heated up water for tea. "After all, he is St. Louis' guest not ours."

"I've had a letter from Belle," Martha said, hoping to redirect the conversation.

"How wonderful, and how does your little girl like San Francisco?" Eunice asked.

"She has been thrilled from what she's described. The Stearns took her to the opera one night, ladies in gowns and men in black suits. Where Belle has always loved singing, she was in heaven."

"Did she describe the dresses?" asked Fanny with interest.

"She said they were satin, silk with lace and jewels worked into designs, every color of the rainbow, and some of the dresses had practically no bodice." Martha smiled at Fanny's look of fascinated shock. "The men wore black suits with tails, white spotless shirts and top hats. She wrote the audience made it one of the most colorful events she'd ever been to. Ladies had fancy fans too, some made from mother-of-pearl or large fluffy feathers."

"Oh my," rhapsodized Fanny, "can't you just see Mr. Stone in one of those suits."

"Portland's got it in mind to be another San Francisco. Silly frippery stuff, but they have parties too," Agatha put in. "Why, last census we had near as many folks as Oregon City."

"It can't be," Eunice said with a frown. "Oregon City has over nine hundred."

"Portland had near eight hundred and that doesn't count the communities right around it, nor the people pouring in every day. You mark my words-- Portland is going to be the place to be if you want your business to grow."

"Why would you say such a thing?" Eunice asked with a frown. "Oregon City was first."

Agatha shook her head. "Don't have nothing to do with it. It'll all come down to navigation. That's what Jacob's always said."

"Hmph," grumbled Eunice not satisfied with an answer that didn't suit her aims.

"Who cares about censuses anyway," Fanny said, smiling broadly. "Tell me more about the clothes in San Francisco. What are the latest fashions?"

Martha poured the hot water into her teapot. "Belle didn't say much more about the clothing, but it wouldn't matter much anyway unless you're planning a trip south. Those fashions aren't going to show up here for a few years."

"I wouldn't be so certain about that, Martha," Agatha said, correcting her. "Times are changing. Oregon's going to change with them. Women in Portland care about what they're wearing in New York and San Francisco."

"I do too," Fanny said, looking pointedly at her mother. "I need more clothing. More up-to-date clothing. No girl can attract a husband wearing old stale clothes." She grinned and Martha saw she clearly knew how to motivate her mother.

"Well then," Agatha suggested with a smile, "you just come on up to Portland and look into our shops. You are going to be surprised at what all we can show you. We have a floor in our store just devoted to women's wear-- well half that floor, but it's expanding. I got to say that's Loraine's doin', but it has worked out to pay for some of our other outlets."

"You know," Eunice said thoughtfully looking back at Martha, "you could sell your dresses for very nice prices. I am pretty sure, that if Belle gave you more information on those evening gowns, you could recreate them. Your dresses always have such a stylish look, some little extra trim or such to make them elegant, give them some oomph like a big city look."

"Oh, I don't know," said Martha skeptically. "Everything I've made is simple."

"They fit you well. Make your figure look really slim." Martha suppressed a smile. "You add just those frippery little touches too. A little flare at the back, a different neckline, or lacy collar and cuffs or just the bits of trim."

"She's right," Agatha said. "We could sell them in our store. As many as you could make."

Martha shook her head. "But everyone sews."

"Not like you. You have a sense of style. If you ever decide to do it for pay, I'd be happy to be a customer." Eunice sipped her tea, adding a little more sugar before she asked, "Oh, I forgot to tell you or did you already hear about the excitement in town?"

"No, what?" Martha asked.

"Well, it happened right in town and in broad daylight. Yesterday afternoon, three men took all the money out of the Oregon City Bank, you know the big one on the corner."

"Took it?" Agatha repeated.

"Robbed it. Killed Hank Jefferies. Town is fit to be tied."

Martha knew she had some money in that bank but was vague on the amount. Fortunately, Amos had believed in never putting it all in one place. Some was still in Missouri and a small amount in a Portland bank. Still, a loss in any bank was something to take into account. She felt especially sorry for those who might've had all they had saved stolen so cavalierly.

"That useless sheriff was gone on some silly errand so he

missed the whole thing. People aren't very happy with that sheriff, I can tell you."

"They got everything in that bank," repeated Loraine.

"Whatever they found. The sheriff got back late last night. He was organizing some sort of band to go after them—shiftless no good that he is."

"Oh my. Oh my," muttered Agatha. "This world just isn't a safe place, not at all safe."

"Most of the time it is," Loraine said, "but there always seem to be those who want to take what others work for."

"Did Horace think they'd have any chance of getting back the money?" Martha asked.

"He didn't see how," Eunice said, helping herself to a cookie as Martha placed a plate of ginger snaps on the table. "I mean it happened yesterday. What's the chance they could follow a trail that is a day old?"

Martha grew cold, thinking of one man who might. She was just grateful he was staying so far from town. It didn't seem likely anyone would think to ask him or know he was here-- except the sheriff. He'd met the sheriff.

"What's wrong, Mama?" asked Loraine, reaching over and touching her shoulder. "You're pale." She touched her mother's hand. "And you've gotten as cold as ice. Are you feeling ill?"

"No," she said, trying to smile, "I do feel a little chilled though for some reason. I suppose thinking about violence that way. We all need some more hot tea." As she refilled cups, she told herself she was being foolish about this. Adam wouldn't be asked to go after a gang of bank robbers. Even if someone did think to ask him, he'd said he'd had enough of tracking men.

"Are you listening to me, Martha?" Eunice interrupted her thoughts.

"I'm sorry. I was woolgathering," she said with a smile. "What did you say?"

"Just that I wanted you to all come to our home for a gathering Friday."

"Any special occasion?" questioned Loraine.

"It's Fanny's birthday, and we thought it would be nice to have a party like you did. My brother, George who owns the stores in Salem, will be visiting. Of course, we'd like Matt, Amy and their baby to come too, if possible." Martha nodded, knowing what she would hear next. "We also want St. Louis and Adam, and that nice Mr. Pollard."

"We'll let them know. What day was it again?" she asked absentmindedly, her mind on something else, something six foot two and proving to be increasingly disruptive to her carefully ordered life.

CHAPTER 16

A dam, Tom Crane, and two men from the town had
followed the trail Adam believed had to be the correct one
through the afternoon, nearly lost it and then picked it up again
as the tracks headed farther into the hills.

Adam stopped his horse. Dismounting, he knelt, studying the
tracks. He touched his finger to one side, letting the dirt fill in a
portion of the track.

"Is that them?" asked Crane.

Adam nodded. "Not in any hurry either."

"How can you tell? How the hell do you even know it's still
them?" one of the men asked belligerently.

Adam didn't take offense. He was used to those who doubted
his skills. Sometimes he himself couldn't explain how he knew
who'd made a set of tracks. Some was learning but sometimes it
was an inner knowing, which was unexplainable. He tried
anyway. "Length of stride. Tracks aren't deep like a running horse.
I'd guess they aren't expecting anyone to come after them, since
they didn't right away. See the nick on the side of the hoof, same
one we caught outside of town. This other horse is digging in

deeper, bigger man. Three horses, traveling at the same gait. Could be coincidence, but I believe it's them."

"Think we'll catch up with them before dark?" the second man asked.

"No," Adam said candidly, looking up and studying the rugged terrain ahead. "I think they'll hole up, but without a full moon, we'll have to too."

"I didn't count on staying out overnight," the first said. "I figured we'd catch them before this."

"That was unlikely," said Crane with a growl. "They had a day's start on us. We're lucky we're coming up on them at all."

"Well, I'm sorry, but I have to go back."

Adam smiled to himself as he remounted his horse, thinking of the response that would have earned in the military. Crane could only huff and puff, but he had no authority to make either of the volunteers stay with him. They both rode for home.

Shaking his head, Adam laughed, "Well, what'd you expect?"

"I'm a lousy judge of men. That's what I expect," Crane grunted, taking off his hat and rubbing his forehead with a handkerchief. "I shouldn't be the sheriff of any town."

Adam absentmindedly massaged his own his neck before he took a sip from his canteen. "You want to quit too?" he asked.

"No, I took the job. I'll see it through. But it is going to be three against two now. How do you feel about that?"

"At this point," Adam said with a cold smile, "I'd go on even without you. I have friends in this area, who might have had money in that bank. Besides there's professional pride."

"Heady stuff that," said Crane, as they began to ride again.

"Yeah, I try to ignore it, but now and again, it nails me," Adam said.

"It's dangerous especially if a sheriff gets it. I try to avoid it myself. That's the sort of thing that can get a fellow killed."

"Or make him a damned good sheriff; so good that no outlaw in his right mind would enter his town."

"I guess you're right. There's two ways of looking at that. What'd you call it? Professional pride?" He chuckled.

They rode on, Adam keeping one eye toward the horizon and the other on the ground in front of him. "I don't know this country that well," he said, seeing the hoof prints begin to take a cut toward the left. "You been up here before?"

"Yeah, but not enough to know where they're heading. Seems like there's nothing ahead, not even homesteader cabins. If they'd of turned left, I'd of figured they were heading maybe toward Champoeg. I don't know why they'd be heading higher into the mountains."

"Maybe, they're thinking of burying their goods, then coming back for it later," Adam mused, rubbing his chin and thoughtfully nudging Joe in the new direction.

"I hope they ain't got wind of us being on their trail," Crane said nervously, loosening his rifle in its scabbard.

"They're still far enough ahead that's not likely."

"It's going to be dark soon. How much longer can you follow the trail?"

Adam smiled, remembering one trail he'd followed into the dark, but that time it was life or death for one of the best friends he'd had. Trailing these men after dark was not needed and would be not only dangerous but increase the risk of losing the sign completely. "I think," he said as he watched the sun go behind the Coast Range, "we're going to have to stop in an hour. I can stay with it that long. After we make camp, we'll see what shows up in the dark. Sometimes a whiff of smoke can lead you straight to them."

As St. Louis rode into the clearing, Martha and Loraine were standing on the porch, watching him. From the moment she'd seen him, Martha had known what he would say. He dismounted and looked at them, managing a smile with what she guessed was an effort. "Got any coffee?" he asked.

"He went with the sheriff, didn't he?" Martha asked bluntly.

St. Louis nodded, slowly climbing the steps. "Gettin' older ever' year."

Agatha came out from the cabin. "Ain't we all," she quipped.

"You know him," St. Louis said, meeting Martha's gaze. "That there Tom Crane come out, tellin' him that if'n he didn't, likely the men'd get clean away. Wasn't nobody else could trail 'em like Adam could."

Martha took a deep breath, to steady her nerves. "Were a lot of men going?"

"No idea, but you'd figure so."

"You don't think it'd be dangerous, do you?" Loraine asked.

St. Louis looked at Martha as he said, "Wal, they've killed one man. I don't expect they'd stop at more. Adam knows that too though; so he'll be watchin' out." They walked into the cabin.

"Those sugar cookies I see over there?" he asked, pointing to the plate on the counter.

Martha managed what she hoped looked like a smile and went for the coffee pot, letting him help himself to cookies. As he chewed, he said, "I'm supposed to stay here for a few days. Figure I can sleep in the loft of the barn."

"Stay here?" Martha frowned. "And what do you mean *supposed to.*""

"Adam's idea, and it's a good one. Three women up here alone. No telling which way those no accounts will end up going. I rode by Matt's and warned him too. "

"But..."

"Better safe than sorry," St. Louis said, taking another cookie. "These are real tasty."

Later that night as the sun sank behind the distant hills, Martha walked out onto the porch. Out there. Somewhere he was. St. Louis followed her. He patted her shoulder before he sat on the bench. "Want to talk?" he asked.

She put her arms around the post that held up the porch roof, tightened her mouth, and shook her head. She ran her hand down the smooth wood, feeling strangely soothed. The sky was reddening. "Going to be a pretty sunset," she said, making an attempt at polite conversation. She wondered where Adam was, what he was doing.

"He's the type always comes back. You know that about him," St. Louis said, ignoring her subterfuge.

"It seems I don't know much about him."

"That's what he was sayin' about you."

"He talked about me to you?" she asked finally.

"Not a lot, but some. No way he could've hid it from me."

"Not easy hiding things from you," she agreed.

"He was talking about heading for Alaska."

She ground her teeth together. "He should do what makes him happy."

"You think that'd be headin' for Alaska?"

She sucked in a breath. "Maybe."

"You know what yore problem is, gal?"

She smiled reluctantly. "Maybe not but I am guessing you're going to tell me."

He chuckled. "You are scared of loving again. All the rest of this is just smoke screen."

"The rest of what?" she asked, feeling a little angry but unsure why.

"Them excuses you been buildin' up in yore head, tellin' yore-self why it can't be between you and him."

"I don't agree, but even if it was so," she said tartly," I have good reason to be afraid. I've lost one man. It wasn't something I want to go through again."

"Might just be there's worse things than losin' someone. Like letting someone go who needs lovin', who you could have loved, and letting go of what you could have had because you was scared."

"There are so many reasons it can't work." Angry at herself, she felt tears in her eyes.

"Maybe. Maybe not, but I'm bettin' that right now none of them seem worth a tinker's damn. Do they?"

"No," she answered in a small voice.

"I thought not. Now we just pray he'll come back, and when he does, Martha?" He looked at her meaningfully.

"For all your words, nothing has changed. He's too young for me. He needs a woman his own age. My daughters would never understand. He lives such a different life. No room for a woman in it." The tears welled over, and she turned from him to hide them.

"You think about it a little bit. Maybe you'll see all you just listed off don't matter none. When it gets down to it, there are only a few things that do. None of them were even on that list of yores."

~

Adam and Tom Crane laid on their bedrolls, eating hard biscuits, darkness turning the night into a place of mystery and the unknown. "You don't think we need a fire?" Crane asked nervously looking out as a coyote yodeled in the distance.

"How long you been sheriffing?" Adam asked with a faint smile.

"This job was first; so a year."

"Well, I've been doing this sort of thing for over twelve years.

If we build a fire, we're asking for trouble. They might scent it and get the idea someone is after them. Put them on their guard or have them take off at night, and while we can't track them in the dark, they could run for it under that cover. Moreover if they build a fire, we might see it or smell it, and then we have the advantage."

"It's just hard, sitting around like this in the dark."

"There's moonlight."

"Not that much in that sliver up there."

"Enough... if we get a whiff of their fire."

"And if not?"

"Then tomorrow we'll catch up with them."

"You thought about what that might mean?"

"You mean shooting?" Adam smiled. Crane wasn't much of a sheriff.

"Of course."

"Oregon City's sheriff job's been a pretty easy job up until now hasn't it?" Adam asked.

"Nothing but a few drunks, petty thefts, a husband beating his wife. There's hasn't been no trouble until the bank. Whoever figured anybody do such a thing?"

"You looked pretty pale when you rode out of town today. Ever killed a man?"

Crane shook his head.

"Ever seen a man who'd been shot to death before?"

"Uh, no..."

"Upset you quite a bit, didn't it?"

"Yeah, well, what'd you expect? Of course, it upset me."

Adam shook his head. "I'll bet you don't like blood either."

Crane seemed to shudder. "I never could take seeing blood."

"Figures. Big men like you, seems like they never can." Adam smiled, using his forearm to pillow his head. He stared up at the patterns in the stars. "Well, with any luck, we won't see any this trip."

"This is strange."

"In what way?"

"I'm the sheriff, but you are acting more like a sheriff than me. You ever do the job before?"

"It's one thing I haven't tried."

"But you've tried plenty of others."

Adam laughed. "You name it; I've probably done it—well, except keeping a store."

"Or settling down," Crane guessed astutely.

"That too."

"Why not?"

"Who knows. Someone said I was a rolling stone, wouldn't want to settle down. I don't think it's been that though."

"Where's your home, Stone?"

"The last place I called home was Ohio."

"You left there early?"

"Fourteen."

Crane whistled. "That's early all right. What'd you do when you left?"

"Headed West, first with buffalo hunters, then I guided wagon trains across. That was a good life for a young man. Once I went to California. Saw San Francisco. Then there wasn't any more need for scouts on the trails. Like Pollard told you, I've been working for the Federals down in the Rogue for too many years."

"So, fighting ain't new to you?"

"No," he said, letting out his breath, "it's not new."

"Ain't you scared about what might happen tomorrow?"

"I don't think about it."

"You ever killed a man?"

Adam thought a moment, debating whether he wanted to tell him, and then deciding it didn't matter, he said, "Yes."

"Was it-- was it hard?"

"It shouldn't be easy."

"Are you a believer?"

191

"In what?"

"In God."

"I don't think about it."

"Everybody thinks about it."

Adam snorted. "Not everybody."

Crane lay back, his hands under his head as he stared into the sky. "I grew up in church. Don't live it though. My sainted mother'd turn over in her grave if she knew the things I've done." When Adam didn't say anything, he went on. "A man's thinking about dying... seems like a good time to think about God."

"Not the way I see it."

"Why not?"

"A man going into battle of any sort needs his wits about him. I suppose if you already believed, it'd be a good time to go to God, but if you don't, it's no time to get distracted. Need to center yourself, not fragment."

"Hmmmm," Crane said, "doesn't seem like the way I've heard it."

Adam grinned. "I'll bet it isn't. Well, what I say is, do what works for you."

Crane groaned. "That's been the one thing I've never figured out."

"No other man can help you come up to it either." He rolled himself into his blankets. "Tomorrow is likely to be a hard day, Crane. Get some sleep."

~

Martha lay in bed, Loraine sleeping peacefully beside her, and tried to think through all the things St. Louis had said. She could not deny he was right about her fear. The rest might matter more than he thought, but the fear was more of loving again than what others might think. One thing was for sure though. It was too late to worry about that one. She was in love again. She stared at the roof over her head.

She knew one thing though and St. Louis couldn't address that. It wasn't just that he was younger and that others would see her as foolish to be with such a man. No, it wasn't even that her daughters would be furious with her. They loved her. She felt confident of that. They would forgive her in time.

No, it was what was happening right at that moment. There would be no security in loving a man like Adam Stone. Just as he was at this moment, he would be off on adventures. She'd be left worrying and fretting-- unable to do anything about any of it. More time with him would only make that harder.

She tried to put out of her mind the feeling of his arms around her, the image of the strong column of his neck, the hard muscularity of his smooth chest, the way his eyes glittered with desire when he looked at her. She didn't want to think about how he made her feel like more of a woman than she'd maybe ever been.

Whatever time he was with her, she would know love. Adam had so much to give. The passion, the fire in his eyes would not give her a soothing relationship as she'd had with Amos, but it would fill places within her woman's heart that had never been filled.

With Amos, she'd known he'd be there, that she could count on him. With Adam, she would never have that. He was like a whirlwind come into her life, throwing everything around, tossing her in directions she'd never intended going, and like a whirlwind, he'd be there and gone.

There were so many problems. She counted on her fingers, age, religion, lifestyle, her children. Children. She had been so relieved when her monthly time came. She was too old for more children, and yet Adam should have them of his own. Thank

God, she wasn't about to give him one that didn't fit into either of their plans.

Adam wanted her to take the risk of loving him, to reach out and take him into her arms in front of the world, at least her world. If she reached out, she'd find only air in her fingers. He was a wandering man, never settling down. She wanted to stay here, stay with her homestead. She couldn't visualize Adam behind a plow, fixing fence all day. He was like a black panther, ready to leap, needing his freedom. Marrying him would be to put a rock around his neck. It would destroy him.

"You're destroying me, lady."

No, no, I don't mean to destroy you.

She rolled over, tucking her knees against her chest, trying to find some position she could finally find sleep. She couldn't let herself think of all he'd said or all she could've said to him. If she did that, she'd never sleep.

For a reason that at first seemed incomprehensible to her, she thought of her Rose of Sharon, just coming into full bloom, the white blossoms delicate and yet surprisingly sturdy. Each generation of the women in her family had valued the shrub, nurtured it in protected places because it couldn't stand the extreme cold. Sometimes it had been raised in covered porches or protected nooks. Somehow, against all odds, it had grown again and again into a full sized bush, full of beautiful white flowers. The cuttings, carefully wrapped in the Conestoga had looked like dead sticks, something no life could come from and yet, here it was-- blooming.

The way of love, which seemed to start from nothing, a piece from something bigger, something that had been nurtured over the years, protected, valued. Without all of that, without the care of generations would it exist at all?

Again and again out of seemingly nothing, love bloomed within the souls of men and women. Sometimes it came slow as it had between her and Amos and sometimes fast as it had seemed to erupt full blown for Adam. Despite the commonsense part of her brain, the reasons she knew it shouldn't, love had bloomed again for her. Could she really throw that away?

Overhead she heard the gentle patter of rain. The skies had been clear when they'd gone to bed. A wind rustled the big fir tree behind the cabin, bringing its limbs against the wall in a noisy display of nature's power. She and Amos had left it there to shelter the cabin, but it seemed sometimes to almost assault the walls.

At first she enjoyed the sound of the drops hitting her roof, and then she began to wonder if it was raining where Adam was. Would he be getting wet, sleeping somewhere on the hard ground and miserable with rain soaking his blankets?

And she was back to the question again. What would she do when he came back? Then another thought, a frightening one, more upsetting than all the others, came out of the darkness. What if he didn't come back?

CHAPTER 17

With first light, Adam had saddled Joe and was ready to go. "Crane," he said, "we got to get a move on." The sky had clouds in it, some that looked capable of a heavy rain. If they lost the tracks in a storm, they'd never find their thieves.

"I'm trying. It just takes some time for me to stoke up my fire." He smiled weakly.

"Look, I'll go ahead. You follow quick as you can. I got the feeling we'll find them this morning."

Crane jumped up, quickly rolling his bedding and throwing it onto his horse. "You ain't leaving me."

Adam smiled. "All right then, but hurry it up."

He found the tracks again; then looked ahead to see where they might be going. The mountains he'd been in with Martha were one direction they could choose to go over the Cascades. He didn't want to catch them up there. He didn't want to kill a man where he'd been with the woman he loved. Likely the only time he would be there with her.

He looked behind him and saw Crane following, lagging a little but determined to keep up.

The tracks disappeared; then he found them again, fresher,

sharper. "Here's where they camped," he pointed out the bent over grasses, the signs of horses being tied to trees. "Not that far ahead now."

"No fire for them last night either," Crane said with some satisfaction.

"Nope." He would let himself think of nothing now but the men ahead. There being three of them, he preferred to have the advantage of surprise to help his and Crane's odds of success. He glanced back at the lagging sheriff and tried to decide how much help he'd be in a fight. He guessed he'd soon know.

The trail broke out into a small clearing, and for the first time Adam could see far enough to catch a glimpse of three men on horses, taking their time as they rode up the next slope.

Adam smiled grimly. "There they are."

"You sure?" Crane asked nervously. "Maybe it's three others."

Adam laughed. "No chance of that. When they see us, they won't be sure we're after them, but let's take no chances. I'll cut around ahead. See how the ground slopes to the right toward a canyon. If I go left, head up into the hills, I can get ahead without them seeing me. They can't cut right, and you'll be behind them. We'll have them."

"You think splitting up is a good idea?"

"I think it's the only way we can be sure to get them."

"Then I ought to be the one going ahead."

"Joe's faster and more sure-footed on rough ground than your sorrel. When I get in place, I'll yell for them to stop. Innocent men would stop. They won't. They will either ride fast toward me or turn and try to run, heading for you. Either way we have them."

"Or they have us." Crane licked his lips, the fear visible on his face.

Adam's smile returned, the humor gone from it. "Either or," he said as he kicked Joe in the side and cut for the upper slope, swinging wide of where the men should be riding.

As he rode, the trees spun past rapidly, and he was left with a blur of terrain. As he broke out onto open ground, he saw he had to cut up the slope a little farther and as though reading his mind, Joe raced up the ground, his hooves seeming to fly. In the heavy trees again, he angled down the hill. The ground was rough, but nothing too demanding for Joe as they cleared a fallen tree with an easy jump. Adam could feel the excited intensity in the big horse.

Below would be the three riders. He forced Joe to his utmost and then knew he'd won when he saw the rocky cut in the mountain ahead of him. "We beat them," he crooned. "Good boy! You did it. "

Adam pulled Joe to a halt. Dismounting, he tied the horse's reins to a small sapling safe from any stray shots. He grabbed his rifle and ran toward the rocky promontory, the spot he'd chosen to confront them. When he got to the top, he saw the first rider about a hundred yards down the trail. He waited.

They appeared to be expecting no trouble at least not from in front of them. He heard one of them laugh before he could make out faces.

A hundred yards-- fifty. He loosened his revolver in its holster, checking its load, glad he'd bought one of the newest Smith & Wessons. He'd jammed extra cartridges for his rifle in his shirt pocket but guessed he wouldn't have time to reload it. This would be over in less than a minute.

As they approached, Adam rose from where he'd been kneeling out of sight. "Law here. Hold where you are, boys," he yelled, his rifle covering them.

"What the hell," one of them yelped, trying to turn his horse.

"Run, and you're a dead man," Adam barked.

"I only see one," another yelled and drew his gun.

No choice for it. Adam squeezed down on the trigger, watching as the man sailed from his saddle as though thrown by an invisible hand.

He grabbed his revolver, aiming and firing as the second outlaw got him in range and let go with a bullet. Adam ducked back and fired, moving down the slope to where he would be able to get a clearer shot.

The bullet caught him on the run, slammed into his side, and sent him sailing in half a fall and half a slide. He rolled over twice, holding on to his gun, never losing consciousness. At the bottom of the slope, he had his revolver up when the outlaw tried to ride him down.

He sighted and pulled the trigger, watching as the man shrieked and tumbled from his saddle.

Adam was numb to the bullet that had hit him. He felt no pain, a condition he didn't expect to last but planned to work for all it was worth. Getting to his feet, he heard shots and tried to rally himself for meeting the last of the outlaws. Then he saw the rider approaching was Tom Crane.

"You trying to get all the glory?" asked Crane. "Weren't you planning to leave any of them for me?"

"I was always a selfish bastard," Adam said as he swayed. Now that it was over, he was beginning to feel the first shock from the impact of the bullet and loss of blood.

"You're hit," Crane said, his face paling as he jumped from his horse.

"You get the other one?"

"I did." By the time Crane got to him, his skin had taken on a greenish cast. Adam managed a smile, remembering the man's admitted weakness at blood.

"Never mind it now. I don't think it's much, probably just creased my ribs. I can look at it later when we make sure they're dead, and that their loot is here."

"You sure?" Crane asked, concerned as Adam stumbled.

"Trust me," Adam said. As he moved down the slope, the sky went black, and he fell flat on his face.

~

Although it was nearly time to go to the Lances for the birthday celebration dinner, Martha felt like doing just about anything but that.

She looked worriedly at St. Louis. "I want you to ride into Oregon City," she said. "We've got to know something. Loraine, Agatha and I will go on down to the Lances, and you come with him or without when you can."

"I'll ride back to my place first," he said, "just to make sure he ain't come home and is there lookin' for me."

"If..." She stopped, unable to go on. It had been two days with no word. Anything could've happened. She couldn't bear to let herself think of the possibilities.

"Ya go on down to their cabin, have some fun. I'll go see what's happenin'. Quit yore worryin'."

Martha tried to smile and failed. "All right. It appears there's nothing else I can do now anyway."

St. Louis gave her an awkward pat on the shoulder. "The boy knows how to take care of himself. Don't you forget that."

She frowned. "He shouldn't have gone off that way."

"You mad at him over it?"

"I might be." Her emotions had gone through so many twists that from hour to hour she had no idea what she was feeling. It made her feel anything but a mature woman. She felt like a silly girl and was more than half mad at the reason for those foolish emotions.

St. Louis grinned. "Women. Can't never please 'em."

"So it's women's fault is it that men ride off on wild adventures?" She managed a laugh though she felt no humor.

"So, if he's there, I tell him to keep right on riding?" he asked, a twinkle in his eyes.

"Of course not," she retorted, forced to smile in spite of herself at the ridiculousness of what he and she both were saying.

She gave St. Louis a hug and a more genuine smile. "Now," she said, "go on. Go find out what happened to that worthless creature."

When St. Louis had ridden out, she went back into the cabin and finished getting ready to go to the Lances. Glancing at the mirror, she patted the smooth bun at the top of her head, irked at the stray locks that seemed determined to spoil the effect of prim and proper lady.

Loraine came out of the bedroom. "I like that dress on you, Mama," she said. "Have I seen it before?"

"Probably not. I made it a few weeks ago. When I didn't have anything else to do."

"It's nice, the black and red print are wonderful with your coloring, and the red embroidered design along that scooped neckline is a nice touch. I think Eunice and Agatha are right. You could sell what you make. Each of your dresses is an original design. Ladies are hungry for that right now."

"Well," Martha said with a smile, "if we lost money in that bank robbery, I might just consider it."

Agatha came out, wrapping a shawl around her bony shoulders. "Did you lose all your money in that robbery?" she asked, having heard only part of the conversation.

"No," Martha replied with a smile, "our money's in several banks, Portland for one, but we might have lost some."

"Shoulda found out," Agatha clucked with disapproval. "Martha, that is purely irresponsible to not know if you lost money."

Martha smiled at the critical tone. "You know what they say about bad news. It comes quickly enough. Don't have to go searching it out."

"Well, still seems a body oughta know about their money."

Martha went over to the counter and picked up the crock of

pickles to take to the Lances. "Shall we go?" she suggested, knowing she wanted to do just about anything but go. She wanted to stay here, waiting until she heard what had happened, but she would go because it was the *right* thing to do. Suddenly she felt very tired of doing the *right* thing but maybe the habit was too ingrained to stop.

It was just a nice stretch of the legs to the Lance's cabin. It took little time before they were there, sipping from glasses of lemonade and being introduced to Eunice's brother, George Simon.

Almost immediately Martha saw what was going on with this community party. George, portly but an attractive enough man, a few years older than Martha, was obviously intended for her to meet. "I'm a bachelor," he said, smiling across at her. "I own three stores in Salem, a livery stable, general goods and a blacksmiths. Do quite well with them all."

"My," said Martha, trying to edge away from him. He followed.

"But you've never married," repeated Agatha with a delighted smile. Matchmaking was clearly on her agenda also.

"That is true. Not that I would not have wished to marry. I've simply been so busy with my stores and then never found the right woman," he said, smiling again at Martha.

"He has a very nice home in Salem, two stories, and a big back yard, perfect for children if he should be so blessed," Eunice put in, patting her brother on the shoulder. "You should see the furnishings. He sent for some of them from San Francisco."

"Amazing," said Martha, wondering where Adam was and whether St. Louis was on his way into Oregon City.

Matt and Amy arrived with their baby in a papoose carrier that St. Louis had made for Laura. Everyone hurried over to admire her. "She's grown just since I saw her," Agatha cooed, touching the baby's tiny fingers.

"You live up the hill, they tell me," said George, still smiling at Martha, showing an even set of white teeth.

"Yes," she said, frowning as she realized everyone was purposely leaving them to themselves. She wondered how she was going to get George to leave her alone.

"Eunice told me you are a widow," he went on, leaning a little toward her.

Martha moved toward the table. "Yes," she said, offering to help Eunice with putting on the food.

"No, dearie. Just visit with George. That's help enough. I've wanted to get him out here earlier to meet you, but he's so busy with all his businesses. George is going to be one of Oregon's most important citizens. Mark my words. Salem wouldn't be Salem without his businesses." She giggled and headed back toward her cabin.

"Aren't any others coming?" Fanny asked

"I'm not sure," Martha said, looking off toward the west and Oregon City and wondering where he was, what had happened.

When the riders approached it was the opposite from where she had expected. Her only warning was a shriek from Loraine. "Here comes St. Louis, and Adam is with him."

St. Louis' demeanor was somber as they rode up, but Adam was smiling until his gaze flicked to the man standing beside Martha.

Dismounting slowly, he said hello to Loraine but brushed on past her to walk to where the tables were set up. He wore a black shirt and pair of black pants Martha had never seen before.

"Sorry I'm late. Had to get cleaned up."

"Yeah," growled St. Louis frowning as he followed him. "Got any place to set?"

"Of course," Eunice said, bringing out a chair for St. Louis.

"How about a few more? Could be other folks need to set too," St. Louis growled. St. Louis was being rude and seemed upset. Unnaturally so. Martha looked from his face to Adam's. Something was going on, but she didn't understand what.

She walked to where Adam was standing. "Did you catch up with the bank robbers," she asked.

His smile was slow in coming. "We did." He looked meaningfully from her to George Simon who had followed to stand very closely beside her.

"Did they still have the money with them?" asked George, smiling at Adam as he introduced himself.

For a moment, Martha thought Adam would refuse to take his hand, but then he slowly reached out, wincing as George vigorously shook it.

"So--" Adam looked back at her, seeming to tilt his head a little as he asked, his voice almost toneless, "What is this? A celebration?"

"Didn't St. Louis tell you?" asked Martha, feeling a need to reach out and touch him, to stroke his cheek, to take away the tiredness she saw in his eyes.

"He said you'd be here, that I was invited, and here I am."

St. Louis pushed a chair toward him. "Wal, then set down. Ya been ridin' the last few days. Need to rest now."

Adam smiled faintly without looking away from Martha. "I'm fine. Quit mothering me."

"It's Fanny's birthday," Martha said. She frowned as she tried to decide what the matter was; he seemed strained, ill at ease, or was he just tired?

"So, old friends getting together for a family celebration," Adam said a wry twist to his lips.

"Yes," said George brightly. "Can I get you something to drink?"

"You got any whiskey?" Adam asked coolly, his blue eyes narrowed as he watched George with what to Martha seemed disconcerting directness.

"Well, no, but there's lemonade and coffee."

Adam looked away, swallowing. "Lemonade. Yes, that would be good."

"Are you all right?" Martha asked, moving closer to him now. Something was definitely wrong.

"Fine. You and George here known each other long?"

"George is a businessman from Salem," Eunice interrupted, as Fanny handed Adam his lemonade.

"He has three stores," Fanny added.

"Three stores," Adam repeated as he looked back at Martha. "Imagine that." He glanced over and saw Matt and Amy with Laura now in her arms. He set the untouched lemonade on the table and smiling, walked slowly over to them. "So this is how she looks cleaned up."

"Yup," Matt said proudly, "Ain't she a beauty."

"Just like her mother and grandmother," Adam muttered, absently brushing his hand past his eyes.

"I think she looks like Matt," Amy said, pulling back the blanket so he could get a better look at her.

"Got his hair all right, but looks to me like she's got Martha's and your eyes." He smiled again, rocking back on his heels a little.

"You said you caught up with the robbers," Horace said. "Does that mean the money too?"

Adam looked at him as though trying to decide what he was asking.

"Any shooting?" Matt asked.

"Some."

"I can't believe our useless sheriff actually did something right for once," Horace chortled. "Where'd you find them?"

"Are you all right?" Loraine asked anxiously.

Adam's smile seemed strained to Martha as he looked back at her; then she realized George had again come to stand behind her.

"Supper is ready," Eunice said, interrupting the questioning. People began trooping into the house to fill their plates.

Adam stood back, leaning his broad shoulders against a large oak, watching silently as the others filed in the door. Martha knew she should go in to the house, should ignore whatever was going on with him, but she could no more have done that then stopped breathing.

With a sigh of relinquishment, a knowledge that she was about to cast caution to the winds and wasn't sorry to see it go, she went to him. "It's obvious you shouldn't be here," she said.

He looked at her as though her words made no sense to him. "Why? This a private thing? Just for family?"

"No! It is not, but you're clearly exhausted. Are you all right?"

"I'm fine," he said, looking over her shoulder at George, who was approaching them. "Here comes your gentleman friend," he said.

"I just met him today, certainly do not call him friend," she hissed. She would've said more but George was there.

"Do you want me to fill a plate for you, Martha?" he asked.

Adam raised his eyebrows as if to say I told you so. Martha glared at Adam. "I'll be there in a minute," she said coldly to George, hoping he would go get his own food.

Instead of leaving, George reached over and gave Adam a friendly slap on the shoulder. "You did a good job, young man," he said smiling. Although George seemed oblivious, Martha didn't miss the way Adam half flinched and his jaw clenched at the man's hearty pat.

"George, would you fill a plate for me after all," Martha asked. He smiled happily and headed off.

"So," Adam said when he'd gone, "man like that can give you security-- big house." He swallowed, half closing his eyes before he added, "Everything another man couldn't."

"Maybe a big house and security aren't all that important," she said. She knew with almost a sense of relief there'd be no going back from this day. She'd suffered too much over this decision and now that it had been made, she was surprisingly at ease with it.

"That doesn't sound like what you've been saying," he

muttered apparently oblivious to what she knew had to be showing in her eyes.

St. Louis walked up. "For God's sake, sit down, Adam," he said as he tried to take Adam's arm. Adam shrugged away, that half smile on his face.

"Think I'm going to get something to drink. I set that lemonade down somewhere, and my mouth's like cotton."

"I'll get it for you," Martha snapped, totally put out with his strange behavior.

"Wouldn't trouble a lady-- with prospects," he said, as he pushed himself away from the tree and began to walk slowly toward the table.

Martha watched him for a moment but could stand it no longer. She marched around him to stand directly in front, blocking his way. "What are you talking about?" she asked, as she stared up at his face, trying to understand the strange set to his lips, the lack of expression in his eyes.

He swallowed again, seemed to try to manage a smile and failed. "That's a real pretty dress. Attract most any man with--"

His long length seemed to crumble before her eyes. As he collapsed in what seemed slow motion, she reached out, her arms coming around him, his weight dragging her to the ground.

St. Louis was at her side almost immediately, kneeling, feeling for the pulse in Adam's neck.

"What is it? What happened?" Martha cried as she cradled Adam's unconscious body in her arms.

"He was shot, that's what. I come up to the cabin, and he was there, just washin' up. He asked about ya and like a fool I told him about this. There was no way this side of heaven to stop him. He was bound he was comin'." He pulled open Adam's shirt, and now Martha could see the white bandage wrapped around his torso, blood staining his left side.

"How serious is this?" she asked horrified at the blood.

"He said it was just a crease, but wouldn't let me look at it, and it's plain to see he's lost blood."

"We'll take him to my cabin," Martha said.

"I'll get his horse," St. Louis said as the others poured out of the house, gathering in a semi-circle around them.

"What's wrong with him?" asked Eunice, and then saw the blood on the bandage. "Oh dear," she gasped, turning away. "I can't stand blood." Loraine stood a distance away, her eyes on them, but she said nothing. Martha felt concern for her daughter but at this moment, Adam's needs took precedent.

CHAPTER 18

Adam's eyes blinked open and into what seemed endless faces and eyes-- all but the one he wanted to see. "Stupid thing," he mumbled, trying to push his body up and aware for the first time that he was being held.

"Don't say a word," Martha hissed, "and lie still. St. Louis is bringing your horse."

He should have known by the scent enveloping him. "Sorry. Didn't mean to ruin the party," he muttered, trying again to sit up. The arms around him tightened and refused to let him rise. He couldn't believe he was so weak that he couldn't break her hold, but it seemed to be the case.

"Don't you think you've lost enough blood? I can't believe your lack of good judgment. Riding all that distance, then not taking to your bed when you got home. Don't you have a lick of sense?"

"Obviously you don't think so."

"You're right about that." She looked around. "Where is St. Louis with that horse?"

"Can I help?" Fanny asked, bending over them. "Bring water or something?"

Amy was already rushing to them. Kneeling beside Adam and her mother, she held a glass of lemonade to his lips. "Drink this," she ordered, watching to make certain he obeyed her.

"I'm fine. Just a little dizziness," Adam muttered; then was forced to swallow or choke.

Matt leaned over. "If you can argue yore way out of what either of these two decides, you are a better man than me."

Adam groaned his acknowledgment of the truth of that statement. "I didn't mean to spoil this day for everyone," he repeated, finally aware of how Martha was holding him, how tenderly she was cradling him in her arms, all the while her words were angry and her tone scathing.

"May I help to carry him?" George asked.

Martha shook her head. "St. Louis and Matt can manage I'm sure."

"I can walk, damn it," Adam snapped. He finally got his arms under him and with a determined effort, managed to push himself to his feet, where he stood, swaying a little but resolute that he was not going to be carried by anybody anywhere.

Martha rose behind him, her arms coming around his waist, providing support without touching his wound.

"I'm fine. Go on back and eat, please," he said. He didn't ever want her to see him weakened, didn't want her pity. And all the while this George, or whatever his name was-- with all those businesses-- watched the whole thing probably with perverse satisfaction.

St. Louis came up with Joe. "I don't know if he can stay on," he said as he held the reins, steadying the horse.

"Don't talk about me as if I'm not here," snapped Adam, fed up with the whole situation. It had been one nightmare after another, the ride into Oregon City, then home, his determination to see her, only to find her with another man. He'd expected it but not so soon. The perfect end to it all was, of course, the ignominy of falling down right under her eyes. All he wanted now was get out of there, get back to St. Louis' where he could crawl into a hole.

"Can you ride as far as my cabin?" Martha asked her arms still around him supporting him.

"I told you, that's not necessary. I'll go back to St. Louis'."

"His place is farther. Mine is just up the hill. Is there something wrong with mine?" she asked.

"No, but what about George?"

She smiled then. "What about him?" she asked.

"You know what I mean," Adam said shrugging and regretting it as it sent a wave of pain through his side.

"Well, I think," Martha said, throwing caution and proper behavior to the wind as, right in front of everyone, she rose on her tiptoes to plant a lingering kiss against his neck, "you belong at my home."

She heard a little feminine gasp and was unsure if the disapproval came from Amy, Loraine or Fanny, but she didn't care. All that mattered was what Adam thought, and she already knew what he thought about such behavior.

Adam half turned then and looked down into her eyes, seeing what she had already shown everyone who was standing in front of them. "Are you sure about this?" he asked.

"No," she told him with a tremulous smile, "not even a little bit."

"That's not an encouraging answer," he muttered, frustrated with his weakness and the pain that seemed to be interfering with his thought processes. It was a fine time to be getting wounded.

"Maybe I can do better," she whispered, "after you are in bed."

"I-- You don't have room for me at your place," he argued, all the while enjoying her arms around him now.

"We'll make room."

St. Louis looked from one determined face to the other. "I

211

think," he said, "the cards has been dealt. You are goin' to her place."

Adam looked into her eyes and saw the love she wasn't hiding from anyone. "I guess so," he said with a wry smile. "I guess so."

"Mother," Amy said, coming up to stand by them, "what is going on?"

"I'll explain it later," Martha said with a sigh. "Or at least try. For now, I am going to get this foolish man to a bed before he falls down again."

Eunice frowned, trying to take hold of Martha's arm. "But what about George?" she asked. "St. Louis can take care of Adam. You stay here."

"No," Martha said firmly with a wide smile, "I'm going to take care of Adam."

~

Matt came back from helping Adam onto his horse—despite Adam's protests. George was watching his sister Eunice who seemed the most upset of anyone. "I can't believe that. I simply can't believe it. She kissed him. Did you see that? She out and out kissed that man."

"Yes," said Loraine with a faint smile, "she did, didn't she?"

"What *is* going on?" asked Amy, her voice reflecting confusion and frustration in equal parts.

Eunice moved over to the table and picked up her plate, sitting down beside Agatha. "Have you ever seen such a thing?" she asked, more to herself than Agatha. George took the other side of the table. Matt assessed his expression as more bemused than upset.

"A time or two," Agatha said with a faint smile, "but it's been a few years."

Horace plopped down beside them. "Are they courting?" he asked, still watching up the hill toward the Stevens cabin.

"Well, I can hardly imagine that could be," snapped Eunice. "He's young enough to be her son."

Horace gave a deep chuckle. "Not hardly."

"Do you approve of this?" Eunice questioned, frowning.

"It isn't for me to approve or disapprove. Just that if Adam gets a woman as strong, beautiful and accomplished as Martha for himself, he'll be a lucky man," Horace said, stabbing a piece of beef with his fork.

Well, whatever the explanation," Amy said, "that can't be that. That's why it's ridiculous even to suggest! She's just mothering him. That's the way Mama is. She's just..."

Loraine put out her hand, taking Amy's arm. "No, Amy. It is not that."

"But Adam was supposed to be for you," Amy wailed.

"And Martha was supposed to be for George," Eunice joined in.

"People don't go to pickin' each other out accordin' to how convenient it is for other folks," Matt drawled, losing all his appetite as he saw this was going to be coming home with him.

"But Mama and Adam?" questioned Amy, shaking her head. "It just can't be. I don't believe it, and I won't unless I hear Mama confess to it herself!"

"Confess it?" snapped Matt. "You make it look like she's done something wrong."

Amy sat fuming, still staring up the hill. Laura began to whimper from where she had been napping in the carrier against a tree, and Matt went over to get her.

"Martha's a fine looking woman," George said with what seemed to Matt to be a thoughtful expression. "You were right about that, Eunice."

"I know," she wailed, putting her hands over her eyes.

George smiled. "You know the old saying-- there's many a miss between the cup and the lip. Well, that happens a lot in life."

"What do you mean?" asked Eunice, raising her head and looking at him hopefully.

"I mean that-- I'm glad you had me meet her, and I didn't get three businesses by giving up at the first sign of competition!" He sat back, still smiling as he contemplated his fingers.

There was nothing about the businessman that Matt found admirable. He was just glad he wasn't about to become his step father-in-law. At that, he smiled as he handled the squirming baby to Amy.

∽

At the cabin, Martha dragged a cot from the bedroom and set it up by the fireplace while St. Louis pushed Adam into a chair at the table.

Yanking his shirt open, the older man growled, "I ain't never seen such foolishness. Pure idjit, that's what ya are."

"It's plain that neither of the two of you believe in tender, loving care," Adam grunted as St. Louis pulled his shirt from his pants and yanked it down over his shoulders, throwing it to the ground.

"I believe in it. When a man's deservin' of it," St. Louis retorted.

"The bed's ready," Martha told them, coming to stand above Adam, resting her hands lightly on his bare shoulders as she watched St. Louis.

"I don't need to lie down in the middle of the day," he grumbled, wincing as St. Louis prodded his side.

"Ya might afore I'm done with ya. Who bandaged this?"

"It's just a gouge. I did it myself," Adam said defensively. "Blood makes Tom sick."

"Why didn't you go to the doctor in town?" Martha asked.

"A doctor wasn't needed."

"Some sheriff, who can't stand the sight of a little blood," grumbled St. Louis with disgust.

"He isn't sure he wants to stay sheriff," Adam muttered as St. Louis and Martha pulled him up and pushed him toward the cot. "This is silly," he said but allowed them to lower him to the bed. He was frustrated to realize it felt good to be lying down as St. Louis cut away the bandage.

"Careful," Adam protested. As the cloth pulled away from the wound, he yelped. "What do you think you're doing? That hurt."

"No joke?" asked St. Louis with a snort. He and Martha stared at the long, ugly groove in Adam's side. "What do ya think?" he asked her. "Looks to me like it's bled a fair amount."

"I think," she said in a small voice, "that for some reason I'm not handling this much better than the sheriff."

St. Louis ignored the failure of his assistant and probed above the torn flesh. "From the way this feels. Right about here." He touched the spot lightly, watching as Adam winced. "I think ya cracked a rib from either the bullet or a fall."

"Just great," Adam growled, irritated that he might be laid up.

"Wal, it ain't my fault. And ya won't like this neither, but we oughta pour alcohol over this torn flesh, or I'm thinkin' bleedin' good or not, after that rough bandagin' job ya are gonna to get an infection to boot."

Adam reluctantly gave a consenting sigh. Martha brought St. Louis an almost full bottle. "Ya want a swig afore I start," St. Louis asked.

Adam shook his head, bracing himself against the burst of pain he expected when the raw alcohol hit the open wound.

Martha knelt beside him, taking his hand into both of hers. "Squeeze down on me, sweetheart," she whispered.

He almost laughed, remembering how recently he had heard those same words as she spoke them to her daughter. "I want to hold your hand tomorrow," he told her with a glint in his eyes, "not break it tonight."

"I don't break all that easily."

He kissed the fingers. "Thanks for the offer anyway."

St. Louis poured the strong alcohol over the wound as Adam twisted against the pain, barely suppressing the oath that rose to his lips. When he could speak, he grated out, "I think you've been just waiting for your chance to do that, old man."

"Maybe so, maybe so."

"I hope you're not expecting a fee for playing doctor. No money."

"None at all?" St. Louis asked with pretended interest as he stood up.

"The Federals don't pay that much." Adam realized it was true. He had little to offer Martha, certainly not three businesses and a fancy house.

"Let that dry in the air for a bit, and I'll go back to my cabin. Get the salve."

"Oh Lord," Adam moaned, shaking his head, "not the salve. The salve you were always putting on anybody that'd stand still for you, including mules."

"Make fun if ya want," St. Louis retorted as he pressed a pad to the wound but didn't bandage it. "About two days from now when ya ain't got an infection, and ya are feeling' fit, then see if ya ain't apologizing." He stalked out of the cabin.

"I think," said Martha, raising Adam's hand to her lips, "that you've offended him." She kissed his palm, placing his hand against her cheek.

"He knows I don't mean anything by it." With a single finger, he lightly stroked along the delicacy of her jaw line.

"Can I get you anything to drink or--" She stopped, struck with the look in his eyes. "Adam," she whispered, feeling suddenly shaky, "you have to quit looking at me like that or--"

"Or what?" His hand changed tactics, drawing her head down. "What will you do?" he asked huskily as he pulled her to where her breath was his.

"I think there would have to be a punishment," she whispered, kissing his lips lightly before nipping the fullness of the lower lip.

"I might like that. What kind?" he teased, stroking his hand down her back.

"Well, not much given you are wounded." She tangled her fingers in his hair. "It wouldn't be good for you."

"You let me be the judge of what is good for me."

"You don't seem to be a very good at that. You're always getting yourself banged up." She smiled and kissed the point of his jaw, resting her hand lightly against his chest.

"What about this George guy," he said, his breath coming a little unevenly not from the pain but from the sensations she was arousing as she lightly kissed down the side of his neck.

"Is there anything about him, other than being Eunice's brother, that is?" she asked, stopping but only momentarily, on her way to his collarbone.

"Yeah, besides that."

"I think, Eunice had some ideas there, but they weren't and are not mine. You're not jealous are you?"

"No, uh maybe. Are you interested in him?" He had to ask it.

"I would have thought I made that obvious to everyone there today, and you were there." She ran her fingers over his chest. "So obvious that no one-- especially not you-- would need to ask."

"A man in pain needs to be humored."

She smiled contentedly. "I might even be in the mood to humor him." She kissed his lips.

"Are you saying what I think you're saying?"

"That depends. What do you think I'm saying?" She kissed his brow, then his eyelids. "Is it that you should take care of yourself? That I'm going to make sure that you do? That there'll be no cutting of wood or riding off on horses until I'm certain you're recovered."

He cupped her chin with his hand. "Are we through playing games?"

"Mmmmmm Maybe not through playing all games." She smiled, her eyes dark with love for him, and he saw all he'd ever wanted to see in those dark depths.

Adam jerked and looked down at his leg. "What the hell is this?" A pensive looking kitten had jumped on his leg and using its claws moved to his groin.

Martha laughed, "Her name is Heaven. Do you like cats, Mr. Stone?"

"I don't know. You sure she's a cat? Looks pretty small for one."

"Well, she's a kitten for now, but she's working her way toward cathood."

"Hmmm, is this a package deal?" He reached down and lightly stroked the soft fur. "Take one, and you get the two?"

"Since she's purring, it appears she has take a liking to you. Do you like her?" Martha grinned at the look of such a ruggedly, virile man with a kitten contentedly curling up and kneading bread. Actually, she thought with a small smile, Heaven has the right idea.

"Since I have designs on her owner, guess I will."

"Well, you wouldn't have to, but--"

"I like cats," he said quickly. "One of these days, when she is one, it'll be fine."

"Well, then, that's one problem out of the way," she said, reaching over and petting the kitten and then letting her fingers take over where Heaven had left off, kneading a little herself.

"So, what about marrying me?" he asked, his breathing

becoming unsteady again as she once more played havoc with his senses.

"There are a few things that need to be resolved."

He didn't like the sounds of that. "As in?"

"I have to talk to Amy and Loraine and eventually Belle. I want my daughters to approve of this, Adam."

"And if they don't?"

"Let's not anticipate that. I believe they will."

"I don't like thinking there are any ifs with us, Martha."

"There aren't, but you are marrying into a family. Have you considered that?"

"Of course, but they won't want me as their father. Just a friend, I expect."

"I agree. There are some other things you and I need to talk about too, Adam. To be sure we are expecting the same thing with this relationship. I'd like us to take the time to do that before we get married. Take it a day at a time. Is that all right with you?"

"Would it matter if it weren't?"

"Of course."

"It makes sense to me. I just don't want you backing out on me."

"I did make it rather public today."

He grinned. "Yes, you did. If you and I are taking our days together, I can wait for anything. Do what you want. Want me to run a quest for you?" he teased.

She laughed and bent over, putting her arms around him, she kissed him, her tongue delving into his mouth as his had hers. When she felt him suck on her tongue, she had to end it. This kind of play would quickly change, and she had Agatha and Loraine soon to come home. In fact...

"Ahem." Agatha Collins interrupted from the doorway.

Martha did not move away from Adam's cot, but she turned her head to watch as Agatha and Loraine entered the room. "You're back sooner than I expected," she said calmly.

"That was obvious," Agatha retorted with a sly smile.

Loraine walked over to the stove; then turned to face her mother. "I-- I'd like to talk to you, Mama, when you can that is."

Adam met Martha's gaze. "I'll be fine," he said.

"All right." Martha rose and followed her daughter outside.

"I am sure you are disappointed," Martha said, not attempting to touch her as they walked toward the barn.

"Not really," said Loraine, "I told you that I wasn't stupid about men any more. I just wanted to tell you that Agatha and I will be leaving in the morning."

Martha stopped walking. "Are you that angry?" she asked in a small voice.

"I'm not mad at all. We had to go back, and we'd thought tomorrow or the next day. It's obvious you need the space now. I am not unhappy with you and Adam. I understand."

"You do?" Martha asked, surprise in her voice.

"I did have a little hint about it. When we came over after Amy's baby was born. You and Adam came down from the woods, and his shirt was not buttoned; you both looked flushed. I'd seen that before with Amy and Matt, and I thought then, but wasn't totally sure. Little things though kept adding up."

"I didn't want to deceive you, Loraine. It was just at that point I didn't think that it could possibly work out the age difference and well, just everything."

"I told you, I understand."

"There are many differences between Adam me. There were then; there still are. Things that may make being together forever not possible."

Loraine smiled softly, staring off toward the distant river. "I wouldn't let any of them stand in my way if I was you," she said after a moment. "It seems to me the way he looks at you, the way you look at him, you have something very special. Don't throw it away. I saw the truth of it when he looked at George Simon standing beside you. I never thought to see the look of despair on Adam Stone's face, but I saw it then. He really loves you, Mama."

"I am so sorry. I didn't want to hurt you," Martha said, tears coming to her eyes as she scanned the face of her oldest daughter.

"Don't be sorry. I never had anything from Adam. You took nothing from me, nothing that was ever mine," Loraine said, smiling through her own tears. "I remember how Papa used to look at you. The way Matt sees Amy and now. Well, truthfully, I never thought I'd see that look on Adam's face, but it's there now. I'd never try to come between that."

Martha drew her into her arms. "How did I raise such a smart daughter?" she asked.

"Well, I've learned some of this the hard way," Loraine said, "but it's going to be worth it. Because I will see that look in a man's eyes, and he'll be looking at me when I see it. If I don't, I'll never marry."

"Loraine, thank you. You've... Well, I was feeling so guilty about the feelings I had for him."

"Guilt is a wasted emotion. I remember hearing you and Papa say that. Wasted unless there is something you can do about it. You can't stop how you feel about Adam and neither can he. And, Mama, I love you both. I wish you all the best."

"I was so sure that you'd be mad at me," Martha said, wiping her eyes.

"Well, I may not be, but Amy is having a hard time with this. So be prepared," Loraine said, shaking her head. "You know how she felt about Papa. This is not easy for her to accept. And Belle, well, you know she never liked Adam. I think they'll come around though."

Martha didn't like thinking about talking to Amy and knew her wise oldest daughter was right about the most difficult obstacle. She would not let it worry her though. It would work out. It had to and Loraine was a good beginning.

CHAPTER 19

E unice and George sat under the spreading oak tree, watching the sun set in the west, neither talking for long moments. Between them were sweet rolls and cups of coffee. Eunice nibbled on one as she moaned. "I can't believe how awful everything worked out."

"It hasn't yet," he reminded her.

"But it probably will. I'd hoped that Adam would be interested in Fanny. I can't believe it's Martha instead that he's had his eye on."

"That's not actually so surprising," George retorted, reaching for his cup of coffee.

"What do you mean by that?" Eunice snarled. "She's clearly too old for him."

George snorted. "Martha is a beautiful, poised woman, with a lovely figure. In short, she is all that most men dream of possessing. A wife that a man could have on his arm and feel proud before the entire community. While Fanny, well, face it, my dear, Fanny is just like you and me."

"That's not a very nice thing to say," Eunice protested.

"But true. When one is unattractive and fat, one must offer

other inducements to entice the customer. Things like bargain rates, bonuses. Do you see what I mean?"

"You are reducing love and courtship to some sort of business lesson."

He smiled. "That's because it is. It is, my dear. Once you learn the rules of making money, you will know the rules to all of life."

"I do not believe that."

"It's true. Isn't that what our sainted father taught us both? You can buy what you want. If you have to bargain, you bargain with chips that you make exceedingly attractive to the other party. You sell for more than it costs. It all works with courtship as well. If you want a man to choose Fanny, you must throw in some attractive bargaining chips."

"That is disgusting." Eunice bit down on another roll.

"Perhaps, but it is the way of life."

She sighed. "I am so disappointed in Martha. In her shocking behavior, and to think I even gave her a kitten... If I'd known the kind of woman she is, I'd have kept Heaven!"

George smiled, dimples appearing in his cheeks. "Don't speak disparagingly of the woman I intend to make my wife, my dear."

"You can't be serious. You saw how she treated Adam today. The way she practically fell all over him. You can't possibly think."

"Can't think what? That she was inspiring today and showed herself to be a woman of deep feeling. She is spirited, beautiful besides being the sort of woman who could serve me well with my colleagues. Considering it all, I shall marry her."

Eunice looked at him with bewilderment. "George, I love you dearly. You are a wonderful man and brother, but you can't seriously think you can compete with a man like Adam Stone. He towers over others, strides through life as though he owns it. He's handsome, brave as we saw again." She stopped and cried. "I wanted him for Fanny," she wailed.

"His very virtues can be his weaknesses."

"George," she said after a moment, "don't you think you are being just a trifle unrealistic here? I mean just a trifle. She is obviously besotted with him, and I saw the look in his eyes when he looked at her just before they left. I don't see how you can think..."

"Because, I understand human nature, Eunice," he said in a patient voice, tutoring her as he had always tried to do on the ways of success, "I know that things aren't always what they seem. Martha is older than Adam. That has to bother her. She has three daughters who may not approve, that is a potential problem. "

"I suppose that's true," she muttered thoughtfully.

"And there are bound to be more problems in their little paradise. Tell me everything you can think of about Mr. Adam Stone."

"I don't know him that well," she sniffed.

George smiled broadly. "If you intended him as a mate for Fanny, I know you too well, dear sister, to not believe you've been learning about Mr. Stone. You've been learning a lot, and I want to know all of it, every last bit."

Matt and Amy lay on their feather tick mattress, she had a light covering over her, but he lay naked, still too hot to sleep. She was repeating for what seemed the hundredth time all the reasons she was upset about her mother and Adam. She concluded with, "He is never going to settle down anywhere. He'll just hurt her. Run around and be shiftless all his life. He drinks. He never seems to have a real job and..."

"Amy," he roared, sitting up and looking down at her, "I've let you talk this all out because I reckoned you needed to get it out of your system, but it's enough now."

"Well, I don't hardly think so," she snapped, sitting up herself so that he had no advantage in towering over her.

He glanced at her beautiful breasts, swinging free of the covering, full with milk for their daughter, and he clenched his teeth against his natural inclination. It was still too soon after the birth of Laura to think such sensual thoughts, and even then the idea of having another child sent waves of terror through him. Her pain had been so great. He didn't want ever to go through that again, and yet not touching her was going to be another form of torture.

"Adam had no right making up to my mother," Amy said, looking out the black window and seeing a crescent moon, hovering over the fir trees.

"Why not?" he asked quietly, resigned now to fighting this out with her. She would never talk it through to her satisfaction.

"That is obvious. He's not right for her. He's a heathen. He's always roaming around. He's too wild, way too wild."

Matt thought a moment. Pulling up one knee, he rested his arm on it. "Amy," he drawled, "if Adam wants your ma, and she wants him, then you are not gonna cause trouble between them."

"I wouldn't do that, but I have a right to make her see that it's impossible."

"No," he ordered sternly, "you don't have any such right. You have to take care of our daughter, our home, yourself, and me. What your ma does with her life is her concern."

"Matt, she's my mother!"

"I know that, baby, but she's also a human being, just like you are. She's got a right to make her own choices, just like you did."

"That was different," she argued, "I didn't have children and wasn't married."

Matt smiled slowly. "None of the three of you, not even Belle, are children any more. And your ma is not married."

"Of course she is." Her words dwindled off. "All right, but not Adam. Not him."

Matt thought for a moment. "If it wasn't for Adam, you wouldn't have Laura or me right now," he said coldly, deliberately.

"You mean when he saved your life. He had to do that."

Matt shook his head. "He did not have to do it. He risked his own life. All he had to do was sit back and do nothing, and you would likely have been his."

"No."

"It's so, and you and I both know it. But that's not the kind of man Adam is. He came."

"You'd have done the same," she argued.

"That's so. I would've." He stopped a moment, smiled. "In the midst of that danger, when he came for me, he was smiling. Risking his life, and all with a crazy man ready to kill both of us and he's smiling. I knew then I'd go through hell for him. You know something else?"

"No, because you've never talked about this before."

"It's not a good memory for me--except for Adam and how he put his own knife into my hand. Doing that likely saved my life but took away one of his own weapons."

Amy swallowed, her fingers stroking Matt's muscular arm.

"And, baby, if your ma loves him, and he loves her, they're gonna be two lucky people, and I want you to steer clear of it."

"But..."

"Nope." He put his fingers over her lips. "I mean it. You talk to your ma, wish her the best, tell her whatever she wants to do is all right by you."

"I don't see how I can do that. I feel like she's betraying Papa's memory."

Matt shook his head, beginning to grow angry for the first time in this argument. "Your pa would be the first one to be glad she's found somebody. Don't you go dragging him into this. He was the salt of this earth, as good a man as ever lived, but he's dead, and he can't be there for her. Amos always liked Adam, and he'd be the first one to say she oughta find another man to love. I'd say that's just what she's done. You should be down on your knees, thanking God. Praying Adam and your mama can work this all out and find a little happiness, and if you try to cause trouble there, you'll have to answer to me."

She wrinkled her nose at him, still irritated but he could see she was weakening in her determination. After a moment, she reached her fingers up his chest, running them around his nipple, causing an immediate involuntary reaction from his body.

"If I do that," she asked huskily, "and I have to answer to you," she reached over and kissed his nipple, tugging on it with her teeth, "just what does that mean?"

"Quit that," he groaned, throwing his head back, trying to force his breath to come evenly as she moved down to kiss his belly. He already ached with need for her, for the release only her love could give him. She was going to make this time of abstinence impossibly frustrating.

"What?" she asked innocently, her fingers stroking down his torso, moving lower and lower.

"Ahhh. You know what," he moaned as her hair began to brush him intimately. He reached down and gripped her arms to force her away from him. "We can't, you can't. It's too soon."

"Maybe for some things," she murmured, "but maybe not for other things." Smiling provocatively, she showed him exactly what she had in mind.

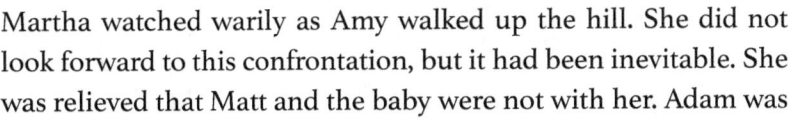

Martha watched warily as Amy walked up the hill. She did not look forward to this confrontation, but it had been inevitable. She was relieved that Matt and the baby were not with her. Adam was sleeping in by the fireplace, and St. Louis was out by the barns. She walked out to meet her daughter where they could talk privately.

"Mama," Amy said as she stopped her dark eyes pensive.

"Well, no point in beating around the bush," Martha said. "I know what you probably want to say and do understand how you must feel."

"Do you?"

"I think so. You don't think this is right for me. That I am making a fool of myself, upsetting the balance of the way things ought to be, and possibly being disloyal to your father."

Amy's face reddened, but she said nothing.

"Is there more?" Martha asked, her voice even, showing no anger or disapproval of what she supposed to be her daughter's rigid attitude.

"It probably would have been," Amy admitted, looking off toward the distant river, "if Matt hadn't talked some sense into me first."

"Matt?"

"He let me talk it out, and then told me I was wrong, and why. It still isn't easy for me. I just can't get used to the idea of you and him together that way, but I know that you are a grown adult."

"Oh," Martha said, letting out the breath she'd been holding.

"I had to find my own happiness and you have to find yours. I know that Papa would have wanted that too."

Martha shook her head. "I wouldn't have believed this. I expected you and Loraine both to be furious with me, and you've both been so strong and mature. I..." She stopped and reached out her arms.

Amy came into them with a little cry. "I'm really happy for you. Honestly I am," she whispered.

"Thank you," Martha said.

They sat on the grass, talking first of the baby and then of the thing most on Amy's mind. "What about the wedding? Have you and he made plans yet?" Martha didn't miss the point that Amy wasn't using his name. She might be working to accept it, but she had a ways to go.

"Adam has asked me, but we are going to wait until we are sure. There are things to work through."

"You will. I know you will and I am glad we won't be losing him to the family."

"I understand this has to be hard for you. It has been for me too."

"Well, I just hope if you get married, he won't expect me to call him Pa," Amy said, laughing.

"I'm sure he won't," Martha responded chuckling at the idea.

"I know Papa wouldn't have wanted you alone," Amy said, obviously forcing the words out. "I really think he would be glad for you both. I won't deny that it's been hard for me to see you be with somebody... well else. Daddy was a loving man, a farsighted one. Maybe Adam is who he'd have wanted for you."

The words Amos had said as he had lain dying came to Martha. *Don't mourn forever. Find another. Write...* She had wondered more than once what else Amos had tried to say. Could it have been to notify Adam. Had he earlier seen what she had not?

She shook her head. She was being foolish, but she remembered how much Amos had always liked Adam. He had tried to talk Adam into homesteading near them but then accepted the young man's firm refusal with no further argument. Could he have sensed how Adam felt? Sometimes men saw things women didn't. Could that have been the rest of what he'd intended to say before his soul left his body? She would never know.

"Mama, I do hope it works out for you." Amy threw her arms around her mother. "I know you have to have been lonely. I am happy for you. Truly I am."

Martha hugged her again. She didn't know. Part of her so

much wanted Adam, wanted forever with him. Except, for Adam, how long was forever?

Two days later, Adam sat on the front porch, watching as Martha picked string beans. "I could help," he offered, not moving.

"You could."

"Tomorrow I better go back to St. Louis'," Adam told her.

"If you think so."

"Then, I'm going to come courting," he said, a glint in his eyes.

"You are, are you?" She smiled.

"I am. You are going to have it all, the flowers, socials. Everything Oregon Territory has to offer."

"Sounds intriguing," she said, sitting back on her heels and pushing her hair behind her ear. She felt the sexual tension between them. They hadn't made love while he'd been staying with her. She was unsure of his reasons, but she'd waited. They did have things to work out, and the white hot heat of sex wouldn't help either of them think straight.

"I hope I can figure out how to do it. I never have before."

"Come on, surely you've courted women."

He grinned. "Never spent long enough wanting a woman to figure it out. But then I never had a woman like you to court either. He looked down the hill. "Are you expecting company?"

"I wasn't."

"Well, you are now."

Martha stood up, straightening her skirt as she recognized George Simon. Adam had already risen on the porch, his eyes narrowed as he watched the approach of the city man.

"How are you fine people today?" Simon asked as he came up to them, wiping the sweat from his ruddy brow. "That's quite the climb."

"You are still visiting Eunice?" Martha asked politely.

"I made a quick trip home, then came back. Just wanted to see how everyone was doing at my businesses. It's time I took a little vacation." He looked up at Adam who was now leaning against a post and added, "Looks like you're taking a vacation too, Adam."

"Adam has been recuperating from his wound," Martha said, wiping off her hands and carrying her basket of beans to the porch.

"Oh, is that why he didn't help you pick beans? I'd be happy to help myself if you need any help that is."

"Adam had offered, Mr. Simon, but I prefer doing it myself," Martha said tartly. "Thank you for your offer though." She stepped up on the porch and patted Adam's arm as she went past, then glanced back. "I'll take these beans in and be right back with something for you both to drink."

Adam watched as she disappeared into the cabin and then turning back to George, he tried to think of something to say. In meeting this man, he'd ended up falling flat; the memory stung.

"Are you nearly recovered?" George asked, sitting down on one of the chairs.

"More or less. St. Louis and I go home tomorrow. Of course, he's been staying here while I have recuperated." He would never compromise Martha with her community.

"Of course," George said with a pleasant smile. "With a lady like Martha Stevens, one would think nothing else."

Adam didn't like the man; but as he had no reason other than jealousy for the feeling, he tried to push the negative feelings away.

Martha came back out with three glasses on a tray. "I make an herbal tea," she said, "which is really quite good, even when it isn't iced. Please try some."

Each man gingerly took a glass and sipped with some caution before they decided it was safe. "Last herbal tea I had from you," Adam said, "didn't taste quite so good."

"Well, of course not," she said, "that was medicinal. This is for pleasure, not healing." She grinned as she added, "Of course, it does do wonders for elimination."

Adam gave her a wary look; and she laughed, reaching out lightly to touch his shoulder as their eyes met.

"You mean," George said, interrupting the moment and shaking his head, with awe in his voice, "that besides being a beautiful woman, an accomplished seamstress, running this homestead, having raised three beautiful daughters, that you also know about natural remedies."

"I have an interest in such."

"Then is that why you so sacrificially took Mr. Stone into your home to doctor his injury. What a noble undertaking, a true Christian offering."

Martha glanced at Adam and saw the flame of anger in his eyes. She smiled. "I cannot let you be deceived, Mr. Simon. I took Mr. Stone into my home because he is an old family friend but moreover because I am very much in love with him."

"Oh."

Adam relaxed back against the post, his eyes still narrowed as he watched Simon.

"Well, of course, that... uh puts a different complexion on things. It surprises me, of course, because Mr. Stone seems so young, but, then, of course, you, yourself, dear lady, are a youthful appearing woman, but I might have expected you to prefer a more-- well let us say, mature gentleman."

Adam made a sound of disgust as Martha tried to smooth the waters. "Adam is quite mature enough."

"Oh, of course, I didn't mean to imply that he was callow or anything like that. It's just I did hear that he doesn't have a job nor has he had a real job-- ever."

"What is tracking or guiding?" Adam asked sarcastically.

"Play for some men?" suggested George with a condescending

smile. "I'd be happy to employ you in one of my stores though if you'd like to get a foot up the ladder in a real profession."

Rolling her eyes to the sky, Martha began to wonder if she would soon be monitoring a battle, which even though Adam was still weakened by blood loss was apt to go badly for George Simon.

"Scouting for a wagon train is hardly play, Mr. Simon," Martha said. "And through the years, many people have relied on Adam's expertise."

"I didn't mean to offend the young man. It's just that it is hardly the sort of job one could do, who hoped to settle down. I mean if you are saying you love Martha-- I expect you are considering settling down. Or were you thinking to continue, uh shall we say moving around?" he asked, smiling benignly at Adam's slowly growing anger.

"I think that's our business to work out," Adam said with a glacial smile.

"Oh, of course, pardon me. I certainly didn't mean to intrude or anything like that. I just have a tendency to say what I think. Sometimes too quickly and without thought." His smile was broad. "I am so sorry if I've offended you in any way."

"How is Eunice?" Martha asked, trying to switch the subject to something safer but unsure what would be.

"So terribly disappointed," George said, his tone reflecting all that disappointment, "she had looked forward to Fanny's little birthday supper and was upset it was ruined." He looked pointedly at Adam.

"It couldn't be avoided," Martha told him, biting her lip when she saw the chagrined expression on Adam's face.

"She understood that. After all, it wasn't your fault that someone was injured... coming there when... well, you know." He looked up at Adam, again smiling. "Of course, it wasn't yours either. You were off... well, trying to do something noble."

"You know something, George," Adam stated, his intense gaze looking down on him, "you smile too much."

"Is there such a thing as too much?" asked George, again smiling. "Happiness is truly a gift from God, and if I've been blessed with it. I simply must smile."

Adam cast his gaze toward the sky, as though hoping for a divine intervention in which Martha knew he didn't believe. She stifled a laugh. "It is nice that God has been so good to you, Mr. Simon."

"George please. May I call you Martha and Adam?"

When Martha nodded, he smiled again. "Yes, God has indeed given me my businesses, my home, my friends. I look to Him for everything, Martha, as I am sure you also do."

"How lovely."

"You've said nothing, Adam," George said. "Do you not also thank the good Lord for all you have or haven't."

"I did thank Wakan Tanka actually, just the other day," Adam said. "I remember it well."

George looked mystified. "Wakan who? What's that?"

"The Lakota name for their creator."

"You thanked a heathen god?" George asked, an expression of amazement replacing the smile for a moment.

Martha was about to intervene when Adam went on, "You know, George, can I tell you something? I wouldn't want to offend you though."

"No, no, my boy, that's fine. Tell me anything you want. I'm here to listen to all."

"Well, in my experience, I've found those who talk the most about God are the ones who do the least."

George's mouth dropped open for just a moment. "You have?" he managed finally.

"Yes, I have."

"Hmmmm, well, uh. Actually." He pulled out his pocket

watch. "I can't believe how the time has flown. I'll come visit again though if I may." With that he was gone.

"He's a self-righteous, pompous twit," Adam said as they watched the heavy-set man make his way back down the hill.

Martha laughed. "Twit?"

"You're not impressed by him, surely?"

"He has three stores. Shouldn't I be?" She giggled.

"He intends to court you too."

"He has not been invited to," she reminded him, coming over to where he leaned against the wall and putting her arms around his lean waist.

"It will take more than not being invited to stop him. I know human nature some. That man is determined, and I don't blame him."

"Well, it's not his determination that matters, now is it?"

"He'll cause trouble if he can."

"Can he?"

"I don't know."

"I suppose he was trying to remind me of what a horrible, big mistake--" She stopped, reached up and bent his head down. "I will be making--if I don't see what awful possibilities await me. If I get--" She kissed him, lightly nipping his lip. "Involved with a ne'er do well like Mr. Stone."

She pulled him with her to the step of the porch. "Definitely a boy like you is unfit for a woman of my, oh so, very mature years." With each word, she added a new variation of kissing.

"Martha I mean to go slow on this and court you," he reminded her.

"And you will, my love."

He tightened his arms around her and kissed her. His tongue delved into her mouth as his hand stroked her full breast. She was so swollen with desire for him that she could barely think.

"I may not be able to," he whispered against her neck, loosening her hair to her chagrin. "I want you so bad."

Her smile was soft and seductive as she began slowly unbuttoning his shirt, teasing her fingers against his bare skin as she undid one button after another, working her way down to his belly. She pushed his shirt apart and he felt her slide her hands inside, pulling him against her, and he forgot about George Simon as she pressed herself against his bare chest.

"As I want you," she said, stroking her fingers along the large muscle that ran down his back. She gave herself over to the pleasure of his caressing lips.

"I think," Adam said thoughtfully, a gleam in his clear eyes as he pulled back just a little, "we better get these problems you are so concerned with, worked out soon, lady. Because the way we're heading here, we don't have long, if you get my drift."

She remembered her own concern about having a baby before she got married. He was right. They needed to work through their possible differences, but the desire between them would not make that easy. Her whole body was aching with need, but it would not help either of them settle their differences and figure out what sort of life they might have when they married—if they married.

CHAPTER 20

George huffed into the cabin, causing Eunice to look up with a start before she settled back to frosting her cake. "What happened?" she asked, swirling the confection higher, shaping it into a pleasing pattern.

"I think I need to try another ploy. Your neighbor lady is indeed besotted with Mr. Stone. What I need to do is come up with a way to make her see that he is not all that she thinks he is."

"George," Eunice said, frowning, "I don't like the tone of your voice."

George settled at the table and steepled his fingers, staring at them. "Don't worry, sister dear. I know what I'm doing."

"What are you thinking?" Eunice asked.

"Perhaps you might be of help." George's eyes turned shrewd.

"Me? How?" Eunice looked at her cake with an expression closely akin to love. "It's a shame to have to cut it," she said, "when it's swirled so perfectly."

"Eunice, pay attention. I tried to subtly lay a little doubt in Martha's head. Perhaps if you followed up on my probing words."

"By doing what?"

"Just a friendly visit and a discussion of Adam's failings. Subtle, of course, so that she doesn't suspect what you are trying to do."

"Hmmmm." Taking a knife from a holder, Eunice sliced into the cake, neatly dividing it into two halves and then slicing again forming a neat triangle. "I'm not at all sure that this will work, George."

"What do you mean? Of course, it will work."

"I don't see how. Adam is such a strong man, so handsome, even dashing." She giggled. "I simply don't see how you'll turn Martha away from a man like that. Even a hero. My word!"

George gave a disgusted snort. "Apart from some purely physical attributes, the man is worth practically nothing in a financial sense. What woman with a little thought would prefer a man who can give her nothing to one who can offer so much? All we have to do is plant some doubts in Martha. Doubts that are justified by his past behavior. When we do that, she will logically turn to the perfect suitor--me."

"I just don't think it will work."

"It had better. Or--" He stopped, not willing to say anything more to Eunice.

"Or what?" she asked, frowning as she looked up at her brother.

"I don't want to go into it, but take my word for it. I will remove Mr. Stone from the competition. One way or another."

"Well," she said, licking a daub of frosting from her finger and smiling at him, "in that case, do you want a piece of cake?"

"Eunice," he asked with exasperation, "what's cake got to do with what I just said?"

"Nothing. I just thought you might like some."

"Well, that's ridiculous. You are not taking me seriously."

"How can you say that, George?"

"Well, I'm telling you something very important. Something

even sinister, possibly life threatening. And you ask me if I want a piece of your silly cake!"

"It does sound rather foolish when you put it that way," she admitted, lowering her head in embarrassment.

"What flavor of cake is it?"

~

A day later as Adam and St. Louis rode away from Martha's, Adam was deep in thought. Finally St. Louis could resist asking no longer. "What's going on in yore head?"

"Just trying to think how I'm going to support a wife. What I'm going to do. Everything I've done up to now isn't of much use when I think of settling down. She has the land, but it was land Amos left her. The homestead act has expired. I don't know that I'd make much of a homesteader anyway."

"You could do it if you wanted and what's wrong with running her place for her? She can do a lot more with a man there."

Adam nodded without much enthusiasm. "I suppose that's what she would like."

"You talked about this yet?"

He shook his head. "She's got so many doubts as it is. I figured it was better to work this out for myself first and then talk to her."

"From what I seen of independent minded women, like Martha, that might not be a smart idea."

"What do you mean?"

"I mean, they like bein' in on the decision makin'. Tellin' them what's goin' to happen ain't usually a good way to make it happen."

Adam rubbed the back of his neck thoughtfully. "I suppose you're right. She's as much as told me that herself. It's just that damned Simon came by yesterday afternoon, and he was laying it on about how I haven't worked at things like a normal man does. I lay awake last night, realizing that if nothing else, he was right about that."

"Don't let him get to ya. You know he's tryin' to lay groundwork for himself."

"That doesn't make what he said wrong." He stared off at the distant mountains. They had always been his goal but no longer. Now his goal was a soft woman in a cabin. He had to find a way to be the man she needed him to be.

"Jest give it some time. The trouble with you, Adam, is that ya got no patience. You decide ya want somethin' and ya go right after it. That's gonna make it plumb hard on the woman in yore life if ya don't let up a little."

"There never was a woman before this," he admitted. "Never anyone who mattered. Never one like Martha."

"Not none?"

Adam shook his head. "There have been women, of course; but truthfully I was never in love until her. I thought for a little that I loved Amy, but I didn't. When Amy told me about Matt, I only remember feeling a mild disappointment and irritation that she'd preferred Matt to me. But when I saw Martha with George at that party, my head felt like it was going to come apart."

St. Louis guffawed. "He ain't no competition for ya, and ya know that."

"I wasn't all that clear headed at the time, and I'd been expecting another man to come along. I thought that a man like him would be easy for her to accept, and he'd make her life comfortable. She had already pushed me away twice. I thought she'd made her decision, and it wasn't going to be me."

They approached St. Louis' cabin and realized a horse was tied to the post and Tom Crane was sitting on the porch, waiting for them.

"About time," he growled, rising as they approached. "I ride all the way out here, and nobody's home. I'm worried that you are dead or dying, and here you ride up, looking like nothing happened to you."

"You disappointed?" Adam joked, dismounting gingerly, favoring his left side. "Well, hell yes, a man gets shot he oughta be stove up for a week at least."

"Well, for your satisfaction, I did get laid up a few days."

St. Louis growled, "I'll take care of the hosses. Why don't you fix us some coffee."

"Yes sir," Adam said with a grin as he walked into the cabin.

"How are you feeling?" Crane asked, bending his head to get through the door as he followed him.

"Not bad. The bullet was just a graze. Except for losing blood, it'd have been nothing, but St. Louis says I cracked a rib, maybe the bullet hit it or when I took that header, and that's been sore." He grabbed kindling and began building a fire in the cookstove. "What brings you up here, other than checking on whether or not I was dead?"

"Somebody anonymously put up a reward, and I figured to tell you."

"Reward? For killing the robbers?" questioned Adam frowning.

"You guessed it."

"Where'd it come from?"

"I don't know. Just it's there waiting, and it's yours."

Something about that struck Adam all wrong. He had not done it for a reward. He was no bounty hunter and didn't intend to become one. He needed to get a start with Martha, but this was not the kind of money he wanted to use for that purpose. He'd build nothing good with blood money. "I don't want it."

"That's just crazy. You deserve it."

Adam had made up his mind whether it made sense to anyone else or no. He knew to some it might have seemed quixotic, illogical, but he was sure in his gut he was right. "Nope," he said as he measured coffee into the coffee pot.

"Don't you even want to know how much it is?" Adam shook his head. "A thousand dollars," he told him anyway. "Man, think what you could do with some quick cash like that," Crane tried a different approach.

Adam couldn't explain it and wasn't going to try. "Give it to one of the churches or if the town's got some charity for feeding the poor, tell them to give it to them."

St. Louis came through the door, "Wal, how ya doin' sheriff?"

"Fine. Although I may not be sheriff much longer."

"Why?"

"Even though they got the whole loot back, the people are put out with me because I wasn't there when the gang robbed the bank. And actually I'm beginning to realize I am not cut out to be a lawman. This last thing convinced me of that. I'd of never caught anybody or got any of the money back if it hadn't of been for Adam. By the time we got to the men, he was more like the sheriff than I was."

"What are ya goin' to do, if ya quit?" asked St. Louis, watching with interest as the coffee began to perk.

"I heard about a new gold strike in California. I like California. Warmer down there"

"Prospecting is one thing I never done. I think it takes a lot of patience, not my long suit."

"A lot of men are heading for California," Crane said, "There's talk it might be as big as the last one."

"Were you there when they had the first big one?"

"In Forty-nine, you mean? I only wish. It seems like I'm always a year or two behind. I get there and all the claims are staked. But my luck is bound to change."

Adam shook his head. "Too much like gambling to me. You put a lot of money down a hole trying to get a few gold nuggets. No way the average man is going to get much, and I've seen how little payoff there is down in the Rogue country. A lot of men have died or killed because of it."

"Somebody has to get it," Crane said with enthusiasm, more enthusiasm than he'd ever shown for his job as sheriff.

"Gold fever," St. Louis muttered, as he poured his coffee. "It eats men up. Almost as bad as love fever."

Adam frowned at him. "Was that comment for me?"

"Take it how ya want."

"You in love, Adam?" asked Crane with interest as he accepted a cup of coffee from him.

"Not that it's any of your business, but yes, I am."

"And you're still turning down the reward money?"

When St. Louis asked about it, the story had to be repeated. Adam expected him to argue with him too, but St. Louis nodded. "Ya done the right thing turnin' it down."

"How do you figure?" asked Crane.

"A man does what's right, but don't want to be paid for spilling blood."

"It's what I do, get paid for that."

"No," Adam said, "you get paid for keeping the law."

St. Louis nodded and smiled. "Ex-actly. Ordinary folk, they oughta do what needs doing and not expect to be paid for it. Just what a man does."

"Makes no sense to me," Crane said, still clearly mystified. "Seems to me that making money's what this country's been built on."

Adam chuckled as St. Louis looked disgusted. "Seems to me," he said, "that kind of thinkin' is exactly the opposite of what this country was built on. Coffee's ready."

Two mornings later, Adam set about the courting of Martha

Stevens. He saddled Joe and with little more than a brief explanation to St. Louis, he rode to her cabin.

She was outside, hoeing in her garden as she saw him approach. Using her wrist, she pushed back her hair. Her dress was faded and badly the worse for wear. She had never looked more beautiful to him. He wondered if there'd ever come a time he would ride up to her and not find his insides turning to mush with his thoughts scattering like the wind? What had he intended to say?

"Good morning," he said as he dismounted.

"What are you doing out riding?" she asked, leaning on the hoe. "Seems to me you promised to take it easy for a few days."

"It's been a few days. A few days too many," he said, taking the hoe from her and kissing her soundly on the lips. "And this is day one in the new plan," he told her as he walked her back to the cabin.

"New plan?"

"I've thought this through. You had a lot of reasons why we shouldn't be together."

"Well, obviously I've thought better of that as we are together," she reminded him, putting her arms around his waist and pulling him to a stop.

"Yes, but you haven't set a date to marry me. Today we start on one of those questions that you say are going to stand between us. We work our way through those things and," he kissed her nose, "in a week or less, we can start making wedding plans."

She shook her head. "I can't believe you. Things can't be worked out that fast."

"Sure they can. We take them one a day. Are there more than seven doubts?"

"I never counted them up, but I don't see how we can really dispose of these kind of things in any set number of days."

"Don't you believe your god created this earth in six days?" He started her walking again.

"The Bible says so."

"You think your obstacles are bigger than creating an earth."

She giggled. "Well, maybe not, but you are definitely not a god."

"I'll give you that. How about though you give my plan a chance, and if it fails, we move onto plan two."

"There's a second plan?" she asked as he pushed her up the steps.

"Yeah, but you don't get to find out what it is unless the first one fails--which it won't."

"You are pretty confident," she said with amusement. "All right, how do we begin?"

"I'll finish hoeing your garden while you pack us a picnic lunch; then we go for a ride into the hills."

"You shouldn't be riding far."

"I won't. We'll just head up the river a ways, find a big pool and picnic there."

"What happens then?" she asked, with a smile.

"I ply you with all the reasons we should get married right away, and you argue with me about everything that stands between us. Then... Well, I guess you'll have to wait to see what happens then."

"It sounds risky."

"It will be. I promise," he said, heading back to finish that hoeing.

"Don't cut off any of my herbs," she warned.

He grinned. "Not a chance. Uh what does that one look like that you put in that herbal tea you fed me last week?"

"Adam!" she remonstrated.

"Just joking."

Half an hour later, they were on horseback and winding their way up the river. Adam pointed toward a knoll ahead of them.

"Oh," she sighed, admiring the doe and her spotted fawn as they bounded gracefully away.

"That one's a late baby," he said.

"So cute. Will it be big enough by winter?" she asked, concern in her voice.

"With a mild winter, probably." He then asked what he really wanted to know. "Has Simon been back?"

"No, but Eunice paid me a call."

"I don't suppose I have to ask what that was about."

"No, I don't suppose you do."

"More of the same? My immaturity, lack of a job and so forth?"

"More or less. She's a little more subtle than her brother, but she seemed to be putting across the same basic points. I don't think her heart was in it; since she still covets you for her Fanny."

"Did any of it change your mind?"

"Of course not, but I have to admit my doubts are big enough already. I don't need anyone else's help," she said, tempering her words with a smile. "They don't relate to money though."

"All right, let's start. No point in waiting. I need to hear what I'm up against."

She glanced over at him, unable to resist admiring the easy way he sat a saddle, the cool blue of his eyes, even the strength of his hands as one held the reins while the other rested lightly on his thigh. Every part of him was beautiful. Definitely the problem wasn't in her attraction to him.

"Where should I start?" she asked, wondering why such a gorgeous man even was interested in her.

"Start with age, one you've shared with me. Do you think I'm immature?"

"It bothers me, but not because of your supposed immaturity." Their horses waded a small stream, the water only a few inches deep with the dryness of the late summer. "Your life experience has probably been greater than mine in many areas."

"Then?"

"I am older, and I'm going to look older and uh older."

"So will I."

"But it's different with a woman."

"Martha, do you think I love you because you're a beautiful woman?"

"I don't know."

"You are beautiful, but it's not just that. There's the way you sass me, the way you love people, stand up others. I saw all of that as we headed to Oregon. Now, I've got added reason. I like how you love me, your sense of humor, your bright, quick mind, and I love the way you laugh. I like the way you know about plants. None of those things are going to go away as you get older. So, you'll have a few more silver hairs, some lines, eventually wrinkles. The truth of it is that for our ages, I'm more beat up than you are."

"I suppose," she said, not convinced.

Adam reined his horse in and reaching out, pulled her against him, almost lifting her from her saddle. "I like the way you look in a pair of pants," he told her with a grin, as he kissed her, "but more than that, I like the fact that you're willing to wear them-- no matter what people think. I even like those damn teas you ply me with."

"All right," she said with a breathless laugh as he set her back firmly in her saddle, "I'll try to realize I'm thinking too physically and let the age thing go." She knew it would be easier said than done, but he was right. It was not something they could change or compromise on anyway. He was no boy, and she was no old lady. If it was not an issue to him, then she'd have to work through it on her own.

"All right, what's next?"

"Aren't we going to get to enjoy any part of this beautiful day?" she asked surprised at her reluctance to discuss all this. Instead of taking the opportunity he had provided for them she wanted only to drink in the day, which was nearly perfect in temperature with a silky blue sky overhead. Towering trees lined the banks of the river. A few golden wildflowers still bloomed in protected shadows. The river rippled over boulders; and beneath a cliff it had cut in the opposite bank, swallows swooped over the water, finding insects for their own picnic. In a month or maybe less, they'd be moving south. Would he also?

"I'll enjoy it more when I know we've worked out what you think is keeping us apart. I love you and I want you to be my wife-- soon."

She sighed. "All right. What do we have in common? We are so different. You say you don't believe in God. I do. I have a homestead, and I like it. You are always on the move, never wanting to settle down. I want time to think things out. You jump right in."

"Wait a minute," he interrupted. "You're swamping me. Let's take this one at a time. Worst case first. What is that?"

"Well..." She thoughtfully considered the various items that seemed to make a marriage between them unlikely. "What about settling down?"

"When I was younger, maybe that was so, that I didn't want to stay in one spot. Felt I had a lot to see and do but that's been wearing thin as I get older."

"What about Alaska?"

He grinned. "It was as far as I could get away from you."

She shook her head and managed a faint smile. "Could you really ever be content living on a homestead? I just can't see you behind a plow. Wouldn't you go crazy with boredom? The life is so simple. There isn't a lot of variety."

"Do you like it?" he asked, enjoying the way her nose crinkled up as she oh so seriously considered the problems.

"Yes, I like it, but I'm a woman."

"What makes you think I wouldn't?" he asked, stalling because he knew this was an issue that wasn't easy resolved. Living on St. Louis' homestead had given him doubts about his own ability to be satisfied with that life, but he wanted her. Somehow he'd find a way to harness his restlessness.

"Just the way you move around the cabin, like a caged cat. How long before you want to go off on the next adventure?"

He looked down toward the river, and he realized where they were. "This is the place. We'll continue this discussion later, if it's all right with you."

CHAPTER 21

Where they stopped, the river made a wide bend. The banks were gradual with a large gravel bar for them to spread out a blanket and sit, eating the simple meal she'd brought, bread, cheese, sliced beef, boiled eggs, and two pears. "That's what you get when you don't alert me to your plans," she said as they ate.

"It's perfect," he said contentedly.

She lay back, looking out at the way the sunlight glinted off the river. After a moment, she said, "It's beautiful here."

He grinned. "I went looking for one to match you. This was not good enough but as close as I could find nearby."

"Match me?"

"Beautiful, fast enough moving water but depths that shadow reflections from the sky and trees, still and yet interesting. All you are, Martha. You are my deep water."

She smiled and turned onto one elbow and looked at him. "And you claim you're not a poet."

"I'm not, but you bring out things in me that nobody else ever did." She bent and lightly kissed his lips. "I won't lie to you," he said. "I have some doubts about how to support you, but I love you, lady. Where you are is home. It's where I want to be."

"You'd never be happy homesteading."

"And how do you know that? Reading tea leaves as well as mixing up all those concoctions of yours?" He grinned as he reached over and lightly kissed her lips.

"I don't need any tea leaves. I just can see you someday feeling tied down by the land, and then you'd be blaming me for tying you to it."

He smiled sensuously. "Tied down huh. I can think of a few places I might not mind you doing that," he teased. "You are too serious, worry too much. We can work all this out. I know we can." He took her free hand and brought it to his lips, teasing it with fleeting kisses, then a gentle nip to the little finger.

"You laugh now, but later you might hate me."

He shook his head. "No, I'll never hate you. I can promise you that, lady. I'll love you until the day I die."

"But--"

"There you go with that word again. Listen to me." He cupped her chin in his large hand and staring up into her troubled eyes, he said, "I know we're going to have to both give up something to make this work. I'm willing to do that. You were married enough years to know that nobody gets it all. We won't either."

"I can't fly with you, Adam. This is where I belong, where I have to be."

"I understand that."

She frowned. "When I think about you being tied to this homestead, it's like tying an anchor around the neck of an eagle."

He grinned at her imagery, "You're living too much in the future, Martha. There are things besides plowing that a man can do with land."

"Like?"

"Ranching. I don't know. Give me some time to think about it. We will work out something if we set our minds to it. I know how much you love this land. I want to do whatever makes you happy."

She sat up, drawing her knees under her. "All right then, leaving that for the moment. What about the religious difference?"

"Is that important to you?" He sat up also and stared at the river rather than face her. "I am not a believer in churches or their concept of god. Will that bother you?"

"Well, I don't have one to go to either right now, but perhaps I will again."

"I wouldn't mind."

"Would you go with me?"

"I might sometimes. I won't promise you to become a member. What I believe or don't believe about God is more outside, more what I feel inside me. A sense of doing what is right, that there is something bigger than us, but I don't see it being in a church."

She thought about that, trying to decide if it truly did trouble her.

"I believe if there is a God, He's out here, Martha, not just in some stuffy little building."

"The building is to worship Him."

"And he needs that?"

She made a face. "People need it."

"Maybe some do, but if it was important to you. I'd go to church with you, but I won't promise to pretend to believe in anything I don't."

"That sounds fair enough."

"Martha, I'd go with you to hell if that's what it took to make you happy," he said with a playful pull to bring her into his arms.

"Uh Eunice told me that a circuit rider was going to be at the Watson's barn. That's down toward Oregon City. Would you go there with me?"

He rubbed his chin and smiled ruefully. "Hell is coming a lot quicker than I'd expected."

She laughed.

"Who is the preacher?" he asked.

"I don't know much. Just that he travels around. He lives down the valley, goes out in the summer, and preaches to whoever will listen. Eunice heard him once in Champoeg and she said he's inspiring to hear."

"When is it?"

"Tomorrow noon," she answered with a little smile.

"Caught in my own web," he said with a smile that said he didn't mind too much. "Yes, I'll go. Now, what else do we have to settle here today?"

"What about children? Would you want children?"

"I honestly had never thought about having children. I suppose you're not eager to start raising another family."

"Sometimes a woman of my age doesn't find it so easy to be able to have a baby," she said, not looking at him. "I don't know how I'd feel if I did." She did know. She knew that having a child by Adam would be exactly what she would want, but there was no point in starting to think that way when it might be impossible.

"It wouldn't matter to me either way. Until you, I never thought about having children of my own. Whatever happened would be all right with me... or didn't happen." he smiled.

"Regarding children, there is another bit of a problem. Belle wrote that she would be able to be here for a week before the new school term begins. I haven't said anything about us because I didn't want her to read it in a letter."

Adam shook his head, with that crooked smile. "As I remember, she wasn't all that fond of me even before I came around to steal her mother."

"She liked you."

"No, she didn't. She made it clear that I didn't treat her the way Matt did. He was her favorite candidate for Amy's hand. "

"I'll talk to Belle when she comes, but to be honest her opinion does worry me because of her being so much younger than the other two. Things that happen to her now could still hurt her future."

"If she says no?" Adam asked quietly, not looking at her.

She reached over, her fingers lightly stroking his jaw. A muscle throbbed, once again, giving away his tension more than the words he spoke. "I won't let her stand between us. I just would prefer she was happy for us."

"You know I have a few doubts of my own?"

"That you might be bored married to me?"

He laughed. "Foolish woman. No, not that. It's Amos."

"Amos?"

"I wonder if you'll be comparing me to him, constantly seeing I don't do things as well."

"Amos was no paragon of virtue. He was just a man like any other."

"He provided you with a good home, even with luxuries. I don't have any of those to give you. Just myself, the fact that I'd die to protect you; that I will work for you, and love you. It doesn't sound like much."

"I'm not asking for material things, Adam."

"Maybe but a man would like to have them to give to the woman he loves. I wish I'd thought more about making money."

"If you had, you wouldn't be who you are. Amos left me enough to not have to worry about that."

He clenched his jaw. "That is little comfort to me, Martha. I don't want to live on another man's sweat."

"What would you want me to do, give it away?" she asked a little irked at his pridefulness.

"Of course, not."

"Well, then?"

"I'm acting dumb?"

She nodded.

"And immature?"

"Don't put words in my mouth."

"Sorry."

She smiled at the nettled tone to his voice. "You don't sound sorry."

Seeing the teasing light in her eyes, he felt his anger disappear. He was being silly. "How can I prove it to you?" he asked, his voice taking on a sensual promise.

"I could think of some ways," she said as he bent her back and loomed over her, his lips only inches from her own.

"Don't take too long," he whispered, kissing her neck, then raining light kisses onto her cheeks, brow and chin before he hovered over her mouth again. She felt the yearning for those firm lips against hers, wanted to melt into him, to forget there was a tomorrow, that things were yet to be settled between them, but he held himself from her.

"What is it?" she asked.

"Just looking at you." His smile was so tender that her heart melted.

She tangled her fingers in his thick dark hair and slowly lowered his head down until their lips were only an inch apart. "I think," she said, as she reached up to kiss his lips, "maybe soon I will need some time to think about all this."

"Time?"

"By myself."

His eyes narrowed, as he swallowed. "No courting?" he asked, trying to keep his voice light.

"We don't need that. We already know how we feel. As you said before, we are not children. I just need to think this idea of marrying again through, and I can't do it when you are with me. When you touch me, my ability to think goes out the window."

"Doesn't that tell you something?" he asked, his eyes darkening.

"Yes, it tells me that I need to be away from you to be able to think about what is best for me and you."

"It sounds risky to me."

She smiled, brushing her lips against his. "You're a man who's used to danger."

"Not this kind." He bent to kiss her. She pressed her tongue against his lips, teasing them to part. He opened for her and she thrust into his mouth. She wanted to possess him, to own him. She knew, by how he lay against her, that he was fully erect. It was a private place. They could...

He lifted his head and sucked in a harsh breath. "Do you know what you're doing to me?"

"I might hazard a guess," she murmured. Her whole body was hot and heavy with wanting, her breath coming unevenly. She drank in the sight of his beautiful face, the proud, sharp jut of his nose, the strong line of jaw and tempting curve of his lips, full now with passion from her kiss. Then she looked up into those eyes, blue as a stormy sky and full of all the depth of love she could ever want.

He shocked her when he pushed away and lay flat breathing heavily.

"Why did you do that?" she asked leaning over him, meeting his troubled gaze.

"Because if you can't take my name, be my wife, I can't take you like this."

She sighed. "Adam. I wish I could right now promise you what you want."

"Maybe if you take that time, you will be able to."

"I hope so."

"Then do your thinking, lady. Whatever it takes, you can have it from me, but do it soon. I need to know what it's going to be for us. I am no boy despite what you might think. I want you for my wife."

~

George stalked into the Lance cabin, bellowing loudly.

"Shut up, George," Eunice said, dragging him back outside. "What is wrong with you? Fanny wasn't feeling well and is trying to take a nap. You have to be quiet."

"Blast Fanny. I needed to talk to you, Eunice."

"All right." She led him away from the cabin to where she'd had the birthday celebration. "Now calm down and tell me what is wrong."

"Everything. Martha is about to make the worst mistake of her life. Did you try talking to her?"

"Yes, I tried, but she didn't listen to me, and frankly I didn't expect her to."

"Eunice," he groaned. "Whose side are you on?"

"I'm on yours, George, but I've been thinking about this and I really don't think you are going to be able to convince Martha that there is something wrong with Adam. She appears to be very much in love with him, and I think it's just a matter of time until she becomes his wife."

"There's got to be a way."

"George," she said, her voice trying to soothe him, "ever since you were a little boy, you have always been unable to let go of whatever you thought you wanted. You demand it even when it isn't reasonable. To be frank, you've been spoiled."

"Eunice!"

"Yes, spoiled, and you have to let go of this idea of Martha.

She is in love with Adam. There will be other ladies for you. Face it; Martha is going to become Mrs. Stone."

"No, I don't believe it. She'll be miserable if she marries that... that stud."

Eunice gasped. "That wasn't very nice, George."

"It's the truth though. That's all he is. She deserves more than that."

"Perhaps, but everyone has to decide these things for themselves, and Martha is the one to make her own decision."

"She won't if I can think of something that will show her what he's really like."

"Like what?" she asked, her voice telling him that she was only humoring him at this point.

"I have several ideas. One thing I think I can tell you about. I put up a reward for the return of the money in Oregon City."

"But you already know the money was returned."

George shook his head at her density. "Of course, I know that," he said impatiently, "but my thought was when he takes the money he'd use it to leave the country."

"Oh, I don't know," she said shaking her head with doubt, "I'm not sure he'd go."

"A man like him. Of course, he will. Perhaps all he's ever wanted was to get his hands on her piece of land now that the claim has been filed."

"How did you know that?"

"It's easy to find out at the land office."

"George, why did you care?"

"Never mind. With some money of his own, well, he'll be down the river and good riddance. When he comes back, she'll be Mrs. Simon."

"George, you are being unrealistic."

He shook his head. "I am thinking this all through quite carefully. And if that doesn't work though, I have another idea for persuading Mr. Stone to leave the country." His eyes squinted as he peered into the distance, working out that idea as he spoke.

"George, I don't like that look in your eyes. You wouldn't hurt him would you?"

He smiled at her. "Not me," he said. "I haven't gotten as far as I have without knowing who to hire for a job."

"George, maybe you should go with me to hear the circuit rider tomorrow."

As though coming out a daze, George asked, "What circuit rider?"

"Joab Powell. He's a genuine man of God, and I think it'd be good for you to go hear him right now."

George rose up to as much height as was possible for him and said, "I am on very good terms with the Lord, Eunice."

"Well, then you'll want to go, won't you?"

"Is Martha going to be there?"

"I told her about it."

"Hmmm, maybe I'll get yet another chance. Yes, I'll go with you to hear this frontier preacher." He smiled then.

Eunice took a step back. "George, you are making me very uncomfortable. I don't like that look on your face. What are you thinking?"

"Less you know the better."

She sighed and shook her head. "Hopefully Pastor Powell can help you see that... you need to accept some things."

He glared at her. "You wouldn't say anything to Martha about your concerns about me, would you?"

"No, blood is thicker than... well, whatever else there is." She didn't look happy but he didn't care. He knew what he had to do if Martha wasn't reasonable.

CHAPTER 22

As Adam drove Martha's wagon into the Watson yard for the revival meeting, he saw rigs parked everywhere with horses tied to all available posts and trees.

"Looks like he's got him a sizeable crowd," crowed St. Louis, sitting on the far side of Martha.

"It's amazing since he doesn't put out posters or advertise in papers. It's all word of mouth," Martha said, echoing his surprise.

"That's a nice barn," Adam said, as the only thing safe for him to comment on. The structure was newly built and imposing, clearly it would have held over a hundred people if needed.

"I think they like to hold it where there is a barn in case it storms. Today looks lovely though."

"What do you know about this Powell?" Adam asked with an unenthusiastic sigh. He didn't expect to enjoy this day, but he knew it was important to Martha that he fully be here and so he would.

"He's a big 'un," St. Louis told him with a grin. "He ain't so tall as you, but... Wal, ya'll see when ya meet him."

"You've heard him speak before?" asked Martha, looking around. "I guess my blue dress fits in all right."

"You were worried about that?" Adam asked thinking there were concerns that might be more important.

She smiled. "A woman likes to fit into the others and I hadn't ever gone to anything like this."

"I seen him once," St. Louis said. "I happened to be where he was speaking and just took a chance. Kind of a funny story about him. There was a blacksmith beyond Champoeg, heard about Powell and said that he better stay away from his section of the valley, warned it'd be unhealthy, if ya know what I mean. Powell heard about that threat; and when he got there, the two of them fought it out. The blacksmith was a tough customer, but old Joab, he won the fight, the man's friendship and his soul."

Adam coughed. "Sounds like a man to avoid."

St. Louis laughed. "Beat the Lord into a man one way or another."

"It's already been tried," Adam said with a grimace.

"You want me to help you carry in the food?" Adam asked as he helped Martha down from the wagon.

"No," she said with a smile, "you just wander around and meet people. I don't have that much."

He smiled at that, remembering the heaping basket of food, from chicken to pickles and everything in between. If that wasn't much food, he'd hate to see an occasion where she brought a lot.

Since the day was neither hot nor cold, the people gathered on a broad, grassy area in front of the barn where they sat mostly on the ground but a few with chairs, waiting for the service to begin. Adam walked around but found no one he knew, no one who wanted to know him, and so he finally settled for standing a bit aloof, observing the crowd and waiting for Martha and St. Louis to find him again.

It had been years since Adam had been to a service like this, and frankly he hadn't ever planned on being to another. He felt even less enthusiasm when he saw George, Horace, Fanny and

Eunice with Martha and St. Louis. All of them found a place to sit together toward the back of the crowd.

"How you feeling these days, Adam?" asked George, smiling fondly at Martha who had come up alongside him. She put her hand on Adam's arm, which he knew was taut.

"Adam's recovered quite well," she said after giving him a little pinch, unseen by anyone else.

He nearly let out a yelp out of pure devilment, but decided it would become an issue later, and besides it was kind of a wifely thing to do and actually improved his mood.

He managed a smile, thinking if he'd had a lick of sense, as St. Louis would've said, he'd have said no to this whole day. Time spent with George Simon did not count high on his list of special happenings.

When Joab Powell rose to stand in front of the congregation, Adam began to understand what St. Louis meant by big. The man was a mammoth, with a voice that boomed across the crowd, allowing nothing to stand in its way. He had to weigh three hundred pounds, but looking closely, Adam didn't think many of those pounds were fat. He was muscled like a grizzly bear, which is what he resembled.

Beginning with prayer, Powell suggested they sing a hymn. As the voices blended in, Joab Powell's could be heard above the ninety or more who sat before him. His fine, deep voice boomed across the people and down the valley. Might even hear that in Oregon City, Adam thought wryly, appreciating in spite of himself the beauty of the man's singing.

"Wal, folks," Powell began, "I figure some of you heard of me. but there's others here who ain't. I wouldn't listen to no man who didn't tell me who he was, where he come from. First off, I got twelve children and live down on the Santiam on a homestead. I ain't no school-educated preacher. I don't read nor write all that fast, but I got me a memory, and I learned the words in this here book." He held the Bible up in front of him. "It's stood me in good times and bad."

He began then to speak of God's word, to tell those listening in no uncertain terms the result of ignoring that word. Because he chewed tobacco, he punctuated his statements with a good healthy spit into a pot, placed conveniently nearby.

Adam admired his ability to work a crowd. He was obviously sincere, and his strength came through in both physical size and powerful belief. His voice rose and fell as he talked about God, about the Word. Sometimes he pleaded; sometimes his voice was like thunder. He played the crowd like a harp, and no one spoke, barely moving as he orated the way to heaven or hell.

Then he stopped talking and silence fell upon them, as heavy and potent as the words had been. He waited a moment before he smiled broadly. "I'm feelin' a powerful hunger here. Might be there's a bite of food back at the cabin. But if there's just a bite of food, I'm goin' to be the most surprised man here, 'cause I know how you ladies put on the fixin's. In fact, I'm expectin' there to be boiled cabbage on that there table. Ya all know how I love boiled cabbage. So, let's pray; then go to it."

When he had finished his prayer, some people rushed up to meet him, while others hurried over to the tables laden with food.

Martha looked up at Adam. "Well, what did you think?"

He nodded. "He's a good speaker." He hoped she wasn't hoping he was going be falling down on his knees to join the *mourner's bench* or be rebaptized in the river below the farm.

"Joab is a wonderful speaker," George put in, taking advantage of Adam's lack of fervor as he followed after them. "He is a true man of God."

"His speaking will be even better in the afternoon," Eunice said.

"By the way, Adam, I heard they offered you a reward for the bank robbers and the return of the money," George said as they filled their plates.

"You heard right," Adam said with little interest as he picked up a stick of celery.

"They did?" Martha asked with surprise.

"I didn't take it. I told them to give it to one of their charities."

"Why would you refuse?" asked George, disbelief in his voice.

"I did what I did as a citizen, not for some reward." Adam took Martha's elbow to guide her to a quiet place to eat if such a thing could be found in this crowd.

"But..." George followed, clearly not ready to give up.

Adam sighed as he looked back at him, resigned to his presence as they sat on the ground.

"Why didn't you take the money? Seems to me a tidy amount to net for capturing three bank robbers," George insisted, unwilling to let the matter drop.

Adam's smile was hard. "I didn't capture them. I killed two. Would you take money for killing a man?"

"Well, it wasn't exactly that, not just that."

"It was exactly that."

"The sheriff gets paid for the same thing."

"No," Adam said, shaking his head as he bit into a piece of the chicken, "he gets paid to keep the peace. If he has to kill someone, that's an unfortunate part of his job. It isn't what he's paid to do."

With that succinct observation, an uneasy silence fell upon them as they ate their meal.

Powell's afternoon message came down harder and with an even more impressive use of that colossal voice as it boomed out the word of God as he interpreted it. Adam listened, aware he liked something about the big man and the way he talked, even if he didn't agree with his assessments of life and a God who became involved with His people. Powell interspersed his message with examples from his own life. He knew the way of the frontier and was at home talking to rough, simple men. His words were simple and plain, not coated with religious terminology, and Adam found he did want to meet him when the service was over.

The crowds were great around him, several people had come forward to be baptized, and Adam realized that he would not be willing to wait until they were all done. Turning away, he was surprised when that booming voice called out to him, "Adam Stone."

Adam turned around slowly, aware that Martha was as surprised as he that Joab Powell had used his name.

Powell came over to them, reaching out his huge hand and shaking Adam's with so much gusto that Adam had to stifle the urge to rub circulation back into it afterward.

"You wondering how I knowed your name?" Powell asked, a big smile on his bearded face.

"An angel told you?" Adam guessed, earning him a not so subtle jab from Martha.

Powell's laugh boomed out. "Not unless St. Louis here's an angel. He told me he was with a big, black-haired galoot who he'd like me to meet. You shore do fit that description, and he give me your name."

"You preach a good message," Adam said with a smile.

"Not good enough to bring you forward though," retorted the burly man with a good natured smile.

"No."

"Never put off for tomorrow what you could do today."

"Good old saying. That in the Bible?" asked Adam with a wry smile.

Laughing, the big man said, "Not in so many words, but it oughta be. It does say never brag about your plans for tomorrow-- wait and see what happens, Proverbs 27." He smiled more broadly as he looked at Martha. "And is this your lovely wife?"

"If I have my way, she will be."

"A good wife's worth anything she costs." Powell stopped and laughed, "In fact, *'if you can find a truly good wife, she is worth more than precious gems.'* That is true for me. My Annie is worth her weight in gold. As with all good women, she's the one who makes my work possible. I am as you might imagine gone a lot. She keeps the home fires burning."

Pushing forward and extending his hand, George, smiled broadly. "I'm George Simon, Pastor, I am so delighted to meet you. I've heard so much about your wonderful work in the valley."

Powell looked steadily at him. "Haven't we already met?" he asked, his gaze keen on the heavyset man.

"Not me, but Eunice, my sister, has been to your meetings. People do say Eunice and I resemble each other."

"I suppose that might be it. It seems though I've met you somewhere."

"I don't think so."

"George claims everything he's got--which is considerable," Adam said with a wry smile, "he owes it all to God."

George smiled weakly. "I do say that."

"How much of it do you give back to him then?" Joab Powell asked.

Thanks to a quick jab in his side, hidden by their entwined arms, Adam resisted the temptation to laugh as George Simon's face whitened and he stumbled over words to avoid having to donate a penny to Powell's ministry.

"Remember the scripture," Powell said, his voice rising with eloquence, "it is harder for a rich man to enter into heaven than a camel to go through the eye of a needle."

"My goodness," George said pulling out his pocket watch and looking at it, then back to Powell. "I didn't realize it was so late. I think we'd best be heading home."

As Adam and Martha walked slowly back toward their wagon, he rubbed her wrist where it rested against his arm. "You know," he said with a grin, "I enjoyed this day more than I'd expected."

Belle descended the steamship plank and Martha could hardly believe that this sophisticated young woman, in a gray traveling suit, blonde hair piled high on her head and wearing a fashionable bonnet, was her fifteen year old daughter.

Only when she saw her mother, did Belle shriek and sound more like the girl who had left home. "Mama," she cried as she wrapped her arms around Martha's waist. "It's so good to see you."

"How are you, baby sister?" Amy asked, putting out her own arms for a hug, while Matt stood back, holding the baby and watching with a satisfied grin.

"I'm not such a baby now," Belle said, smoothing her skirt, her budding woman's figure proving the truth of her words.

"I can see that. You have gotten so beautiful."

"Have you eaten?" asked Martha as Matt handed Amy the baby and took hold of Belle's bags.

"No, and I'm starving."

"Well, then, let's have dinner at Main Street House, and you can tell us about San Francisco."

An hour later, they sat around a table, plates of salad, potatoes and steelhead in front of them. They sipped coffee as Belle regaled them with her experiences in the big city. "It was wonderful. I can hardly wait to go back. The Blacks said they wanted me to come when they next go. They are such sophisticated people and live such exciting lives. Imagine sailing to San Francisco just to buy furniture. They ordered a dining room suite that had come from Hong Kong."

"From your letters, the stores sounded unbelievable," Amy said wistfully.

"Oh they are. Each store sells different things--specializes. For instance one store only sells candy. Every kind you could imagine."

"Did you like Fern's parents?" asked Martha, as she took a bite of salad.

"They're nice. Her father is fat, but he's jolly and good fun. You really have to come to Portland to meet them, all of you."

"Don't sound safe to me," said Matt, laconically.

"Why not?" asked Belle, putting down her fork, almost too excited to eat.

"Because might be Amy wouldn't want to come back, all that fancy furniture and houses might make her want to stay and start one of those literary circles she used to talk about. Laura and me, we wouldn't like that at all."

Belle giggled. "You're funny, Matt. You're always funny."

"Thanks," he drawled dryly.

"So tell me all of your news," Belle said, finally taking a bite of her dinner. "Besides the obvious difference Laura has made. What else is happening at home?"

"Laura is the big difference in our cabin," Amy said, giving her mother a telling glance.

Martha had tried to decide the right way to tell Belle about Adam. They had both decided his coming to meet her was not wise. She couldn't put it off too long though to explain the coming changes in her own life. This wasn't the time. Perhaps laying a little groundwork wouldn't be amiss though. "Adam is visiting. He's staying with St. Louis."

"Adam Stone?" Belle asked with a slight curl of her lip. "He would be here when I come home."

"Don't you like Adam?" asked Amy.

"I have no reason to. He's just so," she paused as though considering her words but didn't pick back up her statement and instead took more bites of her dinner.

"So what?" Amy asked.

Belle chewed thoughtfully. "Well, for one thing, he always treated me like a child. Matt never did that." She turned her beautiful smile on Matt. Martha felt a sense of shock at the level of beauty Belle already had on the cusp of womanhood. Although her other two daughters were very pretty, Belle went beyond that. Was that going to be a problem? Had she made a mistake by letting her have so much freedom?

"Well, maybe you never really knew Adam," Amy suggested turning Martha's thoughts back to the needed conversation.

"I don't want to either. I hope he doesn't come to visit us while I'm there," Belle said, concentrating on her dinner and missing the meaningful exchange of glances between Martha and Amy.

"Adam's my best friend," Matt drawled. "I'm glad whenever he visits."

"You are joking," Belle said, looking up with surprise in her large blue eyes. "He walks around like he owns the world. He's always so cocky and arrogant and why should he be? He's really just a ne'er do well, hardly worth the time to consider anyway, don't you think?" Her tone was lofty as she dismissed Adam as one of those of no consequence and resumed eating.

"Belle, that's no way to talk about anyone else," Martha said, surprised by the extreme dislike her daughter was expressing but even more in the attitudes she seemed to have picked up. Perhaps letting Belle go to San Francisco hadn't been the constructive opportunity she'd expected it to be. It seemed instead that her youngest had become pretentious, with values that conflicted sharply with all she and Amos had strove to teach her.

At the cabin, Belle smiled, as she looked around, approving of the changes that Martha had made since she'd left. She especially approved of the addition of Heaven. "She's so cute," she said, petting the rapidly growing kitten and suddenly becoming for a moment the daughter Martha had sent off nearly six months before.

"I wasn't sure when Eunice brought her, but we've adapted to each other."

"It's good you're not lonely then."

"I haven't been recently," Martha said, taking a deep breath and trying again for the right words to tell Belle about Adam.

"That's good. I worry about you out here, all alone. You really ought to think about moving into town, maybe even Portland, Mama."

"Well, I am unlikely to be alone much longer," Martha said, diving in.

"What do you mean?"

"I mean someone has asked me to marry him."

"But who? I didn't know that there was anyone around. Who?" Belle's voice rose a little her voice taking on an almost childish note, which Martha could not decipher as to whether it was disapproval or excitement.

"Actually, it's Adam."

"Adam? What Adam? Not Stone. You don't mean Adam Stone?" There was no doubt about what the tone meant now.

"Yes, I do."

"But why, when? Why didn't you write me?" Belle asked, obviously trying to understand what she was being told and not finding it easy.

"I didn't want to tell you something so important in a letter, and I knew you were visiting. Besides it isn't a definite decision yet."

"Then, I hope you say no. I don't think it would be a good idea for you, mother. He's too young for you anyway."

"He is younger than I am," Martha agreed, walking over to the stove, "but not so much that it would have to stand in our way."

Belle shook her head with disbelief. "I can't believe this. What does Amy think?"

"She's accepting it."

"What about Loraine?" Belle blazed back at Martha. "Loraine was supposed to be in love with Adam. Not that I ever wanted her to marry him either, but..."

"Loraine knows and is happy for me and for Adam."

"She didn't say anything to me." Belle's large blue eyes were watery with unshed tears.

"Loraine is tactful. I am sure she wanted to give me the chance to do it."

Belle moved away, standing by the door, staring off at the distant mountain, absentmindedly petting the kitten. "I can't believe any of this. How could you do this to Papa?"

"Your father is dead, Belle. I am not doing anything to him."

"He wouldn't want you marrying somebody else. You know he wouldn't have."

Martha sighed as she lit the fire in the stove. "I don't know that and neither do you. Your father was a wise man, and I don't think he would have expected me to live alone the rest of my life."

"Well, maybe not, but Adam?" Belle wailed. "How could you choose Adam?"

"It's hard to explain, sweetheart; but it's a feeling that is there, or it's not."

"And it's there between you and Adam?"

"It is."

Belle shook her head again. "I just can't believe this. I thought I could count on you to be there for me."

"I will be there for you, Belle."

"But he'll be here too."

"What did you hope for? That I'd stay on a shelf?" asked Martha with no condemnation in her voice. "Is that what you wanted? Put me where I would be-- whenever you had time, but not interfere in your life when you didn't? What kind of life would that be for me?"

Tears ran down Belle's cheeks. "Well maybe you did have to remarry, but Adam? Does it have to be Adam?"

"I hope you will give him a chance. I asked him to come to supper, he and St. Louis. It will be tomorrow night, after you and I'd had a chance to visit."

"You wouldn't expect me to call him Papa would you?" Belle asked, her lower lip trembling.

"No, of course not."

Belle sighed, "I don't know. I just don't understand any of this. Just when I think I'm growing up and understanding things, something like this comes up, and it doesn't make any sense to me."

"Can I give you a hug?" asked Martha, and when Belle nodded her permission, she drew her daughter into her arms. "I don't understand a lot of things either," she said finally, "and I'm supposed to be grown up. Maybe we just never do get to a point where we understand everything that is out there."

"I'll try to be nice to him," Belle said against her mother's shoulder. "I really will, but it's going to be hard. I really don't like him."

CHAPTER 23

When Adam walked in the door, he felt the glacial atmosphere and knew that Martha had told her. Belle was not going to accept his presence readily, not tonight or any night. The beautiful girl, who had grown up so much since he'd last seen her had not changed in one thing. She glared at him as he said hello and seemed to dare him to say something to which she could take offense. It didn't help her mood at all when Heaven bounded off her lap and climbed up Adam's pant leg.

Glancing at Martha, he decided not to greet her with any open sign of affection, just as she took the decision from him by putting her arms around him and giving him a light kiss.

At that, the room drew deathly still until St. Louis broke the uncomfortable silence. "Wal now Belle, tell us about San Francisco. How'd it treat ya?"

"Have you ever been there, St. Louis?" she asked, smiling.

"Nope, never did. How about you, Adam?" St. Louis asked, obviously trying to improve the atmosphere.

"Once."

Belle hurried on to talk about what she'd seen, never once looking at Adam as she shared her experiences.

Adam moved away as the others talked. Belle clearly didn't want him part of the conversation. He understood the difficulty for her and moved to the doorway, watching as the sun began to change the color of the horizon to first a pink and then a purple.

He felt Martha's presence before he heard her voice. "She'll be fine with time." She put her hand on his arm.

He shook his head, aware that he didn't share her confidence. Belle was still so much a girl that he wondered if Martha would really do as she said and marry him no matter what her daughter thought of him. It was still hard for him to understand Belle's animosity. It had always been there, but he'd never clearly understood what he'd done to earn it.

When they sat down to dinner, Belle again managed to steer the conversation away from anything to which Adam could contribute. If he said a word, she glared with disapproval, and so he lapsed into a silence.

"What do you think, Adam?" Belle had asked the question twice before Adam realized she was talking to him.

"About what?" he asked, knowing he'd probably committed another cardinal sin in not having heard the question the first time.

"About building a church out here?" Those beautiful blue eyes were coldly on him as though daring him to give any answer. A self-righteous evasion would gain him a pithy reply. *She's out for blood*, he thought, smiling faintly as he considered her.

"Why would you ask me?"

"Why not? You're thinking of moving here. Aren't you?" Her smile was innocence, the expression in those eyes pure venom.

"Could be," he responded, leaning back in his chair.

"Well then, you ought to have an interest in church building. Don't you believe a church is needed?"

"For what?" he asked, taking the bull by the horns.

Belle laughed with mock disbelief. "Why for worshipping God. You do worship God surely?"

"Belle!" Martha snapped.

"No," Adam said raising his hand, "I can answer that question. If I believed in God, the way you do, I still wouldn't think I'd need a building to worship him in."

"Why not?" She dared him to find some fault with her as she sought to bring out the strong difference between him and her mother.

"A church ain't a building, young lady," St. Louis interjected "It's folks. That's all, pure and simple. Folks can worship God in their own ways with or without a church."

"Have you ever been in a church building, Mr. Stone?" Belle asked, glaring at him.

"Yes, ma'am, I have."

"Must not have liked it much then?" He saw then that she was enjoying herself. What a tigress she'd be once fully grown. It'd take quite a man to stand at her side without being swamped by all that female power.

Martha snapped, "Belle."

"It's all right," Adam said, now smiling. "She's got a right to say what she thinks. This isn't really about church though is it?"

"No.".

"It's about your mother and me."

"You know it is."

"You don't like the idea that I asked her to marry me." It wasn't a question.

"No, I do not."

"Well, then if I explained to you about church and me, it wouldn't really change anything would it?"

"No." Belle's full lower lip was pursed out.

St. Louis cleared his throat noisily. "Ya got any more of that there coffee, Martha?"

"Of course," she said, rising with a sigh to go to the stove.

Adam considered carefully what to say next. He decided

talking directly to Belle was the only possible option. "Would you go outside with me a moment, Belle?"

Martha showed her concern on her face but said nothing to stop them. Belle's eyes were hostile, but she nodded her assent. Adam rose and walked out the door, aware that she had followed him.

Outside, he sat on a step, patting the space near him. She refused to sit. "I don't see why we had to come out here?"

"I wanted to know why you don't like me. You never have, and I have never known why."

"It's just you, who you are... and now something more. You're going to take my mother."

"Nobody could do that, Belle."

"I just..." She stopped and stared into the night.

"You know, I wouldn't try to take your father's place with you. I know you're grown up enough now that you wouldn't need or want that, but I would want to be a friend if your mother agrees to marry me."

"Of course, she'll agree," Belle retorted.

"She won't if you don't agree."

"I don't believe that."

"Believe it. Your mother loves you too much to do something that would hurt you."

"So you are trying to be nice to get me to agree?"

"No, I just wanted to know what I'd done. I figured it must be something. I don't remember a time you didn't dislike me." In the distance he heard a horned owl.

"That's true," Belle said, her voice beginning to soften just the tiniest bit.

"I could see why you might not think much of me as a suitor," he said.

"You can?"

"Sure, I don't have much to offer her. I've been a restless man, haven't built up any stake. Your mother has her own doubts whether she can count on me. There are others that could offer her more in a material way."

"Who?" Belle asked with incredulity.

"George Simon, for one."

"Who's that?"

"Eunice Lance's brother. He owns stores in Salem and has expressed a strong interest in your mother. He's made it very clear to her that she'd be making a big mistake by marrying me."

"And that worries *you*?" Belle asked with disbelief in her young voice.

"Yes, but there's nothing I can do about it."

"Do you really love Mama?" Belle asked, not looking at him.

"Very much."

"But you said you loved Amy too."

Adam smiled. "No, I never did. I thought I wanted Amy to be my wife, that's true, but I never asked her to marry me nor told her I loved her."

"Then you didn't?"

"No, I didn't, and it was a good thing for both of us that she was wise enough to know that, and that she loved Matt." He wouldn't tell her of the love he'd carried around for Martha for years because that wouldn't help matters.

"Then you don't just want Mama because you couldn't have Amy?" Belle asked her voice again lapsing into a childish tone.

"No," he said with a laugh. "Is that what you thought?"

"It did occur to me."

"I can see why it might have, but it isn't why I love your mother."

Belle sighed with resignation. "I suppose I've been acting a little immature about all of this."

"No," he said, shaking his head, "I don't think so. I think you've been protective of your mother. I don't know if she'll marry me or not, but if she does, I'd be glad you were protective of her, glad you cared enough."

"You would?"

"Of course."

She was silent for a little time and Adam waited, not wanting to push or prod her. "Maybe it won't be so bad... if you do marry each other," she said finally.

Adam swallowed hard, aware of how hard that had to have been for her to say. "Maybe we can start over, you and me. Pretend we just met," he said. "Think that would be possible?"

"Maybe," she said with a small smile, her gaze meeting his for the first time without hostility.

"All right then. Maybe this time," he said with a grin, "I can avoid the same mistakes as last time."

"How can you," she asked, smiling more broadly, "when you don't know what they were?"

"That's the way it always is with me and women," he admitted with another smile, "I never do know, and usually figure it out after everybody else."

After a few moments, they walked back inside, while not arm and arm. Adam felt relief that if Belle still wasn't thrilled, there was a truce.

Belle stayed a full week with Martha, and it seemed her relationship with Adam improved with each visit he made. Martha was not certain she would eagerly await a marriage, but at least she would accept it. With a sigh of relief, she saw her daughter onto a steamship heading for Portland. As the boat moved away from the dock, Adam asked, "Are you going to be lonely now with her gone?"

"I suppose so for a few days," she admitted, waving until she could see Belle no more.

"And now you don't want to see me again for awhile?" he asked, repeating what she had told him.

"I think it's best. I need time to think very seriously about our future."

"All right then, but I'm going to miss you."

"I know. I will miss you too, but..."

"I know." He managed a smile. "You need time."

"Yes."

Adam came to the cabin door as soon as he saw Martha riding her horse into the yard. He grinned at her unexpected arrival. She'd asked for time to think, and although it had only been two days he hoped that now he'd have her answer.

After she had dismounted, he told her that St. Louis was in town. "Rider came by to tell him he had an important letter. No idea from who, but he figured he wouldn't be back until nightfall, visit his friend and make a day of it."

"Ohh." She looked around as though uneasy at the knowledge that they were alone here and would be that way all day.

He shook his head and smiled down at her. "We've been alone before," he reminded her, all the time admiring the way the pants clung to her slim figure, making her look anything but boyish.

"I know. It's just, but it is best we be alone. We need to talk."

"I figured that's why you'd come. You go on in the cabin, and I'll take care of your mare."

He put the horse in the pen where Joe would have some companionship and watched for a moment as the two horses nuzzled each other in affectionate greeting.

By now, Martha's unnaturally stiff demeanor was beginning to worry him. Had she come to tell him no, that she would not marry him? If it was good news, he couldn't imagine her waiting even a minute to give it to him. Slowly he walked back to the cabin, wondering what he would say, how he would handle it if she told him that it couldn't be. He began marshaling his arguments.

Inside, she was making coffee. He stopped in the doorway,

admiring the slender bend of her body as she measured the water, filling the coffee pot; then he frowned as he noticed that little line between her eyes that always appeared when she was troubled.

She looked up at him, saying nothing, her eyes dark.

"All right," he said, "you wanted time to think. I gather you've had enough."

"Yes," she began but stopped when she looked over his shoulder and said, "I can't believe it. You've got company coming."

"Great," he growled, looking out the open door and seeing two riders. "Looks like one of them is George Simon. I don't recognize the other."

"I don't want to face them here, like this now," she said.

"Since your horse is in the corral, you don't have to. Just duck back in the bedroom. I'll get rid of them."

"Will you? I'd appreciate it. I know it's silly, but I've had all I can take of George and his silly arguments, and I don't want him spreading gossip about you and me being here alone together."

He closed the bedroom door and went to the porch. "What can I do for you?" he asked, when Simon and his friend dismounted. He could imagine no reason for a friendly visit from Simon.

"We had something we wanted to talk to you about," Simon said nervously, looking around as though to make certain they were alone.

"Come on in. Coffee's on." The man riding with Simon seemed unlikely as a friend. Not overly tall, the man had a narrow face, wore a strapped down gun, and his eyes avoided Adam's. He was no storekeeper or banker.

"Now, what do you want?" Adam asked.

"I need to talk to you," Simon said shrugging a pudgy shoulder.

"So you said. You brought a friend along to do that?"

"We had some other business. I thought I could kill two birds with one stone." He giggled as he said that and looked nervously at his friend and then back at Adam.

"All right. Let's get to it."

"I suggest you leave Martha Stevens alone."

Adam crossed his arms across his chest as he studied the storekeeper and then his friend. "Any special reason you'd think I would do that?" he asked.

"You can't be serious about her. You will go on tomorrow or the next day just like your name says rolling stone. You'll just hurt the lady in the meantime."

Adam half smiled at that. "Don't you think that's for her and me to work out?" He began to wonder how much of this conversation Martha was able to hear through the door.

"No, I think as a friend of Martha's, it's for me. Martha needs to find someone more. Well, let's just say she could make a more appropriate relationship."

"Obviously, we don't agree," Adam said quietly, keeping his eye on both the men and wishing he had his revolver closer than the bedroom dresser.

"Then, you're not willing to leave her alone?" Simon asked, his voice breaking, his eyes shooting around the room.

"No."

"You leave me no choice then." He nodded to his friend, who seemed instantly to have a gun in his hand, pointed at Adam's belly.

"You planning on killing me?" asked Adam, eyes narrowed as he looked from the gun back to Simon's nervous face.

"Give me some credit, Stone. Nothing so gruesome as murder." Simon giggled again, clearly uneasy about whatever he planned. He reached into his pocket and pulled out a derringer, which he also pointed at Adam.

Adam laughed with disbelief as he looked at the two men facing him. Simon showed no sign of being a man who had ever done such a thing. His gun wavered so badly that Adam began to worry it might go off accidentally. His companion presented a different situation. He was rough looking, bearded, dirty and had been around enough to be comfortable holding a gun on a man. Adam had no doubts that if he moved wrong, the man would have no hesitation in shooting him.

"With two guns pointing at me, it would seem you have me at a disadvantage," Adam said in a firm voice, "what do you have in mind?" He only hoped that when Martha understood there were two guns out here, she would stay put until it became obvious what was intended. If it wasn't to be an immediate murder, maybe there would be a way out of this without involving her.

"Griggs, keep him covered," Simon instructed, putting away his derringer before he made a wide circle around Adam, giving him no chance to jump him. When he was behind him, Simon ordered, "Put your hands behind your back."

When Adam ignored him, Simon said again, his voice unnaturally high. "Put your hands behind your back and hold your wrists together."

"You're in over your head, Simon. Quit while you're ahead," Adam growled, still not obeying.

"We can hit you over the head, and then it will be quite simple to tie your hands. It is your choice."

"This is a joke, right?" Adam asked, shaking his head but putting his hands behind his back.

"It's no joke. It's part of a very successful, highly thought out plan, which will make you do what you would do anyway if you were a gentleman. It will put you in a situation where you will no longer be able to make the wrong choice."

Adam tightened the muscles in his wrists, increasing their size as much as muscle alone would allow. He only shrugged as he felt a cord cutting into his skin as it was wrapped tightly around his wrists and secured with a knot.

"Are you going to explain this master plan" he asked when

Simon stepped away, satisfied that he had rendered his victim helpless.

"Actually," Simon said, laughing with nervous relief, "I'd be glad to. I am rather proud of it. You are going for a ride with Griggs here. A long ride. It will appear to people around here that you have just taken off again, like the ne'er do well that you are. Martha will become finally disillusioned with you before it is too late."

"Do I come back from this long ride?" questioned Adam with a humorless smile.

"You don't seem nearly as upset as I'd expected," said Simon, watching him for some signs of nervousness, while showing more himself than Adam felt. "Don't you understand what's about to happen to you?"

"Looks like I'm going to be kidnapped," Adam smiled coolly as he began twisting his wrists to loosen the ties that bound them.

"That's right. Doesn't that upset you just a little?"

"Of course," Adam said. "It's never happened to me before; so I don't know what to expect. Want to tell me?"

Simon began puffing up with pride at his own ingenuity in overcoming the big man so easily. "I don't mind at all. Griggs will be taking you with him somewhere down the valley. I don't want to know where. He'll keep you secured, as comfortably as is possible under the circumstances." He giggled again. "Until a month or so has passed. Griggs will take good care of you. Won't you, Griggs?"

The man smiled wolfishly, giving Adam his first uneasy moment. That gun had never been put away. For the first time Adam began to worry, worry that Martha might make an appearance that could prove dangerous. *Please, stay in that room until we leave,* he sent her a silent message. He had total confidence in his ability to get away from this Griggs once they were alone, and suddenly, he was more eager than they to get away from the cabin.

"Well, what's stopping you then?" Adam asked, walking toward the door. "If you've got kidnapping in mind, go to it. You can't do it standing here."

Simon frowned, clearly feeling the situation was being taken from his hands and not understanding how it was happening. "Just a minute here. There's no rush. I'm enjoying this part of it. I sent a false message for your friend to make sure he'd be away most of the day. Just running down that *mail* ought to take him until the afternoon. I'm in no hurry."

"Well, I am," Adam snapped, "let's get out of here or you can forget the whole deal."

"That's ridiculous," the pudgy storekeeper snarled, his voice breaking as he added, "It's not for you to decide whether this gets forgotten or not. I'm in charge here."

"Well, if you're in charge, you're a lousy outlaw." Adam shook his head with disgust. "Once you've committed a crime, you don't stay around someplace waiting for someone to ride up. You get on with it. Isn't that right, Griggs?"

"Yeah. I think we oughta get out of here," Griggs said. "His friend could come back early."

"Oh, all right, but I don't see the rush." Simon walked up behind Adam and, trying to re-establish the dominant role as kidnapper, gave him a push that sent him through the door and nearly to the ground.

Glaring at him, Adam managed to keep his balance as he discovered with bound wrists it wasn't as easy as he'd expected. Both men pushed him down the porch and into the yard.

Before they could progress further, the sound Adam had dreaded hearing came. "That's far enough!" All three men looked back in shock to see Martha on the porch, her legs spread apart, a rifle pointed unwaveringly at George Simon' midsection. Adam noticed irrelevantly that she had his own large revolver shoved into the belt that circled her slender waist.

"Martha," Simon gulped, "what are you doing here? And are

those men's pants you are wearing?" His eyes were riveted on her hips.

"None of your business, George, on either question." She glared at him, the rifle never wavering in its direction. "Now step away from him, both of you."

Griggs hissed, "I can take her."

Martha said sweetly, "He could, George, but I levered a cartridge into the chamber before I came out. You will be the one I shoot-- right between the legs-- where it'll do the most good."

Almost instantly, George's hands went to the pertinent part of his anatomy as though thinking they alone could protect him. "Martha..." he began before she cut him off.

"I mean it, George. I am an excellent shot and trust me, I won't hesitate to use this if need be."

"Do what she says," George ordered Griggs in a quavering voice.

The two men backed away from Adam who moved back toward the porch, careful to stay out of Martha's line of fire. "Throw your guns there on the ground. Your derringer too, George," she ordered, waving her rifle a little to make her point, and watching as they obeyed. "Now get on your horses and get out of here. And George--"

"Yes," he gulped, as he mounted, relieved he was riding away intact.

"Don't ever come back. I don't want ever to see your fat, smiling face again. Not ever."

CHAPTER 24

A s soon as the two men had ridden from the clearing, Adam turned on Martha. "Were you out of your mind!" he snapped. "They might have killed you."

"Me! It was you they were taking away. What did you expect me to do? Nothing? Just let them take you?" She leaned the rifle against the wall, near enough to grab again if needed.

"Damned right." He advanced on her, towering over her angrily. "Now untie me!"

"I don't like that look in your eyes," she said, wrapping her arms around herself and still trembling. It made him more angry to see that.

"Are you thinking of going after them?" she asked tightening her mouth with that stubborn look he'd come to recognize.

"No man does this to me and just rides away. Now untie me."

"Are you serious?" she asked. "After what you just said to me, why should I?"

"Martha!" he hissed, "untie my hands now!"

"No."

He rocked back on his heels, amazement in his eyes. "No? Why the hell not?"

"Because I don't want you to go after them."

"It's what they deserve. You think I should let a man come into my home, pull a gun on me, tie me up, threaten me as well as you, and then walk away?"

"Since you aren't able to think clearly, you can just wait a few minutes to cool off before I untie you," she insisted doggedly.

"Martha!" he bellowed and then decided he didn't need her help. All he had to do was get into the cabin and find a knife. He might get a few nicks, but it would be worth it. He strode up the steps to the cabin, only to find his way blocked by her soft body, pushing his backward. "Martha," he grated out, "get out of my way."

"No, I want to talk."

He looked at her feeling as though one of them had lost their minds. "Now?" he shouted with incredulity. "You want to talk--now? While my hands are tied behind my back? While those men are riding off scot-free. Are you crazy?"

"Possibly, but I think now is a good time."

He suddenly remembered her somber words, the way she'd looked when she'd come up to the cabin. He knew then that she had to have come to tell him she couldn't and wouldn't marry him. Under those circumstances, having his hands tied probably seemed like a good idea to her. Giving into the inevitable, he said, "All right. Have it your way. What is it?"

She picked up the rifle. "Let's go inside." Once inside, she shut the bolt on the door and sat at the table. "I had no idea that George Simon would do such a despicable thing."

"Is that what you want to talk about?" he asked with exasperation.

"No. Of course not, but I just think it's easier if I lead into it gradually." She laced her fingers together and stared at them.

If his wrists hadn't been hurting with the tight cords, he might have been more patient with her, but as it was, he felt a growing frustration that she was going to throw away everything, and it wasn't being eased by his physical discomfort. He pushed the chair out alongside her and sat. "All right," he said trying to sound patient, and knowing he was failing, "we'll do this your way. I had no idea George would try something like this either. Frankly I didn't think he had it in him."

"You admire him for it?" she gasped.

"Not admire, but he does have determination. You have to give him that."

"If I hadn't been here, they'd have forced you off and who knows how that scruffy looking man would have really treated you? He didn't look very nice to me." She pulled his revolver from her belt and set it on the table in front of her.

"You're a good judge of character," he said dryly, "but I think I'd have had something to say about that."

"I don't see how, your hands were tied. You were helpless."

"For then," he agreed, as he continued twisting his wrists, trying to loosen the cords and get his fingers into the knots that would only temporarily hold him.

"Anyway, what I wanted to say, when I rode in here, was..."

"You're not telling me that you won't marry me," he exploded angrily, rising and for the moment forgetting about freeing himself. "I've heard everything you have to say about it, and I don't agree. You love me and are going to marry me, Martha, and that is final!"

"All right," she said in a small voice.

"I want..." He stopped, slumping back down, releasing the knot he had almost gotten loosened. He felt as though all the wind had been knocked from his sails. "All right?" he repeated weakly.

"Yes, I will be your wife. Whenever you want."

"You mean it?"

"Yes."

"But then why have you been so glum?"

"Because I think I'm being selfish, thinking only about what's best for me. I'm worried about how this will be for you, and yet I can't seem to be sensible."

"Cut me loose," he demanded.

"No, you'd still go after them."

"I... oh hell, then kiss me. Convince me you mean it." He waited expectantly as she leaned forward, her lips coming against his in a gentle, sweet kiss, which he promptly changed as he forced her mouth open and slid his tongue inside, teasing and tempting both her and himself. Quickly her arms were around his neck as her own mouth became the aggressor as they kissed, pulled back and kissed again.

"I love you so much, Adam," she whispered, against his neck, her breath a sweet torment against his skin. He felt her fingers at the buttons on his shirt. With frustration, he tried again to free his wrists, but found, his coordination had now gone with her kisses, and his fingers felt like jelly.

Soon, she had his shirt unbuttoned and pushed it apart, baring his chest to her fingers and then her lips as she moved to tempt first one flat nipple and then the other, coaxing them and the rest of his body into a arousal that became all too evident.

"Martha," he groaned, as she reached up and pulled his shirt from his shoulders, leaving it hanging from his bound wrists. Her lips again concentrated on his torso, kissing and touching him, exciting him so greatly that his legs felt weak. "Untie me," he growled, "you are going to drive me crazy."

She smiled as she continued kissing and touching him, running her hand down inside his pants to touch him intimately. She rose then and smiling walked to his bedroom. "I'll drive us both crazy then," she said and beckoned.

He followed her no longer caring about his bound wrists. Once they were inside the bedroom, she shut the door and turned to look back at him. Her smile was pure Delilah. "I think I like you best naked."

He stood as she slowly peeled his pants from him, pushing him to sit on the bed while she pulled off his boots. "Now, lie down," she whispered. He obeyed and watched as she began slowly to unbutton her shirt.

His arousal had been so hard he hadn't imagined it could grow, but it did. Slowly and seductively, she began removing her clothing, taking her time, dropping each item to the floor until finally she stood naked before him. Slowly she pulled the pins from her hair. She was clothed then only in a black cloud as she walked toward him. He could hardly breathe for the beauty she was showing him as she crawled onto the bed.

She smiled. "Would you like..." She didn't need to finish as he nodded. She lifted his head for her kiss as he plunged his tongue into her mouth as he wanted to plunge himself into her waiting warmth. For awhile she played with his body, rubbing her breasts against his chest and then she straddled his hips and held herself just above him.

"Do you want me?" she asked with a teasing smile as she bent and kissed his lips before she lowered herself onto his hard length. He groaned as he felt her totally settle over him. He had never known anything like it. Never imagined anything like it. As she began to move, he lifted his hips to follow her rhythm.

He saw she was enjoying the power, the control she had over their lovemaking. When she contracted her muscles around him, she claimed his lips with a kiss as they climaxed together. For that moment it was as though their bodies were no longer two but one. She fell onto him, then turning to lie beside him, their legs still entwined.

"We are getting married Saturday," he said when he could speak.

"Mmmmmmm whatever you want," she whispered, kissing his cheekbones, his eyes, his jaw and then his mouth.

"Time to untie me," he said.

"I should have done this sooner," she apologized as she untied him with a sigh. "Your wrists are rubbed raw." He rubbed his hands to restore circulation.

"And miss this," he corrected. "Not on your life." He grinned as she smiled and bent to kiss him again.

"So you really will marry me?" he asked again.

"If you want me. I just hope this is truly what you want."

"After this, how can you ask?"

She smiled. "You liked that?"

"Do you have to ask?" he repeated laughing. He pulled her into his arms, holding her tenderly and gently.

"What made up your mind?" he asked as they each found their clothing and began reluctantly dressing.

"Well, it was mostly just thinking of everything you'd said, and of how much I wanted to be with you. I said I needed time to think, but only a day without you began convincing me that I couldn't live without you anymore, not if I had a choice, and I did have a choice. I took another day just to be certain, and I am."

He smiled as they walked out onto the porch. In the distance the mountain peaks had a smattering of first snow. "This winter, you'll be my wife," he said, taking a deep breath and exhaling it loudly. "I can't believe it. When I think of how I spent last Christmas." He stopped, not wanting to darken the mood of this moment.

"Tell me about last Christmas," she asked, reaching up to cup his chin as he so often did with hers, forcing his eyes down to meet hers.

"It's no big thing."

"Then tell me."

He wished he'd never mentioned it. She'd imagine worse than it was if he didn't tell her-- if it could be worse. "I was out with a patrol-- not far behind a bunch of Takelma. Too far though to do any good for the people in the cabin. All we could do was bury the bodies-- a woman, man and three children. God, you don't have any idea what that's like to see the handmade decorations, presents strewn around the room, all destroyed. It's not easy at any time of the year, but at Christmas, it's worse."

"That's horrible," she turned kissing his shoulder in sympathy.

"After that, there was no way of trailing the killers. It was pouring down rain in an icy downpour which changed all too quick to snow. We didn't want to bivouac in the cabin." He shuddered as he remembered the smell of blood and death that had permeated the logs. "So, we went to the barn. The stock had been taken or driven off. We at least found a dry place out of the storm. The Christmas dinner was deer jerky."

"This one will be different," she said with a smile. "Lots of presents, family, warmth, me."

They sat on the stoop, arms around each other. "Will you mind if we're married by a pastor instead of a judge?" she asked.

He grinned. "I want you tied to me for good. So minister is just fine."

"Good. I'd like that."

"I won't disappoint you, Martha. I'll do whatever is my power to make you happy."

She smiled and laughed a little. "Of course, you'll disappoint me and make me cry and go crazy sometimes. I will you too, but that is how life is, Adam. I love you."

~

George Simon rode into the Lance yard somberly, dismounting stiffly. He had paid off Griggs and hoped to never see him again.

Eunice came out of the cabin, a frown on her round face. "Where've you been? she asked.

"Nowhere."

"That just isn't so. You took off so mysteriously. What is going on?

"Nothing. I'll be heading back to Salem in the morning."

"You will? Why now?"

"I've decided I don't want Martha for my wife after all." Nor did he want any more of a life of crime, but he wouldn't tell her that.

"Well, I think that's commonsense for once," Eunice told him, patting him sympathetically on the shoulder.

"Don't pander to me, Eunice."

"You're my brother, George. You have to expect that from me."

He shook his head, sighing deeply. He wished he could confide in her what had happened, but he knew he'd never tell anyone. He felt totally humiliated by his failure. Vividly he remembered Martha's cold face, her angry words, her threat to shoot his-- He only thanked the Good Lord that he'd found out in time what sort of woman she was. He had thought only to help her, keep her from making a disastrous mistake. And what was his reward? The threatening of his very manhood!

No good woman could talk like that, threaten such a devilish thing. Perhaps fooling with all those herbal remedies, she'd gotten into a little Satan worship. He didn't know. All he knew is he hoped he would never see either her or Adam Stone again for the rest of his life. It might take that long to forget the humiliation of this last month, the fool he'd made of himself.

~

As soon as St. Louis returned home, Adam and Martha told him of their plans to his immense satisfaction.

"I'm not sure Amy will be so pleased," she told St. Louis when Adam was building up the fire in the fireplace. With the coming of fall, the days were shorter and the nights were growing chilly enough that a fire was inviting in the evenings.

"Ya just tell her and see. Might be surprised."

"She's been trying to be understanding, but it's not been easy. Since Belle just left, I'm not sure if she or Loraine can get back up here on a week's notice, but we'll try to get them. It's just that now that we've made up our mind, neither Adam nor I want to wait."

"That makes sense. Never put off happiness, I always say."

"Would you ride into Oregon City and ask Pastor Jefferson if he would marry us? I don't think Adam would be comfortable doing that."

"Shore," he said.

Adam interrupted, "Not comfortable doing what?"

"Asking Pastor Jefferson from the Methodist Church if he would marry us," she said, taking hold of his hand, rubbing the back of it along her cheek.

"I will do the asking," Adam insisted. "St. Louis can come with me though to hold me up if he refuses."

"Why would he refuse?" she asked with a tender smile.

"I'm not exactly the prime catch of the year spiritually speaking, and Oregon City kind of sees me as some sort of glorified killer right now. Maybe a temporary hero, but definitely not the man you'd invite to dinner."

She shook her head. "I'm sure it's not that bad."

"I don't know. You kill a man, and I killed two. If I'd been their sheriff, they might have accepted it, but even then, they'd have been leery of me. People shy away from those who kill for a living even if the killing is to protect them."

"They don't know you."

"True and they aren't likely to want to. No, I better talk to the minister myself. Maybe I can talk him into overcoming his own better judgment."

St. Louis laughed. "Ya ain't exactly the most tactful man I ever met, Adam. Ya shore that yore talkin' to him ain't just goin' to convince him that it's the devil himself she's thinkin' of marryin'."

"Thanks a lot," Adam snorted.

"You do need to go, St. Louis," Martha said.

"I got a better idea," St. Louis said, chuckling. "Let's go over to Amy and Matt's and take him along too. Ya can stay with her and the baby."

"Matt!" Adam exploded, "are you saying that Matt'd have a better chance of convincing him than I would?"

"He's got a way with Bible words," St. Louis suggested.

"That's true," Adam admitted, rubbing the side of his nose thoughtfully. "All right. We'll see if Matt's got the time."

"If he ain't, he'll make it for this," St. Louis promised with a grin.

The next morning, the three men rode for Oregon City while Amy and Martha worked on a batch of bread. Amy, hands and arms covered with flour, asked, "Are you sure about this, Mama?"

"Yes, I am. He's a good man, Amy."

"I know that. It's just..."

"It's hard for you. I understand that." Martha went over to pick up the fussing Laura. "My, she grows every time I see her."

Amy smiled, continuing to knead bread dough. "Lifting her is definitely developing some new muscles in my shoulders and arms."

"It has a way of doing that." She carried the baby to a changing table and proceeded to remove the offending diaper.

"What dress are you going to wear?" Amy asked in a small voice, thinking of the one she'd worn to marry Matt.

"I will make something. I have almost a week and I had bought some pale gray silk last spring. That will do nicely."

"You sure you don't want to wear the wedding gown?"

"No, that's for first weddings. Besides I expect Adam would like it better if I wore a special dress just for him, one I hadn't worn before."

"What kind of wedding do you want?" Amy asked, shaping the loaves.

"Small, just us, no friends." She thought of George Simon although she doubted he would dare to show his face. "St. Louis will send Loraine and Belle a wire when he gets to Oregon City, but I doubt they will come. We can have a family dinner afterward, to celebrate."

"What's the rush?" Amy asked, checking the oven to see if it was ready for the bread.

Smiling, Martha thought of Adam and the way he felt in her arms. Before she could try to think of an answer that wouldn't offend her daughter, Amy laughed. "Don't bother answering that question. I can see it written on your face."

Martha flushed. "Don't be embarrassed, Mama," Amy said with a little smile, "I understand very well how you feel." Her voice grew soft.

"Thank you."

"It's been hard for me to think about it, you with another man, but I know this is good. I think it is what Papa would want too," Amy said, reaching out even with the flour covered hands and hugging her mother to her.

"I believe he really would."

Amy shook her head ruefully. "I was foolish when this all started, but at least we got Adam into the family. One way or another," she teased.

It was strange to be talking to Amy as an equal, as another step toward friendship and not just mother-daughter. It was good though. Amy didn't need a mother any more. She needed a friend, and Martha didn't need a daughter so much as she needed a friend. It would seem that without thinking about it, they had taken a step, which would give their relationship a new dimension. *Maybe being human to my children isn't as bad as I'd feared,* Martha thought, remembering back to when Adam had accused her of that fear.

CHAPTER 25

"You don't all have to go with me to talk to him," Adam said tersely as the three men rode into Oregon City.

"Yeah, we do," drawled Matt, sitting his horse as easily as Adam. "We don't go, and anythin' goes wrong, it'll be our heads that roll."

"It won't go wrong," Adam snapped. "You'd think I was a bull in a china shop the way you two carry on. I can talk to a Bible-thumper without offending him."

"See, right there, ya need us," retorted Matt. "You don't call a preacher a Bible-thumper. You call him Pastor or Preacher or Reverend."

"I know that," Adam protested. "I was just saying that to you."

"Well, it wouldn't hurt to practice just what ya are goin' to say," St. Louis suggested. "Tell us, and we'll let ya know if it's all right."

Adam laughed in mock wonderment. "I can't believe this! A preacher is a man, right? What the hell is there about him that makes you two think I can't just talk to him like I would to you?"

"Wal, for one thing," St. Louis said with severity, "ya can't go swearin' around him."

"I know that!"

"Wal, ya are in a habit of doin' it, and don't want to be doing it when ya talk to a man of the cloth."

Adam rolled his eyes skyward. "Heaven help me!"

"That's another thing. Ya don't go makin' fun of them that believes or of the Bible or..."

Adam roared, "Stop! I've heard it all. You can go with me just to see that I can handle this, but no more advice. I've heard enough to last me through two weddings."

"Wal, there ain't goin' to be but one, God willin'," said St. Louis, "and don't go insinuatin' that ya are one of those new fangled folks who believe in divorce, or ya'll be out the door."

"That's enough!" Adam snarled, "you have had enough fun with me on this ride to last me period."

"We're just tryin' to help," assured Matt with a grin.

"Well, that kind of help I can do without—and you two are having way too much fun with this."

"Jest, don't say we didn't warn ya," St. Louis said, shaking his head with mock concern.

"No, I won't. I'll tell you this, if this preacher says no, I'll grab her and take her down to a Chinook medicine man, he'll do it and that will be that."

"Ya shore Miss Martha'd go for that?" asked St. Louis with a broad grin.

"If I grab her," Adam explained patiently as though to a child, "it won't matter if she goes for it or not."

"Last man tried grabbin' something that jest belonged to her, accordin' to what she told me, she threatened to put a bullet where it'd do the most good," St. Louis said with a chuckle. "Imagine what she'd do if'n he was tryin' to grab her herself!"

Chagrined, Adam's face was now the growing red. "She told you about that?"

"Wasn't she supposed to?" St. Louis asked with a loud guffaw.

"What's this all about?" asked Matt, with interest, obviously at a loss in the new direction of the conversation.

"Never mind," said Adam, while St. Louis added, "I'll tell ya about it, later."

Fortunately they arrived at the church before any of them could do physical harm to the other.

"I'd say wait out here," Adam said as he looked at the door marked office, "but I don't suppose it'd do any good."

"Nope. We been sent along to take care of things, and we're a gonna to do it," St. Louis told him. "She'd have our hides if'n we didn't. I don't want to go gettin' shot-- where it'd do the most good." He laughed again at Adam's snort of disgust as he dismounted.

Adam knocked on the door, uncomfortably aware that his two friends were on each side of him.

"Come in." The voice was thin and reedy, and Adam had a sudden bad feeling about this.

When he entered, the pastor rose from behind his desk. "Hello, gentlemen, what can I do for you?" He was gray-haired, tall, thin and had a disapproving look already fixed onto his lined face.

"Good afternoon. My name is Adam Stone. This is St. Louis Jones and Matt Kane."

"Pleased to meet you, I'm sure. My name is James Jefferson."

"Well, Pastor Jefferson, I'm hoping that you would be willing to marry me."

The pastor looked behind them and then cocking his head said, "To one of these two gentlemen?"

St. Louis chortled.

"Uh... no, of course not," Matt said soberly. He saw no humor in anything at this point. "The bride's at home. That is at her daughter's home. We all live out there in the hills between the Clackamas and Molalla Rivers."

"Oh, I see. Well, it would be nice, if I could interview the bride too. It is customary. When were you thinking to schedule the wedding?"

"Saturday."

"Saturday?" he repeated as though he couldn't have heard correctly. "As in this Saturday?"

"Yeah, you got something already scheduled for that day?"

"Why don't you all sit down? Is this your father and brother? No, that couldn't be because the names didn't fit."

"They're friends."

The pastor's thin face widened as he smiled. "Are they here to make sure you do, or don't get married?"

"They're here in case I need help."

"Talking me into this?" the pastor suggested with another smile.

"That ought to not be a problem if your day is free," Adam said gruffly.

"I do have a few questions. You are not of my parish."

"No, I'm not of any parish," he said as St. Louis kicked him in the side of the leg.

"No parish? You're not a member of the Methodist Church?"

"No sir. There are no churches out where we are." He decided that St. Louis was right. At this point painfully truthful would have to give way to mostly tactful.

"Oh, of course. Well, now, what denomination are you both of?"

"His wife's Presbyterian, or at least was before they left Missouri," Matt inserted helpfully.

The pastor smiled again, and looked at Matt. "How is it that you know his wife's denomination, while he apparently does not?"

"Because the bride's daughter is my wife," Matt explained, grinning at the man's expression of confusion.

It was possible to see the wheels turning in the pastor's head, but to his credit, he resisted asking the obvious question as to the age of the bride. Adam almost smiled imagining what he was probably visualizing.

"And so what denomination do you belong to, Mr. Stone?" questioned the pastor.

"Is that important?" Adam said, fighting to hold onto what patience he had.

"Not especially. I just like to know because it has an influence on the marriage ceremony sometimes."

"We don't care what the ceremony says; so long as we end up legally wed," Adam stated, trying to keep his voice level and non-threatening as his friends snickered.

"Uh yes. Now, you are believers, I take it?"

Adam thought a moment, knowing his two friends were waiting for his answer with more interest than the pastor. "What do you mean by believer?" he queried finally as he considered what he could say honestly that wouldn't end up causing the minister to turn him down.

Pastor Jefferson sat back, making a bridge with his fingers as he studied Adam's face. "Do you believe in God?"

If he lied, he'd be married, but if he lied, he didn't know if he could live with himself. "What I believe is not easy to explain," he said after a long moment.

"You are an agnostic?"

What was there about labeling that appealed to people so much? Put everyone in a box. A title for everyone. "I don't know that's a good way to put it."

"Perhaps you could tell me what your belief means for your life? I don't have a belief as a pastor that I will never marry a man or woman, who has no belief in my personal church. I do limit myself to marrying those who I believe have a life code that will make marriage likely to work out. I hope that helps you to understand why I am asking what I am."

Again, Adam could feel three sets of eyes on him, waiting for an answer. He had not put his own code into words or if he had, now they were lost to him. He would try. "I believe in a creator. To be honest, I'm not sure I think he cares what we do as humans."

He felt another kick from St. Louis and a nudge from Matt, but he went on stubbornly.

"The word *right* might say it. I try to live my life right. Do what is right for others as much as I can. I was raised in a church, Pastor Jefferson-- a Lutheran church in Ohio, but I don't go there any more. I did promise my wife-to-be that I'd go with her, when there's a church to go to, and I promised her that she could teach any children we have about God-- her way. I did that because I wanted to make her happy and because I didn't think it would hurt anything since I don't think any god out there cares either. I won't lie about my own beliefs, which are that we can reach God wherever we are, if we can reach him at all."

Pastor Jefferson sat a moment, contemplating, then smiled, rose, and reached out his hand. "What time Saturday, and draw me a map as to where will the wedding be held."

When they were all outside again, Matt grinned. "I thought there for a minute ya were goin' to blow it wide open." He shook his head. "I could just see ya sayin' to him-- Marry us, or it's goin' to be that Chinook medicine man!"

St. Louis chuckled. "It's a pure wonder ya kept yore cool. Ya didn't say everythin' he probably wanted to hear, but he's goin' to marry ya. That's what matters to Martha."

Before they could remount, an angry yell interrupted them. "Hey, Stone," a voice that sounded vaguely familiar, shouted. "I thought that was you I saw riding in." Adam turned and saw Griggs, the man who'd come with Simon to kidnap him. "Hiding in a church these days, huh?" Griggs asked with a sneer. "Well, I got a little score to settle with you."

Slowly, Adam moved away from his horse and his two friends, ignoring St. Louis and Matt's angry hisses to stay with them. "You want something?" He had his revolver on his hip and knew he'd checked the load before they'd ridden out.

"You and that woman made a fool out of me. I don't take

kindly to that. Simon may have wanted to walk away that day, but I didn't like it."

"This isn't your fight. Walk away from it," Adam said in a level tone.

"It is now. We ran that day with our tails between our legs. I don't like remembering that. I need something new to remember." Griggs moved further into the street, his fingers only inches from his large revolver.

Adam heard the door to the pastor's office opening and felt cold going up his spine as he realized the probable results if he got into a shooting with this man. "This is stupid," Adam said, trying again. "I didn't do anything to you."

"It was that bitch, but it don't matter. It's you I see in front of me—for now."

This man was a threat to Martha. Adam took in a calming breath, letting go of anger and any possible fear that he would fail. He no longer cared who was watching, what the consequences would be, or the attitude the good folks of this town had toward him. This man had to die. He moved a little further into the street to avoid stray bullets striking his friends or the church.

"I'm going to enjoy this," Griggs said but not yet reaching for his gun. The eager expression on his face said it'd not be long.

"You just good at talking, Griggs?"

The thin man's grin was an ugly travesty. "If I'd of got you into the woods, you wouldn't of been so high and mighty. I had some interesting plans for you. Pity that they never come to pass, but I can level you here just as well."

Adam wasn't a gunman. Although he had killed, it had never been in a fight of the sort Griggs clearly was demanding. He tightened his lips and watched Grigg's eyes, waiting for the flicker that would tell him he needed to reach for his own revolver. When the moment came, the reaction was so fast that he later couldn't remember getting his gun out. He remembered aiming it and pulling the trigger. He felt a bullet whiz past his head, watched as Griggs staggered back but didn't drop his gun. The man got off another shot, but this time at the sky before he half twisted around, took a step and crumpled to the ground.

Sick with reaction, Adam walked slowly forward, kicking the gun from the fallen man's open hand before he knelt and turned him. There was nothing more to worry about from Griggs if that was his real name. He tried to think through what had happened. Had Simon sent him? He doubted that. He put his gun back in its holster and rose, wondering what the consequences of this one stupid moment would be. Whatever they were, he'd had no choice.

The answer came quickly. Pastor Jefferson followed Matt and St. Louis. They stood, staring down at the dead man. Jefferson spoke first. "Are you all right?"

Adam sucked in a breath trying to steady himself before he spoke. "I didn't want to do this."

St. Louis put his hand on Adam's shoulder. "He didn't hit ya did he?"

"No." He shook his head. "Somebody call the sheriff."

"We're witnesses, of course," said the pastor. "You had no choice. What did that man have against you?"

"He blamed me for something he did, something that went wrong for him. I guess this was how he figured to make it right." He felt sick at the senselessness of it all. It had happened so quickly.

St. Louis looked at him and then back to the man. "He the one that day?"

"Yes."

Matt stared from one to the other. "What is going on here?"

"We'll explain it to ya later. Here come some folks look to be expecting answers for this."

Five men stalked up, looked down at the body in the street and then up at Adam.

"Don't I recognize you?" one of the men asked, removing his hat and scratching his head absently. "Aren't you Adam Stone?"

Adam recognized him as one of the volunteers who had ridden part way in the so-called posse. "Yes, it's me, Sims."

Sims gestured to the other men. "This man is the one that brought back our bank's money. Without him. we'd of never seen none of it. Thanks to our worthless, one-time sheriff."

"Without Crane, I wouldn't have gone," Adam reminded him.

"So that's why the name sounded familiar to me," Pastor Jefferson said. "I just couldn't quite place where I'd heard it before."

Adam sighed, wondering how this was going to affect his wedding. He'd had no choice. A man like Griggs made too dangerous an enemy to leave alive. He might have taken it into his head to go after Martha. Bushwhacking would not have been out of character for a man with no character.

"Where is Sheriff Crane?" Adam asked.

"The cur quit," a fat man in a stiff brown suit growled. "He up and left us flat, heading for California, he said."

"Then how do we settle this so I can go home?" asked Adam.

"We could get the new deputy," Sims suggested, "except who knows where he's at. That man is always ailing with some sickness or another."

A small man, balding moved forward. "I don't think that will be necessary." He reached out his hand. "I'd like the shake the hand of the man who brought back our savings. I'm circuit court judge here. Mason Williams, and I say this is a clear case of self-defense. What do you men say?"

They all nodded agreement. "You can go on home anytime with the grateful thanks of the town," Williams said. "We'll arrange for the burying of this miscreant."

Adam felt relieved. He was beginning to shake as a reaction to the killing. He was eager to get out of Oregon City as quickly as possible.

"Before you go though." It was the fat man again. "We're needing a sheriff here. We'd like you to think about taking the job, Mr. Stone."

"No," Adam said quickly, knowing how little Martha would like living in town. She loved her homestead too much ever to consider moving to where he could take a job of a sheriff. Added to that, she would likely see it as more of his chasing after adventure.

"You won't even think about it?" Judge Williams asked.

"Sorry, can't do it."

The big man sighed. "It's hard finding somebody who can do the job and be trusted. Your record is excellent. Tom Crane advised us to try and talk you into it before he left."

"Thank you for asking, but it won't work."

"Just think about it. The town could give you a offer a good salary with more later."

"Find another man." Adam went over to the hitching rail, and untying his reins, he stepped up into the saddle.

"You'd make a great sheriff," the fat man lamented with a sigh as the townsmen started to relate Grigg's sordid local history. Adam had no interest in listening.

"You are a man used to riding a whirlwind," the pastor said to Adam as the others talked all at once. "I think you want to get off that."

"I suppose that's been so," Adam said. "Sometimes not so easy to do."

"God has a way of working things out."

"Some so believe."

The reverend smiled. "I will see you Saturday at the appointed time. Ride carefully, Adam Stone, Whirlwinds can draw a man into places from which they can't retreat."

Adam knew that truth better than the reverend. He nodded. "Thank you." He nudged his gelding in the side and rode out of town at a gallop. St. Louis and Matt followed in his dust.

When they caught up with him, the three rode in silence for a mile.

"Those folks sure did want you for their sheriff," St. Louis said finally.

"Because I killed a man?" Adam sighed. "It's hard to figure people."

"The man ya killed was a bully in the town and suspected of worse. The folks were scared of him, but none of them could stand up to him."

"Until I come along and conveniently rid the town of their vermin," Adam retorted gloomily.

"Sometimes it just works out that way," Matt drawled.

"Hell, it seems to be working out that way for me too often." Adam frowned, staring off into the distance, not wanting to look into the eyes of his friends.

"It makes sense the town'd want you," Matt drawled. "They know you were with the military; the federals trusted you. You know about guns. Pretty much what they need for a sheriff."

"It seems like it's about all I'm good for."

"That's not true," St. Louis denied. "Ya got a lot of things ya can do besides kill."

"Name one," demanded Adam with a short laugh.

"If you are goin' to get caught up in feelin' sorry for yourself," Matt said, "maybe we can trade off. I can do a pretty good number on that myself."

Adam shook his head, still feeling the black aftermath of having killed, even when it was a man like Griggs. "I just don't know how it's all going to work out with Martha if things like this keep happening," he said, finally sharing his real fear, the fear that he would fail her in some way, or cause her danger because of the way he had lived.

"She understood the problems ya'd have better than ya did yoreself," St. Louis said, "and she's been willin' to put up with ya."

"Nobody can figure out why though," said Matt with a grin.

"Least of all me," Adam admitted with his first smile.

St. Louis reached over and hit him on the shoulder, "What was that for?" Adam growled.

"To remind ya got friends, and next time don't forget it."

"I knew that."

"That's right. Ya got someone to stand by ya with us," St. Louis said.

"Speaking of that," Adam asked, "how about if you stand up with me. Since Matt's going to have to give the bride away."

"I'd be tickled." He shook his head laughing. "I can't believe I'm finally gettin' ya married. Thought for awhile there it'd never happen."

"I want to be the one to tell Martha about this," Adam said breaking another long silence.

"What do ya take us for?" snorted St. Louis in disgust.

"Yeah, do ya think we'd burst in the door and start yelling' to her that there'd been a shootin'?" asked Matt with mock outrage on his face.

"To tell you the truth. Yes."

"That's what I thought," Matt said, shaking his head at the wrongful abuse. "Race you to see who tells her first, St. Louis," he yelled as he kicked his horse into a gallop, followed rapidly by the two others.

By the time they came pounding up to Matt's front door, Adam was leading by solid lengths. He slid Joe to a halt almost at the step, as Martha came out, hands on hips. "There's a baby in this house, boys!" she complained

He was up the step in a bound and had scooped her up into his arms before she could turn around. Whirling her, he said, "Saturday. He'll be here at noon. Are you ready?"

"No, and I won't be until Saturday," she retorted, and then, ignoring the smiling faces, grabbed his ears and pulling his head to hers kissing him soundly on the lips.

He stalked down the steps with her in his arms as the others walked inside, pretending to have seen nothing unusual.

"Put me down, Adam. Where are we going?"

"Just up the hill." He grinned as he carried her to the spot where she'd told him she'd never be able to marry him. "All right now," he ordered as he put her on her feet. "I want to hear you say it again. Humor me."

"Yes, I'll put a ball and chain on you come Saturday."

He thought then of the shooting in Oregon City. "Seeing you always wipes everything else out of my mind. I have something to tell you."

"The minister didn't want to marry us?" she guessed with a troubled look.

"No, he's happy to marry us." Adam looked away. He didn't want to watch her reaction.

"Then?"

He had no way to soften it and so he told her straight out what had happened.

"Fight? What do you mean fight?"

"He had a gun. He wanted to kill me. You would have been next and not just to kill."

"But guns? On the street?" She was trying to get her mind around the concept. "Like a duel?" She knew men carried guns, that Adam often wore one. Yes, sometimes they killed each other, but couldn't seem to imagine it now as Adam was talking so calmly of the event.

"I swear to you, Martha, I tried to talk him out of it until I realized he wouldn't let go if of it. If not then, another time."

She grew pale. "He shot at you?"

"He missed, and I didn't. I killed him. I probably could have winged him but it never would have stopped him. I deliberately killed him."

She felt sick. "And it could have been you killed instead."

Adam shrugged, unable to find an answer that would satisfy

her. It could have gone that way. Griggs was a man used to the gun. It could have gone the other way.

He stood silently. She had to find her way through this by herself. His fear was that it would change how she felt; cause her to turn away from him again. In some ways he wouldn't blame her. It wasn't a side he admired either. Then he damned himself for taking her up to the place she had once turned him down. It could all happen again.

She walked to the little stream and stared at the trickle of water left in it. "I couldn't stand to lose you, Adam," she said finally. "It scares me to think I might have, and I wouldn't have even known you were in danger." She turned and reached for him, wrapping her arms around his waist. He realized then that she'd never even considered leaving him over this.

"I'm sorry. I never meant it to happen," he whispered against her silky black hair, wishing he could pull out the pins, let it fall down across her shoulders and knowing that for now he had to restrain himself. "Just one of those things, him seeing me like that. In another week, maybe he wouldn't have even remembered it had happened, but there and then, well it was too fresh."

"You don't think that George Simon might have been behind it, do you?" she asked, her voice growing cold with her fear.

He shook his head. "They're not the same sort. Simon will only want to forget it ever happened. Griggs dwelt on it. Simon probably will never step across the law again. Griggs walked with violence every day. It was his nature."

"You scare me," she whispered against his chest.

"Me?"

"You know about things I never will. That I can't even imagine. And you are a dangerous man too."

"I have just learned to do what I have had to," he said, his lips against her hair.

"Because of that, you are dangerous. And because I care about you so much, more than I knew was possible, you make me aware how vulnerable I am, how vulnerable that love is. Anything could take it from me. You don't live your life like a normal man. You're always getting involved in something dangerous. I don't blame you for it. It's your nature, but it's frightening to me."

It was no more than he'd thought himself, but he hated hearing the words from her. "Does that mean you are having second thoughts about marrying me?" he asked because he had to.

"No, it's too late for backing out." She smiled up at him. "I love you. I can't turn back time even if I wanted. Besides, it's over, isn't it? I mean Griggs is dead, nothing else is out there waiting for us."

He wished he could assure her of that, but he felt something was out there. He could not see it. He could only feel it. He suppressed the thought. He wanted this woman. He would be the man she needed. He had to be. He lifted her chin so that he could kiss her, "In six days, you'll be my wife. That can't happen too soon."

CHAPTER 26

For Martha the days before her wedding were filled with activity. First, she had the dress to make, and she wanted it to be special for Adam. It might not be her first wedding, but it was his.

She took a length of gray silk and cut it into a bodice hugging style with a softly flared skirt. The neckline was scooped out softly. She spent hours working on the embroidery of little white flowers around its edge, decorated with seed pearls. When she had nearly finished her creation, she felt certain with her black hair and light skin, she would not disappoint the groom.

Constantly having to push Heaven away from the long embroidery threads, she didn't hear Eunice until she had knocked on the door.

"I uh... You're working on a dress," Eunice said as she settled into a rocker.

"For my wedding," Martha said, trying to be hard hearted and failing. "Would you like some coffee. I just made a pot."

"I'd like that a lot, Martha. Uh." She stopped and then blurted out, "I am so sorry about George and me trying to discourage your romance with Mr. Stone. Please forgive me?"

"Did you know what George was planning?"

"I didn't, didn't hear it from George ever, but Horace came back from town with gossip. Pieces of it anyway. It tied to George because Horace said he'd once hired that man. I am so sorry. I had no idea George meant harm by Mr. Stone."

Martha handed her a cup of coffee. "Do you think he put Mr. Griggs up to attacking Adam in Oregon City?"

She shook her head. "George went back to Salem. He seemed humiliated and said he wanted nothing more to do with you. I do believe him."

"I am glad to hear that, Eunice. We're neighbors. I would hate to think there were going to be hard feelings on either of our sides."

"I'm just so sorry for it all. Even when George told me that he no longer wanted you for a wife, it never occurred to me he had gone as far as apparently he had. Is Mr. Stone going to file charges against him?" Martha knotted a silk thread to finish embroidering the last flower. "Because he's my brother. I feel guilty."

"You are not responsible for your brother, Eunice, and Adam has said nothing about filing any charges. I doubt it even occurred to him to do so."

Tears came to Eunice's eyes. "I'm just so sorry. I wasn't a very good neighbor or friend."

"Well, it is past now." Martha shuddered as she thought about the shooting in Oregon City and of how differently the finish might have been. George had brought that about. Griggs would have never challenged Adam if George had not started it all.

"I just feel awful, but there is nothing I can do now," Eunice sniffled.

Martha sighed and smiled. She couldn't blame Eunice. "Well, you could come to our wedding," Martha said.

"Oh, I'd love to, and I'll help too. I'll do anything, Martha."

Martha shook her head, pushing the kitten away again from

the dangling thread. "All right, you do understand not George. I don't ever want to see him again, and if Adam saw him at the wedding, I doubt I could hold him back."

Eunice smiled through her tears. "I understand completely. May I bake the wedding cake? I do have a very good recipe."

Martha nodded her head and smiled. Eunice was a good soul. "No one could make a better one, Eunice. Thank you."

The food for the wedding supper became Martha's priority as soon as she finished the dress. Although Amy had wanted to help, Martha had insisted that she had enough to do with caring for her baby and keeping Matt fed. This was something she was very capable of doing for herself, Adam, and their friends.

First, she shaped yeast breads into different shaped rolls. From her garden she dug enough sweet potatoes to make a candied sweet potato dish. Fresh heads of cabbage and grated carrots provided coleslaw. Before the first freeze, it was such a lush time of the year that it seemed there were ingredients for special dishes everywhere.

For the meat, St. Louis had butchered a steer and brought her a huge roast, which was being marinated and would be roasted the day of the wedding. St. Louis had carried handwritten invitations from her to the closest neighbors and those who had worked for her in the past. She didn't expect many to come. Although she had sent word immediately to Loraine and Belle, she doubted they would receive it in time or be able to come even if they did. She thought that by the time the actual wedding came, she'd be so tired, she wouldn't want a honeymoon, she'd want only to go to bed and sleep a week.

Only on Friday when she saw Loraine, Belle, Jacob, Agatha Collins, and even Clem Johnson arriving in a rented buckboard did she realize how much she had wanted all of her family to be with her. Greeting them with tears and hugs, they all broke down and had a good cry before they began laughing and helping with the remaining preparations.

Clem, who had come out on the wagon train with them, said, "Never figured I'd see Adam gettin' hitched. No way I'd stay away."

"St. Louis will be happy to see you," Martha said smiling broadly.

Belle set herself to finding flowers. "I did this once before," she said with a little laugh, "but the groom got kidnapped. I certainly hope it will go better this time."

Martha might have laughed with everyone else except for her own recent experience with that terror. She remembered only too vividly how she had felt behind the bedroom door when she had first heard Adam being threatened by a gun, and when she had realized with a sinking feeling of horror that he was going to be taken away unless she did something. She had never pointed a gun at a living person, but she had known that day she would shoot to kill if required.

Late at night, Clem at St. Louis', the Collins in bed in her room, she, Belle and Loraine cuddled in the bed in the loft. It would be the last time it'd be just them, and Martha savored it even as she felt excited at the knowledge that in a day she would be Adam Stone's wife.

Martha's wedding day dawned with the promise of a beautiful Indian summer. The leaves were just hinting at a change of color, the sky a turquoise blue. She stood in front of a mirror, trying to decide how to dress her hair. Her first thought was a bun on top of her head and then she knew how Adam would want to see it.

From her own flower bed and the woods, Belle had found a surprising variety of flowers. Many were in vases on the table and mantle, but Martha retrieved two blossoms of the white Rose of Sharon.

Smiling, she slipped the gray, silk dress over her petticoats and chemise, allowing it to fall down over her hips. She brushed out her hair and for once let it fall down her back. With combs, she pulled the sides up, securing a flower with each comb. This was how he would want to see her, how he seemed always to prefer it, flowing down her back, and if it wasn't proper for a woman of her age, well, nothing else she was doing was probably proper either.

Dressed, Martha kept to her room, not wanting Adam to see her before the actual ceremony and knowing she was being foolish in the old superstition. She heard others arriving, knew there would be some guests at least. Then she heard the one voice she had been listening for. Adam was there waiting for her.

"It's time," Matt said as he came to her door and offered her his arm. Feeling as though she needed to gasp for air, Martha looked around the familiar room one last time and then taking Matt's arm, walked out into the sunlight.

Martha almost seemed to glide to Adam, her dress swishing silkily, clinging and yet not clinging at the same time to her gentle curves. Something about the silver fabric made her skin glow with translucence. Her hair falling down her back in a flow of black silk only served to complete the perfect picture.

I can't be shaking, but he knew he was. He'd waited so long for this, dreamt of it at a thousand campfires and never believed it would have a reality in his lifetime, and yet now the dream was walking toward him, dark eyes looking only at him.

"I take it this is the bride," the pastor said with an appreciative grin. "I am pleased to bear witness to this union." Quickly the words were said, the vows given in what seemed only moments, the pastor was pronouncing them man and wife. "You may kiss the bride."

Adam stood as though of stone for a moment, looking down at her; then he smiled and bent, lightly claiming her lips in a proper kiss, prepared to let her go with that. Before he could straighten, her fingers reached up, tangling in his hair, pulling him against her in the kiss he'd dreamed of, a public avowal of her passion for him in a way that was anything but proper.

He heard voices then, congratulating, laughing, talking. Someone was patting him on the back, but all he could think was how a dream had become real. Knowing he was smiling foolishly and unable to stop himself, he let people congratulate him, tried to say things that made sense and knew that beneath it all, he was stunned.

She tucked her hand into the crook of his arm, and as they talked to the various neighbors, relatives and friends, he was aware of a difference. She was his wife; they were together, a pair, acknowledged mates, and she would bear his name. He shook his head, still unable to believe it was real.

"Where the two of ya goin'?" Matt asked after he had kissed the bride and hugged Adam.

Adam felt so befuddled, he nearly asked for what. He and Martha had never discussed a wedding trip. He realized suddenly he should have. He knew where he wanted to go but supposed she would prefer Portland.

"Oh definitely, the upper Clackamas," Martha said. She smiled, her dark eyes pools he could sink into and never come up for air.

"You ready for it again?" he asked, grinning.

"If you promise to not fall off your horse," she teased.

"I didn't fall off. I jumped," he explained patiently. "There's a difference."

"What would you have broken-- if you'd fallen off?" she asked, grinning up at him as Matt laughed.

Amy came up to them, putting her arm around her mother, "We think you have to toss the bouquet now."

Smiling she looked at the three single ladies before her, Fanny, Loraine and Belle. She wanted it to go to Loraine, but she had to be fair and so she turned her back, threw it, and of course, Fanny caught it out of the air. For a heavy-set girl she moved with remarkable agility.

Belle was totally disgusted. "The last wedding the bride didn't even throw the bouquet, and this one, the wrong person catches it," she lamented to Adam.

"Bouquets don't mean much though, except maybe to ladies who don't have much hope of marrying any other way," Adam whispered to her.

"You don't think it really works then," she murmured back, looking over at how Fanny was hugging it to herself.

"Not unless you believe in it," Adam said with a grin, "and then you might as well just believe in yourself, because it's just as potent a magic.

Pastor Jefferson came up to them, "Well, I think I must be leaving. Thank you for allowing me to perform the service. It was a true honor. You have a beautiful bride, Mr. Stone."

"Thank you."

"I was asked to speak to you again, to try and convince you to reconsider the offer of the town," he said clearly reluctant to bring up the subject on such a happy day.

"I told them the answer," Adam said, uncomfortably aware that Martha was standing right behind him listening to the conversation.

"What offer?" she asked, putting her hand onto Adam's arm.

Pastor Jefferson looked from her to Adam. "I guess I shouldn't have brought this up at your wedding," he apologized.

Adam shrugged. "It doesn't matter." He looked down at Martha and said, "The town council of Oregon City offered me the job of their sheriff."

"You didn't tell me about that."

"There was no point. I said no. It wouldn't fit into what we want to do. I couldn't live up here and take care of the town. It's too far away."

"Oh." Her voice was carefully neutral before she said she had to see to the food. The instant she had gone, Eunice Lance walked up to him. "I hope that Martha conveyed to you my regrets about what happened with my brother. It just got out of hand."

Adam's eyes narrowed. "That's one way of describing it."

"I don't know all of what George tried to do, but I am sure he regrets it."

Remembering Martha's gun pointed at George, her threatening words, Adam smiled. "I imagine he does, but what your brother did was dangerous, Mrs. Lance, and could have gotten him killed. It did get another man killed."

She paled. "He was under extreme pressure, just foolish of him, but men do such things," she defended nervously.

"When a man pulls a gun on another, it most often ends in one of them dying. He was lucky." She paled visibly. "Does your brother know his partner in crime is dead?"

"I don't like the way you phrased that."

He smiled. Despite himself, he couldn't dislike this woman. She did seem to mean well, as best she could. It was good that she loved her brother.

"And I don't know what he knows," she went on, "because I haven't talked to him since he went home to Salem."

"You might let him know."

"You won't seek revenge?" He realized this was likely her entire reason for talking to him.

"What's done is done as far as I'm concerned, but there better not be a repeat."

"There wouldn't. George is very uninterested in Martha now."

Adam's humorous grin acknowledged that he believed that to be true. What Martha had done would dampen any would-be suitor's ardor.

Nightfall found the newly married couple high in the mountains, their tent pitched and the darkness settled in all around them. "This is going to be much nicer than our last trip up here," he said, drawing her into his arms.

"You didn't sleep alone every night."

"No, but the exception I was in too much pain to appreciate the situation fully."

"Perhaps we could re-enact it," she suggested.

"You want me to jump off my horse again?" he teased

"Well, we could start after that. Like when I undressed you."

"We could or you could let me tend to you this time." He saw her eyes go soft, and she smiled as she let him lead her to the tent. He had earlier lain down fir boughs and made their quilts into a bed. He drew her down onto it. She was wearing a shirt and her pants, but he began with her boots, then socks. When her feet were bared, he massaged them, erotically and slowly, taking his time, knowing they had all night. They had the rest of their lives.

The waxing moon was just rising, flooding the tent with subdued light. When she tried to reach for him, he stopped her. "Let me play for awhile." And so she lay back and allowed him to unbutton her shirt. He took his time with each button making sure his fingers touched skin all the way down until he pulled the shirt from her pants. He let his fingers just brush the tops of her breasts as he pushed the shirt from them. The chemise top was next to go until her breasts were bared completely, the moonlight outlining them with an unearthly glow. He bent then and took first one, then the other into his mouth, sucking, teasing them with his tongue and hands until the nipples were tight little nubbins, and she was twisting and moaning. He let his hands slide down her chest to her belly, under the pants, teasing her by barely touching where he knew she most wanted.

"Adam?" she begged.

"Oh no. You made me wait a long time for this. Now it's your turn to wait." He kissed her, his tongue teasing hers, then unbuttoned the pants, again so slowly, his fingers touching her skin as much as he could as she twisted under his touch. He pulled the pants down but left the thin pantalets for awhile longer.

"Please," she begged again, but he was in no mood to hurry this. He stroked her through the thin cotton, felt her warmth and heat. She wanted him but not as much as she would.

His own body was so hard with arousal that he could barely stand it, but he wanted them both out of their minds with what they were feeling. That would take time. Finally he pulled off her last covering, leaving her naked. He stopped touching her for a moment. He let his gaze roam over her from head to foot, her face, breasts, belly, pubic hair, thighs, down to her toes and back. He bent then and stroked with his tongue what he had looked at, slowly, working his way over her skin, inch by inch, touching all the places that most had her wriggling.

His proud Martha was now a woman in passionate need. She was where he most wanted—full of desire for him. Her hair was a black cloud around her body, her skin glistened with perspiration. She was soft with wanting him. He clenched his jaw against his own desire. He wanted to be buried within her, but he wanted more to have this night be one they would neither forget.

He stopped touching her while he stripped off his own clothing as she watched. "You are so beautiful, she whispered when he finally was naked and knelt above her, his erection huge and so ready for her.

She would have pulled him to her, but he stopped her again and began slowly touching her body all the places he had before, bringing her back to a fever pitch. She was his to play with, to toy with, her moans of pleasure were making it all but impossible to keep putting off the moment he would enter her.

He was so aroused that his own sensations were beginning to warn him that to wait longer would have him going off before he finished the game. He forced his mind to control his body as it had so many times before in less pleasurable situations.

"Spread your legs," he whispered. When she had obeyed, he

bent and used his tongue and mouth to give her just a little more pleasure before he positioned himself to finally do what they both wanted. He lowered himself over her, felt her hands on his shaft as she guided him into her heat. She was so wet and ready, throbbing with warmth. The sensations forced him stop again while he got back control.

He kissed her as he plunged his tongue into her mouth. When he began to move, she was with him, her hands stroking his body, cupping his buttocks. She brought her legs up around him, locking her ankles at his back. They again found their rhythm as his speed increased, the pressure building coming closer and closer to culmination.

When he heard her cries of release, felt the inner contraction of her muscles in her climax, he let himself go and it nearly exploded as his orgasm seemed to fill his entire body. When he finally came back to reality, he was lying beside her, still within.

"That first night, when you came back, seeing you naked, the firelight glowing off your muscles, your body so beautiful, so all male," she whispered, kissing his sweat slicked neck. "I wanted you then, so bad I thought I'd die." She laughed. "Tonight I know how."

Riding their horses down into the hot springs fork of the river, was like coming home. They pitched their tent where they had before, walking to the steaming springs, their arms around each other.

"I'm going to enjoy this a lot more today." He kissed the top of her shiny hair. "Last time I couldn't stop thinking about you here, lying in this water, and I wasn't there."

"You mean, you're not going fishing while I use the hot water?" she teased, her tone sounding shocked.

"I plan on giving you a bath in them myself," he promised, kissing her neck and then her shoulder as he pulled her shirt wider.

"That sounds positively decadent, Mr. Stone," she protested, her own lips finding the indent at the base of his neck.

"As it should, Mrs. Stone."

"Well, don't make promises you can't keep," she said, ducking away from him.

"Who says I can't keep this one?" he asked, stalking after her.

"I don't know. I..." She sighed in surrender as she felt his fingers at the buttons of her blouse, the soft autumn air bathing her bare skin as he stripped her. "But Adam, what if someone comes?" she asked as she returned the favor by stripping off his clothing.

"I'll kill them," he promised, his lips sealing hers.

Later as they dressed, he told her the salmon might be in the river and asked her to go fishing with him. "I'll watch, but I've never fished," she said.

"Then it's time you learned."

"But I don't know if I want to learn. Fish are smelly and slimy and..."

He had her hand and was dragging her up the river with him. "Fish are beautiful, silvery, slick and you will find you enjoy it once you learn how."

"But Adam," she protested, pulling back.

"Nope, I take this as a challenge. Every lady should be able to cast out and bring in a salmon at least once in her life."

Soon she was standing beside him on the bank of the river, trying to see into the water where he pointed. "See it. See that silver. Have you ever seen anything prettier?" he asked, excitement in his voice.

"Well uh..."

He quickly adjusted his pole, tying a large fly to the hook. "I've had a fair amount of luck with this lovely." He smiled up at her as he worked.

"I can imagine," she said, looking at it and wondering why any fish in its right mind would think it looked edible.

Nothing would do for it but that she had to take the pole in her hands. He positioned each hand and then taking hold of it himself, he drew the pole back and threw it out, letting the line out between his fingers. "Watch how I do it," he said, not letting go of her or the pole. Cast after cast they made together. "Now do it by yourself," he said finally.

Sighing because she knew she was going to have to do this, and she was still not convinced she wanted to, she brought her shoulders up, using the full upper strength of her body as she flicked the pole and line, trying to make the outfit do what she'd felt happened each time with him.

Somehow though instead of sliding smoothly forward, she couldn't make the pole go beyond her head.

"You're hung up," he said, his voice still patient.

"What does that mean?"

"It means your hook is in the tree behind us not the water in front of us."

"Oh."

"I can't believe you've never fished before," he commented as he climbed the tree and somehow working the hook and his precious fly free.

"It's true," she admitted, hoping he wouldn't fall or break a limb-- mostly not his-- before he got back to the ground.

"All right," he said as he again stood beside her. "Try again."

"Are you sure? Maybe this just isn't my thing."

"It's everybody's thing," he said, still smiling, but a little thinly.

"I just seem to be doing it all wrong."

"Let's just try casting differently. I was trying to get you to put your line way out there. Instead, try a lateral cast, just skimming out across the water. Don't forget to let go of the line as it sails past your shoulder."

"All right," she muttered, hoping she would remember exactly the right moment to release her thumb on the reel. She whipped the long pole back and then using both arms, tried to do as he had instructed. Only once again the line was hung up on something.

"Hold it," he yelled.

"I did it again. Didn't I?"

"No," he grunted, "not this time. This time you hooked something."

"I did, but what? I didn't see the line go into the water." She peered forward as though to see if it had somehow magically gotten into the water.

"That's because," he muttered, "what you hooked was me."

She turned slowly to look and saw that the hook was imbedded through his thin cotton shirt and into the back of his arm. "Oh no," she cried, dropping the pole. "How do we get it out?"

A muscle began to jerk in his jaw. "We cut it out."

"You can't be serious."

"I am serious and since I can't reach it. You're going to have to do it."

"Adam," she wailed, "I don't want to do this. It will hurt you."

"Not as much as pulling it out would," he grimaced, still trying to smile.

"All right." She reached down and took the knife from his belt. "What do I do?"

"Just a little ways, just enough to edge the barb out. Take it easy. Ouch!"

Victoriously, she held the freed hook. "I have it."

"I'm just glad I wasn't using a baited hook," he muttered.

"What?"

"Nothing. All right, now, ready to try again."

"You can't want me to try again," she said her mouth dropping open.

"I am a patient man, my love. You haven't hooked a fish yet. Just a tree and me."

"But, I don't care if I hook a fish. Can't you be the fisherman in the family, and I'll just be the watcher and cooker of fish."

"Maybe, after you've caught one. Now," he ordered, "cast like I showed you, and I'll stand out of your way—well out of it."

This time she was successful in getting the hook into the water, and she stood, impatiently waiting. "How long does this usually take?" she asked, glancing back at him.

"Sometimes all day. Sometimes just a few minutes. Keep your eyes on the tip of the pole. Make your hands sensitive to what it's telling you."

"How will I know?" she started to ask and realized the pole was beginning to jerk. "Adam," she shrieked, "I think, maybe there's something on it."

"Lift the tip, hold onto the line," he ordered as he started toward her.

She turned back again to smile and suddenly the pole was jerked from her hands by a violent tug. "Adam!"

He took one look into the river at his precious pole being propelled away from him before he jumped, boots and all.

"Adam!" she yelled as she watched his body hit the surface of the river, his hands already reaching out for his pole. "What are you doing?"

"What does it look like I'm doing?" he bellowed. His hands closed over the pole. "And Martha."

"Yes?"

"You can forget the rest of the fishing lesson for today."

He found his footing and began to play the thrashing fish. Pulling the line, the fish rolled into the swifter water. Releasing the tension, he carefully moved downstream to avoid the fish taking all of his line. Good hand-woven, oiled line was hard to find, and he wasn't going to let a little error in judgment cost him the line he had bartered from an old riverboat captain in San Francisco.

He knew with time he could work the flashy beast into the still waters at the lower end of the hole, lift its head with tip of the pole and slip his fingers into the gills and out the mouth and the prize would be his.

"Are you mad at me?" she asked anxiously, watching as dripping wet, he straightened, his whole body concentrating on maintaining his balance on the rocky bottom and holding onto the flopping fish.

"No. This is the largest trout I've seen."

"I thought you said it was a salmon? It is pretty with that red stripe down its side. When can we eat it?" she asked, almost unable to contain her excitement at the whole event, which had been miraculously resurrected even though it had seemed doomed from the beginning.

"It would probably taste better if we cleaned it and cooked it first," he said dryly as he brought it to shore. "Maybe I'll smoke part of it and take it back with us, St. Louis'd love that. He's as bad as a bear for going after smoked salmon."

"There you said it again. Is it a salmon or a trout?"

"It's a big trout that came back from the ocean with the early salmon run."

Wading ashore, dripping water, he laid the fish in the grass, drew out his knife and slit its full belly from vent to chin. In one shift motion, Adam's thumb and fore-fingers lifted out the gills and entrails.

"I didn't realize they did that."

"Not just men go on adventures," he said with a smile.

CHAPTER 27

Later they leaned back against a fallen tree, watching as the fish fillets cooked, secured between green maple branches, over the open campfire. Adam's boots were hung on nearby branches, not too near the fire, but close enough to begin drying. His shirt dangled from yet another branch.

"I still feel guilty." She gestured toward his bare feet.

"It wasn't your fault. Could've happened to anybody."

"I don't know why I dropped the pole."

"Buck fever. It happens easily the first time. The feel of a big fish on your line is something nobody can prepare you for."

"You've been very understanding."

He grinned at her. "I'm in a mellow mood. Of course, if I'd lost that pole and line, I might not have been so understanding."

"And I wouldn't blame you."

He looked up at the alder branches overhead, their leaves just beginning to turn yellow and sighed. "This is paradise, or as close as we'll ever come on this earth."

"It is beautiful up here. The air is as clear as I remembered it."

"It kind of reminds me of a poem my mother used to read to me when I was a child. I memorized part of it."

"You memorized poetry," she repeated, amazement in her voice.

He shook his head ruefully. "Why is it nobody ever figures I've got anything to me but a gun."

"Well tell me the poem."

"It's by Lord Byron. I don't remember what it was out of, but here it is. 'There is a pleasure in the pathless woods. There is a rapture on the lonely shore, There is society where none intrudes. By the deep sea, and music in its roar: I love not Man the less, but Nature more.'"

"That is lovely," she said, awe in her voice. "I never expected to hear poetry from your lips."

"Well, you won't-- at least not that I wrote," he said, pulling her against him.

"You do quite well with words of love."

"Just with words?" he asked, his lips now so close that she could feel his breath in her mouth.

"Well... and a few other things," she whispered, tangling her fingers in his thick black hair.

His lips lightly touched hers, drew away and then came back as she pulled him tight against her, her lips seeking and demanding his response, a response he was only too eager to give her. Adam parted her mouth with his tongue; his hand cupped one rounded breast as he leaned her back against the ground.

The noise from the woods penetrated his love-fogged brain as he pushed up and thrust Martha behind him in one swift movement.

"What is it?" she gasped.

"I don't know." He reached for his revolver as he tried to peer into the woods.

When he saw the three Indians coming toward him, smiles on their faces, he relaxed. "Men from the Molalla tribe." He put his pistol into Martha's hand. "I don't expect any trouble but you keep this," he said.

"Indians--"

"Don't worry, they're friendly. Probably up here gathering huckleberries and smelled our fish cooking. Just stay quiet and let me do the talking."

"As if I could," she muttered, watching as he strode barefoot and bare-chested toward them, his hand raised in a gesture of friendship. From what Martha could see, the men wore very little clothing except for what appeared to be a short apron or skirt tied around their waists.

Adam spoke to them, gestured at the fire and fish. She wished she understood something of what he was saying, but gestures seemed to carry most of the conversation.

After a few moments, he used his Bowie knife to cut off a hunk of the fish to hand to them, accepting a gift in return. The men all raised their hands again in what apparently was a sign of friendship, and then the Indians disappeared back into the woods from which they had come

"What was that all about?" she asked, still shaking a little in reaction to what she hadn't understood.

He smiled as he dropped down beside her. "Just a neighborly greeting." He handed her the buckskin sack and when she looked inside, she saw it was full of huckleberries. "This was a father and his two sons. The rest of their family are over the ridge. They wanted to be sure who we were."

"Did you know them?" she asked, eating a berry.

"No, but they spoke a little Chinook."

"Could you teach me something useful?" she asked, smiling as she watched him lean over the fire, testing the fish for doneness.

"How about *mika tikeh muckamuck?*"

"Which means?"

"Would you like something to eat?" He held out a bite of the fish, and she ate it from his fingers, nipping them lightly in the process.

331

"Was that nice?" he asked, taking a chunk of the fish for himself. "Isn't that called biting the hand that feeds you?"

"Mmmm," she agreed as he fed her another bite and this time she held his finger lightly in her mouth, sucking it, her gaze never leaving his.

"Maybe," he said, putting down the fish, "I'm not so hungry after all."

Later they lay together, watching the fire, contentedly enjoying the sounds of the night and the river beyond. "Adam," she whispered."

"Yeah?"

"Why didn't you tell me about the job in Oregon City?"

"There was no reason."

"Shouldn't I have heard about it?"

"I suppose so. I'm not used to this business of there being an us, when it comes to making decisions." He was silent a moment. "It didn't amount to much. They asked me. I said no."

"Why did you say no?"

"Because it wouldn't have been anything you would have wanted. We'd have had to live in town. I didn't think you'd like me wearing and using a gun all the time."

"It's like you said though. It's not just me or you any more. It's us. And this is a question of what you'd want as much as what I'd want."

He sighed, staring into the fire as he thought. "I don't know what I'd want. It'd be challenging to be a sheriff. Maybe I'd have liked it. Maybe not, but I can't see how it would work for you, Martha. You have your place, and you love it. It is beautiful up there, so quiet and peaceful. You've got your daughter and grand-daughter with you. I don't want a marriage where we live apart all the time. I couldn't see you being happy in a town."

"I don't know, maybe you're right," she whispered, putting her arms around his neck. "Do you resent me because you had to refuse the job?"

He turned her so that she could look into his blue eyes and see the truth of what he was saying. "Of course not. I'd never resent you for anything, lady. I am so besotted at having you for my wife that I'd pull the damned plow myself, if that's what it took."

"I hardly think that would be necessary. Although..." She felt of the muscles in his arms, admiring the hardness and size. "You could probably do it if you wanted." She followed her fingers with her lips, first kissing and then lightly stroking with her tongue.

"You know something," he whispered, slowly opening her shirt.

"Mmmm.

"You're insatiable."

"Is that bad?" she asked, moving to kiss his chest.

"No, no that's good, very good." He sighed as she moved down his chest with that clever tongue. "It's just a good thing..." He groaned and managed to somehow finish his expressing his thought, punctuated by more than a few sighs of appreciation, "...a good thing I didn't know it all those years ago, or I'd have totally gone crazy when I thought of you."

Martha awoke in the middle of the night, unsure what had disturbed her sleep until she heard Adam moan. He was restlessly twisting, as though fighting an imaginary enemy. His naked body was bathed in sweat.

"Adam," she said softly, fearing that if she awoke him too quickly he would be even more disturbed.

He seemed not to hear her. "No," he cried, his voice distorted in anger or pain, "not that... Don't! Dear Lord, no!"

"Adam," she said a little more loudly, touching his shoulder, amazed at the tension in his muscles. Whatever his nightmare was, it was not one easy to escape.

She shook him lightly. "You're having a bad dream," she whispered against his neck, trying to bring him to awareness.

He opened dazed looking eyes. What had he been seeing in that dream? "Sorry," he mumbled, running his fingers through his wet hair.

"What was it?" she asked. She shifted her position and took him into her arms.

"Isn't that supposed to be bad luck to tell a dream?"

"I don't believe in superstition. I think it's important to talk about it, figure out what happened and why. Sometimes dreams can tell us things about our days."

He ran his fingers through his hair. "Maybe seeing the Molallas triggered it. Just a dream about when I was with a patrol." He stopped, as though trying to see back into the images.

"Something that really happened?"

"A mix, I think. I don't know. I'm sorry I woke you."

"Do you have such nightmares often?"

He shook his head. "I haven't for awhile. It's always about trying to fix something, but I never can. I get tangled up in something that blocks me from helping and then just have to watch."

She stroked him, kissing his forehead. "We all have nightmares sometimes."

"I guess. You were there. You were blaming me, leaving me over it."

"I won't leave you," she promised. His skin was clammy with sweat drying on it.

"I hope it wasn't an omen." He tried to joke but she saw it was a real fear.

"It wasn't. You know what I think?" she asked.

"No." He tried to smile and achieved a cross between a real smile and a grimace.

"I think we could both do with the hot water down at the river."

"In the middle of the night? Is that proper?" he teased.

"Yes sir, in the middle of the night. The moon's high enough we can see to get there, and it will relax us both, help us go back to sleep." He sat up to reach for his pants. "You need those to walk down there?" she asked, smiling innocently. Her face was illuminated by the moonlight, her black hair a cloud around it, as she rose to stand above him, her body magnificently nude and glorying in being so with him.

He looked at her with a wry smile. "No, we don't need anything."

"Now, how do you feel?" she asked as they submerged themselves in the steaming water.

"Like I married a very wise woman as well as a passionate one."

"I guess I didn't warn you about that side of my personality."

"It does explain why Amos always seemed like such a contented man," Adam quipped as he reached for her. After a moment, he asked, "It doesn't explain though why you didn't have ten children."

Martha smiled, a little embarrassed now. "Well, actually, Amos wore something when we decided we didn't want more children."

"A condom?" Adam asked.

"Yes. You've heard about them too."

He grinned. "I told you I went to San Francisco. A man hears about everything there. So Amos knew about them?"

She shook her head. "Actually, it was my mother. She was a mid-wife and made it her business to learn about new ideas, especially for some of the girls that shouldn't have children quite so soon. There are herbs, of course, but none of them are always effective, and they are poisonous—which is why they sometimes work to end an unwanted pregnancy."

"So I have a very wise wife."

She sank deeper in the water, enjoying the heat permeating

her limbs. After a moment, he asked, "Are we likely to have been making a mistake in my not wearing anything so far?"

"Do you mind if it wasn't?"

"No, I wouldn't." He grinned at her. "I do have such a device, but I didn't have the brains to bring it with me, and before you can ask. I'll tell you. It's never been used."

She laughed. "That's good to hear. How do you know it's still all right? They do get old."

"I... uh got a new one before I left California the last time. There was a store where..."

Shaking her head, she laughed again, interrupting him, "I can't believe you. You certainly had this all planned out."

"No," he admitted ruefully, "if I had, I'd have used it. From the time I first saw you again, I forgot all about it, and everything else. You pushed my sanity out the window, lady, and I'm not sure when I'll get it back."

"Poor baby," she cooed, reaching out and massaging his neck muscles. "Life has been very difficult for you recently."

"No," he said, his tone suddenly very sober. "It's been very good for me *recently*. It was before that that it was difficult."

The next two days were filled with swimming, fishing and making love. Little by little Adam told Martha things about his childhood about his mother, which helped her to understand the man he was. She shared her own growing up, the way she'd eloped with Amos due to his family's disapproval. There had been no real wedding for her until with him. He no longer felt threatened by Amos, secure in the love Martha offered him, but he didn't mind hearing when something between them was a first for her also.

When it came time to leave the high country, he felt they had strengthened their connection and were more truly one. They were ready to head back to the world of problems and people. He would have to work out a place for himself on the homestead, find a way to earn his keep and support her. He didn't mind what

Amos had left her, but didn't want them living on that. He would work it out.

When they arrived at the cabin, Martha dismounted first, watching as Heaven jumped down from a windowsill and bounded up to greet her. "Did St. Louis take good care of you?" she asked, petting the ecstatically purring little cat.

Adam took the horses to the barn, feeling a strange sense of homecoming, something he hadn't remembered experiencing in years. Nothing had been home. There'd never been anyone waiting. When he looked back at the cabin and saw a whiff of smoke beginning to come from the chimney, he wondered how he'd lived so many years without this. The thing is he knew it would never have been this way with any woman but this one.

The cabin was as warm and cozy as he'd remembered, but there was a difference now. This was his home as well as hers. He looked around it, memorizing the furniture, its arrangement. He didn't realize what he'd been doing or why until he thought about how temporary everything had been in his life.

He stepped up behind Martha who was putting together flour and other ingredients on a counter, slipping his arms around her waist. "I love you," he whispered, his breath nudging her ear.

She smiled. "I love you too and am glad you are happy."

"I am. It's so damned good to be coming home, knowing I have a home to come to." She turned in his arms, holding her flour coated hands safely above his shoulders as she kissed him.

The next morning, Adam began working at the myriad of chores that always needed to be done around a farm. The main project was to cut wood for their winter. Several logs and saplings had already been downed. He could chop them up in quick order.

Speculatively, he looked up at one particularly tall tree, just beyond the edge of their woods. Martha had come out to watch him work. "I think I'll cut down that one tomorrow," he told her.

"We can split it later in the winter when it dries out and freezes."

"I'd rather you didn't."

"Why? It doesn't look that healthy to me."

"It's not that." How could she explain the terror in her heart when she thought about him cutting down that tree? "Amos was killed cutting down a big one, like that." She put her arms around him.

He put down his ax and put his arms around her. "I won't get killed, Martha. That won't happen again."

"Nobody can promise that." He realized she was crying.

"No, but we can't live in fear of it either."

"I know... I'm sorry. I was being silly."

"I understand, but I won't die on you." He would not let life do that to him. He'd finally gotten his dream, and he did not intend to die before he'd had the chance to drink of it fully.

"I'm sorry."

"It's all right. I'm glad you love me enough to care. Now let go of me, woman, so I can go back to work."

"How quickly the honeymoon is over," she lamented as she started back up the path. Suddenly she was swung up into the air and over his shoulder, the air almost knocked from her lungs. "Adam!" she shrieked as he started for the cabin.

"What?" he asked laughing.

"Put me down!"

"I will."

"I mean now!"

"Nope."

"Adam!"

He only laughed as he said, "You will beg me to forgive you for saying that about the romance being over. Before this afternoon is gone, you'll be begging for mercy."

She laughed too, as she watched the scenery bounce by at a

new angle. "We'll see who's begging for mercy," she muttered under her breath.

"What'd you say, my love?" he asked as he kicked open the door to the cabin, strode into the bedroom and threw her on the feather mattress.

"I said," she repeated, smiling up at him as she watched him begin to unbutton his shirt, "we'll see who begs for mercy."

"This sounds like a challenge," he told her, watching with avid eyes as she began taking off her dress.

Hours later, they still lay nestled together. She sighed with contentment as she said, "Well?"

"I wouldn't call that begging," he said, trying to control the laughter in his voice. "Maybe a little moaning."

"Begging," she whispered, against his ear, "it was begging, and you know it. Want me to prove it?"

"Lord lady, if you prove anything more to me today, I'll be a dead man, and we'll never get the extension on that corral."

Martha smiled and getting out of bed, she pulled on a robe and disappeared into the kitchen.

"What are you doing?" he asked, hating to give up the softness of the bed, the memories that now accompanied that softness.

"Just starting a fire so I can fix us a light supper."

He sighed, knowing he had to get up and still procrastinating. He looked up at the wood rafters above his head and thought then of the man who'd built this cabin. The man who'd slept in this bed with Martha. Up the Clackamas he'd conquered his jealousy of Amos and here in the bed, he felt he came to peace with the spirit of the man. If Amos knew what had happened, if he somehow could see his family, Adam felt he approved.

Smiling foolishly, he pulled on his pants and padded out to the main room where Martha was stirring something in a pan. He put his arms around her waist and kissed her neck.

"Are scrambled eggs enough?" she asked, arching her neck to allow him fuller access.

"Mmmmmmm." He pulled her robe apart to get at the swell of her shoulder.

"I don't even know what kinds of foods you like," Martha said as she moved away to slice bread for toast.

"Anything you fix, I'll eat."

"Anything?" she questioned with that dangerous glint in her eyes.

"Nearly. There are a few things I don't like but not many."

"Like for instance?"

"Well, I'm not over fond of artichokes, asparagus, broccoli."

She interrupted, "Those are all vegetables that are good for you."

"Maybe so, but you asked what I don't like."

"I suppose your true favorites are things like apple pie, chocolate cake."

He grinned. "I think you have the idea. Homemade ice cream's good too."

"Not very healthy though. Those are all desserts."

"I know. I do love dessert," he whispered suggestively, pulling her against him, liking the way her curves fit perfectly into his angles.

"And you say I'm insatiable," she said, rolling her eyes skyward.

"Maybe, we're both insatiable," he suggested, nibbling on a sensitive earlobe.

~

The next morning Adam split more logs for corral posts before he came in at Martha's call to lunch. "What do you like to do in the evenings?" she asked as they ate lunch, their eyes playing games, their legs brushing against one another's.

He raised his eyebrows. "As in?"

She blushed. "I mean usually-- or other than."

"I haven't had a lot of family evenings to compare. What would you like?"

"Do you like to play games?"

"Some kinds," he drawled with a reminiscent grin.

"We can't do *that* all the time. So..."

Adam shook his head. "I think we've been giving it a damn good try, but I'm willing to try something else. What kind of games?"

"Checkers or chess."

"Might be interesting," he agreed, finishing up his sandwich. "If the stakes were right."

"Stakes? I never played checkers for stakes."

"Then maybe you've got something to learn, Mrs. Stone. I'll meet you after dinner for a game of strip checkers."

"Strip checkers. I've never heard of it."

"You will-- after tonight." He kissed the tip of her nose and went back out to finish the corral.

After dinner had been eaten and cleared up, they sat down at the table, and Martha set up the checkers board. "Do you want black or red?" she asked.

"Black, of course," he said with a grin, enjoying the sight of her bent over the board, separating out the colored pieces. She was wearing a simple cotton dress, which seemed just right for what he had in mind.

When the board was set up, he explained the rules. "For every three men you lose, you remove a piece of clothing. Whoever loses the game loses it all if they haven't already."

"Adam," she said with a smile of disbelief. "You don't really mean."

"I sure do. You want to play any game, you got to make the stakes worthwhile."

She stared at him for a moment, her eyes running over the way the cotton plaid shirt hung off his broad shoulders, hinting at the muscular chest beneath it. "All right," she said finally, licking her lips. "I suppose there's nothing wrong with your idea. Although it does sound like gambling."

"For the best stakes," he promised, eyes glittering.

The first move was his and little by little they moved their pieces out into the board, evenly exchanging men until each had lost two. Smiling, he jumped her man, which meant she was about to lose an item of clothing. Expectantly he watched, thinking the dress would be the first to go. With disappointment he saw her reach down and unfasten a stocking, pulling it from a trim leg and putting it onto the chair between them. She then looked back at the board and jumped four of his men in one move.

His eyes gaped at her as he saw what she'd done. "I believe," she said with a smile of satisfaction, "that you owe me *two* items."

He looked down at his narrowed company of men and wished he'd put on socks after he'd cleaned up. He settled for removing his shirt and belt, laying them beside her stocking. He felt fortunate he'd chosen to wear long johns because of working outside. Still he was at a disadvantage.

The game settled into a series of carefully calculated moves as Adam and Martha each managed to lose another man before each gained a king. "Do kings count extra?" Martha asked as she jumped his.

"Just per man," he grumbled, rising to remove his pants.

"i was hoping the game was over," she said, her eyes traveling down his body with unhidden satisfaction.

"Not yet," he promised, determined to do more effective battle with the new king he'd gained.

Two more moves and he had three more of her pieces. He

looked at her expectantly before he realized that, of course, the other stocking would go next. "This isn't fair," he complained. "You wear more clothes than I do."

"You should have thought of that before you suggested the stakes," she said with a complacent smile as she looked on his nearly nude body with clear satisfaction. The long johns didn't hide much.

His luck improved with the next moves, and she stood to pull off her dress, doing such a slow striptease that he almost lost interest in the game completely as the dress shimmied off to reveal a thin chemise, which barely covered her breasts, and a long petticoat.

Now all he could think about was pulling down the straps of that chemise, and it cost him as he lost another king. If he lost one more piece, he was finished; but she still had two items of clothing for certain and he wasn't sure about a third. He shook his head with frustration as she began crowding his king against the edge of the playing board. Ruthlessly she swept down with another king. He tried to counter with one of his own pieces but it was to no avail. His king went.

"I believe, that means I win," she said, rising to help him to remove the long johns as he reached for the strap of her chemise. She backed away. "Ah no, I win. I get the pleasure of seeing you first."

Standing in the light of their fireplace, he edged the long johns down slowly, smiling as he saw the look of desire in her eyes and knew that while he might have lost the game; he hadn't lost the match.

When he stood naked, the firelight gleaming on his skin, shadows accenting his masculinity, dazedly she remembered that first night, the night she'd turned away from his nudity, the night she'd first begun to realize her body could come alive again.

Martha sighed with pleasure as Adam reached out and slipped the straps of her chemise from her shoulders, undid the ties of her petticoat and allowed both to drop to the floor, revealing that she had only worn the two undergarments. Lying down before the fire, they made slow love, enjoying and reveling in each other as the firelight flickered. Afterward, they lay entwined, not wanting the moment to end.

"I could lose like this every night," he suggested, kissing her forehead as a benediction.

"I wouldn't object," she promised, nuzzling under his neck and wrapping her arms snugly around him.

Adam froze and abruptly sat up.

"What is it?" she asked, reaching for her clothing.

"We got visitors. A single, no, two riders." He pulled on his pants. "You go on in the bedroom and get dressed. I'll see who it is." When she had closed the door, Adam loosely threw a shirt over his shoulders. With gun in hand, he opened the door.

CHAPTER 28

Through the bedroom door, Martha recognized St. Louis but then an unknown deep male voice. By the time she went out to join them, Adam had lit more oil lamps and was heating up coffee from their supper.

"Honey," he said, his face grim, "this is Lieutenant Phillips."

"I'm glad to meet you, Lieutenant," she said, looking at the tall, thin young man, his uniform showing signs of the hard riding he'd done. She frowned as she tried to understand why St. Louis had brought a military man to their cabin after dark.

"I heard you've just been married, Ma'am," the young lieutenant said, "Mr. Stone is a very fortunate man."

"Thank you," she said, looking from St. Louis to Adam and trying to understand what was going on. They both wore glum looks.

"What is happening?" she asked as she walked up behind Adam who was kneeling in front of the fireplace stoking the fire.

"Phillips is stationed at Fort Lane," he said.

"There's been more trouble down there?" she guessed.

"When isn't there?" Adam said rising with a grimace

"More white settlers were killed," Lieutenant Phillips said. "A wagon train, going across the Siskiyou Mountains was hit. Two men and a woman killed."

Adam's lips curled with disgust. "And, of course, the special volunteers had to react to that. An excuse that could not be missed!"

The lieutenant put up his hands in mock protection. "Back off, I never asked for this assignment. I just want to do my duty and get out of it in one piece."

"What is happening now?" asked Martha, beginning to feel a shiver of apprehension. This was not just about what was happening down there.

"The whole region is a powder keg," Adam said, glaring at the hapless lieutenant. "And if you are heading back, you won't get out of it in one piece. All the miners, out of work because of the dry season, are standing around, ready to have more hanging parties, to burn out every Indian, peaceful or not. The military still doesn't know what it's doing, and basically I am sure it's the same situation I left."

"Major Lawton has come up from Yreka and is calling for public meetings." Lieutenant Phillips spoke in a low voice, obviously not comfortable with being at this cabin any more than Adam wanted him here, but determined to relay all the information he had committed to bringing.

"*Major* Lawton," Adam snorted, "that's a good one. A self-designated major. I suppose he wants a simple solution to the problem, extermination of all the tribes, peaceful or otherwise for a start. Forget treaties, forget who got there first, use whatever excuse you can to get what you want! Isn't that about what he has in mind?"

"Sounds like about it." He handed Adam a letter.

Adam looked at the handwriting before he threw the letter down on the table.

"Aren't you going to read it?" asked St. Louis, moving into the light for the first time.

"Later," Adam said.

"Have you eaten?" asked Martha looking at the lieutenant.

"Yes, ma'am. Mr. Jones gave me something at his cabin. Thank you though."

"I suppose," Adam snapped, "that if anyone spoke for the Indians at the meeting, he was drummed out of the room."

"Adam, it isn't this young man's fault," Martha said.

Adam shook his head. "I suppose not. Just so damned frustrating."

"Well, you were right about that, Mr. Stone." Phillips took the cup of coffee Martha poured for him. "One man tried to speak up and tell the people they should try and behave like Christians, but there's been threats against his life and talk that he should leave the valley. Fear and anger are rampant."

"What was the result of the meeting?" Adam asked.

The lieutenant stared darkly into his cup. "The volunteers mounted up at night. They rode to Butte Creek, near the reservation."

"Damn them to hell," Adam groaned.

"Yes, I'm afraid so. They opened fire shortly before dawn on the Indians camped along the stream." He paused a moment sipping from his cup. "No easy way to say it. They killed eight men, fifteen women and children."

"Children too?" Martha repeated.

"Yes, ma'am. They claimed it was too dark to tell the difference."

"What a lie," Adam snarled. "Makes for easier killing if they can't fight back. Is that the all of it?" he asked. He walked to the window to stare out at the black of the night.

"No, other volunteers attacked different Indian groups in the valley. The people on the reservation were terrified and fled with their weapons."

"Oh hell," Adam muttered, "now there'll be innocent blood shed on both sides."

"It's already begun," Phillips said, "as the Indians fled."

Adam shook his head in disgust. "When does it end?"

"Lieutenant Pollard is hoping you can come back, get us in touch with the Indian leaders so that we can work out a peaceful solution. Nobody with us down there has been able to find them in those mountains. You know what they are like. The hope is if we can talk to them, well..."

Adam shook his head again, smiling coldly. "There won't be a peaceful solution. Not now. Every illegal act, every murder in the valley has been blamed on the Indians, whether they did it or not. The settlers want blood, and they won't quit until they have all of it."

"I'd like to disagree, but..." Martha was surprised at the expression on the lieutenant's face. Suddenly he didn't seem so young.

"What can Pollard offer them? A quicker death?" Adam asked with a sigh.

"He thinks, if he can get to the Indians before the volunteers get to them, he can round them back up, bring them to safety. Otherwise, they'll be massacred all up and down the Rogue and Illinois Rivers."

"How could one man, Adam, make that kind of difference?" Martha asked, feeling a shiver up her spine at what she was hearing. Adam had told her how it had been. She had seen the results in his nightmares. That was in the past though, not the future. Please, God, not the present.

"Look, lieutenant," Adam said, his voice steely hard, "I want to read the letter. Get out of here. I'll talk to you in the morning."

Martha looked at Adam, seeing the expressionless look in his eyes, and snapped her own mouth shut rather than to say what she had thought about his rudeness.

"I'll wait only a day for your answer at Mr. Jones' homestead," the lieutenant said, rising and walking from the cabin.

St. Louis nodded sympathetically but said nothing as he followed the officer out the door.

When they were alone, Martha sank into a chair, unwilling to let her mind accept what was happening.

"Let's go to bed, Martha," Adam said, his voice so low she could barely hear it.

"Aren't you going to read the letter?"

"In the morning. It's not going anywhere." He walked into the bedroom, stared at the bed.

"Adam," she said, as she blew out the oil lamps in the main room, "don't you want to talk about it?" She stood at the door, waiting for his decision.

"Later, not now." He stripped, throwing his clothes onto the floor and then watched as she undressed. When she crawled into bed with him, he said, "I'm sorry if I'm hurting you. I just can't talk about it yet."

"It's all right. I think I understand some of what you must feel from what you've told me," she whispered, kissing him lightly before she blew out the light.

"All I want right now," he murmured, his lips against her hair, "is to hold you in my arms. Just that."

Another of Adam's nightmares awoke Martha during the night as he thrashed his way through the Siskiyous. She felt again her helplessness to make it better. After that, she knew he lay awake until dawn because she did the same thing, lying quietly beside him. She wished she could comfort him, say something to help; but this was something he would have to work through on his own. She understood how powerless he must feel at knowing he could do nothing, at thinking of the death and destruction he'd already seen, with more yet to come.

In the morning at first light, Adam got dressed and left the bedroom to read the letter. When he had finished, he walked outside to watch the sun come up, holding the letter limply in his hand.

"Who was it from?" Martha asked, a robe wrapped loosely around her body. The morning air was crisp, a light frost was visible on the grass.

"John."

"What did he want?"

"Me."

"What are you going to do?"

"I am trying to decide what I can live with for the rest of my life."

She leaned her head against his shoulder for a moment and then went back into the house to make coffee and cook breakfast. He stared bleakly at the landscape. John needed him. He wasn't a man to beg, to use friendship, but he had. It meant he was scared not just for himself. Adam didn't want to think about whether he could help. He was not sure. But if he tried to help, what would it do to his life?

"May I read the letter?" she asked as he came back inside and sat at the table.

He handed it to her. There was nothing in the letter, which Phillips had not told him-- except John's personal plea for his help. That and John's belief he could make a difference, could save lives on both sides. His friend was in desperate need of an experienced tracker. *They are hiding, so scared, Adam. You may be able to reach them, stop this from happening to the babies, to the innocents.'*

Adam tried again to think if he could live with himself if he didn't try. He did not believe he could stop the tragedy unfolding, not really. The settlers were bound to have every Indian out of that country. They wouldn't rest until they were all dead.

He could hear the sound of salt pork crackling in a pan, the odor of it doing nothing to tempt him to an appetite. He had everything he'd ever wanted with Martha. He didn't want to leave it to go back to hell. But the dreams were telling him something. If he ignored this call, would he ever sleep through a night again? He could go down, help find the Indians, talk to their leaders and hopefully be back before Christmas. It was forever and at the same time nothing in time. He moved restlessly around the room, finally leaning on the door jamb to watch her at the stove.

"It's a difficult request to refuse," she said, her voice quiet.

"It is."

"Then you have no intention of refusing," she said, not asking a question so much as making a statement.

He grimaced as he considered what she'd said, wondering what her attitude was going to be. Would she understand if he went? Would she believe he was just using it as an excuse to run off? He knew the truth, that he wasn't seeking adventure, but how could she know. To her it would mean Simon had been right about him all along. He could read none of what she was thinking from her set expression.

"You breakfast is ready." She brought his filled plate to the table.

"I don't have much of an appetite."

"You have to eat."

He wondered how much he could force himself to eat before his stomach rebelled.

"You are going to go, aren't you?" she asked, again not really asking.

He sighed, staring at the biscuits, at anything but her white face. "I wish it was otherwise. You know how little I want to do this. I've tried to think of a way around it. I don't think I have a choice."

"You have one, but you already made it."

He pushed himself away from the table. "You think I want to do this?"

"Yes."

"How could you believe that? I have everything here that I want. I don't want to go back, to face what is down there."

"Then don't go."

"And how do I live with my conscience? How do I live with dead eyes staring at me in my dreams, condemning me because I didn't try?"

She threw up her hands. "And what do you think you, one man can accomplish, except maybe get himself killed?"

"John is right. I can speak to some of the leaders. I can track the families trying to flee, let them know there is somewhere safe to go." He only hoped that was true.

Then she said what he had expected. "You want to go because you want the excitement."

"If you believe that, you don't know me at all."

"I think that is obvious."

His thoughts were bleak as he considered the alternatives that seemed possible. He could stay here, with her and try to live with himself later. He could go, taking the chance that he would have nothing to come back to when he did return-- if he did. He didn't think it was possible to make her understand why he felt as he did. If she had seen what he had, she would understand, but he was glad she had not. He wouldn't try to tell her what a butchered child looked like. How it felt to have them haunting her dreams.

He looked at her for a long moment; then got up and walked into the bedroom.

"Adam," she said, raising her voice desperately as she followed him, "what are you doing?"

"There is no point in putting this off. I have to go, and I am. I will be back as soon as I can." He began throwing his few clothes into a saddlebag.

She stood in the doorway as though frozen. "If you go, don't bother coming back."

He clenched his jaw as he closed up the bag. "I am your husband now. I am going, and I will be back."

"Not to me, you won't," she cried, turning to run from the room.

He closed the distance between them in two long strides. Reaching out, he pulled her into his arms. She pushed against him, but his arms were like steel vices as he held her. His eyes narrowed, as he looked into hers. He brought his lips down, claiming hers in an angry, almost violent kiss. "I love you, and I will be back," he repeated as he let her go, striding from the room.

As fast as it was humanly possible, he saddled Joe, tied his bag and bedroll onto the back of the saddle and rode from the homestead. If he didn't go now, didn't leave immediately, he would never be able to. If he didn't go, he would never be whole again. He would blame both her and himself. He had to hope she would come to understand. He kicked Joe into a run.

At St. Louis' cabin, he roused out the young lieutenant. "I'm going and right now. Are you coming with me or later?"

St. Louis watched as Phillips threw a saddle on his horse. "Ya sure about this?" St. Louis asked, his eyes showing his concern.

"I would like to have it be otherwise, but I don't have a choice," Adam said with a cold smile, not wanting another argument from the older man.

"I didn't say ya did."

"Please look after her," Adam said as he stepped up into the saddle. "Tell her I'll be back... And, Elijah, I'm going to buy another horse in Oregon City. I don't want to take Joe with me this time. He's getting too old for what I expect down there. Will you pick him up at the stable just south of town?"

St. Louis showed no surprise at his use of his real name. "Ya know I will but don't ya want a horse ya know ya can trust?"

"I need to know he's back here more."

"Ya are expecting trouble down there, the kind you don't want to lose yore horse in." It was not a question.

"I'm expecting hell," Adam told him, as he swung Joe around and rode off at a fast gallop, leaving the lieutenant to follow.

~

With afternoon, Martha saw the horseman approaching. She dried her tears. She knew it wasn't Adam. She sat back forlornly on the bench and waited as St. Louis tied his horse to the post. "Ya all right?" he asked.

"No."

"Didn't figure ya would be. If it's any satisfaction, ya sent him off in the same state."

Tears ran down her cheeks. "I thought I could stop him, save his life. I couldn't. He didn't love me enough to stop."

"Martha, ya married a man, not a boy. Didn't ya know he'd do what he had to do?"

"If he had loved me, he'd have stayed," she said stubbornly.

"Gal, there are things people do because they are right, higher things than what they might want to do for themselves. You can see Adam was doing that as he saw it, can't you?"

"I can't see anything right now." She began to cry again. "He left me. That's all I can see, and I hate him for it. He made me love him, and then he left me."

"So you wanted to wear the pants in your family, huh? Maybe figured because Adam was younger, you could make his decisions for him?"

"It wasn't that."

"Then what was it?"

"I wanted him with me. I didn't want to lose another husband." Her lips quivered. She felt weak inside as though he was already dead. In the distance she could see the rain clouds beginning to build up over the coast range. It was going to storm. The land needed a good heavy rain.

"Martha, if you wanted a boy for a husband, you didn't pick one. Adam is a man who picks his own paths. He's got to do what he knows is right. You should have known that about him. He didn't feel he had a choice on this, and I can't say I blame him."

"I lost one husband. I don't want to lose another."

"So ya sent him off thinkin' ya were done with him?"

She didn't like hearing it described that way. "What can one man do?" she argued knowing she was being stubborn but still so hurt at what had happened that she couldn't stop herself.

"What a dozen can or a thousand. He can do what he knows is right. Those Indians are humans. Their lives matter too. Ya do know that?"

She tried to stop the sobs but couldn't. St. Louis took her in his arms, letting her cry it out. "I'm sorry," she said when she finally stopped and dried her eyes, blowing her nose. "I'm a fool. I never should have let myself love him. My own fault. I blame only me. Not Adam. I knew what he was when I married him. Knew this would happen." She was sounding bitter, and she knew that too but couldn't stop the flow of words.

"So you wish you hadn't married a scalawag?

"That's not what he is." She managed a little laugh among her sniffles. "You know I don't think that."

"Then what are ya goin' to do about it?"

"There's nothing I can do. He's gone."

"Ya could send him a letter."

"The last one we sent took a year to reach him."

"It'd be worth a try. He was feeling pretty down when he rode out. Might be a letter will get to him, and it will help him get through what's ahead."

She began to cry again. "I don't know if I can do that. I love him, but..."

"You can't accept the man he is?" St. Louis finished for her.

"It's not that."

"It's not? Seems to me that is exactly what it is. People will always be needing Adam. When he sees he can help, he will go. That's who he is. You don't like that he'd not always be there, servin' yore needs?"

"You make me sound selfish."

"It's not one way or another, Martha. You married a man can do something about things that others can't. Ya knew that. Ya also knew it'd cost ya. I know it was hard to lose Amos. I saw what it did to you, how you grew stronger after it."

"And now it's happening again."

"Not yet it ain't. Martha, girl, you know as well as anyone he could be killed right on this place. You too."

"That's not the same as inviting it to happen."

"You think that's what he did?"

"No, of course not. I read John's letter. I saw the weight he laid on Adam. It isn't that I don't feel bad for those people." She knew she was trying to justify what she was feeling.

"Ya see them as people?"

"Of course, I do." She felt offended.

"I won't argue with ya about what he did. Iffn ya decide you want to write a letter, I'll take it into Oregon City and mail it when I pick up Joe."

"Pick up Joe?" she echoed.

"He said he wouldn't take him down. He was buying another horse in town."

"Why?" she asked in a small voice.

"You know why, don't you?"

"I wish... I wish I'd sent him off differently." She began to cry

"He's going to come back, gal. The question for you is whether you can live with what he's like because you also know it'll come again once in awhile. The call and he'll have to go."

"I may not have a choice in it. He might not come back." She took a deep breath, trying to stop more tears.

"Have some faith, gal."

"Do you think if I rode into Oregon City I could catch him?"

St. Louis shook his head. "He was riding like the devil was on his tail. No man or woman could keep up with him when he's like that. No, a letter's the best way."

"I don't even know what I'd say if I was to write one."

"Wal, I sure can't help ya with that."

CHAPTER 29

Adam rode into Fort Lane and out with the first patrol heading up the Rogue. All the military men who'd been serving in these mountains felt the same sense of defeat and frustration that he did. Pollard was already out somewhere. Phillips led the patrol Adam guided.

They wound their way up through the hills, camping and talking little as they tried to find indications of where the Indians were and get to them before the volunteers or militia did. The risk, of course, was that the Indians would be in no mood to talk and very much in the mood to strike back.

The third afternoon, they caught up with a group of volunteers led by Michael Thorne. "You military are always too late," Thorne castigated Phillips.

"And you, volunteers, are always right on time for killing women and children," Adam snapped, barely holding onto his temper, as he dismounted and tried to study what sign had not been ruined by the vigilantes.

"Who do you think you are?" Thorne asked.

"I think I'm the tracker, and you don't want to know what I think you are."

Thorne was off his horse and lunging at Adam when he saw the gun leveled at his nose. "Fight like a man," Thorne growled.

Adam smiled, his gun never wavering. "Fight a man, who is a man, maybe. Killers of babies don't deserve that kind of respect."

Thorne's eyes showed his fury, his desire to rip Adam limb from limb, but the gun leveled on his nose left him no option except to get back on his own horse. "When you don't have that gun," he promised.

"I know," Adam snapped, "with no gun, you'd kill me. Helpless victims are your style aren't they, Thorne?"

After he had ridden off, Phillips said, "I'm not sure that was wise, making him an enemy that way."

"If this job requires making a man like that into a friend, it's even worse than I figured."

Phillips chuckled. "He is a snake."

"A vicious one, and a man like that wouldn't be your friend no matter what. Might as well know him as your enemy."

"Mr. Stone, do you think we are close to a band of hostiles?"

Adam knelt, studying the tracks again. "It's Adam, and I doubt these are hostiles. Women and children most likely, the old, and I think we are about an hour behind."

"I haven't served in this region long enough to know, Adam, but do you expect these people to come back peacefully with us?"

Adam stepped into his saddle, satisfied with the responsiveness of the solid bay gelding, as he held steady for him. "This group likely won't have much to fight with, Lieutenant, but they also won't want to go. If someone was going to put you on a reservation, a long ways from your spiritual places, the places you'd been born, the places you hunted and gathered your food, and the places your ancestors were buried, would you go peacefully?"

"I don't suppose I would," the young man admitted, drinking from his canteen.

"Then I think we better be prepared whichever way it goes," Adam said, checking his revolver's load.

The terrain through which they rode was rugged, changing dramatically from one slope of the hillside to another. In some areas the underbrush was thick, making distant visibility all but impossible. In other places loose rock was a hazard to horses and men. Madrona, fir, sugar pine, and poison oak were in ample abundance, and even though it was late fall in the high country, the poison oak was to be avoided as it was as potent as ever and fully capable of leaving a man in misery. There was enough misery to go around without adding weeping rashes.

Adam hunched his jacket around his shoulders. It was growing cold in the hills, another couple of weeks at most and there'd would be snow at the higher elevations. He didn't envy the Indians or the soldiers if they were in these mountains then.

He thought of Martha, wondering what she was doing, if she was still angry. He'd also thought of writing her a letter, but the idea of receiving an answer that showed no forgiveness, a letter that took away his hope was more than he could bear. It was easier to have the hope that she would be able to forgive, than it would be to have it taken away by a demand for a divorce. If he had to hear that, he wanted it to be when he was back up there and had a chance of changing her mind.

Adam stopped to check for sign. "Others joined with this band," he said as he looked into the direction they appeared to be heading. He saw no movement.

"Where are we?" Lieutenant Phillips asked.

"That down there is Grave Creek."

"I hope the name isn't symbolic," the lieutenant said wryly.

Adam smiled humorlessly. "We should rest the horses and then push down into the watershed, and I think we'll find them. Whether or not they're in the mood to talk or fight, I can't predict." The lieutenant passed the word down the line. The men dismounted, leaning back to take what might be their last break in some time.

"This is only my second assignment. I saw no action on the

Plains. I was reassigned here and arrived two months ago, and frankly, it's been a lot to take in." He moved over to sit beside Adam under the edge of a tall sugar pine. The ground was cold but not wet. "Never fought Indians before—other than in a textbook."

"I'd have never guessed it," Adam said with a little laugh, "that is if you didn't keep telling me, every now and again." He reached into a small bag and took out paper and a small sack of tobacco. With precision, he poured a line of tobacco onto the paper, rolled, licked, and lit it, drawing deep on the smoke.

In the past, he'd quit smoking several times, but somehow in the last week, he'd found a cigarette to be about the only thing that offered him a moment of respite. Looking over at the lieutenant, he asked, "You smoke?"

"It's one vice I haven't tried."

Adam smiled. "Want to try it now?"

"I've never rolled one."

"Nothing to it," Adam said rolling another and handing it to the young man.

"Thank you," he said as they leaned back, smoking silently.

"You never told me your first name," Adam said.

"Randall. Rand to my friends."

"Well, Randall, you are about to go down into that canyon and lead your men into what possibly could be a battle. I see sign of about twenty with that bunch who could be warriors. If you've never done anything like this before, how do you plan to proceed?"

"I just thought I'd follow the book."

"West Point?" Adam asked, shaking his head as he blew smoke out into the cold air. He watched as it drifted downward, caught above a low bush.

"Yes sir." He coughed as he inhaled the smoke but kept on determinedly drawing on the cigarette.

"Well, West Point won't prepare you for fighting Indians,

Randall. The tribes don't have a set of rules they all operate by. Their tactics are nothing like the European wars you likely studied."

"I did know that, sir."

Adam smiled shaking his head. "Remember, it's Adam."

"All right, Adam," Phillips said, smiling, "if you start calling me Rand."

As they proceeded down into the canyon, fighting their way through the undergrowth, they came across another company of the military, led by a Major Montgomery.

"We were on our way to Vancouver Barracks, being transferred north, but we've seen a large encampment below. We sent for reinforcements. Lucky we found you," Montgomery said.

The men gathered, regrouped into squads. Adam sat on his haunches, silently watching, nerves on edge. Waiting had never been easy for him even when it was necessary. Major Montgomery briefed them on what he expected. "There would be as many as one hundred and fifty camped down there."

"Of which most are women, the elderly, and children," Adam reminded him.

"They can kill too."

Adam hadn't expected to like this man. "So are you planning to give them a chance to surrender peacefully?"

"And give up the surprise, I hardly think so," Montgomery said with amazement reflected in his voice.

"How do you know they are hostiles?"

"We trailed some from the south. Besides if they weren't wild, they'd already be at the fort where they belong."

Adam knew it was no use arguing with this by the book commander, but he had to try anyway. "I could go down and try talking to them, to see if they will surrender. That is what I was asked to do here."

"There will be no talking."

The next morning was spent first fighting the underbrush and then trying to find some indication of where the Indians were before they melted into the same underbrush, going a hundred different directions. The squads had spread out, and when Adam heard firing, he knew one had found trouble. He had stayed with Phillips, and they made their way toward the sound of the guns as fast as the rugged terrain would allow them.

When bullets began flying in their direction, Adam and the lieutenant stopped his platoon and found enough protection to begin firing back. Several wounded men made their way behind their lines as the firing continued. There were no obvious targets for the soldiers, but they kept up a barrage into the thicket.

With nightfall, the gunfire stopped. There would be no fires or supper. The men regrouped, grabbed blankets, wrapped themselves in them and slept as they could, leaving guards to watch for a night attack, something that was unusual for the Indians of this area but not impossible.

Adam lay in his blanket, another cigarette between his lips, fighting against allowing himself to think again of Martha. It was likely that the morning would see real fighting. The Indians had only been testing them. These warriors were not only fighting for their land but their soul. It wouldn't go down easy. The possible fighting numbers appeared to be as large as the commander had guessed. They were not running. Maybe too many women and children for them to run. Maybe they just didn't have anywhere to go.

His mind wandered to the blanket he and Martha had shared high on the Clackamas. The thought of her warm body in his arms was enough to keep him from sleep until finally the light began to appear in the east.

Sitting back on his haunches, he smoked one last cigarette as the men around him got themselves ready. He did not have a good feeling about this day. How does a man get himself ready to die? Adam rose, grinding the remains of the cigarette into the ground with the toe of his boot.

This time, the soldiers moved forward, carrying the battle to the enemy. When the soldiers realized they were being flanked, they dug in. The enemy still seemed mostly invisible in the thicket. Adam fired his revolver when he could see a target until he was forced to duck back and reload. When he looked up again, he saw a soldier fall, mortally wounded. With the Indians all around, there would be no retreat, at least not until or unless the hostiles pulled back.

Phillips crawled over to Adam, a black smudge on one cheek. The woods through which they'd fought their way had made his uniform less than regulation. "What now?"

"Where's the major?" asked Adam, reloading.

"I don't know. I haven't seen him. I think he's over to the left, but..."

"Shoot if you see a target." Adam hated it. This wasn't what he had come for. How had he gotten himself sucked into killing when he had come hoping to save lives?

"Don't you think we ought to retreat?" Phillips asked, his voice low, but carrying enough that the nearest trooper could not help but overhear.

"Where to?" Adam asked shaking his head. "They're all around us, besides our casualties aren't that high. Just hold steady, Rand."

"But..."

"Look, if you run now, you're more likely to get killed than if you hold."

"I wouldn't run," Phillips argued with a wry smile, "just strategically retreat."

Adam laughed. "The Indians might not see the difference. Sometimes it's the only way you hold your own with them. Let them see you aren't giving up. They have to see they can't win and that they will all be killed eventually. They really don't understand what they face with the full force of the United States eventually to come against them. Get some rest."

Phillips stared at him and then straightening his weary shoulders smiled. "I'll trust in your wisdom."

The hours of fighting, gunshots, screams, powder and smoke seemed to go on forever and then some of the men began to break. Volunteers had been interspersed with the soldiers, and they began edging backward, away from the firing. "We can't stay down here when it gets dark," one muttered and then another.

As they pulled back, more fell with fatal or disabling bullet wounds. Adam dragged one badly wounded man with him as he moved to where Phillips was hunkered down. There appeared to be no shots coming from the north. Perhaps it was time to get out of the hole they were in. He nudged Phillips. "Time to go."

"But you said," Phillips argued, sighting down the barrel of his gun as he fired at a movement to his left.

"Rand, there's one more thing to learn about Indians. When you are outnumbered and in a bad location then, if you see a way clear, you move out of the situation to live to fight another day. So get off your butt and head toward the north for that strategic retreat you wanted earlier. It looks to be open that way."

Phillips shook his head but stood up just as one of the Indians fired. The force of the bullet threw the young officer back a step and half turned his body. "Are you sure I shouldn't have stayed there?" he quipped as he grasped his left arm with his right, the blood seeping through his fingers.

Adam pushed his hand aside and grabbed hold of his sleeve, ripping it open. The wound was a deep groove right alongside the bicep and didn't appear to have entered the arm. "This might just get you home," he observed as he ripped off a piece of his own shirt to tie around the wound and stop the bleeding.

Phillips grimaced but said nothing. When Adam bent to pick up the unconscious man he'd been dragging, Phillips took the man's other arm. "You sure you're up to that?" Adam asked.

"I got no breath to waste with arguing," Phillips muttered with a twisted smile, not letting go of his half of the unconscious trooper.

At their horses, they counted the wounded and injured, finding that nine soldiers had been killed and twenty-seven wounded. That had been a less than successful attack. Hard to say how many of the Indians had been hit. Phillips started off to get further orders and Adam grabbed him by his uninjured arm. "You sit. You can't take that injury for granted, or you'll be losing your arm. Infection is a nasty thing."

Phillips frowned but subsided back where Adam pushed him. "It's nothing," he complained as Adam took off the rough bandage.

"You got a medic traveling with you?"

"Yes, but he's got more serious things to worry about than this. I've got a pint of whiskey in my saddlebag. Maybe if we pour it over this, it'll take care of that infection you're so concerned about."

Adam shook his head as he went for the whiskey, picking up clean dressings from the medic who was indeed treating the more serious injuries. "I can't believe I am saying this," Adam said when he got back to the wounded lieutenant, "but I'm wishing we had some of St. Louis' salve."

Phillips grunted and twisted away as the whiskey was poured over the wound. "St. Louis salve, never heard of it," he said when he could.

"The man you met, not the place. He swears by it for everything from flea bite to gangrene, I think." Adam tied the bandage neatly around the upper arm, securing it tightly enough to hold.

"Sounds, uh better than whiskey," Phillips said, taking a swig from the bottle when Adam handed it to him.

"Doesn't hurt any less." He grinned. Phillips handed him the bottle, and they both took a couple more swallows.

"I doubt," Phillips said, rising slowly, testing his legs, "that this graze'll cause me much trouble, but it's possible that you saved my life back there."

Adam snorted. "It was just a flesh wound."

"No, I mean you steadied my nerves. You knew what we ought to do when I didn't. Thanks. For all my so-called training, I'm a greenhorn at this. It makes it tough out here when there's no time to learn anything without it costing somebody. None of this looks like the book."

"Look, Rand, this situation would test a man who'd been out fighting Indians for twenty years. Don't blame yourself if you don't know what to do. Nobody else does either. Some just pretend they do."

Phillips grinned at him, rolling down his sleeve. "You tell it your way, I'll tell it mine," he said with a little smile as he reached out to shake Adam's hand.

Back at the main camp, the cold wind coming even more cuttingly, Major Montgomery was complaining to all who would listen. "This campaign is going to take all the bloody winter."

Adam grimaced at the truth of his statement. They had gained nothing with the men they had lost, and the Indians could now disappear into the brush with nobody following as they went all the directions of the wind. Adam would be here again at Christmas from the way it was looking, out on another lonely patrol instead of in bed with the woman he loved. The pain of this one would be much greater because he now knew he had another place he could have been, a place warm and filled with love. Instead, he stood on a lonely ridge, shivering with the cold and asking himself what he had accomplished by coming.

Martha sat by the fireplace, a shawl wrapped around her shoulders as she stared into the flames, ignoring the fabric for a new dress that lay across her legs. She had promised Eunice that she would finish this in time for Thanksgiving, but she had no enthusiasm for it. All she could think of was the cold outside her door and wonder where Adam was. Did he have shelter? Was he safe?

She had sent two letters south, but heard nothing in reply. She had no way of knowing if he'd gotten them and wasn't willing to reply or if they weren't reaching him. In each letter, she'd reassured him of her love, begged for his forgiveness, and told him to come home to her when he could.

Mentally, again and again she castigated herself as having been uncaring. *What kind of man did you expect you had married?* she thought. An old poem by Richard Lovelace kept coming into her mind. It was of a man going off to war, leaving behind a woman who hadn't understood any better than she had. It had ended with the words, "I could not love thee, dear, so much, Loved I not honour more."

The words cut into her, condemning her for she grasped their truth now as she'd never understood them before. A woman didn't think about honor so much-- not until a man forced her to look at it and realize that without it she wouldn't have loved him so completely either. Adam was the kind of man he was and that was what she loved. If it cost her his presence, if it left her a widow again, she could only think how glad she was that they'd had the days together they had. In the letters she'd written him, she'd tried to explain that to him, make him see that she did understand. If only he received the letters.

She had been disappointed when her monthly time had come. She had hoped against hope that perhaps she might have been pregnant. Even raising a child alone would have been better than losing every part of him.

A knock at her door roused her from her reverie, and she opened it to see Eunice standing, bundled warmly in a slicker, dripping water from a scarf bundled around her head, and holding a bundle wrapped in a small tarp. "Eunice," Martha said, ushering her into the cabin. "I can't believe you'd come out in such weather."

"This was such an unexpected storm that I was worried about you up here all alone."

"At least it's not snowing, and Adam piled up a remarkable stack of wood for the time he was here," Martha said, pouring a cup of coffee for Eunice and topping off her own. "Plus Matt or St. Louis come by to check every day or so."

"That reassures me some. Have you heard from Mr. Stone?" she unwrapped her bundle, which was a plate of fragrant, obviously freshly made cinnamon rolls and plopped down on a chair beside the fire.

Martha felt defensive. "No, but the mails are unreliable at this time of the year. For that matter, down there they aren't that dependable at any time of the year. I don't have any real address for him."

"You'd hear if anything happened to him." Eunice daintily picked up one of the rolls taking a bite after that reassuring comment.

"I suppose so," Martha said, gathering her shawl more tightly around her.

"You're his wife now. They always notify the widows."

Martha smiled a little, wondering if Eunice was trying to be helpful.

"Of course," Eunice added, "they might not know he was married."

"Is Fanny enjoying Portland?" Martha asked, to redirect the conversation to something less painful as she sipped coffee.

"From her letters. It sounds like it. She visited Loraine, but maybe your daughter told you about that."

"No," Martha said, "not yet."

"Well, they went to a Sunday service together, and Fanny said Loraine has a very nice young man who seems smitten with her."

"She did tell me about that," Martha said smiling as Loraine had added she didn't return his interest, but she hoped he would remain a good friend.

St. Louis rode up to the door, stomping his way into the house as he took coffee and one of Eunice's baked delights. "Ya still wanting to make a trip into Oregon City?" he asked Martha after he'd gotten settled.

"Yes."

"Wal, I figure tomorrow'll be a good day for me. How's it for ya?"

"It would be fine. If this rain would let up, it would be even better."

"Wal, don't go lookin' for that because it figures to rain now until March."

"Why are you going to Oregon City?" Eunice asked.

"I have business," Martha said, not caring to share her news with the local gossip just yet.

"Anything important?"

"At the bank, among other things," Martha said, smiling at Eunice's determination. She and her brother obviously shared more than their weight in common.

When Eunice had finally given up and gone home, St. Louis shook his head. "That woman," he said, "she's a caution."

"She means well, I believe," Martha said as she began stitching up a seam, taking tiny, fine stitches that would hold no matter what the stresses were on them.

"Why didn't ya tell her why ya were goin' into town?"

"Because I'm not certain I'm doing the right thing. I want time in town to see, and maybe talk to some people."

St. Louis grinned. "Wal, for what it's worth, I think you're doin' the right thing."

"You do?"

"Yup, I do. He didn't even give it a thought figurin' how you wouldn't want it, but that job is cut out for him. It don't hurt to go seein' if it's still open. The folks weren't all that pleased with the shiftless deputy last time I heard."

"I should have gone sooner. I just couldn't seem to think about anything sensible right after he left."

"What are ya fixin' to do for Thanksgiving and Christmas?" St. Louis asked, pouring himself another cup of coffee.

"I counted on you being with us," she said, watching as he nodded his assent. "It'll be quiet. I don't know if Loraine or Belle will be back. I'd want Agatha and Jacob also, but I suspect a lot will depend on the weather. Of course, there will be Matt, Amy and little Laura, but I have the feeling now that Adam won't be back until spring." She stopped, unwilling to go on because her fear was that he might not be back even then. Perhaps he would be killed, and his last memories of her would be harsh, cutting words. She shook her head, knowing she couldn't think that way. She had to make plans for the future and that required going into Oregon City as soon as she could.

"If ya find a house in Oregon City, what are ya goin' to do with this one?"

"Keep it for now. Lease the land if I can. We fulfilled the requirements for a claim. The land is ours," Martha said, looking around. "I don't think I'm ready to think about selling it and maybe Adam won't like being a sheriff after all."

"That's possible, but I wouldn't want to bet on it. Seems to me it was a job he was born to do."

Martha sighed, "Then this place could be a retreat, a place to come to sometimes to get away from everything. I don't know. Maybe eventually we will sell it, just not yet."

CHAPTER 30

A dam stared with cold eyes at Major Montgomery as he
began giving orders for the next day's march. The man was
angry, and in a hurry to conclude this so that he could proceed
onto Vancouver. His lack of caution was not doing anything for
Adam's confidence in his leadership.

"You think you can find them for us?" he snapped at Adam.

"They will have split up. We can find some." Adam said,
taking a drag on his cigarette, "but we already found them several
times for all the good it did."

Montgomery glared at him. "Well then, find them again!"

"We'd do better if I went out alone to try and explain things
to them."

"I don't negotiate with savages. I want this finished."

Adam shrugged and walked away. Saddling his horse, he
thought again, of what he had committed to do. This was working
out to be as bad as the massacre he'd feared, and he had found
nothing he could do that would stop it.

With frustration, he rode along the ridge, watching the
wooded land ahead for any indication of human activity. It was

his job to find them, but he was uncertain what the result would be when he did.

Not finding the Indians could possibly prove as fatal to them as finding them. Soon the first heavy snows would be falling, and this high in the mountains, people with little food, no extra clothing or supplies, no plank lodges would have little chance of surviving for long.

Down in the canyon, on the other side of the river, he saw movement. Trying to decide if it was a deer or a person, he held his mount steady. More activity. He sat quietly, leaning against the pommel of his saddle, wondering if he wanted to tell the over-eager military what he'd seen.

Reporting back to the major, he felt like a Judas, but he'd had no real choice. He'd been hired by the military, given his word to help them find the tribes. It wasn't his option as to what was to be done when they were found, but none of it made him feel better about it. Leaving the Indians could end up with massacred civilians. There was no winning any more.

As he watched the soldiers settle themselves on the bluffs above the Indians and begin firing down as though they were targets and not humans, he felt a rage grow within. Angrily, he strode up to the major, who had just shouted an order to one of his men. Adam grabbed his arm and swung the man around.

"I thought we were trying to bring them in peaceably. You aren't giving these poor devils a chance."

Montgomery smiled coldly, looking down at Adam's hand still on his arm. "These people had their chance. They left the reservation. I already told you how it would be. Any out here are hostiles and are to be treated as such."

Adam had been through too much over the last weeks, too many disappointments; too many times he'd been told it was the way it had to be. Angrily, he grabbed the front of the major's uniform, his fist held in front of the man's arrogant nose as he growled, "They are human beings, Major. Not animals."

"Take your hands off my uniform."

"Are you listening to me?" Adam snarled, tempted almost beyond reason to hit his smug face even if it cost him time in the brig.

A slight movement behind him was only enough warning to allow him to throw his arm up in defense as a pistol lashed out, striking his head. Driven to his knees, he tried to rise only to have another blinding pain take away all his senses.

It was nearly dark when Adam came to. Lying there, he tried to remember what had happened. He was first aware he was going to have a blinding headache and second that he'd done a stupid thing in attacking the major. It had accomplished nothing except to get him in trouble with the military. He tried to put his hand to his head and wasn't surprised to find his wrists and ankles had been shackled.

Swallowing hard, his mouth dry, without a lot of possible choices, he lay back and wondered what kind of mess he'd gotten himself into. The major didn't look like the forgiving kind. Would he attempt to court-martial a private citizen? They probably could try since he was under government contract of sorts.

Looking around he saw that he'd been dumped into a corner of the camp, out of sight and hopefully out of mind. No one guarded him, but then with heavy chains on his wrists and ankles, that was hardly necessary.

He closed his eyes. From long experience of living under bad conditions, he had learned to take sleep wherever and however he could find it. Right now he was helpless to do anything else anyway.

A nasty voice close to his ear awoke him. "Got yourself in a real bind didn't ya?"

Adam opened his eyes, only mildly surprised that he was

looking up into the face of Thorne, who was squatting beside him. A quick look around told him that no one was paying any attention to what the volunteer might be saying or doing to the prisoner.

Thorne laughed coarsely. "It don't hurt my feelin's to see ya in chains. Nope, not atall." He reached down and grasped the front of Adam's shirt in his fist, pulling him up almost to his nose.

Adam smiled, his eyes meeting Thorne's. "Think it'll be worth it?" he asked.

"What do you mean?" the man asked, twisting the shirt so that it pressed against Adam's throat, making breathing a bit of a challenge.

"I mean..." He choked and then managed to say, "A little more of that and you'll be finding yourself right beside me."

"How do you figure that?" he asked, one hand reaching out to lightly slap Adam's cheek.

"Interfering with a prisoner of the US Army. The military doesn't take kindly to it. I've seen men whipped for less."

Thorne let go of his shirt, allowing Adam to drop back to the ground. "Nobody'd know or care what I did to the likes of you. Attacking an officer. You think that major's goin' to care if I beat the holy crap out of you."

Adam smiled. "Guess you can find out. Won't hurt my feelings any to see you in chains."

Thorne seemed to be considering. "The major hates you now."

"Could be, but he's the kind who likes to control everything around him, but hey, don't take my word for it. Try it for yourself."

Thorne glared at him with frustration. Reaching down, he cuffed Adam hard across the side of his face, snapping his head back with the force of the blow.

Adam was furious but hid it. He'd not give the dog satisfaction. "If that's all the better you can do, and it is, I'm going back to sleep," he said and closed his eyes shutting out the frustrated face of Thorne.

When he opened them again, Rand Phillips was the one beside him. "So, you're awake," Phillips said with a smile, sitting back on his haunches.

"Yeah, you're a lot better looking than the last man here."

"And who was that?"

"Thorne. He was trying to take advantage of what he saw as a beneficial situation for him.

"The vermin."

"You are good at character analysis."

"Are you planning to attack the major again?"

"I didn't attack him the first time."

"That's up for debate. You are to stay away from him."

"Suits me fine."

"Good." Phillips brought forth a key from his pocket and proceeded to free him. Adam rubbed his wrists to restore circulation. "That wasn't a very smart thing you did," Phillips said.

"Then it was right in line," Adam grunted, grimacing as he stood up, every muscle in his body aching.

"Nobody can attack the United States Army and win. You know that."

"I wasn't after the whole army, just one man, and I hadn't attacked him. I was just thinking about it real hard."

"You put your hands on him."

"I should've put them on harder. It would have made this more worthwhile."

"Well, it's to your good fortune that you didn't. The major does not want to see your face again and has decided to forget the incident, that is, officially." Adam half smiled, sure that there was more to come, and he was not disappointed. "He won't report it, but you've just assured yourself the worst winter of your life."

"It's was headed that way anyway." Adam rubbed the back of

his head, feeling a good sized lump where the gun barrel had clipped him.

"Well, then you won't be disappointed." Phillips smiled ruefully. "I tried to make him forget the whole thing. Your record almost did it for me, but you humiliated him when you grabbed him that way and in front of his men. He's the type who doesn't take well to that."

"So, what's the result?"

"You will stay out in the field going out with every patrol. You are to be based at Camp Leland instead of the fort so that Major Montgomery, who has been temporarily diverted from Fort Vancouver by this mess, doesn't have to see your face, and to assure himself that you will be just as uncomfortable as possible. I think his own disappointment is adding to his desire to make your life miserable."

"The fort wasn't exactly my idea of paradise anyway," Adam said shrugging.

"It'll be your job to bring in as many Indians as you can. Talk to them, convince them to go to Lane. The major says since you like Indians so much, you can live like them."

"Nice man, the major."

"There's something more." Phillips stared at the ground. "There is no easy way to say this. We received word that John Pollard was killed."

Adam closed his eyes. "When?"

"It happened four days ago. Down river. From what I heard, it was a fluke. He was hit, nobody knows by who or where it came from. He never knew what hit him."

"Lord," Adam whispered, sinking back to sit on the ground. "He should have quit," he muttered, wondering if Pollard had had a premonition of this. He remembered the desperate letter that had sealed his own fate, the plea for help that Adam had doubted his ability to deliver but which had come too late to help John anyway.

He closed his eyes, the pain from this blow every bit as great as the one, which had flattened him in front of the major.

～

Martha stood in the middle of the tidy parlor, looking around trying to imagine her own things softening the bare walls. A few pieces of furniture, draped in sheets were scattered around the room. The coldness of the unlived-in rooms would be easily alleviated by the fireplace in the parlor and woodstove in the kitchen. The larger of the three bedrooms upstairs also had a fireplace.

St. Louis strode over to check the marble-faced fireplace. "Looks like everything's in workin' order," he drawled.

"It does." She looked out the windows and could see the Willamette River and town below. Although it wasn't the Clackamas, at least she could still see a river. "They told me that the man died, and his wife didn't want to stay on here."

"Where'd she go?"

"I guess back East. Pastor Jefferson says he thinks we could get it at a good price. It will include the furniture we see. If later we want to sell, we could turn a tidy profit." She stared at the porch, trying to visualize Adam sitting on it, rocking on the swing. Would he like this house with the big maple trees in the front yard?

St. Louis chuckled. "Those folks down at the town hall were shore eager at the idea of gettin' Adam as their sheriff. I think they'd wait 'til hell freezes over if that's what it'd take."

"I can understand that," Martha said, touching the faded curtains at the windows. "That deputy looked inept to me also. I'd hate to depend on him protecting anybody." She pulled the dust

378

laden curtains down, deciding that sewing new ones would be her first project.

"Ya made up yore mind then?" he asked as he followed her from window to window.

"Yes, I'm going to buy it, and make it into a home."

"Ya think you're goin' to like it in town?"

"I like a challenge, myself. I think that I'll like living wherever Adam is, and wherever he's going to be happy. I knew he wasn't cut out for farming. It would have been like chaining him to a heavy weight and watching it drag him into the ground. This, well at least it will be something challenging for him."

St. Louis shook his head, smiling at her. "I'll never understand women," he growled. "I figured ya was set out there on that farm and nothin' would've blasted ya from it."

"I thought so too," she admitted, "but a whirlwind came into my life, uprooted everything, and suddenly the little farm doesn't seem so necessary."

"Where ya goin' to live this winter?"

"I think until after Christmas, I'll stay at the cabin. I want to be with as much of my family as is possible, and be there in case Adam does get back sooner than I expect. After that, I'll move in here and fix this up. I still haven't heard from him, but he said he'd come back, and I'm counting on that especially after he reads my letters."

"Ya wrote him again?"

"I'm going to keep writing, with the hope that one reaches him. I had hoped to hear something back, but so far it's as though he dropped into a dark void."

"He's not much for writing."

"I know that, but just a word to tell me that he's well would be enough."

She walked out into the kitchen, admiring the large, many-paned windows. Mornings would see sunlight there, filtered by big maple trees. It would be a nice place to work, to prepare meals, to wait for her husband to come home.

St. Louis put his hand on her shoulder, giving her a soothing pat. "He's goin' to be home afore ya know it."

"I hope so. I can't help worrying though with winter harder there, and the reports of attacks that we read in the *Argus*. It doesn't seem encouraging."

"They sensationalize everything. Ya know how them papers are. Things have a way of workin' themselves out. Just keep prayin' to God that He's lookin' out for him. Your man will be back with the spring."

His tender words brought the tears to her eyes. Turning into his wool coat, she let herself cry. "I believe that, but it's hard. I just wish I'd sent him off with my love, and not--"

"Don't go blaming yourself for what ya can't change." He patted her shoulder, trying to offer what consolation he could.

"I accused him of going down there for excitement," she said. "I said he wanted to go."

"Wish I could help, gal, but just have faith. In time it'll be all right."

She stopped her tears. "I will and I'll stay busy. I have a plan now and I can make it work. I know I can." Tears weren't going to help. She had done too much of that. She needed to set ground for the future, for when he came back. He would come back.

Adam's winter was proving every bit as damning as Major Montgomery had hoped. Every day, except in a blizzard, he went out, sometimes with a small patrol, often by himself. He talked to the Indians he met, explaining to them in sign language and his limited Chinook, about the demands of the military. Slowly he began to learn more of their tongue, enough to converse in a limited, halting fashion.

Only once was he physically attacked. A large brave, a Shasta, lunged at him. Adam wrestled him to the ground, taking care not to hurt him any more than was required. He held no animosity toward any of them even though likely one had killed Pollard. He understood they were fighting for their lives, their land, their sacred ground; and in their place, he would have done the same thing.

Most of the ones he met were dejected by the time he got to them, seeing that they could not run, and ready to hear of a safe place, of a way to be protected from the elements and from the vigilantes who also sporadically roamed the hills. Many headed down the canyon toward the fort to give themselves up. Their choice was to stay in these hills, starve, die of diseases, or to take a chance on the mercy of the white government. Some were already sick with tuberculosis or measles.

With the long hard days, the driving frustration and the loneliness of being so far from the woman he loved and often alone, Adam thought about what he wanted, about Martha the most but also about the meaning of life. He had gone from believing he'd made a mistake in coming to knowing he had done what he needed to do. Maybe it hadn't worked out to save John, but he was needed. Perhaps he could save very few lives, but a man did what he knew. He couldn't second guess the future.

On lonely patrols, he began to find it satisfying to talk as though someone was listening. He still had little faith that any god cared much what happened to him, but it felt comforting to talk as though someone rode with him. Maybe an angel, maybe a ghost, perhaps even John.

"I don't know if you are here today or not, but see that draw ahead, I got to know whether I ought to go on up it, or head off to the left. What's your thought?"

"This is good fishing country, if a man didn't have to watch his back every minute, that is. Those pools there-- salmon come up them. Shastas love them as much as me. Wonder if you appreciate what it's like to get a big strike on your line." He laughed. "Maybe I am going crazy." He imagined what a sight he had to be presenting, a heavily bearded man riding along, leather pants, an ice crusted wool coat, and talking to himself.

From all Adam had heard and there wasn't frequent news, the major still held a grudge against him, one that wasn't likely to be forgotten soon. None of it mattered. He felt the sting of regret about John, wishing he'd been able to talk him into leaving before he was killed. Pollard hadn't even heard he'd been married. It would have been satisfying to tell him. So he did.

He lost track of the days and had no idea when Christmas came and went. He felt no satisfaction, no comfort, nor did he expect to find any. It had been as hard as he'd anticipated. Many nights, like this one, found him camping alone, back in the hills.

He scraped out a hollow for himself underneath a pine tree and kicked snow away from a patch of grass for his horse, the horse he didn't intend to name. "No getting fond of you," he muttered as he brushed the animal down and tethered him. "Not that I'd have to tie you to keep you here. This is probably the only grass inside of five miles."

Rolled into his blankets, sleep soon found him and shortly after that Martha walked into his dreams. She came toward him on a rocky beach, a glowing river behind her, her arms outstretched in love, her lips calling his name. Smiling he walked toward her, pulling her into his arms, kissing her lips, telling her he would love her forever. Lying back, he stripped off her blouse, baring her breasts to the sunlight and his touch. 'You're so beautiful,' he whispered, kissing her again, feeling her body strain against his, and then she pushed him away. At first he thought it was playful, but she snapped, 'You never really loved me. I'm going to divorce you and marry George. He'll be there for me, and he has three houses and three stores.' 'Martha,' he had bellowed, only to wake and realize it was all a dream, and he was lying, sweating in his blankets.

Lying in the dark, staring up at a clear, starlit night, he wondered if he'd ever hold her again. He'd go back, as he promised her, but would she be so convinced that he would do this again that she would turn from him? Maybe her mind had already been made up.

If it is, he thought with a dark promise to himself, *I'll change it back. I did it before, I can do it again. Once I leave this country, and I will leave this country, with the spring thaw, army or no, Indians or no, I'm going home.*

He lay back and tried again to remember making love to her. Closing his eyes, he let himself feel her touch, her soft skin, the roundness of her breasts under his hand, in his mouth. Perhaps he was torturing himself but it was almost as though she was there beside him.

∼

A bit after midnight, Martha awoke abruptly from a dream. Tears ran down her cheeks. Adam had been kissing her, making love to her, his body hard against hers. It took her a moment to realize it had not happened. It might never happen again. She could barely contain her feeling of loss that he wasn't beside her and had to look over to be certain the bed was empty except for her and Heaven. It had seemed so real.

She rolled over and tried again to sleep, but it didn't come. She forced her mind to other things. Every thought carried her back to him. She wanted him so badly. All right, think of something else, anything. No, not anything, something good.

Christmas had been good, not as quiet as she had expected

with Amy, Matt, Laura, St. Louis, the Lances and a new couple, the Doolings with their two small children. It had been a day filled with food, laughter, enjoying Laura learning to crawl, roast chicken, stuffing, mashed potatoes, gravy, sweet potatoes, apple pies and as much coffee as even St. Louis could drink. The rain had beat a steady tattoo on the roof, but it had been cozy and friendly inside as they talked and laughed.

Around her family Martha kept her pain and fear to herself. She managed to smile, forced herself not to wonder where Adam was spending his Christmas. Was he sheltered, soaking wet, in snow? Was he sick, wounded? Was anyone caring for him? It did no good to tell others how she felt. Who could help any of it? She just had to get through it and pray that he would return, that they would have more good memories to share someday, that Christmas the coming year wouldn't be like this one. She tried not to let herself think that maybe she'd never have him in her arms again. Maybe like that poem by Blake, the hour had been all they were ever to know.

She remembered with a smile her surprise Christmas gift. When it had come time to unwrap the gifts, most had been expected, simple gifts, handmade-- quilts, carved wooden toys, new dresses, shirts, a crocheted tablecloth, wrapped fruit, rum fruitcake. But one had not been. St. Louis had brought Martha a large wrapped bundle. "This is from Adam."

"But how could it be," she had asked. "He didn't know he was going to be gone in time to leave anything."

St. Louis had explained it was something Adam had planned awhile back. When she had opened the flour sack wrappings, she had found a soft, golden pelt. St. Louis had said it was the cougar Adam had shot. "He wanted ya to have it for a rug or a muff or some such thing. Whatever ya'd want." She had run her fingers over the soft fur, looking down at it, admiring the texture, the slickness, thought of the time when he had shot it, and had forced herself not to cry.

She had brought it with her when she moved to Oregon City the week after Christmas. She had half expected Amy to argue with her about the move. It seemed her daughter had accepted the change to her life. There were no arguments, just help in packing.

Lying in her new brass bed, which she had bought for the Oregon City home, Martha struggled with a suddenly sleepless night as she remembered how it had been with Adam, what touching him was like, how his skin felt so silky for a man.

It could not be that their time was over. They had to have a chance to make their dreams come true, to give them both a new life. She didn't want their last angry words to be all they would ever have. She couldn't think that way; and so she lay planning a future together, a future that in her darkest moments she feared would ever be.

CHAPTER 31

January was cold and snowy in the Rogue Country, the days short, the nights long. Adam continued his mostly solitary forays into the hills, although more and more he found no one. The various tribes and bands had yielded to the might of the US Military, the frigid winter, and were gathered where the Federal troops wanted them.

It was well into February when a courier came to Camp Leland with a message from Lane. "You are ordered back to Lane," said the curt missive, with no explanation for what had happened or why. Saddling his horse, Adam started out immediately, unsure of what to expect when he got to there.

Phillips was the first to greet him, almost before he'd dismounted. As Adam rolled them both a cigarette, Phillips explained the situation. "We've got over four hundred Indians here, Toquahear's people. Superintendent Palmer has decided that because of the local attitude, the only safe place for them is to take them north to a reservation on the Yamhill River."

Adam frowned, inhaling deeply of his cigarette, he looked at Phillips. "How are they going to get there?"

"One hundred troopers, myself included, and you are going to take them on foot."

"On foot," Adam repeated with disbelief. "These people were sick before they left the mountains, some dying. They don't have adequate clothing. A lot of them won't make it if they try to walk that far in the dead of winter."

"Those are the orders," Phillips said, rocking back on his heels.

"Is this being done to assure that more die?" Adam asked bitterly.

"It's because we can't protect them here. They won't stay on the reservation when the weather warms. The idea is to get them away from here, away from the people who want to kill them."

"Away from where they have their spirit quests, away from their burials, away from the places they dig the camas, away from their hunting grounds," Adam finished.

"Look, the decision to do this wasn't mine. I just carry out orders. If you refuse to go, you'll be back up on the Rogue or worse."

Adam shook his head with disbelief. "If I refused this, I'd go home."

"I don't think so," said Phillips, gesturing toward the officer's building. "You signed a contract."

"I did not. I came, but I signed nothing."

"Montgomery will forge your signature if need be. He'd take great pleasure in having you thrown in the brig if you say no to this. He'd like any excuse to do that. The man's not overly pleased that he's stuck here himself. It seems that hating you has added something pleasurable to his life."

Adam stared off at the distant Coast range. "So I have him to thank for this assignment?"

"No," Phillips admitted. Adam saw how pale he was, his eyes bleak. The winter had been a hard one for every man on this assignment. "You have me. I asked for you."

Adam shook his head ruefully. "All right, I'll do it, but it'll only be because I'll likely be the only man traveling with them, who'd like to keep them alive to make the end of the march."

"No," Phillips said, grimacing, "not the only one, but maybe one of two or three."

The next morning, with no delay, they started on the trail north. It was late February, the ground frozen, the land locked in winter, light sleet falling, but none of that was considered cause for delay as the troopers and their charges began their northward exodus. All but thirty-four of the oldest and sickest natives set out from their homeland on foot.

Adam gritted his teeth as he saw the small children, some seeming to be wandering with no parents, the elderly, the sick, some walking well, but many stumbling as they set out for their new home, one they would not have chosen for themselves. The people had clothing that little protected them from the elements, most wrapped in blankets against the biting cold.

Each day seemed worse than the one before. The weather was bleak, wind blowing when the rain didn't come down, drenching all of them with its steady downpour. And even that was almost a relief because of the alternative of traveling in snow or sleet.

Adam watched one of the small boys as he stumbled. Unable to stand any more, Adam dismounted and picked the child up. For a moment, the little boy stared at him as though frightened. Adam could imagine with his shaggy beard, he was probably a scary sight, but when he was again mounted with the child in front of him, the boy settled down. There was no smile, no words of gratitude, and Adam didn't expect them. All of this misery was due to the white man. The child had no reason or maybe any energy to feel grateful.

He piled on two more children and then walked leading his horse. From that time on, he frequently allowed some of the children or ill Indians to ride, and he noticed Phillips and other troopers doing likewise. The misery of the Indians, already weakened by their time in the mountains, was almost enough to bring out the benevolence in even the most hardened soul. Almost. There was so little they could do to make this trek easier on the people. Even if every soldier gave up his mount, there weren't enough to take all the sick and weak.

Six days out, a group of volunteers rode up behind them. Adam turned his head, wondering what they were up to. He took the children from his saddle and handed the smallest one back to her mother who stared at him with bleak, expressionless eyes. He mounted up and rode back with Lieutenant Phillips.

"Just goin' to make sure you get them out of here and none of them gets away to come to our homes," one large, surly man said, staring belligerently at Phillips and then Adam.

"Thank you," Phillips said, obviously working to keep a polite edge to his voice, "but we don't need or want help."

"You don't get it, soldier boy. We know how the military has bungled everything else. We'll make sure you don't bungle this. There's been word that there's been an attack on the coast."

"The Tututni?" asked Adam, fighting back his inclination to hit this loudmouthed volunteer.

"I don't know what they call themselves, but they're stirring up trouble. Rumor come up, that they hit the Gold Beach Guards."

"The ones camped directly across from their village?" asked Phillips, obviously working to keep his own temper under control as the crude volunteer spit tobacco juice next to his boots.

"Whatever happened down there," Adam said curly, "has nothing to do with these people. They are under the protection of the United States government and are peacefully leaving their land. We don't need your help and would appreciate it if you got the hell out of here."

"No. We'll just ride along with you. Ain't no law against that is there?" a tall skinny man asked snidely.

Adam and Phillips looked at each other in frustration. There was no law that could make the volunteers leave unless they caused trouble.

"Think they'll be a problem?" Phillips asked as they rode back to the front of the column.

"Most likely," Adam said his own mood dour. If there was more trouble, would he ever get out of this country?

A gunshot sent them galloping their horses to the back of the line where the volunteers were talking loudly and gesturing. Adam dismounted and knelt at the side of a fallen Indian. A hole in the center of his back didn't leave Adam any hope for the man and when he turned him over, he saw that he was dead.

The loudmouthed volunteer stood his ground. "One of the bucks tried to run away. I shot him."

A young woman with a child on her back began to wail. She stood by the man, not reaching down and touching him. Her voice the only indication that she understood his life had departed him. Her cry was a keening reminder of all the tragedy that had befallen these people.

Adam straightened, the anger that had been growing in him was nearly at the boiling point. "Run away?" he repeated with disgust, "Where would he have run to? You killed an innocent, unarmed man, and you ought to be arrested."

"For killin' an Injun? I oughta get a medal for it." He grinned showing tobacco stained teeth.

"What's your name?" Adam asked, stalking over to him.

For the first time the volunteer looked nervous. "What's it to you?"

He grabbed him by the coat collar and asked it again despite the guns that were now pointed at him by the man's friends.

"Sam Weiner."

"Well, Sam Weiner, you just murdered a man, in cold blood. You shot him in the back." When Weiner tried to twist away, Adam held him, pushing him back against a tree. "That man has a family, Weiner, a wife, children, parents. He was a human being. He had hopes and dreams, but you don't care about any of that, do you? You just want to go home and brag that you killed an Indian."

Weiner reached down trying to pull Adam's hands from his coat. Adam shoved him backward, backhanding him so hard that he fell to the ground, wiping his mouth where blood had began to trickle at the corner.

"Are we arresting him?" he asked Phillips, his voice cutting like a steel knife.

"Not yet. I have to have permission."

"I can't believe this. You have to have permission to arrest a murderer."

"I'll send a messenger back," Phillips said, "but my orders were to deliver the Indians and not to stir up trouble with the locals."

Adam let his shoulders sag as he looked at him with stunned incredulity. "When you send your damned messenger," he growled, stomping away, "tell them that I quit. When your Indians are delivered, I'm through."

"But..."

Adam turned to look back at him. He forced a smile that he knew held no humor. "I've had all of this country I ever want. When we get to Yamhill, that's it, even if I have to desert as you see it; and if you had a brain in your head, you'd do the same!"

With the night, Adam made his way back through the Indians. Their faces were sullen as they wordlessly stared at him. He understood their hostility, the hopelessness they must be feeling, but he was determined to talk with the family of the man they'd buried along the trail. Somehow he wanted them to understand that there were people who did care. They would find more in their new home.

When he found the woman, her child now lying beside her on the ground, wrapped in all the covering she had to give it, he tried a few words of Chinook; then the other words he'd learned, but she didn't understand any of it. A man strode up, his face frozen, his stance belligerent. "I speak English," the stocky man said.

"I just wanted her to understand I'm sorry."

"You're sorry?" the man asked incredulously. "What good is your sorry? Will that bring back her man? Will that give her back her home? Or her father who lies dead, his body lost in the forests? What good is your sorry?"

Adam understood that truth as well as any man. "There isn't anything any of us can do about this. I don't have any more power over what is happening here than you do."

"Yes," the man said, his frozen face back in place, "but when this is over, you can go home."

Adam only stared at the man, shivering himself with the cold. After a moment, he knew there was nothing more he could say. This man would never understand nor would the weeping woman because he didn't understand himself.

As he walked back to where his horse and bedroll waited, despair engulfed him. Was it true? Did he have a home to return to? There was every possibility, that because of what he had done, he would have no more home than these people did. He wrapped himself in his blanket but was too cold to sleep. He could only lie on the cold, wet ground, hating people of little tolerance, hating the conditions that had forced this march upon both him and these people.

From then on Adam steeled himself to not think, not imagine anything. He no longer thought of Martha or of home. He thought only of finishing the seemingly endless march. The volunteers continued to follow them from a little distance now, and Adam's only satisfaction came when permission to arrest Sam Weiner finally came.

He rode back with the detail that put the killer under guard.

Weiner was incredulous when they told him. "But he was an Indian," he muttered.

"He was a man," Adam said, still sitting on his horse as he watched the irons being attached to the man's wrists. "When will you people ever understand that? They're people." He didn't imagine much would be done to Weiner, not with any trial in Oregon Territory, but at least he'd know some discomfort now over what he had done.

The march went on. At night the temperatures dipped to freezing, the ground froze hard. Even if Adam had not been sleeping cold, sleep would have been difficult to come by. The nights were marked with coughing and the crying of children.

The people were forced to wade across the many streams through the valleys they traveled. When they reached the Umpqua River, it was raging past from the rains and a recent snow melt in the mountains, the water a murky brown. To ford it would be a challenge even for healthy people, let alone with those who were nearly at the end of their strength.

Adam and Phillips dismounted, staring at the current, the uneven rocky bottom. "I don't know how we're going to get the sick ones, the children across this," Phillips said through clenched teeth, the weight of their trek falling more heavily on him every day as his face seemed to have aged in only these few weeks.

Adam sat back on his haunches as he rolled and lit a cigarette. "We'll have to use a guide rope, to keep those who can swim or walk from being carried downstream. The weak ones, the children we'll take across on our horses, returning until we get them all. It's the only way."

"That water looks cold."

Adam nodded, taking a drag on the cigarette before he handed it to Phillips. "That's because it is cold."

Phillips looked at him through the smoke. "I was afraid you'd say that." He stared at it again, the frothy brown water not anything like it might have been during the summer or even later in the spring. "I don't suppose it's particularly deep," he suggested hopefully as he handed the cigarette back to Adam.

"There's only one way to find out." Adam gave Phillips one end of his lariat. "You keep a good grip on this. I don't want to have to do this twice." Mounting his gelding, he edged the reluctant bay to the bank and with a strong booted kick to his side, they lunged into the full current of the river, working their way across. The river was bitterly cold, the air above not much warmer. By the time Adam had gotten across and secured the rope, he was shivering violently. He had to keep active now if he wasn't going to get sick himself. Keeping active meant getting back into that water.

As he started back, he heard Phillips yell. "Johnson, Taylor and Berringer, you go across and build up bonfires, big ones. Gather all the wood you can find and build 'em high."

Repeatedly, Adam, Phillips and the troopers made their way across the Umpqua supporting children, women, trying to hold as many as possible above the waters. The stronger men and women made their own way across the river by swimming along the rope.

In the darkening evening, the air below freezing, the only bright part to their ordeal was the promise of the huge bonfires, casting light and heat into the night sky. As the people were lowered to the ground, they made their way to the only warmth they would find. For Adam and the troopers, there was no such promise until the last person had crossed. Only then could they stand by a fire, stripping off as much wet clothing as possible and trying to warm their bodies.

"Y-you know, you aren't all w-wrong about the m-military," Phillips said shivering so much he could barely talk.

"You j-just figuring th-that out?" Adam asked, his own teeth chattering. He and Phillips had stripped to their long johns and would have gone further if there hadn't been women among the

Indians. *False modesty will get you pneumonia,* he thought, but left the long johns on. He found it hard to believe he would ever be warm again. His hands and feet had long since lost feeling. He wasn't eager for the pain when that feeling returned.

Phillips reached over and began vigorously massaging Adam's shoulders and chest with a rough towel, which had been miraculously kept dry through the many crossings.

Adam grinned. "Not a b-bad idea... for a city b-boy," he grunted as he returned the favor. Slowly their bodies began to warm.

"They don't tell you about these kinds of assignments at West Point," Rand said with a small laugh as he hunkered down, accepting again one of Adam's rolled cigarettes. "My father never had this kind of experience or he lied to me. He pushed hard for me to be a soldier. In the beginning, I never saw a real option. It was the family trade." He took a long draw on the cigarette.

"Maybe it was lucky my father was a ne-er do well. Not a crook or anything but just failed at everything he tried," Adam said squatting beside Rand. A private brought them two cups of hot coffee, which further restored warmth. "Given his failures, there were no expectations, except maybe negative ones."

Phillips opened up his saddlebag and brought out a whiskey bottle. He held it over Adam's cup, and Adam nodded as he poured a liberal dollop into both cups.

"That could be its own set of expectations," Rand said.

"'I guess so." Adam laughed, as the hard liquor and coffee hit his stomach, sending up a glow from someplace. "My mother sure did figure I'd end up like him, and maybe she's been right."

"At least you have a home, a beautiful wife. You're a fortunate man in that."

"Yeah, or I will be if I still have any of that."

Phillips stared at the fire. "Your wife was that upset at your going?"

"She said if I went not to bother coming back."

Phillips shook his head. "Women say a lot of things they don't mean when they're angry. Not that I've had such a great experience with women. The military becomes a man's mistress."

Adam shook his head. "Any man claims he's an expert on women is probably a liar anyway, but I can't forget the sound of her voice, the anger, and I haven't heard anything since I left. It doesn't give me a lot of encouragement."

Phillips seemed lost in thought. He almost said something and then swallowed hard as he evidently decided against it. When he opened his mouth again, Adam spoke first. "You got a woman, Rand?"

"No. Oh there was one once, where I thought maybe. She didn't like the military life, the separations, the worry. I never asked her to marry me, and she married my best friend."

"Was that hard to take?"

"I didn't love her. So, no. Besides, I didn't see how I could do this and leave a family behind. At least this way, there's nobody who cares."

"How about your parents?"

"My mother's dead, and my father's remarried. He has another son now. Maybe one that'll live up to what he wants more than I ever could."

"West Point wasn't enough for him?"

"Nothing ever was."

Adam shook his head as he smoked, thinking again of Martha and how he had let her down. "Before I left, I tried to make Martha see why I had to go. Now I wonder if I did have to." He fought against the depression that threatened to swallow him. "She asked what difference I thought one man could make. It wasn't a bad question."

"You probably saved my life. That's a difference to me," Phillips said, moving to warm the other side of his body. "There are people traveling with us, who would not make it except for what you've put into it. I think you said it before. If nobody tried to help, where would we be?"

"I don't know," Adam said with a humorless laugh, "where?"

Rand smiled at him through the mingled smoke of their cigarettes. "Don't ask me. I figured you'd know."

~

Looking around her new home, Martha felt a sense of pride in what she'd accomplished in two months. New curtains hung at all the windows, starched and white. With the help of a handyman in the community, she'd put up wallpaper in the parlor, a pale green with a tiny white flower. The furniture was a mix of the pieces, which had been left by the previous owner and those she found in Oregon City and Portland when she'd visited her daughters. She'd been reluctant to take the ferry down the river, afraid Adam would return while she was gone, In the end she'd needed the break, needed to stop looking at the road, wondering if it was him, whenever she saw a rider; then facing disappointment that it wasn't.

The front porch swing was newly painted white and ready to be used in the evenings. Although it was too early to plant seeds, Martha had worked up several small beds, eagerly anticipating the time when the soil would warm enough to allow her to begin making the garden as fully hers as the home now was. She had taken a cutting from her Rose of Sharon. Only time would tell if it would take in this new soil.

The neighbors to the left of her were an elderly couple, Alvin and Mary Jones, whose children lived down the valley. On the other side were a couple closer to her own age, Virgil and Annie Buxman. Virgil was a heavy-set, husky man, who sat on the town council and was instrumental in ensuring Adam the job of sheriff. Annie, a little too rounded in the hips, her personality as bouncy as her walk, had been quickly over to meet Martha, repeating her visits frequently.

The knock on the door this time was one Martha expected. Annie, Clarice Sims and Elfrida Jefferson had invited themselves to tea. Martha had greeted the social invasion with a combination of humor and resignation. She'd never been much for small talk, and she didn't know how this afternoon would go. These might be friends though; so she had dressed carefully, braiding her hair into a coronet on top of her head and wearing a dark blue dress with white trim, appropriately lady-like and sober for the wife of their future sheriff.

Elfrida was silver-haired, her figure as straight as the back of a chair, her posture as stiff. Clarice, a small woman, almost bird-like walked around the room before she joined the others in the kitchen. "I just love this house," she repeated, again and again.

When the ladies were finally seated at the round oak table, Annie said, "Martha, we simply must have you join the Woman's Circle."

Martha poured each lady a cup of tea, giving herself a moment to gather her thoughts. "Explain it to me again." She handed the sugar bowl to Annie who added two teaspoons before she passed it to Clarice. The last time this topic of the Woman's Circle had come up, Martha, who had never been much of a joiner, had managed to evade a decision, but she'd have to find out what it was eventually. Town life did have its complications.

"It's a group of ladies, we're all members, who get together and attend to various charitable needs in the community. Our group was instrumental in establishing the first public library over ten years ago. We try to look at the needs of the community and come up with projects that will be beneficial. Our major concern right now is making sure our new school is growing and teaching what is needful."

"On a personal note, we also discuss new books we've read or political comments that seem to be affecting our community," Clarice added.

"Mmmm," Martha said noncommittally.

"We play bridge too," Elfrida put in. "Not every meeting, but at least once a month. Do you play bridge?"

"I'm afraid I never learned."

"It's simple to learn. You'll just love the game," Clarice chirped.

Martha smiled as she thought of the last game she'd played, strip checkers. She rather doubted that would qualify her for membership in the Women's Circle.

"Our civic involvement is important to the city and our children," Annie added, sipping from her tea.

"I can imagine," Martha commented absentmindedly, her mind really out the window and wondering if the rain would soon stop.

"It is. We're always in need of new ideas and women with experience in social causes."

"I'm afraid I haven't had much experience in anything like that."

"Perhaps you have and just don't know it. It's truly amazing the way women can make a difference in a community, bring in the finer things so to speak. Besides as the new sheriff's wife, it will be your responsibility to become involved in a positive way."

Martha smiled neutrally. She was determined that she would become no more involved than she deemed beneficial and right now she wasn't certain how much that should be. Everything would depend on Adam when he came back.

"I heard that you do tailoring," Elfrida mentioned.

"I sew."

Elfrida asked, "Did you make the dress you're wearing?"

"Yes."

"Well, it's just lovely. So demure. So stylish in a chic sort of way."

"There really is a need in Oregon City for quality clothing. Even though my husband is nearly sure that the capitol is going to be permanently located in Salem," Annie said with a bitter twist to her voice, "we still will have our social obligations, and your stylish dresses would do much to improve the atmosphere of them."

"I don't know." Talking about clothing came close to boring Martha to death. She wondered just how deep the political discussions were in this women's group. "Would you like more tea?" she asked.

All three nodded.

Elfrida said, "Your sewing has a definite flare, Martha. We've all commented on it in the month you've been here and attending our church."

"How nice," Martha said. She understood if she was going to make her life interesting here in town, and she felt it would be possible to do so, she had to find some interests that expanded her own and didn't revolve around who wore what dress to what social gathering.

When the ladies had gone, Martha sat, staring out the river and at the gray sky, wondering where Adam was and whether he was sleeping under a roof or out in the open. *Come home,* she mouthed the words to the air, to the wind. *Time to come home, my love, to me.*

CHAPTER 32

The attitude of the settlers, which they passed as they traveled north, proved as difficult as had it had been in the Rogue Valley. Many of the whites in the Umpqua and Lower Willamette valleys feared the decision to bring peoples they considered savages into their proximity.

Adam continued to walk as much as he could, sparing the weaker Indians by letting them ride his horse. The walking, the sparse meals took their toll on his body. He developed a nagging cough, and the weight dropped from him until he was just sinewy muscle and bone.

Through one of the communities they passed, they learned of a massacre at Gold Beach. Whites who'd been gathered for a George Washington Birthday dance in Gold Beach had been attacked. By dawn, twenty-three white people had been killed, a woman and her two daughters carried off.

Adam grimaced at the news. The Indians might have thought they won a battle, but they assured their own defeat by having killed the local Indian agent. The newspapers that he and Phillips managed to get their hands on were playing this up as a huge Indian war, never mind that there weren't that many Indians left in those hills. It made for exciting copy, and the army was sufficiently pressured to send more forces south to take care of the problem.

Their own march into hell continued, the temperatures so low at night, that Adam shivered in his sleep, no matter how curled up to find warmth. But all earthly hells come to an end, one way or another, and after thirty-two days and two hundred and sixty-one miles, they delivered their charges to their temporary reservation.

Adam saddled his horse, ready to ride northeast, to learn if he had a home. Phillips stopped him. "Hold up." He shook Adam's hand. "On behalf of the US government, I thank you for your help and wish we could talk you into going south with us. On a personal level, I wish you luck and understand completely why you are not going to do that." He gave a short laugh. "I put it in writing that you completed your agreement—which you never signed, of course."

"If you had any brains, Rand, you'd quit the military," Adam said. "I tried to talk John into getting out, but he wouldn't listen. It's not a good life for any man."

"You might be right."

"So, do it."

"I wish I could explain why it becomes something you don't quit. You just are. I admit it's not perfect, but no life is."

"You have me there."

"I feel what I do makes a difference. If someday I stop feeling that way, I will quit."

"Well, if you get up our way, come see us. I've got a daughter who's so beautiful you won't believe it."

Rand raised his brows. "You've got a daughter. If you do, she couldn't be old enough for me. What kind of man do you think I am?"

Adam laughed. "She's my wife's daughter. Loraine lives in Portland. Real pretty lady, smart too."

"If she looks anything like your wife, I could believe that," Phillips said with a wry grin. "I just might take you up on that someday."

Adam shook his head. "And, Rand, think about getting out. Getting a life where somebody else doesn't pull your strings— half the time for stupid reasons."

Rand just smiled.

"I tried to tell John the same thing and look where he ended up, six feet under and making no difference to anybody."

"He got you down there."

"And maybe cost me my home and marriage."

"You think it could?"

Adam thought again of the long winter and no word. "It could have." He remembered the last thing Martha had said to him. Did he have a home-- anymore than these poor Indians who had been displaced?

"I shouldn't tell you this," Phillips said, "I could end up court-martialed if you repeat it. I wouldn't be much of a friend though if I didn't tell you."

"Get to your point, Rand. I need to get out of here."

"I'd have told you earlier but don't even know it's true. It is said that Montgomery ordered any mail coming to you routed through him. He said he didn't want subversive mails to enflame the situation. There might have been letters, Adam. There might not have been; but if there had, Montgomery easily could have destroyed them."

Adam hated Montgomery for his small-mindedness. Maybe Martha had written although it was equally likely she had served him with divorce papers. No way to know which. If it had been the latter, he guessed he had been better off not knowing. Maybe Montgomery had done him a favor.

"Thanks for telling me," he said. "I guess I'll find out soon enough."

"Good luck with it. I know the major is a small man, but I believe we all get what is coming to us. We reap what we sow."

"Wish I thought that way," Adam said with a laugh, and then he wondered if he did. Perhaps he didn't deserve Martha.

In a drizzling rain, he rode with one determination. If Martha was planning on divorcing him, he would fight it. He'd do whatever was required to get back his wife, to have the dream he'd dreamed for so long. Despite his resolve not to lose her, not to lose hope, he felt an aching loneliness, worse than he'd experienced in all the years he'd spent by solitary campfires.

As Adam rode up to their cabin, his first concern was the lack of smoke from the chimney. His heart seemed to drop into his boots as he realized the animals were gone from the corral. Scarcely daring to breathe, he tied his horse to the rail and walked across the porch. He couldn't let himself think that something had happened to her, the thought was intolerable. He tried the door and found it locked. Moving down, he concentrated on one of the windows. He pried it open and slipped inside the dark cabin.

His boots echoed hollowly in the empty room. Most of the furniture was in place, but what had made it a home was gone. Where was she? God, he hoped she hadn't gotten sick and died. He couldn't even let himself imagine that, but no one had lived in this cabin in months. Then he saw the envelope on the table and walked toward it, knowing he was holding his breath as he picked it up. His name in Martha's handwriting.

His hand was shaking as he opened the envelope. It took him a moment to understand the words. "Adam, I am in Oregon City. Please come when you get home." She had not signed it, but she had drawn a map on the bottom of the page.

He scanned the words again. Looking around the room,

almost literally seeing nothing, he tried to understand the two sentences. From the tension and pressure of trying to get here, he found himself hard put to reason through what she was telling him. Except there was nothing to understand. The note told him nothing. Not why wasn't she here. Not what was going on. He felt almost physically ill as he stared again at the brief missive.

He went back out through the window, carrying his letter with him. With a grimace of pain he wondered if she'd already divorced him. Was she living elsewhere with a new husband and didn't want him to learn it from a note.

Stepping into the saddle, he kicked the bay into a lope, heading directly for Oregon City. He had no interest in seeing St. Louis or Matt and Amy. All he could think of was getting to Martha and finding out what was going through that beautiful head of hers. If she thought it would be easy getting rid of him, she had another *think* coming.

Riding into Oregon City, it was almost dark, and he had a hard time following her little map. Rain was pouring again, reminding him of the first time they'd spent a night together. That night, he'd wanted to kiss her so badly he had almost been able to taste it. He wondered bleakly what she would have for him this night.

He tied his horse to what he believed to be the right porch pillar, staring up at the house. As he mounted the steps, he could scarcely think. It was a nice enough house; except, what possessed her to be here? A new man? He wouldn't think that way, but why come into town? When he did knock, would it be a man answering the door. He couldn't let himself believe that was possible, or he'd go insane.

Water running off his clothing in rivulets, he had to work up the courage to knock. When he finally did, he stood back a little, almost shadowed by the brim of his hat and the gathering night as he heard her steps coming across the floor and then her voice. "Who is it?"

"Adam."

The door swung open, and she was framed in the lamplight, her eyes huge as she looked at him. She wore a thin wrapper, belted at the waist, outlining her body against the light. Her hair hung loose down her back. She hesitated only a moment as her eyes scanned his bearded face before she had crossed the threshold and was clinging to him, ignoring the fact that he had to be soaking her robe with his wet clothing. His arms came around her, closing convulsively as he held her.

"It's you. It finally is you," she cried, reaching up and pulling his head down where she could kiss his cold, wet lips. He felt as though life was flowing into his body with that kiss.

Her hands were now drawing him inside, back into the warmth that he'd known only with her. "I'm dripping water all over your floor," he muttered inanely, aware that he was shaking and uncertain if it was from the cold or her nearness.

She smiled then, her eyes warm with the light he'd dreamt of seeing for months. "Then," she said, her voice husky, "you have to get out of those clothes."

"I got to take care of my horse first."

"You're so cold. Your hands are like ice," she complained. "I'll get dressed and see to your horse."

"No." He was firm. He wanted her in this house, waiting for him, not outside, getting soaked.

"There's a small barn out back, she said, relinquishing her hold on him. "Joe is there with my mare. When you're finished, come back-- to me."

He worked as fast as he could, but the gelding deserved better than being left wet and he took the time to rub him down, added time to rub Joe's nose and give the three horses each a pitchfork of hay. As he worked, his thoughts never left the task. When he had finished, he walked back into the house, and she was waiting for him, her gaze not letting go of his as she reached up and stripped off his coat, throwing it to the floor. In moments she had unbuttoned the equally wet shirt and pulled it off. "Move closer to the fire," she ordered when she saw him shivering. "I'll be right back."

He stood in front of the fireplace, realizing that under his feet was his cougar pelt. St. Louis had obviously finished it and given it to her. He stepped back, not wanting to mar it by the water still running from boots and pants.

Heaven came over and sniffed of his leg, seeming to decide that she did remember and accept him as she rubbed against him. "You've grown up," he said, reaching down and petting her sleek length before he stared back at the flames in the fireplace, wondering how long it would be before Martha was back.

Martha walked back into the room, a large quilt in her arms and stopped, staring at him, at how thin he was and yet how wondrously male he looked as the light of the fireplace outlined every muscle in his gaunt torso and arms.

When he turned to look at her, she saw the questions in his eyes, but there would be time for those later. Now she wanted him dry and warm and in her arms.

She pushed him into one of their new chairs. "I'll wreck the fancy upholstery," he protested, "I'm wet and dirtier than you can imagine. It's been many months since I've been clean."

"And you have a huge beard," she agreed. "We'll take care of first one and then the other, but you sit on this chair now. Upholstery isn't that important to either of us."

He gave her a sketch of a smile, still unsure of what was going on with her, of what had possessed her to be in this house.

Kneeling in front of him, she pulled his boots off and then reached up to unbutton his pants. He stood up, feeling his insides turn over at the thought of her touching him so intimately. When he tried to brush her hands aside, to unfasten his own buttons, she laughed and determinedly stripped him of everything wet and in the process, everything until he stood before her naked.

He'd gone through too many emotional upheavals and was too tired to do anything except allow her whatever she wanted.

"I put on water for a bath," she murmured. Her eyes almost seemed to glow as she stared up at him before she handed him the quilt to wrap around himself.

"First tell me why you're here and not out at the cabin."

"I'll explain everything in time. There are things I want to know too, but not now, my love. Now isn't for talking," she whispered, her fingers lightly stroking his bearded face.

"But, Martha."

She pressed her fingers on his lips, sealing them gently. "Are you hungry?"

He tried to remember the last time he'd eaten, maybe the day before. He had gotten out of the habit of eating. "I just need you," he said.

"Well, you have me." She smiled then and disappeared into the kitchen. He heard water splashing. "It's ready," she called.

He wrapped the quilt more securely around himself. Walking into the room, he saw painted white cupboards, a large cook stove, a round oak table with matching chairs, gingham curtains at the window, and a hip bath sitting in the center of the floor. The steam rising from it indicated it would be a hot bath. Lord, he'd been dirty and cold so long, he'd forgotten what it felt like to be clean and warm.

"It's not as good as the hot springs," she whispered when she had him folded into the water as best his long length would allow. She soaped up a wash cloth and began washing his chest, "but it's the best we can do, down here."

He closed his eyes as he felt waves of pleasure coming over him at the warmth of the water and the sweetness of her ministrations. She shifted her efforts to his arms, the cloth swirling, caressing his skin, washing away not only the grime and chill that had been a part of him for so many months but also the iciness that had gripped him for months.

"I wasn't sure if you still wanted me."

She caught his bearded face between her palms, holding him so that he looked into her eyes. "I am so sorry for what I said that day. I just was afraid, Adam. I wanted to keep you from going. I was wrong."

"Maybe not wrong," he said. "I thought I had to go, but I don't know anymore."

"Adam, you wouldn't be you, if you didn't try to help where you could. I am so sorry I tried to stop you. I just didn't want to lose you. Please forgive me."

He felt moisture in his eyes, knowing his weakness was not going to make keeping control of his emotions easy. "I could forgive you anything," he whispered finally, trying to keep his voice from breaking.

"I love you, Adam. I never stopped. I wrote. Didn't you get any of my letters?"

"No, nothing." He thought of the vindictive commander and knew where the letters had likely ended up. "I should have written too, but I was afraid of what you'd say. I didn't want to hear you wanted a divorce when I was down there and couldn't do anything to stop it."

"No, I never wanted a divorce. I wrote you six letters. I wish you'd gotten them. Than you'd have known."

"I wish I had too." He closed his eyes for a moment; then remembered something else. "That note at the cabin was pretty curt. I didn't know what to expect after I got that. I couldn't figure out why you weren't there."

"I wasn't sure who all might end up in there. I didn't know what to say. I admit I thought you had to have gotten at least one of my letters; and when you didn't answer, I thought perhaps you were still mad at me. I still can't believe not even one got through. Where were you?"

"In the mountains most of the time, but that wasn't the problem. After I got up here, I was told an officer down there, who I'd offended, may have blocked them. Then again, they might be floating around somewhere."

She flushed. "I certainly hope he didn't open them."

For the first time he grinned in amusement. "Did I miss a lot?"

"Well, there might have been a few reminders about marital pleasures," she said with an embarrassed smile.

"Then if he read them, he likely hated me worse knowing what I had waiting."

"Maybe also jealous of your lovemaking prowess," she said with a laugh. She bent and began washing his feet, working her way up his calves to his thighs where he stopped her with a gentle smile. "You do that," he said, "and I won't last to get out of this tub."

Turning to his head, she gently washed his shoulder length black hair, sudsing it, massaging his scalp as he laid back, his eyes closed with the pleasure she was giving.

"This beard has to go," she told him as she pulled him to his feet.

"Why? You don't like the idea of a bear kissing you?"

"Well, if you are the bear, I guess I could get used to it, but I'd miss your handsome face." A pail of rinse water had been heating. After testing it, she made him bend over a little so she could pour the first onto his head and then the rest of his body, rinsing off the soap. When he stepped from the tub, she took a large bath towel and began vigorously drying him, arousing more warmth in his loins.

She handed him the quilt to wrap himself in before he sat in one of the kitchen chairs. "I could shave you," she suggested thoughtfully as she reached down and ran her fingers lightly over that heavily bearded jaw.

"I'm not sick, Martha, and can do it myself."

"Would you mind if I did?" she asked with that Madonna-like smile that made it impossible to say no.

"Can you do it?" he asked, pretending to consider her request although he knew even if she cut his throat, he wouldn't stop her.

She got out his razor. "I collected the rest of your things from there before I came here," she told him as she began running the razor over the strop to sharpen its edge.

"Pretty sure of yourself." He smiled softly, his eyes half closed.

"I couldn't think any other way. I would doubt and be afraid, but I made myself believe you'd be back in the spring," she said, her hand lightly caressing his cheek. "It was the only thing that made it possible for me to go on living."

"I wasn't so sure what would be waiting for me, but I knew I wouldn't give you up. I was going to win you back whatever it took," he said with a smile. He let himself relax as she tipped his head back a little and began to lather his beard, tilting his head this way and that as she smoothly brought the razor down onto his skin, skimming away the beard as she worked across his face. God, he was home. He could hardly believe it.

When she had finished, she ran her fingers over the enhanced planes of his face. "You've lost a lot of weight, my love."

"Some."

"It was bad down there?"

"Yes." Later he knew he'd have to talk about it, think about what he didn't want to remember, but for now, for this moment, he didn't want to relive what he'd seen, the hopelessness he had felt when he thought about the existence the Indians would be facing, those that survived. All he wanted to do now was to touch her, to feel the warmth of her body against his; melting away the coldness that had seemed so much a part of him that he had doubted he would ever be free of it.

She insisted then on his eating something, cut thin slices of roast, cheese, and put them between slices of bread. He didn't really want food, but made himself eat. He would have to begin rebuilding the strength the winter had taken.

When he had finished, she pulled him from the chair and

drew him back into the parlor and the warmth of the fire. She
threw the quilt onto the floor and drew him down to it and into
her arms. He reached over, pulling her tightly against his naked
body. He kissed her, running his lips around her mouth, plunging
his tongue within. They lay before the fire, kissing, tasting and
coming again to know each other.

She tangled her fingers in the long black hair. "If you keep
this up," she whispered, her lips nuzzling his earlobe, "you'll have
hair as long as mine."

"I'll get it cut," he promised, "I thought of doing it but just
couldn't take time away from getting to you." He reached down,
untying her belt, allowing her wrapper to fall open, revealing a
thin, linen garment, which showed every line and curve of her
body to perfection. Her nipples pushing erectly at the filmy
fabric. Smiling faintly, he asked, "Is this new?"

"I made it for when you got back."

"How did you know I'd be here tonight?" He pushed the filmy
material up her thigh, allowing his hand to cradle the gentle fullness of her hips.

She took a breath, closing her eyes at the pleasure of his
touch. "I didn't. I've been waiting-- night after night. Day after day,
hoping each would be the one." She felt him lift the garment
from her, leaving her open to his touch a thousand different
places as lips, tongue and hand stroked her to a near mindless
pleasure.

He buried his head into her breast. He ran his lips over her
breast, first one than the other, kissing and sucking as she arched
her back, giving him more access.

She bent to his chest, her tongue licking a flat nipple and
taking it into her mouth. "I was so afraid something would
happen to you before you could get back to me. I sometimes
feared you wouldn't come because of what I'd said."

"I'll always will come back. I just don't ever want to go again,"
he promised, kissing her long and hard.

Slowly with the sureness of knowing each other's bodies, and the knowledge that they now had all the time in the world, their lips and hands stroked and reassured, building again that paradise that only they could enter. When they were both ready, she straddled his hips. "Let me do the work this time," she whispered as she proved true to her word bringing him and then her to the heights he'd not let himself remember in the months apart. Groans of pleasure filled the small room with the sounds of love, the sounds of renewed life.

Later as they lay together half wrapped in the quilt, he stroked her thigh lightly as he asked, "Now, tell me why you aren't at the cabin?"

She opened her eyes, smiling sleepily. "Are you sure you wouldn't rather wait until tomorrow to hear all of this? There's a wonderful feather tick and brass bed upstairs. It's been waiting for us to use it together."

He was tired, almost exhausted and suddenly the thought of that bed became a temptation he couldn't resist. So long as they were together, he could wait to hear whatever had caused her to move off the homestead and to this home. Nothing mattered except that he was in her arms.

Arms around each other, they climbed the stairs to what was their bedroom, Heaven bounding ahead of them. Almost as soon as he fell onto the soft mattress, he was asleep, leaving Martha awake as she studied his face, seeing the new lines in his cheeks, the signs of the suffering. Leaning on one elbow, she traced his face lightly with her fingers, memorizing each new plane, reassuring herself that he was there and his arms were around her.

With morning, she woke to find his lips on hers, his hands caressing her into wakefulness. Smiling, she knew there was no way she'd rather wake as she gave herself to his embrace, her own lips and hands increasing the fire that was slowly building within them. Afterward, they lay, sweat slicked limbs entwined, as they savored the afterglow of lovemaking.

"All right now," he said huskily, his lips against her ear, "tell me what you've done."

She smiled a little uncertainly now. It had all seemed so obvious when he wasn't here; when he wasn't such a big, forceful presence in her bed.

His virile, patently male body sprawled beside her in its naked splendor, only partially covered by the blankets. It made her remember he had his own ideas on things. She'd already seen that clearly demonstrated. Perhaps he wouldn't like her planning as she had. "Well," she began hesitantly, sitting cross-legged on the bed so that she could face him, "when you left, I began to think."

"Yes?" he said encouragingly.

"What I thought was, that you wouldn't be happy home-steading, being a farmer."

"I thought we'd worked that all out."

"We had, except when you weren't here with me, I wasn't so sure about it, and I began thinking about that job as sheriff."

He sat up now, the sheet loosely draped around his waist as he put his full attention onto what she was saying.

A little nervously, she went on, her eyes intently trying to read his expression. "Well, when I thought about that, I thought what a good sheriff you would make and how if you were going to be sheriff, we couldn't really live out in the country so far away."

"But I'd already told them no," he reminded her, his blue eyes intense as he leaned back against the brass headboard, studying her.

"I know, but I thought you probably said that because of me. Was that so?"

"Maybe."

"Anyway, after you'd gone, and I'd had this chance to think. I made the decision to come into town and ask if the job was still open."

"Are you saying you went to the council?"

"Actually that is what I did. More or less." She still was not sure if he was pleased or unhappy with her. Perhaps Adam didn't like his woman taking matters into her own hands.

"And?"

"The long and short is the job was still open, and they said they'd keep it that way until you got back from your job with the military. You can't believe what an inefficient deputy they have now, and they're all really eager to have you take the job."

"What about this house?"

She wished he had made it more clear how he felt about the first part of what she'd done. "Reverend Jefferson helped me find it. It was a very good price, and if you later on decide you don't like being a sheriff after all, we can sell it for a profit. At least that's what Reverend Jefferson thought. The town is really boom-ing, even if it isn't going to be the capitol."

"You bought this house?" His voice reflected his disbelief.

"Yes, with double lots," she said, nodding her dark head, black hair falling down her back and over her shoulders. "Are you mad at me for doing this without talking to you first?"

"No, just shocked. I thought that homestead was your dream, didn't imagine you'd ever want to leave it."

She looked up into his eyes, her own beginning to fill with tears. Leaning forward him, she laid her head against his chest. "I didn't either," she said as he pulled her into his arms.

"Then why?" His palm reached down and forced her to look up at him.

"Because, Adam, now you are my dream, and I just couldn't imagine you wanting to farm. I didn't want you tied to another man's dream. I wanted you to have your own. I hoped this could be a part of it."

He crooked one corner of his mouth as he shook his head. "Come here," he ordered.

"Then it's all right."

"It's more than all right. What did I do to deserve a wife like you?" he asked, bending to kiss her tenderly.

"Did you think that when you rode away from here last fall?" she asked, with a little smile of her own.

His smile broadening, he quipped wryly, "Yes, as a matter of fact I did."

EPILOGUE

December 1856

"Now just ya calm down, women been havin' babies for well, all the time man's been livin' here on this earth."

Adam looked at St. Louis. "Yeah, but--"

"No, buts. Martha is goin' to be just fine. Ya heard what the doctor said when he come down a minute ago."

"I know." He turned away, running his fingers through his tangled hair, trying to get control of himself.

"Just relax Adam. This here's goin' to be a Christmas baby. That's a blessin' don't ya know that?"

Adam scowled at him. "I'm not a heathen."

"Wal, then prove it, relax. No, that's not right because I think every man has a hard time relaxing when the woman he loves is having his baby."

At every little noise from upstairs, Adam jumped up, his face a picture of woe as he stared at the stairwell. "I should be up there."

"The doctor said for ya to stay down here."

There was a knock at the door. "Damn, who'd be coming here

now?" muttered Adam to himself as he opened it to see Virgil Buxman and his wife, standing there, grinning ear to ear.

"Merry Christmas," said Virgil thrusting a gift into Adam's unwilling hands.

"What's this?" Adam asked, holding the gift as though it was filled with gun powder.

"Just a little present of appreciation for our sheriff and his wife, showing you how much we all value all that you've brought to Oregon City this last year."

"I haven't done anything," Adam said, uncomfortably aware that he ought to invite them in but because of what was going on upstairs, he didn't want to have anyone in the house, watching him unravel-- that is no one except an old friend.

Buxman laughed. "You call it nothing, we call it bringing peace, arresting trouble makers, keeping the rifraff in line. Our town hasn't been so peaceful, well, since it got founded."

"Where's Martha?" asked Annie, observing Adam's nervous mannerisms and the paleness of his skin.

"She's upstairs. The doctor's with her."

"The baby's coming?" asked Annie her voice rising with her excitement.

"Yes."

She grabbed her husband's arm. "Then we won't intrude, not unless you need us."

"No," Adam said too quickly and then laughing nervously apologized. "I'm not handling this well."

Annie smiled as she dragged Virgil from the house. "We understand completely. Do keep us informed."

When he'd closed the door, Adam leaned weakly against it. "I understand now how Matt felt. Damn, I feel like I could faint too."

St. Louis grinned as he patted him sympathetically on the shoulder. "Just think, boy. Pretty soon, ya'll be holdin' yore son in yore arms. Now ain't that a thing worth goin' through a little sufferin' for?"

"If it was my suffering," Adam groaned when he heard a cry from Martha.

"Wal, that ain't the way God set it up and ya are lucky about that. Cause I don't think there's a man born that could handle it like the women do."

"Yeah," Adam grunted, not convinced.

"What ya goin' to name yore son?"

Adam took a couple of deep breaths, trying to keep himself from the dizziness that seemed to threaten him. After a moment, he growled, "What is it that always makes you so sure it's going to be a boy? I remember you saying the same thing to Matt, so sure it would be a boy."

"Wal, I was wrong that time, but this time it's a boy."

"Martha seems to think it'll be a girl."

"That's just cause she ain't had no boys to show her the difference."

Adam shook his head, walking over to the fireplace and staring deeply into it. "What time were Amy and Matt coming again?"

"In the mornin'," St. Louis told him, shaking his head at Adam's misery. "I only told ya that three times in the last hour."

"I forgot."

When he heard the wail of a baby, he looked at St. Louis and then ran for the stairs, taking them three at a time as he rushed to the bedroom where his child had just been born.

Looking in the door, he felt as though his heart had stopped when he looked at Martha, her hair a black mass around her face as she held their baby. She saw him, and smiled, "Look," she said, putting out a hand for him to come closer, "He's got your hair."

Adam fell to his knees beside the bed. "He?" he repeated, his voice breaking, "We have a son?"

Martha pointed to the pertinent organs and said, "Looks like a son to me."

The doctor grinned, completing his work and standing up. "It's a fine boy, you have, sheriff. What are you going to call him?"

Adam reached down and touched his son's fingers. Martha smiled up at him, her heart in her eyes, her son cradled in her arms. "Well, what is it to be?" she asked.

"Elijah. Elijah Amos Stone for two good men."

The End

To be notified of upcoming new book releases or snippets of works in progress go to:
http://Raintrueax.blogspot.com

The Stevens women stories continue in 'Going Home' and 'Love Waits'.

www.ingramcontent.com/pod-product-compliance
Lightning Source LLC
Chambersburg PA
CBHW060138260626
47160CB00001B/27